Aim High

An Eddie Malloy Mystery

Joe McNally

The Eddie Malloy Series
in order of publication

Warned Off
Hunted
Blood Ties
Running Scared
The Third Degree
Dead Ringer
Aim High

Eddie also appears in *Bet Your Life* alongside
Frankie Houlihan who makes his debut in
For Your Sins

Author's note

This is a work of fiction. Names, characters, places and incidents are
either a work of the imagination of the author or are used fictitiously, and
any resemblance to actual persons, living or dead, business
establishments, events or locales is entirely coincidental.

For my sons, Ryan and Kevin, with love

ONE

Eddie Malloy hurried from the jockey's changing room at Worcester at 5.17pm on a Friday in late July. He'd had one winner, three losers, a hot shower, and not much to eat. He got in his car and took the phone from the glove box.

A text from Sonny Beltrami, in the coded letters they'd agreed, told him Sonny was heading for one of their secret meeting places. Eddie sighed, flipped the sun-visor down, and joined the line of traffic leaving the track.

Sonny Beltrami had left Worcester racecourse one hour before Eddie. He rode a black BMW K1600GT motorcycle, and never broke the speed limits. If a cop stopped Sonny, he might find the deerskin pouch containing that day's take: one hundred thousand pounds.

Sonny did not know that a man carrying a large well-worn camera bag had followed him.

As Eddie reached the M5 motorway, his friend, Peter McCarthy, was alone in his London office. He was awaiting a call from his boss, Nic Buley, chief executive of the BHA, the British Horseracing Authority.

Buley finished a call on a telephone in his office that was not linked to the BHA official network. He sat staring at the door for a few seconds, unblinking, then he dialled McCarthy's extension number. 'You can come up now.'

McCarthy took the lift. He was 52 and forty pounds overweight. The commitments he'd made to himself to use the stairs more often invariably faded when faced with the climb.

Buley was opening his office door as McCarthy approached. Both men forced a smile.

'Peter. Good to see you. Come in. Apologies for the wait.'

'That's okay.'

Buley rolled a high-backed leather chair across the wooden floor. McCarthy was careful sitting down. He'd been embarrassed before when his bulk had unbalanced the chair and almost spun it from beneath him.

Buley settled at his desk opposite McCarthy. 'Kellagher, Sampson and Blackaby,' he said.

McCarthy nodded. Buley said, 'I want them in court by August fifteenth.'

'Why?'

'That's the first anniversary of my appointment. I promised that cleaning up racing would be my top priority. Time to show I wasn't bluffing.'

McCarthy began sweating. Buley, who consumed no more than 2,000 calories daily, and worked out every morning, had switched off the air conditioning to increase McCarthy's discomfort.

McCarthy said, 'We're at least four months away from court with this…probably nearer six.'

'Not we. You.'

'What does that mean?'

'You should have had this ready to go by now. You've been on it more than two years.'

'It's been the toughest case in our history. We need to get evidence that will stand up in a court full of people who know little about racing. We need rock solid, easily explained detail, built on facts.'

Buley straightened, opening his hands toward McCarthy. 'You're head of integrity. It's your job to get those facts.'

McCarthy leant forward. 'And that's what we've been doing. Painstakingly. And we're getting there.'

'Not quickly enough.'

'Nic, you can't put deadlines on cases like this!'

'It's a project, same as any other in business. What do you want me to do, let it run forever?'

'It's not what I want or what you want, it's what will get us a conviction.'

Buley, elbows on desk, clasped his fingers again and said, 'August fifteenth.'

McCarthy stared at him. 'The police won't accept that.'

'I'll deal with the police.'

McCarthy shook his head. 'I'm afraid I can't support you if you want to go ahead so soon.'

Buley smiled. 'Then I'll find someone who can.'

McCarthy waited for more. Buley just kept smiling. McCarthy said, 'Meaning?'

'Clear your desk. I'll draft a statement with the PR team over the weekend and announce your departure Monday.' Buley was hard-faced. McCarthy stared at him. 'Seriously?'

'Seriously. We'll agree a compensation package in line with your length of service and tied to a compromise agreement.'

'Nic…I've worked in security here for twenty-eight years.'

'The BHA hasn't been around for twenty-eight years. I know you were with the BHB and the Jockey Club, but maybe that's part of the whole problem. Old habits die hard. Times have moved on. Adapt or die…etcetera.'

'Are you saying that I shouldn't come to work on Monday?'

'Or any other day. Spend the weekend making new plans. It'll do you good, the change.' Buley stood. 'Now, if you don't mind, I have a couple more hours work to do.'

McCarthy got to his feet. Sweat darkened his blue shirt and, in the sunlight through the window his face glistened. Buley reached across with his right hand, as though sealing another deal. 'Someone will be in touch to run the statement past you, so you can field any calls from the press.'

McCarthy, dazed, slowly shook hands and turned away.

When the big man left his office, Buley hit redial on the private phone. 'Job done.' He said.

'Good. Phone Lisle. Get him ready for a midweek announcement.'

'You're sure he'll bite?'

'He'll think Christmas has come in July.'

Buley rang Broc Lisle and listened to his voicemail message: "This is Broc Lisle. Thanks for calling. I'm in studio for a *Newsnight* recording on the Iraq uprising. I'll return your call between 19.15 and 19.25. Please leave your name and number."

Buley left his, then hung up and said, 'Jeez, and people call me anal.'

TWO

Broc Lisle was at BBC HQ, having his make-up finished. The young man working on him said, 'Long time since I saw a moustache like that, if you don't mind me saying. Bridge on the River Kwai and The Great Escape.'

Lisle smiled. 'Oddly, I was clean-shaven all the time I was in the army. It was only when I started making a living at this that I grew it. And I'll tell you why, though you might have heard this, being in the business. Stop me if you have. It's about John Travolta.'

'Go on,' the boy worked to highlight Lisle's cheekbones, which were already prominent. Lisle was square-jawed, too, and allowed enough grey in his hair to convey experience and inflate his air of gravitas. The only thing betraying him, and telling of his impending 58th birthday, was the loose skin on his neck. But a high collar helped. His dark brown tie and suit completed his media persona. If he'd been able to continue wearing a uniform after retiring as an army major, he'd have done so.

Lisle said, 'A reporter was shadowing Travolta one day on set. They had to move from Travolta's trailer for a meeting with the director. A limousine waited outside the trailer and Travolta and the reporter got in. They travelled a hundred yards and got out again. Mystified, the reporter looked at Travolta who put an arm around his shoulder and said, "It's not enough to be a star. You've got to act like a star." Hence my moustache. I'm not a star, by any means, but that taught me a lesson about looking the part and it's helped make me what you guys call the "go-to" man for comment on military and international security issues.'

'Good story. I'll use that. I'll cut it to fifty yards though.'

Lisle chuckled.

When Eddie Malloy reached the abandoned graveyard in the woods near the village of Slad, Sonny Beltrami was waiting. As Eddie opened the creaky south gate behind the ruins of the church, he could hear Sonny singing *My Melancholy Baby*. Eddie smiled. All Sonny's songs were melancholy.

Sonny's big frame, dressed in motorcycle leathers, rested on an oak trunk felled in a storm. The evening sun lit most of the dead tree, but Sonny sat in the shade. Eddie chose the sunny side and straddled the wood. 'Not topping up your tan?' Eddie said.

Sonny shook his head, singing the last line out before he replied. 'Doesn't suit the song, my friend. Ambience is everything in a performance.'

Eddie looked around. 'There's nobody listening to your performance, Sonny. None of these poor folk have heard anything for a long time.'

Sonny sat forward, sweeping back his white hair, accentuating that Latin skin colour Eddie envied. Sonny was sixty, but looked ten years younger. He kept himself fit, although he claimed that was under doctor's orders for the sake of his lifelong diabetes. Eddie sometimes wondered if Sonny's illness had nurtured the melancholy.

Sonny said, 'Don't be so sure nobody's listening.' He scanned the mossy headstones. 'Think of all the spirits circling this place. Most of these people would never have left Slad village. Their world would have been the five square miles around this valley. Their ghosts won't be far away.'

'Maybe you could have sung them a happier song, then?'

'I'll bring my fiddle next time, and play a jig.'

Sonny got to his feet, not bothering to brush the green debris from the back of his shining leathers. He reached inside his jacket and pulled out a deerskin pouch from which he drew two bundles of banknotes. 'One hundred grand dead,' he said.

Eddie took it.

In the trees beyond the graveyard perimeter, the man who'd followed Sonny squeezed the shutter button on his camera, silently gathering twelve frames a second through the 400mm lens.

'Want your commission now?' Eddie asked Sonny.

'Nah. Mave can square it up at the end of the month. I always thought I wanted money. Now I've got it, I don't know what to do with it.'

'Why don't you rent a big band and a theatre, and sing to some live people for a change?'

Sonny smiled, looking around at the headstones. 'The dead don't boo.'

'They don't clap, either. And who'd boo you? You've got a voice like honey.' Eddie got up, stuffing the cash in his pockets. Sonny put an arm around his shoulder and they walked. Sonny said, 'The best audience is the one in your head, Eddie. You can change it as you please.'

'So, who's your favourite audience?'

'Depends how I'm feeling. Often it's just one woman, sitting in the dark, watching. All I ever see is her face, but she's comfortable, and she understands my whole life just from hearing me sing that song.'

'Anybody I know?'

Sonny's smile was slow and sad. 'You weren't even born, my friend…somebody from a long, long time ago.'

They stopped just through the gate. Eddie reached to shake hands. Sonny took a step forward and hugged him, then wandered away in silence.

The man in the trees cursed himself silently for missing the picture of the hug. His name was Jonty Saroyan. When a viewfinder enclosed his eye, it eclipsed his heart and soul. There was no photo he wouldn't take. Stripped of his camera, he was affable and childlike, a dreamer and a fool.

When the sound of Sonny's BMW cracked the silence, Jonty made the call: 'The big man's leaving now.'

THREE

Eddie reached his house in the valley, hemmed in by small hills and four hundred acres of woodland. He locked the front door behind him, dragged the heavy seagrass mat aside with his boot-heel, and opened the floor safe while pulling the money from his pockets. He couldn't cram in more than fifty grand.

He cursed and hauled it all out, then sat on the floor and counted it, his frustration increasing in ten-grand increments.

The sun had just gone down, so Eddie knew there was a fair chance Maven Judge would be out of bed and ready to start work. He sat at his PC and pinged her. 'All well?' she asked, not looking at her webcam, as usual, eyes on screen, fingers blurring across her keyboard.

'No. All is not well, Mave.'

Still she didn't look at him. 'What's up?'

'I just counted the cash I'm holding for you.'

'And?'

'Three hundred and forty five grand. The rubber bands have broken on some of it. Most of the notes are grubby. I opened the safe and it was like a burst drain of money.'

'Filthy lucre, eh? Take what you need and get a bigger safe.'

'I don't want a bigger bloody safe! I want you to take at least three hundred of this off my hands. *You* get a bigger safe!'

'Keep the head, and I'll buy you a hat.'

'Mave, it's not funny. There's nobody around this house all day. If anybody breaks in, they could be in another country by the time I got home.'

'The cameras would pick them up'

'Then what? I ring the cops and say, could you help me find this guy who just stole a third of a million in used banknotes from my house?'

She stopped the keyboard work and looked at him. 'Okay. I'll call Sonny and ask him to bring me two-fifty from it.'

'I left him about an hour ago. It was when I tried to cram the cash he gave me into the safe that I realized I'm not cut out for this.'

'You and Sonny are the only guys I trust. You're the only ones I know.'

Eddie watched that big-nosed plain face. Her brown hair would be tied back in the usual ponytail. If she smiled, he'd see those crooked crossed teeth. Maven Judge had won fortunes betting throughout this summer jumps season. She could have had Hollywood teeth and a nose job, but Eddie liked her as she was. He loved the fact that the notion of changing her looks never seemed to have crossed her mind. Eddie rubbed his tired eyes. 'Let me sleep on it, Mave. I'm wound up.'

'Never.' She smiled now, full and wide, no bashfulness in showing those teeth. Eddie smiled too. 'See,' she said, 'it's not all bad. I noticed you had a winner at Worcester.'

'Yep. That's fifty-seven for the season.'

'See. That's what happens, Edward, when you apply yourself.'

'Under duress. Needs must, and all that.'

'Well, take some commission from the bets.'

'Mave, I can't! I've told you, if I take no reward, I'm breaking no rules.'

'Well, stop bloody moaning, then!'

He smiled again, and she said she'd call back when she'd made the pick-up arrangements with Sonny.

Mave had helped Eddie when a friend of his, Jimmy Sherrick, died. She'd been pestering Eddie for two years to help her perfect her betting system, and Eddie believed Maven Judge was a genius. She could do anything with software, hack the toughest of security systems, and cruise through mental challenges. Eddie had told her that her brain was a six-lane highway to everyone else's single-track road.

After Jimmy's case, Eddie owed Maven the favour she'd been seeking for so long. This was to be his summer of repayment.

FOUR

Mave had been calling Sonny every half hour to try and arrange the pick-up. At nine o'clock, worried, she rang Eddie.

'Mave. He's probably gone to a bar to spend some of his commission.'

'He rarely drinks. And he never ignores my voicemails or texts. The reason he chose that place in Salisbury was because of the signal strength. The phone just rings out.'

'Give him another hour or so.'

'Will you wait up?'

'Of course.'

By midnight, she'd had no response. The longer she waited for word, the more upset she got. Eddie watched her strained face on the screen, and said, 'Want me to drive down and check the caravan?'

'Would you? I'm just scared he's had a hypo and he's lying somewhere.'

Eddie was confident Sonny wouldn't have allowed that to happen. Type one diabetes was as much a part of Sonny as his limbs were. He'd managed the illness perfectly all his life and never took chances. But Eddie sensed Mave was beyond logical debate. She just wanted the reassurance. And one thing wasn't sitting right with Eddie...the fact that Sonny had hugged him before parting that evening. He'd never done that before.

Eddie told Mave he would call when he reached Sonny's place. 'It'll take me an hour.'

'Okay. I'll be here.'

Sonny's southern base was a thirty-five foot static caravan on a pleasant site on the outskirts of Salisbury. The gates were closed. Eddie pressed the buzzer for security and explained about Sonny's illness.

His caravan was in darkness. His big black motorcycle was nowhere to be seen. Eddie persuaded the security guard to get the master key to the caravan. Sonny wasn't there. Nothing had been disturbed. Eddie called Mave and she asked if he had any idea what route home Sonny would have taken from the graveyard.

'No way of knowing, Mave.' He considered mentioning that Sonny had seemed a bit more heavy-hearted than usual, but it was pointless worrying her further. Anyway, that was just Sonny. He'd been singing. Maybe Eddie had simply read things wrong, given the surroundings. It was all about the ambience, as Sonny had said.

'Do you think anyone could have followed him from the track?' Mave asked.

'He's been very careful. So have I.'

'I know, I'm just-'

'If anyone had followed him to mug him, they'd have done it before he handed the cash over, wouldn't they? Not much point in it afterward.'

'Unless they didn't see him give it to you?'

'True.'

'Should I call the police?'

'I don't think you should, Mave. He's a well-adjusted adult who doesn't take alcohol or drugs and he's been "missing" for about seven hours. They'd tell you to ring back in a week.'

'It's just not him, Eddie. You know that!'

'I know. But it's three in the morning. You've done what you can. Let's see what daylight brings. If he hasn't turned up by the time I leave Stratford tomorrow, I'll drive straight to your place.'

She sighed. 'Okay. If I hear from him in the next few hours, should I call you?'

'Please. I'll leave my phone on.'

FIVE

The usual stream of banter criss-crossed the Stratford changing room. Underlying the chatter was an edginess about three jockeys who'd been suspended by the BHA that morning pending possible prosecution on charges of race-fixing.

Racing wasn't clean. It wasn't straight. But Eddie and his fellow riders knew the villains. They lived a close life in those changing rooms up and down the country, and a jockey is first to realize when others in a race aren't trying to win. But Eddie believed the sport was ninety-five percent straight, and there was nothing he could do about the other five percent except avoid associating with them.

Riley Duggan, head popping through black and yellow silks, fixed his hair and said, 'Shock move by the BHA, Eddie, eh?'

'Yep. Not like them to exceed the speed of a tortoise.'

'You hoping those three get warned off?' Riley asked.

A dangerous question. Eddie was one of just ninety-five professional jump jockeys in the UK. More amateur jockeys than pros held riding licences. And there were a hundred or so young conditional jockeys, jumping's equivalent of apprentices. They all lived and worked in a cramped, competitive, dangerous world. A careless remark about someone would soon reach that person. Riley wasn't trying to lead Eddie into any kind of verbal trap; he was a straightforward guy who just said what he was thinking.

Eddie pulled his boots on. 'I've got enough to worry about with my own career to give theirs any thought, Riley.'

Three hours later, winnerless, but fresh and showered, Eddie walked through the car park, bordered by meadows. The sounds and smells of harvesting immersed him. It was one of those rare summer evenings with no haze or humidity. Eddie got his phone from the glove box and called Mave. 'Any news on Sonny?'

'Nothing. I've spent most of the day calling hospitals.'

He wanted to reassure her, but encouraging words would offer no comfort. 'I'll be there in a couple of hours, Mave.'

'You staying?'

'For as long as it takes.'

'See you soon.'

The day's warmth lasted, and when Mave's white house came into Eddie's view, the bottom half of it rippled in a heat haze. The sea beyond was flat calm. A perfect setting, except for a missing friend.

Mave heard Eddie drive into the yard behind the house, and came to meet him. She put her arms around his neck. He hugged her just tightly enough to hold her comfortably for as long as she needed the support.

They stood linked and silent for over a minute. The only sounds came from sea birds. He could sense her distress and that oddly consoling feeling of being attached to her, of fitting together naturally, of silent communication. She felt it too. Eddie knew that. 'Do you want to walk?' he asked.

'Let's have some coffee first. You've had a long drive.'

'Fill a flask. Bring a blanket. We'll sit on the headland.'

When Eddie first met Maven Judge, she'd told him she lived in a cliff shack. That's what he'd expected to see on his first visit that spring as he drove the final narrow road on the edge of the Lleyn Peninsula in North Wales.

Mave's "shack" turned out to be an old whitewashed farmhouse, its walls two-feet thick to thwart the weather when it blasted up the sheer cliff over Hell's Mouth bay.

They wandered into the evening sunshine, Eddie carrying a big old rug rolled up on his shoulder. Mave walked alongside swinging a plastic bag in which mugs and spoons and flask rattled in the remarkable stillness. 'Heaviest blanket I've ever seen, this,' Eddie said. She smiled sadly, glad at his attempt to make her feel better. But her head was down, watching her boots trail through the grass.

They settled twenty yards from the cliff edge. Birds rose, then dropped from sight as though bouncing from below the cliffs. Eddie poured coffee. Maven watched the horizon. Eddie pointed to what looked like mountains away across the Irish Sea. 'Is that a mirage, or am I seeing things?'

She smiled again. 'You're doing your best, Eddie. That's the Wicklow Mountains. A rare sight. There's usually a haze or sea weather.'

'It's been a diamond of a day.'

She nodded.

'Weather-wise, I mean.'

'I know.' She drank and turned to him. 'What do we do next?'

He shrugged. 'Wait, I suppose.'

'Somebody's got Sonny, haven't they?'

'Maybe. How many winning bets has he placed on track since you started?'

'Thirty-two'

'Losers?'

'Two.'

'Between what he delivered to me and dropped off here, how much has he carried?'

'More than four million.'

Eddie pulled a long strand of grass and twisted it and stared at the ground.

'I don't like it when you go silent on me,' Mave said. 'Do you think you were followed from the track yesterday?'

'Possibly, but what would be the point of following me? You've never bet in any race I've ridden in. Sonny's the one who's been moving among the bookies collecting the cash.'

'That's what I can't work out…why they let Sonny get to you with the money.'

'Maybe they were waiting for him at the caravan. Maybe they expected him to have the money.'

'But he didn't, so what's the point of holding him? They're onto this, aren't they? The betting,' she said.

'They could be.'

'I've been stupid, and complacent, and careless, and Sonny's taking the consequences,' she said.

'Mave, it was never going to be risk-free. Sonny knew that. It was one of the reasons he liked doing it. If somebody's got him, they'll be making a call to us soon.'

'There won't be any call. Sonny won't talk.'

'He won't need to. If they've been tracking us for a while, they'll know I'm getting the cash.'

'But that's why it makes no sense. They didn't stop Sonny before he handed it over to you.'

'They'll have bigger plans than a one-off mugging.'

'If I've heard nothing by midnight, I'm calling the police.'

'Okay.'

She turned. 'You're humouring me.'

He nodded.

She said, 'The money doesn't matter anymore. The system doesn't matter. I can do something else.'

'I know you can. And I know the money doesn't matter. But all the police will be able to do is the same as us…wait for the call. And the call's going to say don't involve the cops.'

She looked away again. Eddie said, 'This is probably a couple of fly boys who think I'm easy meat. Give them a chance to show their hand.'

'You got a signal?'

He checked his phone. 'One bar.'

She stood up. 'We'd best get back then. You get four at the house, don't you?'

Eddie looked at her as he squinted against the sinking sun. 'Mave, why are you dusting off your jeans? You've been sitting on an inch-thick rug.'

'Habit, I suppose. Come on.' She gathered the coffee things. Eddie crawled to the edge of the rug and pulled up the corner to look at the underside.

'Eddie…what are you doing?'

'Looking for the start button. I thought we'd fly back, on our magic carpet.' She took three quick steps toward him and raised her boot to his shoulder, pushing him over to roll in the grass. 'Move your arse, Malloy.'

He lay looking up at her. 'You know you could have injured me? Me, your rug carrier. Your slave.'

'Get up, or I'll roll you off the edge of the cliff.'

'You and whose army?'

She ran at him. He jumped up and she chased him round the rug. A couple walking a dog stopped and watched Eddie and Maven running in circles against the setting sun.

SIX

As night came on, Peter McCarthy moved from the garden chair into his house. Since his wife Jean had died last winter, his dread at coming home to an empty house had grown. Unable to face it on the day he'd lost his job, Mac had checked into a London hotel and drank himself to sleep.

He couldn't stay away for ever, but he could spend as much time in the garden as the weather allowed, and that's what he'd done on this Saturday.

Mac still wore the suit he'd left the office in the day before. Left it for the last time. At least he wouldn't have to tell Jean. He stared at the cold fireplace. He didn't have to tell anybody. They had no close friends. His office colleagues would make what they wanted of the news on Monday.

The news.

The reality of dealing with the press came back to him. Oh yes, he *would* have to tell somebody. But tell them what? He'd resigned? He'd been fired?

He recalled what Buley had said about sending him the proposed press release for comment. That comment would be governed by his compromise agreement. And his payoff would be tied to that compromise agreement, the compromise in question being the one he'd make to sell his silence.

Mac stood and walked to the window to look down the valley at the twinkling lights in Lambourn. This career in racing, at the heart of it here in the Valley of the Racehorse, was what he'd worked for. This was his life. Had been his life…this, and Jean. He didn't need money. The compromise agreement could lie unsigned for all he cared. Then, when the case against the three bent jockeys fell through he could gloat, unfettered by any contract. He could issue a big fat public I TOLD YOU SO! To Nic Buley.

But Mac knew he would not do that. In his world, no matter how primitive your feelings, regardless of your lust for revenge, it was not the done thing.

The stiff upper lip trumped personal wounds.

Dignity ruled.

Anyway, Jean's absence relegated all else to the boundaries. The trouble was, Mac had to keep reminding himself of that.

Eddie and Mave sat through the dusk and into the night with lamps lighting the corners and logs crackling in the stove. It was warm outside, but thick walls kept the house cool. They needed the brightness of a fire, the lunging flames sparking optimism and fight. Eddie listened as Mave unravelled the years of her life. 'I can't recall not knowing Sonny. He was around our house all the time. I remember him jamming with dad. Dad's Stratocaster didn't go too well with Sonny's accordion or his fiddle, but they always seemed to be smiling. And dad would finish a bottle of red and Sonny would try and talk him into playing some of the old Italian tunes he remembered, the ones his Dad taught him.

'Sonny was born here. His mum and dad came over during the war and started a fish and chip shop in Glasgow. Dad went up there when he was still a teenager, trying to get gigs. Sonny was at one of the auditions. They went to a party that night and that was it. The Elderly Brothers, Dad used to call them. They got together and started touring the working men's clubs in the north of England. They were getting so many gigs, they rented a house in Halifax and that was it. Until dad met mum.' Mave smiled. 'I remember mum telling me how hard he tried to persuade her to move into the digs in Halifax rather than them getting a place of their own. It took her a year to drag him away from Sonny. I wish, I wish, I wish he'd just have played with Sonny and no one else.' She stared into the fire.

Mave's father, Jack, was asked to fill in one night as lead guitarist for a band he'd never worked with before. Their equipment was faulty and he'd been electrocuted on stage and killed. He was thirty-five.

Mave told how Sonny had never missed a day visiting her and her mother in the months after her father's death. As the years passed, they'd kept in touch with calls and letters and visits. Her mother died on what would have been her dad's forty-seventh birthday. And Sonny returned once more to help Mave through.

Eddie knew how happy it had made Mave to be able to offer Sonny this job as her 'special agent'. It had brought new life to him in his retirement. But she'd never foreseen this threat. Eddie realized he should have anticipated it.

They had made Sonny as anonymous as possible on the racecourse; dressed in drab clothes, and flat caps, spreading the bets around many bookmakers. No lumpy wagers with any single bookie. No conversations with them. Note each bookie and work through a cycle so that the same one wasn't bet with again for at least a month.

But racetracks have no filtering system for villains. From rogues to royalty, this was the sport's audience. Ninety-nine percent of racegoers were decent people, but skulking among them were spivs and pickpockets, thieves and junkies and sharpies seeking information and 'contacts'. Men on the make. And women.

The call came at ten o'clock. Mave jumped to her feet, looking to her phone. But it was Eddie's that rang. He recognized the city code as Birmingham. Mave sat still and unblinking as he answered it.

'Eddie Malloy?'

'That's me.'

'We've got your pal here.'

'Is he all right?'

'For now, he is.'

'What do you want?'

'The same information you give Sonny.'

'Okay. We'll work something out. We should meet.'

'We will.'

'When?' Eddie asked.

'Name it.'

'Tomorrow.'

'Okay. You're riding at Market Rasen. I'll see you there. Wait in your car after racing. Leave the doors open. I'll get in the back.'

'You sure?' Eddie said.

'What's the problem?'

'Well, if I'm going to start giving you tips and you're going to bet them, are you happy for all the faces to see us together?'

'Fair point. Where, then?'

'You know the golf course close to the track?'

'Yes.'

'A wood borders the eastern side of it. A decent road runs through the wood. Drive down off the main drag and take a right at the fork. You'll be able to see one of the tees on the golf course. I'll meet you there half an hour after the last.'

'No cops. No company. Just you and me. I've got some very sharp pictures of you on five different occasions taking lumps of cash from Sonny. I've got video too. You won't want to be joining your mates at the Old Bailey.'

'Can I speak to Sonny?'

'I'm in a pay phone. No room for two. Sonny's okay. He's being looked after.'

'I'm glad to hear that. I'll see you tomorrow.'

Mave waved frantically and mimicked an injection in her arm. Eddie said to the caller, 'Does Sonny have enough medication?'

'Yes. He's fine. Sonny's an asset. We'll look after him.'

'He's not a fucking asset. He's my friend, and if anything happens to him, you can put your photos on a poster in Trafalgar Square for all I care. Then you'd better leave the country.'

'No violence, Mister Malloy. It never solves anything.'

'Well, that's a popular saying, but it's not true. Violence solves a lot of things. A lot. Keep my friend safe. I'll see you tomorrow.'

'The car I'll be driving won't be traceable. Save yourself any preparation. Let's just meet and get a civilized deal done.'

'Is that it?'

'That's it.'

Eddie hung up and walked across and put his hand on Mave's shoulder. 'Looks like we've been outed, Maven.'

'What was that about pictures?'

Eddie told her.

She shut her eyes, and raised her chin, stretching her neck and groaning. 'Oh, Eddie, I'm sorry! Now you're in trouble as well as Sonny.'

'No trouble. He sounds like an amateur. We'll fix this before the week's out.'

She sat shaking her head.

'I'll make some strong coffee,' Eddie said.

Mave traced the caller's number: a pay phone outside New Street railway station. 'We should have recorded it,' she said, 'I could have taken a voice print.'

'Why? I'm meeting him tomorrow. There's every chance I'll know his face. He must be a racecourse regular to have sussed what was happening. I'll know his face, then it shouldn't be hard to put a name to it.'

'Then what?'

'Then we do the deal for Sonny and figure out how to get those pictures off him. If he really does have pictures.'

She watched Eddie pace the fireside rug. The logs were embers now, the dull yellow glow reflecting in his shoes. Mave read his mind. 'Eddie, we need to do this the easiest way. The safest way. No point getting yourself wound up.'

'I know.'

'I know you know, but it's making no difference to you. Go to bed.'

'Can't sleep.'

'Whiskey?'

'Please.'

'Will you sit down to drink it?'

'I will.'

She brought two glasses. Eddie sat in the chair across from her and laid his head back. 'You got any recording gear I could wear tomorrow?'

'Plenty.'

'Can you rig me something up now?' She rose and left the room, and he sat staring at the empty high-backed old chair she'd been nesting in.

Half an hour later, Eddie lay in bed, still angry. Angry at himself for not thinking things through, and angry at the people who believed kidnapping and blackmail were okay. He had tested the bug Mave built. Six times. No more sloppy preparation. He was going to try and make this episode short and not at all sweet for the captors of Sonny Beltrami.

SEVEN

They left Mave's Shack soon after dawn, driving through a sea mist that covered the wheels and made it look as though the car was floating eastward off the headland. Market Rasen racecourse was on the opposite coast, five hours' drive away. Maven sat wrapped in a tartan blanket. Her body clock was set to sleep mode from dawn to dusk, and she tried to get comfortable.

'Nice blanket.' Eddie said.

'Mmm.'

'Where'd you get it?'

'Blanket shop.'

'How come it didn't make an appearance yesterday when I asked for one for the picnic?'

'Because I didn't want two grass stains in it shaped like your arse bones.'

'So I had to lug the rug.'

'About all you're good for, rug lugging.'

'Say rug lugger six times.'

She tried. She failed. They laughed.

He let her settle into sleep, her skinny legs drawn beneath her, curled up like a child. The mist lifted as they left the coast behind and drove toward the rising sun.

They reached Market Rasen just before noon. The only movement from Mave during the journey had been with the gentle rocking of the car as it rounded bends and crossed uneven ground. Stationary now. Engine off. Still she slept.

Eddie shook her softly and she uncurled and looked at him and stretched and yawned. 'We here?'

'We're here. At the golf course. This is where you get off.'

'Any water?' Mave asked. Eddie passed her a bottle from the back seat. 'Put it in your bag.'

'I can buy some in the club house.'

'Just be careful not to lean against the wall. Somebody might think you're a golf club and pick you up and swing you.'

'Ha, ha. That's shapeism, or weightism or some ism or other that's probably against the law.'

Eddie knew that banter helped her nerves. But he worried what she'd do on her own for the next four hours. She opened the back door to reach for her holdall with the gear in it. 'See you later,' she said.

'Mave. Go easy. Take no chances. A two minute video clip should be enough. I'll make him get out of the car and come to mine.'

'I know. I know. You told me three hundred times last night.'

'And remember. I can't take my phone into the track. If anything goes wrong, leave me a voicemail.'

'Eddie! You do all the wisecracking to take my mind off things, then you switch straight to scare the shit out of me mode. You'd make a crap psychologist. See you later.' She closed the door and he watched in his wing mirror as she wandered toward the big club-house.

The talk in the weighing room was of how soon the three jockeys, Kellagher, Sampson and Blackaby, would face trial. Eddie overheard someone say McCarthy had been sacked. He borrowed a copy of *The Racing Post* and read the formal statement: the usual gushing appreciation from Buley about all McCarthy had done in his long career and how relieved his friends at the BHA were to see him leave in one piece to spend more time with his family.

What family? The poor bastard was on his own! Eddie was angry that Mac had lost his job, and frustrated that the big man hadn't called to tell him. He was even angrier with Buley as he knew Mac had been stitched up. Eddie asked the clerk of the scales if he could use the landline to make an urgent call.

McCarthy didn't answer. Eddie left a voicemail: 'Mac, why didn't you phone me? When did this happen? Jeez…what are you going to do now? Look, I'll get down there to see you as soon as I can, but call me this evening, okay?'

Eddie had three mounts booked for Dil Grant, a Canadian horseman who'd found his way to England via Hollywood bit parts, rodeo shows and seducing widows on Atlantic cruise ships. The widows supplied most of Dil's horses and paid his training fees promptly, but he was always grubbing for cash. Dil's life lurched from crisis to crisis and Eddie had concluded that the trainer couldn't live without chaos.

Dil legged Eddie up on Scamperalong, a compact little gelding likely to be suited by the tight right-handed track and the fast going.

And he was.

Eddie led nine rivals throughout, forty hooves rattling out a four and a half minute drum roll on the firm ground. Scamperalong scampered along and became Skipalong each time he met a hurdle, jumping it with skill and exuberance. Eddie's favourite part of riding a winner for Dil Grant was seeing how it opened up Dil's world again, that bright smile childlike and untainted, because everything Dil had dreamed of had once more become possible.

Eddie's other two mounts finished unplaced. He had no ride in the last, so he sat in the sun by the weighing room, scanning faces in a futile search for someone who looked guilty about kidnapping. Half an hour later, he drove out of the car park, bug in place at waist height, behind his belt.

He passed the golf club and turned right at the sign saying Dog Kennel Wood. Eddie knew this place because he'd once pulled in to nap for half an hour before the long drive home.

His eyes adjusted to the forest gloom as he cruised slowly along. Mave would be watching. There'd been no voicemails, so he had to assume all was well, and leave the rest to her.

He took a right at the junction and rolled along to the back of the 13th tee. He pulled in tight to the verge, lowered the window and switched off the engine.

Birdsong.

The scent of pine.

A muffled cry of "Fore right!"

Eddie watched his mirrors, not wanting to appear nervous by looking round. He settled back, fingering the bug again, and checking his flies. In the right wing mirror, he saw a green Range Rover approach, travelling fast. He sat up quickly, released the handbrake and shoved the gearstick to neutral in case the car hit him from behind.

But it stopped under hard braking about ten feet back, spraying wood chips and raising a dust cloud. Eddie wondered how long he'd need to wait before the man came to him, allowing Mave to get a video clip.

No time at all.

And it wasn't a man.

She was tall and slim, a catwalk swagger in fast forward as she tossed her long red hair and swung her arms in a short-sleeved blouse as white and glossy as a daylight moon. Jeans, boots. No jacket. No bag. No intention of getting in the back. She opened Eddie's passenger door and sat down and slammed it shut.

She didn't smile. Her facial bones looked like they'd been drawn in by a pencil artist. Sharp jawline and chin, high cheeks and deep brows. Eddie would have bet eastern European but for her red shining hair, fringed as sharply as her brow, hanging straight and heavy at the sides to touch the bicep-high cuffs of the blouse.

'You look much different from how you sounded on the phone,' Eddie said.

'I don't keep dogs so I can bark myself.'

'You're in charge?'

'That's right.'

He watched her. She held his gaze. 'Okay, what's the deal?' he asked.

'I want in on the racket you're running.'

'What racket would that be?'

'Come on, Malloy. We've still got Sonny.'

'I know that. I just want it clear that I'm not running any racket. I collect money for a friend of Sonny's. Sonny brings it to me. I take it to our mutual friend.'

'You tell Sonny what horses to bet.'

'I don't. That would be breaking the rules of racing. Sonny gets the info elsewhere, he does his job, and I take the money and pass it on.'

'Why doesn't Sonny take it direct to his friend?'

'To try to keep his friend's life uncomplicated.'

She watched Eddie, then did that wild and wilful head toss again, throwing in a hard look. Eddie sensed she was in charge of nothing. 'So it's Sonny's friend passing on the tips?' she said.

'Listen, I don't know anything about tips. A while back, Sonny asked me to help him out. I agreed.'

'Help him out by telling him which races were fixed.'

He turned in the seat to face her. 'Did Sonny tell you he was betting on fixed races?'

'He's told us nothing. But it doesn't take much working out. We've been watching him for a long time and he's yet to back a loser.'

'How much do you know about racing?' Eddie asked.

'Enough.'

'Not enough. Far from enough. You've no idea who Sonny's working for?' The doubt that had been in her eyes changed to a flash of fear. 'He's working for you.'

Eddie shook his head. 'If only. Do you seriously think that if I knew that every bet Sonny placed was likely to win, that I'd still be riding horses for a living?'

She watched him. 'Who does he work for?'

'I'd be doing you a big favour if I told you, and I don't think I owe you any favours.'

The anxiety level in her green eyes was rising. Eddie said, 'I'll do you one favour. Go straight to wherever you're holding Sonny and put him in this nice car of yours and take him back to where you found him, treating him gently along the way. And remember to tell him how sorry you are for making such a mistake. Then barricade your house and hope for the best.'

She did the hair flick thing again, and raised her chin. 'You're bluffing.'

Eddie shrugged. 'Don't say I didn't try.'

'We've got those pictures of you. And we've already got a buyer.'

'Good for you. Sell them. I've nothing to hide.'

'Then why did you agree to meet me?'

'Because your friend sounded what you obviously are…amateur. And I wanted Sonny out with the minimum of fuss. I now need to go and tell Sonny's friend. And that means there'll be a lot of fuss. A lot. You'd best get yourself back and start building those barricades.'

She opened the door. 'I'll call you later, Mister Malloy.'

'Okay. That call had better be to tell me that Sonny's out.' He watched her in the mirror. The swagger had gone. She walked staring at the ground. She turned and came toward the car again. Eddie rolled the window down. 'Don't try to follow me,' she said.

'Okay.'

'I'll be checking.'

'I won't follow you. No need.'

She turned away, moving faster this time and resuming her toughness once back in the car with an aggressive, wheel-spinning reverse. Eddie waited. Mave popped up by the open window and shouted 'Boo!'

He smiled.

'You didn't even flinch,' she said.

'Mave, the best bet of the week was that you'd do that. Get in and tell me about your day.'

EIGHT

After the long drive back to Mave's house, Eddie made tea and sandwiches. Mave cared little for doing anything unless technology was involved. Eddie brought a tray of stuff to her desk and pulled up a chair. She always worked in the gloom, a short desk lamp shone for Eddie's benefit only. On her PC screen, she zoomed in on a map of the UK with a single tiny red light animation flashing in the West Midlands.

'You got it?' Eddie asked.

'Looks like Chaddesley Corbett.'

'There's a point to point meeting there. Martin Tate's old yard's close by.'

She closed in and switched to Google Earth and they spiralled down from space to a house lying in about three acres at the bottom of a dead end lane just off the A448. Two vehicles were in the picture, neither one the Range Rover that Mave had stuck a tracker on.

'Could be their place,' Eddie said, 'or just some safe house where they're holding Sonny. Can you find out who lives there?'

'If it's changed hands in the last ten years or so, it'll have been on the Internet. Once I've got the address and postcode, I can find out who owns it.'

'Crack on.'

The redhead rang at ten-forty and the recording app Mave had put on Eddie's phone kicked in. 'You call your friend and tell him if he wants to see Sonny again, we'd better get the name of the next horse that's going to win,' she said.

Eddie sighed. 'Okay. To use an old cliché, it's your funeral.'

'When will it be?'

'The funeral?'

'The tip!'

'Calm down. I don't know.'

'Tell him we need to know within forty-eight hours.'

'I will pass that on,' Eddie said.

'I'll call you in the morning.'

'You do that.' Eddie hung up. Mave checked the dialling code of the pay phone. 'Bromsgrove.'

'About ten minutes' drive from that house.' Eddie pointed to the Google Earth picture.

'We could be there in three hours. How are you at sleeping in cars?' she asked.

'Depends how you are at driving?'

'I'm good. I don't brake much.'

'Others do, then, no doubt.'

'Only the scaredy cats.'

'I'll drive.'

'You've already done ten hours today, Eddie. I've slept. My working day's just starting.'

They watched each other.

'Do I get the blanket this time?' Eddie asked.

She nodded.

'No rug?'

'No rug. And I'll fill the coffee flask.'

'Lordy! Manual labour for Maven Judge. Whatever next?'

Ten minutes later, they were locking the house up. Maven said. 'Wait! I forgot.' She hurried back in, and came out with three cushions. Eddie smiled. 'Very thoughtful of you, Mave. A blanket and cushions. I'll think I'm at The Ritz.'

'They're not for you.' She opened the driver's door and stacked them on the seat before climbing in and adjusting them. Even at that, her chin only reached the top of the steering wheel. Eddie got in the back and said 'Drive down to the harbour first.'

'Why?'

'See if there's a sub docked that can lend us a spare periscope.'

'Very funny. I can see fine now.'

'You look like you can see three yards of bonnet and a yard of road.'

'Did I at any point today criticize your driving?'

'Tough thing to do when you're prone. And snoring.'

'I don't snore!'

'No, I suppose you don't. More like a purring noise.'

'Shut up, Malloy, and go to sleep.' She turned the key and wrestled with the gearstick. 'How do you get this heap into first?'

'It's an automatic.'

'Oh. Right.'

'Can you reach the mirror to adjust it?'

'I can reach you to slap you!' She adjusted the mirrors and they set off. 'Which way is it?'

'Mave. Stop.'

She looked down to find the brake and stamped on it, bouncing the coffee flask onto the floor.

'When did you last drive a car?'

'When I passed my test.'

'How old were you?'

'Seventeen.'

'How old are you now?'

'Thirty-four.' Their eyes met in the mirror and she shrugged. 'I thought it was like riding a bike. It just came back to you.'

'Move over.'

'You need to sleep, Eddie.'

'I'd rather be tired and alive than asleep and dead.' Eddie got out as Mave slid across. She settled with the blanket around her. 'I'll stay awake, and talk to you,' she said.

'What a treat.'

NINE

As the satnav announced "destination reached", they made one pass at the top of the dead-end lane. Lights were on in the house. It was too dark and too far along to see if the Range Rover was in the driveway. They turned off onto a track in the woods and parked. 'You coming?' Eddie asked. Maven nodded, nerves sealing her voice box. She undid her seat belt.

'Be careful closing the door.' Eddie said. They walked back along the road, listening for vehicles, eyes adjusting to the rural blackness.

'I can see better now we're out of the woods,' Maven said.

'Courtesy of your ancestors. Your pupils dilate as you get used to the darkness.'

They walked in silent apprehension until they saw the lights in the house through the trees. Maven whispered, 'What are you going to do?'

'I don't know, yet.'

Ten more paces. They heard a vehicle approach. Eddie took Maven by the arm and they stepped onto the grass verge and into the hawthorn bushes. Eddie sensed her holding her breath. The car flashed by. They got back on the road.

'What if they're armed?' Said Maven

'They're amateurs. They'll be more afraid than we are.'

'Than I am, you mean.'

Eddie smiled.

The gate to the wide driveway lay open. The surface was loose, heavy gravel. A van was parked five paces inside the entrance. A gate in the front hedge led to a door via a row of circular stepping stones. Light came from the windows on either side of the door, but other than the stepping stones, gravel surrounded the house. Eddie signalled Mave to follow, and they retreated. Eddie said, 'We'll have to go round the back through the fields. The gravel at the front will make too much noise.'

'Okay.'

Dew had formed already in the meadow they crossed. Mave looked at the sky. 'The clouds are breaking up. Do you think they could see us by moonlight? '

'I'd be more worried about the dogs picking up our scent...our sound.'

'How do you know they've got dogs? '

'Most country folk do.'

'Watch-dogs?'

'We'll soon find out.'

The property was unprotected at the rear. No hedges. No gravel. A railed paddock backed onto the house. They ducked through the gaps in the wooden spars. A strip of light showed near the centre of the big window where the curtains hadn't been fully closed. All Eddie could see through the gap was a coffee table with bottles of alcohol on it. No sound came from inside. Eddie led Mave to the side opposite the driveway where a windowful of pale light fell on the Range Rover Maven had tagged that afternoon.

Eddie turned to her and smiled. She looked petrified. Eddie whispered, 'Do you want to go back to the car and wait for me? '

'No.'

'Stop worrying.'

They stayed close to the wall. The window was too high for Eddie to see through. He signalled to Mave that he'd lift her. She nodded. Eddie bent and hugged her hips from behind and slowly raised her to the corner of the window. 'Nobody,' she whispered. 'That's the kitchen.'

Eddie lowered her. She seemed less afraid. That didn't last long. When she saw him try the handle on the kitchen door, Eddie heard her sharp intake of breath. The door opened. Eddie gestured for her to follow.

Inside.

Door closed behind them.

No noise except the buzz of snoring…it sounded as though it was coming from the next room. They crossed to the door which lay open a few inches. Eddie could feel Maven close behind. He eased the door halfway ajar and waited. Nothing. Leaning forward, Eddie looked inside. Two people. Asleep in chairs. The redhead was one. The snorer was a man whose chin was on his chest, thick dark hair hung over his face. His ankles were crossed, his knees wide apart. Beside him, on the green rug, was a glass with a mouthful of red wine in it. The redhead held an empty glass in her lap with both hands. Eddie walked over and took the glass from her. She stirred for a moment, then closed her eyes again.

'Wake up.' Eddie said. She shifted sideways on the sofa, the overhead light glinting in her hair. She stared at Eddie, and her sleepy eyes filled with panic and she tried to rise. Eddie pushed her back down. 'Jonty!' She cried. Eddie turned to look at him. Slowly he raised his head and narrowed his eyes against the light, then lifted a hand to shade them as though trying to block the sun. The redhead looked afraid. Eddie said, 'Where's Sonny?'

'Jonty!' She was angry now. Eddie hauled him from the chair by the lapels of his leather jacket, and turned, swinging him, keeping him off balance, then dumped him on the sofa beside the redhead.

'Where is Sonny? I won't ask again.'

She looked at Jonty, then at Eddie. 'He's in the darkroom upstairs.'

'The darkroom?' Eddie said.

'For pictures,' Jonty said, 'developing.'

Eddie stepped back. 'Lead the way.' She got up, barefoot. Eddie kicked Jonty's ankle. 'You too.' He slid to the edge of the cushion and pushed himself to his feet. Eddie looked round at Maven and smiled.

Jonty unlocked the door of the darkroom. Eddie made him and the redhead go in first and turn on the light. Eddie followed, then took a step back, bumping Mave. 'Jeez! What's that smell?' Eddie asked.

'Developing chemicals. Sorry. We kept the fan on during the day.'

Mave went to Sonny who was shackled to a radiator. He smiled at her the way he always did, and she knew everything was okay. 'Are you all right?' Mave asked.

'Bit of a headache, but I'll live.'

Eddie said, 'Have you been locked up with this smell since they brought you here?'

'No, Jonty's right. They had the fan on most of the time.'

Eddie turned to the bedraggled Jonty. 'Most of the time! What are you doing with a darkroom anyway? Haven't you heard of digital?'

'I use both. As, I'm afraid, you'll soon see.'

It took them ten hungover minutes between them to find the keys to the handcuffs locking Sonny to the radiator. Mave sat with him, a hand on his shoulder, while they waited. She said, 'You seem kind of disappointed the excitement's all over.'

Sonny chuckled. 'I suppose I am.

Back in the big living room, they learned that the woman's name was Nina. She sat again on the sofa with Jonty. Sonny stood, his arm around Maven's shoulder. Eddie sat where Jonty had been and watched him and Nina. Jonty was fully awake now, thin-faced, big-eyed, his prominent Adam's apple bobbing as he tried to swallow. 'Can I get some water?'

'Any weapons in the house? Eddie asked. Sonny said, 'They had a shotgun.' Eddie looked at Jonty. 'It's under the stairs.'

Within ten minutes, Eddie had the gun, Jonty had his water, Nina had a large measure of gin, and the others had coffee. Sonny also had an apology from his captors. Jonty and Nina had a problem, and from the story they told, Eddie discovered he had an even bigger one.

TEN

Jonty Saroyan was a freelance photo-journalist. He'd been working on a magazine piece about the decline of the traditional bookmaker. He'd noticed Sonny one time too many collecting a bundle of notes from a bookie. Jonty followed him. Not only had he a file of pictures of Eddie accepting money from Sonny, he'd a hundred more of Sonny taking wads of cash from various bookies. Each picture was time stamped. Jonty had sold copies of the pictures to a tabloid journalist called Barney Scolder.

'Sorry,' said Jonty, 'we've been pretty desperate.' He and Nina had met a year ago. She told them that her marriage to a man called Onur Olusu had soured after five years and that he had kidnapped their son Zeki, and taken him to Turkey. As she explained this, Eddie glanced at Sonny, who seemed unruffled, even sympathetic.

'So,' Nina said, 'we need to pay a private investigator to find Zeki and bring him back. With all this corruption stuff coming up in the courts, we thought the papers would pay a lot for those pictures. But we could only get ten grand. That's when I had the idea of trying to get in on whatever scheme you were running. I'm sorry. I'm at my wit's end worrying.'

Eddie said, 'So you thought you'd bugger up Sonny's life and ruin mine, as yours wasn't going so well?'

'We thought you were a crook,' said Jonty.

'Did you ask Sonny? '

Nina nodded.

'And, he obviously told you the same as I did, that I was collecting the money for a friend. I knew nothing about the horses he was betting. Sonny knew nothing until he got a phone call.' Another nod, then Nina said quietly, 'We didn't believe that.'

'Do you believe it now? 'Eddie said. Nina looked at Jonty and he tried to prompt her with his eyes. She turned to Eddie. 'I suppose so.'

Eddie said, 'You need to get those pictures back.' Jonty put his arm across her shoulders and said, 'We've already paid the money as a deposit to the guy who's going to find Zeki.'

Eddie shook his head in disbelief. Maven watched him, and Eddie could see she wanted to speak, to offer them the money to pay the journalist for the pictures. But she stayed silent.

Eddie said, 'Then tell Barney Scolder the pictures were faked.' The couple looked at each other. Jonty said, 'Can you give us some time to try and think this through?'

'I doubt that's going to make any difference, is it?'

Jonty rubbed his face, beard shadow crackling lightly. 'Probably not.'

'How well do you know Scolder?' Eddie asked.

'Not that well.'

'Has he asked you to testify that the photos are genuine and that you followed Sonny etcetera, if it all comes to court? '

'Yes.'

'Did you sign a contract with his paper to do that? '

He pursed his lips and looked at Eddie. 'Yes.'

'Fuck.' Eddie said quietly, and stared at the floor.

Dawn was breaking when Sonny drove Eddie's car out of the woods. Mave was in the passenger seat. Eddie lay in the back hoping for some sleep on the way back to Maven's Shack. Eddie was due to ride at Catterick and he worried about dozing off at the wheel on the way there. Sonny offered to drive him to the races.

'Thanks, Sonny. But given that we're both likely to be featuring on the front page of a Sunday newspaper sometime soon, it might be best if you're not seen chauffeuring me around.'

'I'll drive you.' Maven said.

'I'd rather walk. Barefoot.'

Sonny smiled and insisted. 'We'll be okay. It'll give us a chance to make some plans.'

'What, like leaving the country?'

Sonny chuckled. 'We'll figure something out, Eddie. Don't worry.'

Eddie gathered the blanket and tried to settle. His best hope for sleep was the rocking of the car and exhaustion. Maybe that would be enough to slow Eddie's frantic mind and let him sleep. The biggest bully among the rabble of negative thoughts was the memory of Eddie being warned off. Five years in the wilderness, just when Eddie was at the top of the tree.

Seven years ago, Eddie's licence was returned, and he was just managing to make a decent living again from riding. He lay in the back seat knowing this could finish him.

ELEVEN

Broc Lisle rose at dawn and began the routine he'd followed since leaving the army. He emptied his bladder, pulled on black shiny compression underwear, and picked up a 16kg kettlebell. After twenty minutes of exercising, he lay on a yoga mat to rest and stretch and plan the blocks of time in his day.

First was a breakfast meeting with Nic Buley who had contacted him out of the blue to discuss 'an opportunity.' The research he'd done on Buley indicated that the CEO of the British Horseracing Authority was an ambitious man, like himself. Though Buley was just 37. Lisle envied him that.

Sweat puddled below his neck.

Lisle thought of his father, who had been a racing man. He'd won the Grand Military Cup at Sandown and young Lisle had been there with his mother, watching from a private box. He recalled that even at ten, discipline and dignity decreed that he applaud politely rather than jump up and down shouting his father home on the big black horse.

That seemed like ten lifetimes ago. Now dementia had robbed his father of any discipline or dignity. His days were spent haunting the corridors of a nursing home. Wandering like a lost soul, his face pained and questioning, his eyes seeking escape.

It was a fine nursing home. And the sale of the family house in Berkshire would finance Lisle senior's care as long as he lived. Broc had no concerns about money. What troubled him was the aimless wandering. When his father had first been admitted to the home, Broc had visited every night. An only child, his mother long dead, Broc was the sole family carer. And he would have borne it bravely had he not been confronted every night with the sight of his father groping his way along the walls of that place, touching every door, trying every handle, searching for a way out, seeking a response from a dementia-riddled brain, a plan, some method of escape.

It so distressed his son, that Broc had eased himself down to twice-weekly visits. After long nights of soul-searching, Broc had decided that the nightly visits were of little benefit to his father, but of serious detriment to his own mental health.

Twice a week he could handle. Whatever proposal Buley had for him, it would need to allow for those two visits.

Lisle sat up on the exercise mat. Then got to his feet without using his hands. Core strength. How old would he be when the ability to do this deserted him? How long could dementia be delayed if he looked after his physical fitness as well as he'd always done?

He shaved at the sink, spending more time working around his pencil moustache than on the rest of his face.

Lisle stepped into the warm shower for three minutes of washing with unscented soap. Gel left oil on the skin, preventing it from drying properly. He spun the shower dial to 'coldest' and forced himself to stand for thirty seconds.

One thing age could not rob him of was exhilaration when stepping out of a freezing shower. It lasted a long time. Lisle believed it fuelled his day.

He recorded his first voicemail message to cover the meeting with Buley, then opened a white noise app and chose the sound of men parading on a barracks square. Slowly, he dressed, doing everything by looking at his reflection in the wardrobe mirror. He knotted his tie, centred it, then stood to attention and saluted himself, and smiled.

He turned away and switched off the marching men.

For breakfast, Lisle ate one orange, then took a dozen vitamin pills. Five minutes later he locked up the small flat in North London and walked to Manor House underground station, mentally switching on what he called his 'encounter counter'. He kept a record of the number of people per day who recognized him from his media work. Many spoke to him. Some just looked for a few seconds. A few were borderline "I think I know him but can't recall his name." Lisle counted them all. His record was 247.

Coffee was all the breakfast Eddie Malloy could risk as he had to do ten stones in the handicap hurdle. Sonny ate bacon and eggs in his usual unhurried manner. His short internment hadn't seemed to bother him. He'd been confident Mave and Eddie would get him out, even if it meant paying, and he'd been carrying plenty of insulin. The affection Maven held him in had left him in no doubt she would do exactly for him as he would have done for her.

But he insisted on driving Eddie to Catterick races. 'I'll drop you a mile from the track. Nobody will see us, and you can get a nice warm up walking in.' Maven had offered to pay the taxi fare for the 400 mile round trip.

She seemed suddenly lost. For years she'd worked toward perfecting this betting plan, shunning not just publicity, but daylight. Night was what she knew. In the dark she was comfortable, especially out here on the western rim of the country.

Now the plan had backfired. On her friends.

She was a genius. She'd won more than four million pounds. But she was lost. Sitting at the table, her back to the window and the morning sun, Eddie squinted against the light to watch her. She said, 'Do you want me to see this journalist and make him an offer he can't refuse?'

'That'll just drop me deeper in it.'

'He won't know who's offering.'

'But he will know that somebody thinks the pictures are worth more than he paid, and for them to have any value, I must be guilty.'

A silhouetted nod from Mave. 'I'm sorry, Eddie. I should have thought this through properly.'

'Not your fault. I was the one who didn't do the thinking.'

'But I'm the one who's been nagging you for the past two years to join me.'

'Your plan was to wait until I retired. Remember? '

'I should have stuck to that. I'm sorry.'

'Spilt milk,' Sonny said, 'No point crying over it now. We'll fix it.' He smiled a big dazzling denture smile and mopped yolk with the last of his bread. The excitement seemed to have flushed away his natural melancholy.

The interior of the car was hot. Eddie lowered the window as they pulled away, and they waved to Mave. Sonny clicked to open the other windows, and the smell and the sound of the sea filled the car and he slowed to savour it. Smiling, he turned to Eddie and began singing *Oh What a Beautiful Morning.*

By the time Sonny dropped Eddie, they'd discussed all the possibilities with the pictures. Timewise, Eddie believed he had until the end of the upcoming trial of the jockeys at The Old Bailey. The *Racing Post*'s reporter reckoned it would begin on August 3rd and that it could run for weeks, maybe months.

It would be pointless publishing the pictures before the end of the trial. If the three jockeys were convicted, Scolder's paper would run Eddie's story as "the one that got away". If the three were found not guilty, the line would be that the sport was still crooked.

So Eddie had some time. What he was going to do with it, he hadn't yet worked out.

The wasting Eddie had done to make ten stones paid off as he rode the winner of the big hurdle race. Normally he'd stay at the track until racing had finished, but Eddie had nothing booked after the fourth race, and he had a mile to walk to meet Sonny.

On the drive back, Sonny told Eddie he planned to stay with Mave for a week. Eddie decided to head south and home.

As Eddie packed his bag, Mave watched. She said, 'Come and have a picnic with me on the cliff before you go.'

'Ahh, the old rug-lugging ruse again.'

'No. I'll bring my blanket this time. My best blanket.'

Eddie turned to look at her. 'Your best one?'

'Promise.'

'Okay.'

It was early evening, much breezier than last time and the tide was at full flow, sending echoes up from the rocks of Hell's Mouth Bay. Mave's face held many words...she was just finding them hard to say. 'Do you want me to stay?' Eddie asked.

'I don't particularly want you to go. I don't *need* you to stay, if that's what you mean. I don't even need Sonny to stay now that I know he's all right.'

'So spit it out. What's up? '

Her hair blew across her face and she moved a rubber band from her wrist to tie it up in a single flourish, like a magician. 'Well, one of the reasons I wanted you in on this as a partner was to try and reduce the chance of you getting mixed up in any more of your investigations. Your luck is going to run out. Simple statistics.'

'It just did.'

'I know. And rather than prevent it, I caused it.'

Eddie shuffled closer to her. 'Tell you what, you were right about this blanket. The rug was much better.' Eddie poured coffee from the flask. 'Listen Mave, drop all this guilt stuff. It's not like you. Man up, as the saying goes.'

She punched Eddie's shoulder. 'It's not so much you I feel guilty about, it's my poor judgement. A child could have seen this coming.'

'Well that makes two of us, as I said before, so forget it.'

She shook her head, and pulled daisies, throwing them to the wind. 'I'm done with this now. No more bets.'

'That's the opposite of what I need.'

She looked at him. Eddie said, 'When the pictures get published and they haul me in, I know you'll speak up for me.'

'Of course!'

'We'll it's time to start building some evidence that your system is completely independent of any input from me. Open online accounts with every bookmaker and get as much on as you can. By the time my case comes up, you'll have a list of closed accounts with every bet listed. Just make sure you don't bet in any race I'm riding in.'

'Okay.'

'You'll be exposed after that, but you can go back to using Sonny.'

'No. It's too dangerous. I'll either figure out something fool proof or chuck it completely.'

'And do what? '

She looked across the sea. 'Who knows? Travel, maybe.'

'Well, remember to keep enough money for driving lessons. Or a chauffeur. Or compensation for the public.'

She smiled. 'You could be my chauffeur.'

'The perfect job. Driving a woman who sleeps all day. You'd best get a motorhome.'

'I might just do that.'

TWELVE

It was close to midnight when Eddie drove down the rough track to his house in the small valley. Bats whizzed through the beams from the security light. As Eddie got out of the car, an animal screamed from the forest as jaws closed on it.

Bad omen, Eddie thought.

The house was cool but smelt musty. Eddie made coffee, and pinged Mave, as ordered, to tell her he was home. Then Eddie sat in the small back room, which he'd christened the Snug. His fireplace was there, and the room was dominated by a large picture window offering a view of the long garden and the woods beyond.

He sat in darkness, playing chess in his head with the potential moves he could make before Barney Scolder made his with the pictures.

Peter McCarthy came to his mind. The big man had not returned Eddie's call. Eddie guessed that Mac's resignation was tied to the surprise announcement that Kellagher, Sampson and Blackaby were to be prosecuted.

He rang Mac's home number. 'Eddie, I'm sorry. It's been frantic. Come to my house in the morning for breakfast. It's better we talk face to face.'

In the morning Eddie set off, reflecting on how long it had been since Mac had invited him to his isolated cottage on the hill. Mac didn't 'do' visitors. Eddie knew that Jean McCarthy had suffered agoraphobia for many years. Mac had been protective of her privacy. Now, nine months on from Jean's death, Mac remained reclusive.

Jean had died suddenly, after a minor operation went wrong and she contracted pancreatitis. Complications quickly set in, the worst of them necrosis. Ten days after going into hospital for a two-hour appointment, Mac's wife died in the intensive care unit.

Eddie wondered how Mac would cope without his job while still grieving for his wife. The big man had survived for years by adjusting, by making few waves, by compiling victories in his name from the accomplishments of others. But he did so in such a way that Eddie found it endearing. Eddie had done him many favours and most had been returned.

Eddie saw Mac at the window as he pulled to a halt in the wide driveway. Mac raised a hand. By the time Eddie was out of the car, Mac was opening the front door, which was framed by a trellis of roses, and Eddie walked through a tunnel of scent.

'Beautiful morning again,' Mac said, shaking hands.

'It is. How are you?' Eddie looked Mac up and down. 'I'll never get used to seeing you in just a sweater and cords.'

Mac smiled sadly. 'I think it'll be a while before I stop reaching in the wardrobe for my suit in the mornings.'

'It'll pass. At least you're not stuck in an office on a day like this. Especially the same office as that prick, Buley.'

'True. Come in. I'll put the kettle on.'

They sat in the garden, old cast iron chairs turned east toward the sun, coffee pot on the table alongside Mac's favourite pastries.

Mac said, 'How are you?'

'Surviving, with a tale to tell. But you go first.'

Mac raised his shoulders and opened his hands, then broke eye contact to look at ground. 'There's not much to say, Eddie. Nic Buley and I have had a few disagreements as you know...We just reached a point on Friday that was, well, completely unacceptable to me.'

'This court case?'

Mac nodded, as though reluctant to continue. Eddie said, 'Even the lads were surprised when they heard it was suddenly going to court.'

'An astounding decision, and uncharacteristic of Buley, I must say. It seems his narcissism has got the better of his usual guile.'

Mac told him about Buley's ambition to have the case started before the first anniversary of his appointment.

'Crazy, Mac. But it doesn't surprise me. He'd have wanted you lined up to take the fall, you see. That's where it made sense to him. But you called his bluff. Don't be surprised if he comes begging you to go back.'

'Not now. It's gone public. He'll blunder blindly on and worry about a scapegoat later.'

Eddie nodded toward the table. 'I think you'd best eat that last Danish before the wasps do.'

Mac picked it up. Eddie said, 'So what do you think you'll do, now?'

Mac shrugged and chewed. Eddie said, 'All those years of experience. They'll stand you in good stead. They'll be queuing up to offer you a job.'

Mac smiled sadly, 'Kind words, my friend. If only. I'm fifty. And fat. And from a different epoch. I hear people in London saying how hard it is to get a job in your mid-thirties. Fifty's ancient these days.'

'I know plenty rich owners, Mac. I'll tell them a good man's going to waste.'

'No, you won't. I mean, I'm grateful for the thought, but I don't want someone creating a job for me out of sympathy. Money's not an issue. I'll find something, maybe do some charity work.'

Eddie sighed and clasped his hands as he leant toward the big man. 'Well, don't rule out a recall once Buley makes a balls of this. He'll have nobody to hide behind, so he'll need to go. Whoever takes over would be crazy not to ask you back.'

'We'll see, Eddie. We'll see. Anyway, tell me about your troubles.'

Eddie told him about the pictures, and Mac reacted with all those expressions Eddie knew so well, manipulating his face while chewing, leaving Eddie in no doubt he was in as deep as he'd feared.

Mac drained the coffee mug and set it down and looked at Eddie. 'What are you going to do?'

'I was hoping you might have some ideas.'

'You were always the ideas man, Eddie.'

'Well, I'm stuck. If I try to get the pictures back, he'll think I'm guilty. If I don't, they'll publish.'

He nodded slowly, wiping his hands and mouth with a napkin. He said, 'If it's any consolation, I'm pretty sure the BHA *will* lose this case at the Old Bailey.'

'Why? Apart from Buley being a dickhead, that is?'

'Various reasons. Insufficient evidence. Lack of a deep understanding of the intricacies by the prosecution, inexperienced witnesses, and crucially, not a damned thing on Jordan Ivory, who's behind it all.'

'The big bookie?'

'The big criminal. But one without a single conviction. And that's what's made the case so difficult. We know those three are working for Ivory, but unless one of them admits it, or someone in Ivory's camp turns, all we have is circumstantial evidence. It will be hard enough for experts to agree on how those three were manipulating results. To expect a jury with no experience of racing to interpret race footage and betting market fluctuations, well, it's a total waste of time and money.'

'But that's the mystery here, Mac. Buley must know this. He wouldn't have needed you to tell him. Could he have something up his sleeve to make him look the hero come court time?'

'Well, the whole department has spent more than two years trying to build a solid case. We believe it centres on Ivory. Until there's hard evidence of his involvement with those three, I can't envisage anyone, Buley or anybody else, coming up with an ace by August third.'

'That's when the court case starts, isn't it?'

'So I'm told.'

Eddie watched him. 'You've been well stitched up here, Mac. They manage to get rid of you on Friday, which was, what, the twenty-fourth of July, and just over a week later the case is in court?'

'I was thinking that myself. The deadline Buley mentioned was the fifteenth. That's one year on from his appointment.'

'You spoke to any of your police contacts?'

Mac lowered his head. 'Not yet.'

'I don't suppose you've had much of an appetite for it. Sorry.'

Mac raised a hand. 'Don't worry.'

Eddie stood up. 'Look, Mac, I'll let you get on. Just leave Buley and the BHA to mess everything up without you.'

Mac, grunting, got to his feet. 'What about you? Is there anything I can help you with over these pictures?'

'Forget that too. If Buley's prosecution gets thrown out, it'll make things tough for Scolder's newspaper. Any quick attempt at dropping another jockey in it will look pretty lame to the public.'

'Well, I hope you're right. But, I'm around if you need me.'

Eddie reached to shake hands. 'Same goes here. You know that. I'm just ten minutes away if you want some company. We never close.' He smiled. Mac did too.

THIRTEEN

Over the next three weeks, Maven Judge steadily built her online portfolio of betting accounts. She joined an online tipping forum under an assumed name and began proofing her tips. Sonny resumed betting on the racecourse, but delivered the winnings to Mave in person.

At the start of her project, Mave had bought Sonny three static caravans: one in the south, at Salisbury: one in the midlands at Stourport and one in the northwest at Formby. As the summer wore on, Mave noticed that Sonny had settled in the Stourport site, and always travelled back there no matter where he'd been that day.

All Eddie could do was wait and watch the court case play out at the Old Bailey, while his frustration over Jonty and Nina grew. Driving home from Newton Abbot one evening in late August, Eddie got to thinking again about Sonny's kidnappers. He was angry that they'd escaped punishment while he continued to roast on the spit until Scolder decided to use the pictures.

If Eddie called the cops to report the kidnapping, the details of the photos would come out. And the bets. Mave would be outed, as would Sonny, and all for no benefit to Eddie. Also, he realized that his resentment was for what they did, rather than who they were. She'd been desperate. Jonty had wanted to help her. Neither knew Eddie. It was nothing personal.

But wherever Eddie turned with this, he ended up in a corner.

Since the prosecution of Kellagher, Sampson and Blackaby had begun, much of the talk in the changing room was of the court case. Three weeks in, most of the guys thought it was swinging in favour of the prosecution. Eddie said little. He wanted bent jockeys out of the business, but a "not guilty" verdict would neuter Scolder's story with the pictures.

There was an hour of daylight left as Eddie turned off the M4, and he decided he'd drop in to see how Mac was doing. He'd made a point of visiting at least twice a week since Mac had lost his job.

The big man was in the garden, as Eddie turned into the driveway. Mac was pacing the paths in the large rose beds, same old corduroys on, same worn brogues. Eddie walked toward him. 'You're beginning to look like a proper countryman with your flowers and that old hands-behind-the-back stooped walk. Beats rushing around in the city, eh?'

Mac smiled. 'How was Newton Abbot?'

'A winner-free zone.'

'Well, you're in one piece. That's invariably the best result of all.'

'True. But that long drive has left me with a desperate thirst for coffee.'

'Come inside. I'll put the kettle on.'

Seated at the kitchen table, Mac said. 'What's the word in the changing room on this case?'

'It seems to swing with regularity. Latest is that the prosecution is just on top.'

'What happens daily won't matter in the end. Come summing up time, when the jury files out, that's when they'll realize just how hard it is for ordinary folk to cut through all the racing jargon and the so-called expert interpretation of different rides.'

'No doubt, you're right. The lads seem to have taken to Broc Lisle. They love it when he swings into professional presenter mode for the press. He seems quite a character.'

'I feel for the man. He doesn't seem to understand that Buley's making him look a clown as the official spokesman. Buley's slipped quietly into the background and left the poor bugger to it.'

'Slithered, not slipped, Mac. Buley's a snake. He'll probably try to wriggle out of this when the case turns against the BHA.'

Mac looked at Eddie. 'From what I hear, I'm not sure he'll be able to.'

'Go on.'

'Not for publication...'

Eddie nodded. 'As ever. Soul of discretion.'

Mac said, 'Buley has offered the police three hundred grand to help with their costs.'

'Wow! I take it the defence don't know that?'

'Not yet.'

Eddie smiled, 'But some little bird is going to tell them?'

He shook his head. 'I'm not the vengeful type, you know that. I'm just sad they've ballsed this up.'

'Who told you about this...this bribe?'

'An old friend in the Met.'

'How are the police going to justify accepting money, effectively from the prosecution side?'

'They'll manage that all right on the grounds of public interest and budgetary demands. How they'll handle the PR aspect of implied bias, well, I don't know.'

'Desperate stuff from Buley though. All he's doing is proving your judgement spot on.'

'Maybe. But I'm told the funding was agreed and paid a while before I left. That's how they were able to bring the case at such short notice.'

'So, let me get this right...Buley has been so desperate to chalk up a result within a year of joining the BHA that he has persuaded the board to ante up almost a third of a million of racing's money to try and get a conviction that he'll claim sole credit for?'

'That sounds a fair summary.'

'And everyone else at the BHA stays mum. Everybody except you, which he'd have known, so he engineered your resignation?'

Mac shrugged. Eddie leant toward him. 'Mac, does that not make you very angry?'

'Sometimes,' Mac said quietly, lowering his head.

Eddie put both hands on the table and craned his neck low to try and look into McCarthy's eyes. 'Sometimes? Sometimes? I'm fucking livid about it, full stop!'

Mac nodded. Eddie grasped Mac's arm. 'Listen, let's do something about this! I know you've got other things on your mind, but this is not right!'

Mac looked up. 'What? What shall we do?'

'Something! You can't just sit here day after day or walk in the bloody garden or stand gazing down the valley at what used to be. Come on, Mac, fight!'

Mac smiled sadly. 'I always admired your guts. Whatever differences we had over the years, whatever problems you caused me, I always stood in awe at the fire in your belly. Does it never fade?'

'No it doesn't bloody fade when stuff like this is going on. You don't need fire in your belly, or guts or anything but a sense of fairness and the determination not to let them get away with it.'

Mac watched him flare then said quietly, 'But, in the end, Eddie, it doesn't matter. It's an insignificant scene played out on a tiny stage, and everyone will forget it the day after the decision.'

'I won't. And you shouldn't!'

The big man sat back and sighed. 'Perspective, Eddie. And perception. Yours differs from mine. And mine from many others.'

'So we just stand aside? Where does that leave us? Where does it leave the world if everybody just says that's how it is?'

'Fair point.'

'Think about it, Mac. If Buley gets away with this, who'll be next? Who'll be the next Peter McCarthy in his sights?'

Mac straightened and nodded slowly.

'Good,' Eddie said.

'What?'

'Your jaw muscles clenched when I said that.'

'They did?'

'Hard. There's life in you yet, old man. Let's get together and get Buley.'

Eddie stood. Mac looked up at him. 'Let me think about it.'

'You do that. Think about Buley's next innocent victim.'

Mac walked out with Eddie and raised a hand as he drove away. Then he looked down the valley, and beyond, to the churchyard where his wife lay.

FOURTEEN

When Eddie arrived home, he noticed Mave had pinged him on their secure PC link. He pinged her back. 'Sonny had an idea,' she said.

'I'm listening.'

'Give Nina Raine the next six tips live.'

'Raine…I guess she went back to her maiden name after the Turkish guy left her?'

'She'd never changed it, according to Sonny.'

'I think our Sonny has a soft spot for this Nina Raine.'

'In a fatherly way, I'm sure. Oddly enough, he's been using the Stourport site for a few weeks now. Always goes back there, and I needn't tell you it's not a million miles away from the house they took him to.'

'Jeez. I hope he's not developed one of these captive captor relationships, what do you call them?'

'Stockholm syndrome.'

'That's the one.'

'I doubt it. He was only there for forty-eight hours. I think he just feels for her with the loss of her son.'

'Maybe. I'll reserve judgement, I think. Anyway, go on, what's the plan?'

'I link to her PC next time I'm running the software, and let her see it make the selection live, so she knows for certain you're not involved.'

'And Sonny does the talking, so she doesn't know it's you who's behind it?'

'You got it.'

'And if she gets half a dozen winners, she can pay to get her son back?'

'I believe that was part of Sonny's thinking,' Mave said.

'Big softy, right enough.'

She smiled. 'Huh, listen to you!'

'So we prove to her and Jonty that I had nothing to do with the selections and none of the races was fixed, and come publication time, they speak up for me?'

'Correct. And I record and date every online session. And I then offer the BHA the same opportunity, to see the system working.'

They watched each other through the webcams. 'Well?' Mave asked.

'Worth a try. Want me to make contact?'

'Better if Sonny does it. You shouldn't be seen to be trying to influence them if they're going to be witnesses on your behalf.'

'Witnesses I wouldn't have needed if they hadn't set me up. Something tells me the world has suddenly turned upside down, Mave.'

'Well, we need to play the cards we're dealt.'

'True. Too late to call for a new deck, I suppose.'

'You'd still have ended up with the joker.'

Sonny phoned Eddie next morning and told him that Nina Raine had wept 'sore and long' with relief when he'd made her the offer. Nina had been preparing to make the trip to Turkey to search for Zeki.

The thought that something good would come of all this raised Eddie's spirits and he was in a better frame of mind as he drove to Stratford.

On his second ride, on the favourite in the handicap 'chase, Eddie smiled as they galloped toward the last fence. He had led all the way and was still ten lengths clear. His mount had jumped perfectly throughout giving him a rare experience: a flawless round in the late August sunshine doing the thing he loved above all.

His mount landed well balanced at the last and got away from the fence still galloping. Then Eddie saw a loose horse coming straight at him on the run-in. The animal had lost its rider on the first circuit, and rather than stay with the field, as most loose horses do, he'd become confused on getting to his feet and set off in the opposite direction.

Now he was on a collision course.

Eddie's horse was tiring. Eddie eased him toward the rail to try and keep him straight and give the other one the width of the track.

The loose horse would have missed them but for the collective gasp of shock from the stands spooking the chestnut who half ducked, half tried to turn, and cannoned into the bay gelding. Eddie came off in a sideways somersault and dropped right on top of the plastic rail just where it was strengthened by a vertical support. Eddie heard the snap of his collarbone and felt the stab of pain at the same time.

The ambulance driver was old enough to remember concrete posts and thick wooden rails on racetracks, and he left Eddie in no doubt he was a lucky man to be riding in these days of health and safety. Eddie consoled myself with that, plus the bonus of the break having happened before the proper winter season. He'd be back in the saddle well before then.

And in Newmarket, a boy who was dear to him would be eking out the last of his school holidays.

FIFTEEN

The Malloy family tree was tangled and scarred. A couple of years after Eddie had been banished at sixteen by a father who'd hoped he'd never see him again, Eddie's schoolgirl sister Marie, had borne a child.

Twelve years later, she'd been forced to tell Eddie about it. The shame. The birth. The adoption. The wiping of everything from family history. And last year Eddie had found her son and brought him 'home'.

But Marie did not want the boy.

At the time, she was nursing their mother, who was grieving for her dead husband. Caught in a tightening vise between two generations, Marie had chosen the one she'd known all her twenty-seven years.

So her son Kim had stayed with Eddie and 'Aunt' Laura for a year at Laura's racing yard on the north east coast of England. And life had been good through that spring and summer.

Eddie had thought Laura was 'the one'. After many false starts, he believed he'd found his partner. That promise held for a few months. But Laura was too big a character for Eddie Malloy. She was all confidence and independence and certainty as she blasted through life. 'They should have named a hurricane after you,' Eddie had told her.

She turned out to be Eddie's earthquake.

Living with her exposed his fault lines, and on their wildest days those cracks in Eddie's personality widened. In the calm periods, the fissures showed no signs of closing, of healing. Laura could live with them. Eddie couldn't. Eddie's fragility could not withstand the burden of expectation.

But Laura had never tired of the project that was Eddie Malloy. Eddie, as always, slunk away seeking sanctuary. Isolation. And that withdrawal was made easier, practically and emotionally, by the death of his mother. Her legacy provided the money for Eddie to build a house, a den, a retreat in a place of relative safety. And Eddie's nephew, Kim, had the option of moving to Lambourn to live with Eddie, or to move in with his birth mother, and try to rebuild his life and hers.

For Kim, duty came first, and he chose Marie, his mother, newly bereft of her own mother. Alone. Eddie promised to help them. He never shirked from healing others. So long as the emotional stethoscope was measuring the shortcomings of someone else, Eddie could cope just fine.

A year had passed since then. In that time, Eddie had been careful not to intrude too often, to give Kim and his mother a chance to build their relationship. If things worked out in the coming days, this would be the longest period he'd have spent with them as a family.

Eddie knew jockeys who had ridden with a broken collar bone, so driving with one, supported by a figure of eight brace, was nothing to complain about.

Kim sat astride the front wall waiting for him, the boy's smile and his black hair gleaming in the afternoon sun. Eddie rolled the window down as he slowed, and he saw an old saddle beneath Kim, the stuffing squeezing out through tattered leather. 'Is that attached to you or the wall?'

'Well, I've been here for an hour and my bum got too sore just sitting on the wall.'

'We need to toughen you up.'

Kim slid out of the saddle and walked alongside the car as Eddie steered into the drive and parked. Kim was thirteen and, Eddie thought, at that horribly awkward stage of wanting to do the adult thing. He held out his hand. Eddie shook it then grabbed him, intent on swinging him around, but the bolt of pain reminded him of the broken clavicle. Eddie settled for a hug and lowered Kim gently as the front door opened. Marie. Smiling. Smiling effortlessly…the first time Eddie could recall her doing that since she'd been a child.

She went to him. 'Will that collarbone stand another hug?' Eddie opened his arms as far as the brace would allow.

Kim and Eddie went for a long ride together. The boy's heart was set on being a jockey. He knew his uncle would help when the time came. They rode along the Devil's Ditch in the quiet of late afternoon, surrounded by hundreds of acres of Newmarket heath. After an hour spent talking about horses, Eddie asked how things were with his mother. Kim smiled across at him as they went at a steady walk. 'Marie, you mean? That's what she told me to call her.'

'Since when?'

'Just last week,'

'How do you feel about that?'

'I'm not sure. She said she knows how much I loved my adoptive mother, and she'd always felt awkward when I called her mum. But I've been wondering if she kind of wants to keep some distance between us.'

'Do you want me to speak to her about it? '

'No, thanks. It'll work its own way out. I'd rather talk to her about my real father than about what I call her, but she just says we'll talk about that "in good time", whatever that means. You never knew him, did you?'

'Never did. I was up and away by the time your mother met him. I guess she's told you about that part of the family history, me leaving home?'

Kim nodded, quiet again then said, 'Do you want to talk about it?'

Eddie looked at him, realizing the boy was uncomfortable with the subject but wanted to give Eddie the chance to unburden himself. And Eddie loved him all the more for it. 'Not now,' Eddie said, 'But thanks for asking. I've never really talked to anyone about it. Someday I will. And watch out, it might just be you.'

Kim smiled. 'I don't mind. It must have been a horrible thing for you. When I think about it, my stomach flips and I feel I might be sick.'

'It was a horrible thing for all of us, and it affected everybody in different ways. Your mother, too. It can't have been easy for you since you decided to try and make a go of things with her. Though it looks to me you're both doing pretty well on it.'

'We are. It's been much harder for her. She's been carrying a ton of guilt for years. It's been easier for me, I think.' Eddie felt an odd mixture of sadness, happiness and admiration for him then. His mother had effectively rejected him twice and here he was trying to heal her wounds as well as his own.

Eddie looked across at him as they held that steady walking pace in the heart of a wide empty land. 'I'm proud of you, Kim. Proud just to know you, never mind to be your uncle.' Kim blushed and shrugged and looked away, then said, 'I'll race you to that big tree at the end of the row!'

Eddie smiled. 'Okay.'

'And don't be letting me win. Try your hardest.'

'I always do. Always.'

'Ready? '

Eddie kicked his horse and yelled and got the drop on his nephew, leading him by a couple of lengths as they galloped west toward the sun.

SIXTEEN

That night, Eddie sat with his sister in the kitchen, the only room where Eddie felt comfortable. The dark formal sitting rooms, gloomy stairway and the four bedrooms upstairs held no warmth for him. He remembered his first visit when his parents were still alive. Eddie had been a reluctant caller on what he'd thought a mission of mercy. There had been no prodigal son moment, only resentment from Eddie's father, and a cool reception from his mother, who never dared cross her husband.

Now they were gone, but their spirits remained.

Eddie looked across the wide pine table at Marie, her dark hair tied back, eyes a vivid blue with more life in them than Eddie had ever seen. He was struck by how pretty she was. Family troubles had separated them for fifteen years. When Eddie had first met her again as an adult, she'd been surly and defensive. Since Kim had come back into her life, she'd bloomed. The furrows had gone from her brow, the cynicism from her eyes, and Eddie saw much more of her fine teeth in frequent smiles.

She sipped white wine and nodded toward the strapping on Eddie's injury. 'Your collarbone survived a gallop with Kim, okay?'

'Ahh, I'm soft compared with some of the lads. They'd ride with broken legs if the doc would let them.'

'You're his one and only, you know, Eddie. You're the best in his eyes.'

'He's a great kid. I wish I could see more of him.'

'You're welcome here, anytime. You know that.'

'I do. But I need to make sure Kim, and you, are kept out of the scrapes I keep getting myself into. We almost lost Kim once before.'

'Those scrapes, as you call them, seem to go with the sport. You won't be free of them until you retire. And knowing you, you'll still find ways of getting mixed up with other people's problems. You're a natural-born angry young man…well maybe not so young these days.' She smiled and drank again.

Eddie raised his glass of water, 'Cheers, Sis.' He told her about the pictures and about Mave and Sonny and Nina Raine, and the chances of him being made to look like a cheat by the media, feeling lousy as her old frown gradually returned. 'Sorry, Marie.'

'You were only trying to help', she said quietly as she rested her chin on her hands and stared at the table.

Eddie said, 'I don't know if I should tell Kim.'

She looked up sharply. 'He wouldn't believe a bad word against you, no matter how many newspapers printed it.'

'I know. I'm more afraid of him losing his temper and wanting to pitch in to help.'

'It sounds like you've got a good plan together already.'

Eddie nodded, then reached across and rested his hand on hers. He said, 'I'd best tell him. The plan could easily go wrong. I'd rather he was prepared, especially with all the shit he'll get from other kids.'

She slid her hand from under his and picked up her wine glass and drank, then nodded. 'Okay.'

'He'll still be awake, won't he?'

'He reads himself to sleep. Been through the whole Dick Francis series.'

'Could be worse. Might be Playboy.'

'That was your favourite at that age, was it? I doubt they even do it anymore.'

'You're probably right.'

'Anyway. Kim finds racing a lot more exciting than women.'

Eddie got up and pushed the chair in. 'It won't last. Trust me.'
She smiled and said, 'And that's when life's real troubles start.'
Eddie went upstairs.

SEVENTEEN

Broc Lisle sat watching his father. This was the first time Lisle had visited and found him seated in his room. The staff told Lisle that his father's endless walking was finally taking a toll on his energy levels. He was resting more often.

'Getting tired, father?' Lisle said, smiling and leaning forward to put himself directly in his father's eyeline. That was the only time he had a chance of getting a response of some kind. Occasionally, the old man even raised a smile or managed a few intelligible words. Although dementia had set in, Lisle senior had come into the home as a result of a brain injury.

Waiting to cross a London street on his mobility scooter, a kindly driver had stopped to wave him across. Seething behind this kindly driver was an impatient one who was cursing this fool for stopping in the middle of the road for no apparent reason.

He swung his car out and stamped on the pedal for maximum noise and speed to show this moron how to use the roads.

That's when Lisle senior's scooter emerged into his path.

A £500 fine and a six-month driving ban for a man whose impatience had ruined the life of another. But it did not alter Broc Lisle's world view. He had seen many bad things done to people, few of them deserved, and quite a number driven by bloodlust and cruelty.

Why me? Why him? Why us? Pointless questions, Lisle knew. Pointless.

Broc Lisle lightly kissed his father's head. 'I'll see you on Friday. Less walking, more rest. You hear?'

Lisle left Manor Park underground and waited for a break in the traffic. His 'encounter counter' antenna was still working, and he checked those passing in vehicles as well as the pedestrians on the other side of the crossing. Since he'd taken this BHA job, his mental encounter graph was on a steady downslope. It was important to him that he acknowledged this, otherwise, what was the point of keeping figures? Where was the pleasure in celebrating highs?

He crossed and turned west toward his flat. Light from the setting sun highlighted the roof from behind, and Lisle slowly shook his head. 'I need a big sky,' he muttered.

He locked the door behind him, undressed and showered.

Wearing a clean white shirt and soft twill trousers, he sat by his telephone and searched for Cynthia's number. This job was not working out as he'd hoped. Mister Buley had been making himself less accessible. Jordan Ivory's name was coming up with increasing frequency as the Old Bailey case was slipping. Lisle needed more information on both.

Lisle had known his lack of experience in racing would be a drawback. But he had broken that down and considered it and judged it surmountable. What he did understand keenly was when the odds were in his favour. This had been a marginal decision, taking this job, and he now believed his original calculations had been wrong. The odds had been against him, because Mister Buley had not supplied a comprehensive set of data. Worse, Mister Buley had obscured some important facts.

But Broc Lisle would see it through. A change of odds was much less important than implementing orders. Persistence would see him through. Persistence and innovation…

He found the number and dialled…Persistence…Innovation…And some cherished friends. 'Cynthia?'

'Broc! How lovely to hear from you.'

EIGHTEEN

At home with Kim and Marie, eating with them, helping with the horses, working the day through, trying to muck in as best he could with a strapped clavicle, Eddie began to sense the rhythm of their lives.

Marie had been ten when Eddie left home in Cumbria. Since then they had seen little of each other. The estrangement was not just one of time or distance; adulthood had messed them up too. Or was it that childhood had planted the bad seed and the years had cultivated it?

By the time they met again they couldn't get to emotional grips with each other, couldn't find a way through the fog, the dense clutter of the past. When their father died, Eddie had persuaded Marie to move in with mother here at the stud. But he had done that through selfishness, a motive Marie had taken too long to recognize and Eddie had taken too long to acknowledge.

Marie's initial rejection of Kim had enraged Eddie, stirring an anger that had always been with him. One born of injustice. A childhood cruelty. Marie had known about it. She'd used it to skewer Eddie, as well as her own son. There had never been a formal truce.

Eddie was discovering that the key to slowly unwinding the gnarled and wasted years, was the patience and remarkable wisdom of a thirteen-year-old boy who wanted his mother to find peace for the first time in her life.

Eddie knew that if anyone was entitled to harbour resentment, Kim was. If anyone was owed answers, Kim was. If anyone deserved nurturing it was Kim. Yet here he worked quietly at putting back together something that two adults didn't know how to fix. When Eddie had discovered Kim's existence, his worry was how the boy was to be looked after. Now here was Kim looking after them.

They'd all been in the kitchen for an hour, talking. Kim ruffled Eddie's hair - an old joke between them - and said goodnight. Then he kissed Marie and hugged her, emotionally tucking her in even though she sat in the kitchen and he was the one bound for bed.

As the creak of each stair grew fainter, Eddie watched Marie's smile which had barely faded. 'He's some kid,' Eddie said.

She nodded slowly, still smiling. 'He reminds me of you sometimes. In some ways.' Her mind was back in Cumbria twenty years ago.

'He asked me about his father. When we were out riding.' Eddie spoke softly, careful to let her see he wasn't trying to pick a fight.

She opened her hands on the table, as if about to start explaining. Then up they went to finger-comb her hair. 'He's never mentioned it to me,' she said. 'I didn't know if he was being protective or just wanted to cut things off.'

'What do *you* want?' Eddie asked.

Her chin tilted sharply forward as she looked at him, hands still supporting her head, fingers lost in her hair. 'I want to tell him that his father was the only man, the only boy I ever loved. I want to tell him that when I was stopped from seeing him I tore my hair out in clumps and tried to block the toilet with it as some sort of revenge. I want to tell him that when I met Rory Campbell I felt like I'd been hauled aboard a rescue ship after a lifetime of clinging to wreckage. I want to tell him that my parents ripped me away from Rory and threw me back overboard, and while I was still trying to survive they took his son away from me.'

Eddie watched her. She straightened slowly and smoothed her hair. 'That's what I want to tell Kim.'

'He'll still be awake. I think he'd very much like to hear it.'

'Someday, Eddie.'

'I think if you go up and tell Kim what you just told me, he'll love you even more than he does now. And he'll feel a hell of a lot better about himself, and more importantly, about his father. Did you ever see him again?'

She smiled. 'Some evenings I'd slip out and stand at the bottom of the lane near his house, watching and hoping he'd come out to the ice cream van when it stopped outside.'

'Did he never try to contact you?'

'He sent me a letter, through a friend. I still have it.'

'You look like a girl again, just talking about him.'

Her smile held sadness and nostalgia. 'We were fourteen. Everybody used to give me all that puppy love crap and tell me I'd get over it. I never did. Never will.'

She pursed her lips. The longing in her eyes pumped another hit of hatred of Eddie's parents into him, tempered by a tenderness for Marie that left him unsure whether to weep or scream with frustration. Eddie leaned forward and put a hand on her bare forearm. 'Marie, do one thing for me and for you and for Kim…go upstairs now and tell him what you just told me.'

She shook her head slowly. 'He'd be awake all night.'

'He'd be a boy who'd finally know how wanted he was by his mother and father. How much would that have meant to you at that age? How much would it have meant to us? Wouldn't you have liked to hear it?'

She looked up, as though their mother still lay alive and listening in that old upstairs room. Marie's eyes were wet and glistening in the overhead light. 'Yes,' she said quietly. 'I'd like to have heard that more than anything else in the world.'

She rose and walked, closing the door behind her. Again the stairs creaked. Eddie heard the bedroom door click open, then voices, and Eddie got up and went out into the night.

He crossed the yard toward the barn under a crescent moon, light-footed and light-hearted and enjoying a sense of achievement he'd ever experienced. Way better than riding the winner of the biggest race. How strange, he thought, how strange.

NINETEEN

Nic Buley was alone in the BHA building in High Holborn, London. The only light burning was in his office. It was close to midnight. He'd been waiting an hour for the promised call on his private line. He passed the time remembering with fondness how, in his previous job, the chairman of the BHA had phoned from New York at three in the morning with the intention of leaving a voicemail.

Buley had been stranded in the office by a public transport strike and had decided to sleep there. He answered the phone. The BHA chairman had asked if he was actually still at work, and Buley had said he was, on a vital project. That lie had helped him get this job. The man whose call he was waiting for now, would decide if Buley would keep this job. Buley blanched as he realized that the man would decide whether he was ever to hold any job of merit again.

The call came on the stroke of midnight. The man said, 'You can go home.'

'Now? I mean, do you mean for now? For tonight?'

'I don't mean permanently, if that's what you're afraid of. You're doing a good job. A degree of finesse will be required to see things out in the Old Bailey, then get Lisle to fall on his sword as planned.'

'He might need to be pushed onto it, or at least helped a little. He's proving quite resourceful.'

'He's a clown. You know it, and I know it. The public likes him. He was an appropriate appointment at the time. But you've manoeuvred him perfectly, haven't you?'

'So far, I suppose. But he's much more level-headed than he comes across at times. If he hits a dead-end, he just backtracks like some automaton and keeps looking until he finds another way.'

'That's known as blundering blindly.'

'I don't think we should under-rate him.'

'Buley, do not let him affect this verdict.'

'I won't.'

'You don't sound too confident. Do what you need to.'

'I will.'

'And keep your bloody nerve, man!'

Buley nodded. The phone clicked. The empty tone purred in his ear, and he held the phone there and stared at his reflection in the plate glass window.

By the time Eddie's collarbone had healed, Mave had backed two winners, as had Nina Raine. Eddie passed his medical inspection at Ludlow and won on his first ride, though he was breathing as heavily as the horse come the finish. Missing just a week's race-riding takes the edge off your fitness. Eddie was still blowing when he reached the changing room. Dinky Cobb said, 'Sit down, Eddie. I'll get the oxygen mask!'

Eddie sat and smiled at him. 'Very funny.'

'You're an old man now, remember.'

'Keep this up and you won't live to be an old man!' Eddie threw a boot at him. Dinky sidestepped and laughed, and everyone in the room smiled, because Dinky's laugh was one of those deep-bellied ones which gets to everybody. The sound was all the funnier coming from his tiny frame. He was an elf with a giant's laugh. Dinky was a rare guy in that he was easily light enough to ride on the Flat, where horses carry much less weight than those racing over jumps. But Dinky had chosen jump racing purely for the thrill of it.

Listening to the laughter, and watching the faces of these men who risked their lives every day, Eddie took a few seconds to let it sink in. These would be the precious times come retirement. Eddie had noticed too how much lighter the atmosphere in the changing room had been since the trial had started at the Old Bailey. No jockey could claim sainthood, but the absence of three colleagues they all knew to be consistently crooked, had allowed everyone to breathe more easily.

Reports from court suggested the three might be back soon. The BHA's case had been strengthening as Broc Lisle worked on making the evidence more 'jury-friendly'. But it had taken an unexpected hit when the press discovered the BHA had paid the police almost a third of a million pounds "to assist with expenses in a vital and unique prosecution." The defence had portrayed it as bribery.

Eddie thought of Mac, and wondered if the big man had changed his mind and used his press contacts to mortally wound the BHA's case. No, that wasn't Mac. He wouldn't change character this late in life. So who else had it in for the BHA?

Eddie dropped in at Mac's place on the way home. No car. No signs of life. He waited five minutes, then left. As he turned out of the driveway, Mac came over the brow of the hill in his Merc. He considered honking, or flashing Eddie, but he left it too late as Eddie's car took a right-hand bend at speed. Mac, tutted. 'That fellow will take one risk too many one day,' he said aloud.

A message on Eddie's PC told him he'd missed a ping from Mave. He clicked to return it.

She accepted, waving her small hand at the webcam. 'Mister Malloy. I see your first one back was a winner.'

'T'was.'

'Well done.'

'Thank you.'

'We have one for tomorrow.'

'Not at Worcester, I hope?'

'Afraid so. But it's in the last, so you're not riding in it.'

'Not yet. I might pick up a spare.'

'Leave early. Feign injury. Fall asleep on the toilet.'

'Keep trying, Mave.'

'Listen, everything's going to plan. This'll be my third big bet with all the online guys so we're building a solid audit trail for your defence. Sonny will be at the track with twenty-five grand and Nina and her hubby are placing their bets in the betting shops.'

'How long do you intend to keep giving her tips?'

'Until she has enough to move to Turkey and look for her son.'

'How much is enough?'

She stopped typing and stared at the webcam. 'Eddie, what is this, the third degree?'

'It pisses me off that they're getting what they wanted free of charge after kidnapping Sonny. Remember how you felt when he went missing? Remember who buggered up your long term plans by selling pictures to Barney Scolder?'

'But we're stuck with that, aren't we? Now we're swapping indignation for outdignation.'

'Very funny.'

'What's the point of being bitter? You'll just poison yourself.'

'Mave, I'm not bitter! Just…well, pissed off.'

'Forget it. Put it behind you. We are where we are, let's just concentrate on digging our way out.'

'Okay.'

'Good. When are you next up this way?'

'I'm at Haydock on Friday. I could drive across after that.'

'Stay over. It looks like we'll know where we are with this corruption case in London by then. Scolder will be closer to a decision on playing his hand with the pictures. Where are you on Saturday?'

'Chepstow.'

'Well, you can have a lovely early morning drive the length of Wales.'

'All twisting roads and sheep.'

'A metaphor for life, Eddie.'
'A motofor, I think you mean.'
'See you on Friday.'

TWENTY

Eddie roamed the silent house in the early hours, resisting the temptation to disturb Mave. He knew she was trying to get her sleeping habits back to normal.

He made coffee and got his doodling pad and pen. He had to act. He'd never been able to live with indecision. He sketched Scolder's name. He drew a judge's wig, then a gallows, and began a solitary game of hangman. Whatever the papers were forecasting about the trial, Eddie knew he couldn't wait out the weeks before the verdict, before publication of the pictures that could finish him. He had to confront Scolder. He'd do it come daylight. Eddie cut the rope on the hanging man with a slice of ink from the black pen and went to bed.

As Eddie drove to Worcester in the morning sunshine, he called Barney Scolder on the number Jonty had given him. It went straight to voicemail. Eddie left a message.

A minute later, Mac called him. 'Good morning. How's the collarbone? I hear you had a winner yesterday, so I'm guessing it's half healed, at least.'

'Morning, Mac. Nah, I'm too old now to ride with anything short of full repair. Those days are long gone.'

'I'd hate to see your litany of complaints once you reach my age.'

'Litany…that's another word of yours I like, Mac. I'll add it to my list.'

'Please do.'

'What's happening? I dropped by your place last night.'

'That's why I'm calling you. Was it something urgent?'

'No, it was just…How did you know I'd been there?'

'I recognized the tread mark of your tyres. Your nearside rear just impinged on a section of soil by the front lawn. I noticed it this morning.'

'You're kidding me, Mac?'

'Why would I?'

'You noticed and identified a short tyre mark?'

'Well, nothing unusual there. I've been in the investigation business since you were knee-high to a Shetland pony. I know you've always questioned my competence, but I have picked up a few tricks in my time.'

'Jeez. Well kudos to you, Mac. I'll dine out on that one.'

'All in a day's work, Eddie. Anyway, what was it you wanted?'

'Just to see if you were okay. I've been in Newmarket for a couple of weeks with family. I should have called you while I was away.'

'Not at all. Most kind of you. Very thoughtful. But I've been fine. In fact, last night when you dropped by, I was with an old colleague who was sounding me out for a meeting with Broc Lisle.'

'Lisle wants to see you?'

'Tomorrow.'

'Interesting. Any idea what it's about?'

'None, I'm afraid. But it won't be long until I find out.'

'Maybe Lisle thinks you leaked that news of the police pay-out to the press?'

'Hmm. I hadn't thought of that.'

'I'm only kidding, Mac. First, how would he know you knew? Second, a few phone calls would soon teach him that you're not the type for revenge, as you said yourself.'

'Unless one of those phone calls was to you, Eddie, who, if I recall correctly, suggested right away that I would drop the BHA straight in it.'

'What happened there was that I was thinking aloud about what I would have done. Bollocks to all this revenge served cold stuff.'

'Ahh, it's not the temperature that pays dividends, it's the timing.'

'I'll try to remember that. Listen, it could be that Lisle is after your help with this case. They've got to be very close to losing it after that bribe story came out. Let Lisle sink. And the BHA.'

'Eddie, I have two years of my life invested in that case. Those three are guilty and they're going to walk unless the BHA can shore things up and fight back.'

'So why should you help? Buley gave Lisle your job. They owe you, you don't owe them. Come on, Mac!'

He hesitated. 'Well…it's not as though I'm doing anything else.'

'Mac, Buley hung you out to dry, and now he's sending Lisle back to see if there's any juice left in you before they abandon you again! Give them nothing!'

'I've said I'd meet him. I can't back out now.'

'Well, meet him. Tell him you don't come cheap. You've spent your life nailing villains in racing, tell him you're a consultant now. If they can pay the cops three hundred grand, they can pay you fifty for anything you've got.'

'I'll think about it.'

'Mac, you're saying that to get me off the phone. Seriously, you've got to make a living now. No more paycheques. Charge the bastards.'

'I'll raise it.'

'Well raise it before you tell him anything. And get a contract.'

'You want to be my agent?'

'Gladly. You could get a job as an Indian tracker, you old fox. I'd take my fifteen percent.'

'You would, too, wouldn't you?' Eddie could hear the smile back in Mac's voice.

'I would, Mac. I'd nail Lisle and Buley so high on the wall they'd have nosebleeds. Can I drop by tonight on the way home?'

'If you promise not to harangue me like a harpy.'

'I'll be logical and analytical.'

'That'll be a first.'

Eddie cut the Bluetooth connection and smiled. Action, at last. How desperate must Lisle be? They had all the files for the case in the BHA's office. He'd want Mac's personal insights, maybe more. And what about Mac and that tyre track? That was something else…something else.

TWENTY-ONE

Eddie reached Worcester well before the first race, dumped his kitbag in the changing room and walked behind the main stands, where he sat on the concrete steps on the south bank of the River Severn and called Scolder again. Jockeys in the UK are not allowed to use mobile phones on the racecourse within a 'restricted period'. Eddie had an hour before the restricted period began. He redialled Scolder's number. It rang this time. Eddie watched the sun glint on the Severn. 'Barney,' he answered, all busyness and authority.

'It's Eddie Malloy.'

'Who?'

'Eddie Malloy. The guy who left you a message this morning. The guy you've got a hundred pictures of. The guy you're planning to defame at the cost of a big lawsuit for your paper.'

'And I'm the guy who has a shitload of work to do today without taking calls from cranks. Where'd you get my number?'

'From Jonty Saroyan. Jonty who sold you the ten grand pup, remember?'

'It barks awful loud for a pup, Eddie.'

'And white elephants are the same size as grey ones.'

'What do you want?'

'I want to save us both a lot of hassle.'

'I like hassle.'

'Not this kind, you won't.'

'No, no, no! I've never run into a breed of hassle I don't like. I thrive on it. Thrive.'

'That's a relief. I won't feel so guilty when you find yourself unemployable.'

'Then we're both happy, Mister Malloy. I'll go now, if you don't mind. Unless, that is, you want to do a full page confession?'

'Goodbye, Barney. At least I tried.' Eddie hung up and switched off the phone.

A man in a Canadian canoe came under the bridge away to Eddie's left, his Panama hat bright in the sun. Eddie watched him stroke steadily up the middle of the river, through the morning peace. Come the rains, the Severn would rise here, as it always did, and spill across concrete onto the racecourse, a perfect flood plain. The water level would rise to cover the white rails and leave the top half of the winning post standing like some kind of dull red-bulbed lighthouse.

But now, toward the end of summer, the Severn was low and still, and the man in the Panama hat cleaved steadily through the water as though he'd been doing it for a thousand years. He looked up at Eddie and smiled and cried out 'Good morning!' with the delight of an aged Tom Sawyer. The man's beard was long and white, his face wrinkled and tanned. Eddie waved. 'Good morning to you. Where are you headed?'

'Who knows?' It echoed back at him from the high walls of the grandstand. Eddie nodded and smiled. The long canoe held several well-worn packs. Maybe he lived on the river. Eddie envied him his solitude, his simplicity and his appetite for adventure…he watched the boat's slow wash settle and fade until no sign of its passing remained.

Eddie rose and walked slowly to the car to lock up his phone. Barney Scolder was a fine bluffer or a confident man. Strangely, Eddie felt better for confronting him, even though it had come to nothing. The battle was on.

Eddie finished second in the handicap hurdle. His other two mounts were well beaten. Though sweaty and grimy, Eddie decided to skip the clean-up. He could shower when he got home. His sole aim was to be off the racetrack when Sonny was moving among the rows of bookies, betting on Mave's selection in the last. Eddie didn't know the horse's name, and didn't want to know.

As those riding in the final race were getting ready, Eddie was stuffing gear in his kitbag. He opened the side zipper to get his car keys and realized he was going nowhere.

The main car park at Worcester is encircled by the track, and the crossing would already be closed for safety. Eddie went into rewind and pulled his towel and toilet bag out, then headed for the showers. He made a point of talking too much to the valets and the handful of jocks as he got dressed. On the TV, the last race was being shown. Eddie might just need someone to recall that he was safely inside the changing room as the race played out, with no opportunity to affect the result.

As the guys weighed in after the race, Eddie took his leave, congratulating Andrew Bellis, who'd ridden the winner, the five-to-two second favourite. There was every chance that had been Mave's selection.

On the way out, Eddie had to pass the rows of bookmakers. Most were paying their customers while their clerks dismantled the 'joints' to pack them away.

Eddie saw Sonny Beltrami, looking stooped and aged beyond his sixty years. He moved slowly from bookie to bookie, collecting what Eddie knew would be bundles of cash. Sonny, head down, hadn't seen Eddie. He wandered slowly away from the line of bookies toward the car park, pulling his deerskin bag from inside his jacket and working the notes into it as he walked.

Eddie knew Sonny was too smart to speak to him, but he stayed two hundred yards back just in case. As Sonny followed the stragglers toward the car park, he seemed steadily to straighten, to unstoop, to grow. His faltering gait eased and as he crossed the inside track toward the car park, he strode out, white-haired head high, straight-backed and confident.

Odd behaviour. When Eddie had been collecting cash from him, Sonny had been warned to play the old man at all times; unthreatening, quiet, anonymous. Now here he was, walking tall, and confident like a general about to accept surrender.

Then Eddie saw why, and he ducked in behind a white van to avoid being seen by Nina Raine, her red hair glinting as she raised her face to Sonny's kiss.

TWENTY-TWO

Heading south on the M5 in the late afternoon sunshine, Eddie smiled and shook his head and said a silent well, well, well. Stockholm syndrome Plus. She was half his age and had seemed to Eddie manipulative from the start. Eddie thought her good looking in that chiselled, fine-boned way, but it was a professional prettiness, as though she'd worked on herself in the way a trainer would prepare a horse. There was no warmth in her. Mave came to his mind. Mave was real. Nina Raine was a robot in comparison.

But the choice was Sonny's. So long as the relationship didn't threaten Eddie's future, or deceive Mave, then Eddie would leave him to it. He would keep it from Mave, for now. Eddie was glad in a way; *Melancholy Baby* would be deleted from Sonny's repertoire for a while.

When Eddie got to Mac's place, the big man looked sharp, clean and eager. They shook hands, and Mac returned to his laptop which lay open on a table in the corner. 'Give me two minutes, Eddie, and I'll make coffee.'

'No hurry. You look like you're on a mission.'

'Just reminding myself of a few things before I see Lisle.'

'Where are you meeting him?'

'He's coming here.'

'When?'

'Tomorrow. Noon. On his own. You want a coffee?'

'Water would be fine.'

They went into the garden, to sit at the cast iron table, below darkening clouds. Mac moved with purpose. He'd been adrift since losing his job and now Lisle had thrown him a lifeline.

'Mac, you're getting back into the zone with this.'

He crossed his legs and looked at Eddie. 'Is that good or bad?'

'It depends on what you agree with Lisle. Has he said what he wants?'

'Just to talk.'

'How well do you know him?'

'I don't.'

'So how are you going to play it?'

'I'll wait and see what he has to say.'

Eddie pushed his water glass aside and leaned across the table. 'Mac, I promised not to give you a hard time. It's your choice if you want to work for free. But for all you know, Lisle might already be looking for a scapegoat.'

'As in?'

'As in you.'

'I was the one who didn't want the case brought to court this year, remember?'

'And don't you think Lisle and Buley will find a way of spinning that? Who else knows you opposed the prosecution?'

'Nobody else. It was between me and Buley.'

'Exactly.'

Mac crossed his arms, and his head went down.

'Mac, look, I might be wrong. Maybe he'll be begging for your help. Just be careful, that's all. Things are bad enough for you just now and when your luck is out, it tends to stay that way for a long time.'

Back at home, Eddie pinged Mave and told her about his conversation with Barney Scolder.

'Was he bluffing?'

'If he was, he's good at it.'

'Well, everything's building up nicely here, evidence-wise. With Nina and Jonty to speak for you, I think you can relax. What's the chat on the Old Bailey case?'

'BHA are struggling big time. They need to prove this guy Ivory was masterminding it, and nobody's talking.'

'Ivory? That his real name?'

'Jordan Ivory. Precious, eh?'

'Very funny. A mastermindish name though.'

'Maybe, but a scary man by all accounts. Witnesses are hard to come by, and if they find any, they will not be the talkative type.'

'Do you think those three were involved with him?'

'If they were, that's their business.'

Mave looked at her webcam. 'I'm not trying to catch you out. I'm your friend, remember?'

'Sorry, Mave. I just spent some time with Mac. Made me edgy.'

'I thought he'd retired.'

'It's a long story.'

'Is he helping you out?'

'I'm trying to help him out.' Eddie told Mave about the Lisle meeting.

'Mac would speak for you, though, wouldn't he, if it comes down to it?'

'Sure. But I doubt anyone would listen.'

'Well, the way things are going, we'll have enough ammunition anyway to blow Scolder away.'

'Good. What about you? You going to stick with this now, once everything's cleared up?'

'With the betting programme?'

'Yep.'

'I don't know yet. Sonny's coming up tomorrow. I might talk to him about it.'

'Social visit?'

'I don't know. He called earlier saying he needed to see me about something. Could be anything, knowing Sonny.'

'Could be.'

'What about you? You still planning to stay over Friday night?'

'Unless the shit hits the fan before then.'

'You expecting it to?'

'I'm always expecting it to.'

'I think things are going to get easier from now, you know.'

'Don't tempt fate, Mave.'

TWENTY-THREE

Broc Lisle got out of his car in Mac's driveway and watched the big man walk toward him. Lisle saw that spark of recognition he was so used to, but he could not count it as Mister McCarthy knew who he was. They shook hands. 'Welcome,' Mac said, 'How do you do?'

'How do you do?' Lisle shook his hand warmly then looked around. 'Visibility is superb for September, eh? Most unusual.'

'Last night's rains cleared the haze,' Mac said.

Lisle turned on one heel, a neat full circle, smiling and looking up. 'A big sky. You have the precious privilege of a big sky, Mister McCarthy. Was that in your mind when you moved here?'

'Well, not directly. We wanted privacy and a nice view down the valley. A large garden.'

'Look up, is my advice to you, if you don't mind me offering it. With such a big sky, complacency can creep in. Remember your London days. Remember them each time you walk out that door. How much of the sky did you see in London?'

'Very little.'

'Treasure this.'

Mac looked up. 'I hadn't thought of it that way.' He watched Lisle spin again, smiling. Mac said, 'You won't mind if we hold our meeting in the garden, then, Mister Lisle?'

'It will be a rare pleasure. I don't care for offices. Do you?'

They walked. 'Well, again, I never really thought about that. I've spent most of my years in an office job.'

'May I congratulate you on the fact that it did not damage your judgement? It seems you left your job at the right time and for the right reasons. And I'm grateful you've agreed to see me, given the circumstances.'

'I had a lot of time invested in the case. I'm curious, too.'

'I'll enlighten you as best I can, beneath the light of the sun.'

At Mave's, on Friday evening, the log fire cast the only light as they ate supper and drank whiskey, Mave spearing black olives with a toothpick, said, 'Sonny's looking for a big favour.'

Eddie watched and waited.

'He's going to Turkey with Nina Raine to help look for her son. He wants to know if it's okay to fly back whenever there's a job on, bet the horse for Nina, and head back with the cash.'

'How do you feel about that?'

She shrugged and made a face.

'You agreed?'

'I'd never deny him anything. I'm sad I won't see him so often, and happy that he's in love.'

'He said that?'

'He didn't have to.'

'What about Jonty Saroyan?'

'Did a runner. He was betting the horses I was giving Nina, without her knowledge. Filled his boots then strapped them up and strode out.'

'A most reliable witness then, if I ever need him.'

'I doubt you'd find him anyway, and the judge would soon suss him. Better if he stays away.'

'And when will Sonny suss Nina?'

She shrugged, 'Who knows? But he's bewitched, though not bothered nor bewildered. Long may he enjoy it.'

'She's using him.'

'Sonny will be sixty-one in a month. He's thirty-one in his head, a head that holds a brain now fizzing with chemicals, making him certain of everything in the way that only the deluded can be. That's love.'

'Speaking from fond memory?'

'Deep study.'

'Deep longing?'

She hesitated, 'Sometimes.'

'Platonic's underrated, you know.'

She looked at him over the rim of her glass, 'It's boring too.'

Eddie smiled. 'So going back to the Sonny side, when's the Turkey trip?'

'They fly out tomorrow. He's packing as we speak.'

'Will Nina Raine come home and testify if I need her to?'

'Sonny says they both will.'

'Do you think you'll have enough bets placed online to shore up that side of the evidence?'

'Plenty. And I'll carry on recording all the screen sessions with Nina, showing the system working.'

'So how long will you keep it going?'

'Until Sonny and Nina have enough to find her son and pay whatever legal bills they'll have to get him back home.'

Eddie nodded slowly. 'Then you'll quit?'

'Then I'll quit.'

'Forever?'

'Never say never, I suppose, but that's the plan.'

'And you'll set off to see the world?'

She nodded slowly and sipped whiskey, then said, 'Well, I'll start with Wales.'

'Scaredy cat.'

She shrugged. 'What's that saying…a journey of ten thousand miles starts with a single step?'

'Or in your case, a single car crash into the side of this house as you reverse.'

She smiled. 'I've already booked a refresher course in driving.'

'God help your instructor.'

Mave made a funny face. Eddie shuffled forward, the half inch of whiskey swilling in his glass, and he raised it in a toast: 'May he, or she, rest in peace.'

Mave poured what was left in her glass over Eddie's head.

TWENTY-FOUR

On September 8th, Eddie had the choice of travelling north to Sedgefield for three rides, or east to Fakenham for two. Fakenham wasn't that far from Newmarket and Kim had three days remaining of his summer holiday. Eddie decided to head east, ride at Fakenham, then spend the evening with Kim and Marie. He rang Marie to tell her he was planning to surprise Kim.

'It must be something in our genes,' Marie said, 'thinking up surprises. I was planning to take him to Cumbria tomorrow for a couple of days.'

Kim had been raised on a farm in Cumbria by his adoptive parents. 'Has he asked to go back to the farm?' Eddie said.

'No. He hasn't asked specifically. But you can hear the longing in his voice the odd time he talks about it.'

'I've offered, more than once. I got the impression he doesn't want to go back in case he can't drag himself away again. He told me that after his dad died, he'd planned to hide out at the farm until the authorities lost interest. Then he believed he could just run it as his dad had done. I know he loved the place.'

'I think he still does. You're making me wonder now whether it would be a bad idea to surprise him.'

'It might be better asking him in advance, Marie. It's your call, in the end. But, well, I don't know…I'll leave it to you.'

'I was thinking of taking him to Greystoke.' Marie had to stop herself from holding her breath.

'To Kyrtlebank?' Kyrtlebank had been the leasehold farm where Eddie and Marie had been raised. Eddie would never have referred to it as home. The nearest village was Greystoke.

'Maybe.'

'Why?'

'Don't be mad, Eddie…I don't know why. Maybe I won't go. But I want him to see where his father used to live. Rory, his biological father.'

That changed things for Eddie. He knew it would be Marie's first step in helping Kim find his father. And Eddie had no doubt about the longing in his sister's heart for the boy she had loved and that time she had been happy and no longer clinging to the wreckage that was the remains of the Malloy family.

'I'm sorry,' he said, 'I didn't mean to be sharp with you. The place haunts me. I don't want Kim tainted by being anywhere around it.'

'Eddie, you can't blame the farm or the land around it. That was beautiful. It was always beautiful, don't you think?'

'I can't see it that way, Marie. I'm sorry. I never will.'

'It was them, Eddie. Mum and dad. It wasn't Kyrtlebank. There was promise there. For me, at least. *Hope.* I spent a long time there hoping.'

'Then ask him first, Marie, will you? Once you're on the road, once he realizes where you're going, ask him if he wants to go there. Don't force it on him. He'd settle for Greystoke. He doesn't have to see Kyrtlebank.'

'I won't force him. I promise.'

'Where will you stay?'

'At the Greystoke Inn. I've booked two rooms. Make Kim feel properly grown up.'

'Want me to arrange a stable visit for him to the Richards' yard?'

'That would be brilliant, if you could.'

'He'll love it. Proper yard. Proper people. I'll phone them now and call you back with the details. But when you're settled in tomorrow night, get Kim to ring me, will you?'

'Do you think I'd be able to stop him?'

TWENTY-FIVE

Eddie had committed to Fakenham, and that's where he stood in the changing room with other jockeys watching Nic Buley on Sky News. Buley was outside the Old Bailey burbling his usual buzz words in his supposed defence of the BHA's decision to seek a criminal prosecution. The three jockeys had just been found not guilty of conspiracy to defraud. Blackaby, Sampson and Kellagher were free to resume riding.

Not much was said in the changing room, though Eddie heard the word farce more often than any other. He grabbed his bag and hurried to the car to call Maven Judge. The trial result had caught many off guard, Eddie included. It took fourteen rings before Mave answered. 'I'm sorry if I woke you, Mave.'

'What's wrong?'

'The trial's over. Not guilty on all three. The judge stopped it and directed the jury to acquit as there was no case to answer.'

'Sudden.' She yawned.

'Want me to give you a few minutes to wake up properly?'

'No...Well, let me make some coffee to clear my brain. Give me five minutes. I'll call you back.'

'I'm heading home. I'll ring you when I hit the motorway.'

'Okay.'

Pulling away from the exit, Eddie cursed the timing. Where was Sonny? Was Nina Raine still with him? Where was Jonty Saroyan?

Three witnesses who could be vital to him keeping his licence. Eddie's phone lit up: Barney Scolder.

Eddie composed himself and hit the answer button. 'Mister Scolder. What can I do for you?'

'Just wanted to offer you the chance to comment on the story we're running on Sunday alongside those lovely colour pictures of you and Sonny Beltrami.'

'My comment's the same as when we last spoke.'

'Remind me.'

'Publish what you want. You were stitched up by Saroyan. Not only will you be on the end of a lawsuit, but you'll be on the end of a lot of pointed fingers from your mates who'll be pissing themselves laughing.'

'Is that it?'

'That's it.'

'Well, you've got my number.'

'I have. I'll pass it to my lawyers.'

'You're a sound bluffer, Malloy, I'll give you that.'

'Goodbye.' Eddie cut him off, confident there was doubt in Scolder now. He'd be calling Jonty Saroyan and Jonty, if he was still playing out the cash he'd won from Mave's tips, would not be answering.

Eddie rang Mave and told her.

'Jeez. Scolder didn't hang about.'

'They'll have had the story ready for a long time.'

'Like they do with obituaries?'

Eddie smiled. 'Your sense of humour never fails you when I'm in the shit, Mave.'

'I work hard at it, believe me.'

'You heard from Sonny?'

'Not a word since the last bet.'

'Any idea where he is?'

'I'd love to say with Raine in Spain, but they were thoughtless and went to Turkey, ruining my rhyme.'

'Will you ring him, please?'

'I already left him a message and emailed him too.'

'Thanks, Mave.'

'Don't worry. I've got the bet data and the recordings with Nina Raine. Want me to call Scolder and arrange to meet him?'

'Then you'd be outed.'

'It doesn't matter. I've got more money than I'll ever need.'

'And you've got a bullet-proof winning system. Unfortunately it's alongside a non-bullet-proof body.'

'We can worry about that later.'

'No we can't. We can make sure we don't have to worry about it at all by keeping this out of the papers. I can do a deal with the BHA to protect your identity.'

'Really? The same BHA you constantly slag off as being useless? The same BHA who've spent a fortune bringing a worthless prosecution against three jockeys everyone knows are bent, yet still can't get a conviction? You'd trust them with my identity?'

'Mmm. Maybe not.'

'At least Scolder sounds competent.'

'Mave, don't call Scolder. Okay?'

'Okay! Okay!'

'I'll drop in and see Mac on the way home.'

'I'll have another coffee and get to thinking.'

'Good.'

'And listen, Eddie, if it comes to lawsuits against newspapers, what's mine is yours. There's plenty here to pay for the best.'

'Thanks, Mave. I doubt it will come to that. Getting Saroyan to retract before Sunday would kill the story. Let's try and find out where he is.'

'Okay. I'll work on that. Let me know what Mac says.'

'I will.'

TWENTY-SIX

In the deep dusk, as Eddie pulled in through Mac's gates, he recalled that Mac had warned him this was exactly how the case would end, a dismissal by the judge.

Mac's driveway was empty. The house was in darkness. Eddie got out and walked to the back to check for lights. None. The gravel crunching under his shoes seemed loud as he returned to the car. Lambourn's small cluster of streetlights glowed down the valley. Eddie called Mac's number.

'Eddie.'

'I'm at your place.'

'I'm five minutes away.'

'See you soon.'

Eddie rolled down the window and switched off the car lights, and watched the half-moon on the rise over the woods. Autumn. The air blew cool, gusting here on the hill. Winter waited with its usual promise for Eddie of big races, of hope, of renewal.

Spring was nature's renewal; winter was Eddie's. It had always been. The cold, the falls, the wasting to make weights, the best horses returning from summer breaks…inspiration for him. Even the wasting nourished Eddie in a strange way. It deprived his body, but fed his spirit, challenged him, brought him out fighting, restored all his confidence. Whatever race-riding could throw at him, Eddie could handle. If you've achieved something even once, you can do it again. And again.

But a licence suspension was almost certain now. At least Eddie could use the time to track down Jonty Saroyan. Mave was much more confident than Eddie was about the evidence she'd built on Eddie's behalf. Saroyan was the key.

A cloud covered the moon. Mac's headlights swung in and filled Eddie's mirror. Eddie got out.

With three lamps lit in the living room and the paraffin smell of white firelighters in the air, they settled in easy chairs, drinking coffee. Mac loosened his tie and laid his head back to stare at the ceiling and a long sigh came out of him. 'You okay?' Eddie said.

'Been to the cemetery. My first visit this week. Been getting lazy on it, so I sat with Jean until the sun went down.'

Had Mac not been a friend, Eddie would have found some platitude to spout. But the big man was entitled to the respect of silence. He rarely spoke of his personal life or his feelings. Mac stared at the blueish fire flames as they enveloped a split log. 'Strange how you adjust to living with someone so long,' he said. 'You become blind. Deaf and blind to how they feel and who they are. You're only interested in how they react to you within the relationship, not as people themselves, not as individuals. I wish I could have seen through the shell. I knew Jean was ill, but that just became part of us, part of a joint life. To me, that is. It was way bigger than that to her, but as long as I could file it in a drawer in my mind and accept it, then life just rolled on. Mine rolled on. Jean's was ebbing away. Under my eyes…Shameful.'

Eddie watched him. Mac watched the fire. 'You're being awful hard on yourself, Mac. If it wasn't for the operation, well…what I mean is, you couldn't have known.' Eddie said.

Mac nodded slowly, still staring at the blooming flames. They sat in silence until the coffee was done and Eddie stood and took his empty cup. 'I'll wash up.'

'Thanks.'

Eddie washed and dried in the bright kitchen and found the cupboard where the cups lived. He stood in the doorway watching Mac. 'That's it, Guvnor,' Eddie said, echoing a saying from his past when evening stables had finished and the horses were locked up for the night. Mac smiled. 'Sit down, Eddie and let's try and sort your troubles out now.'

'Mine can wait, Mac. They're insignificant.'

'Not to you.'

'They can wait.'

Elbows on his knees, he looked up at Eddie. 'We've got a relationship too, you know.'

'I didn't know you cared.'

'I've taken it for granted over the years.'

'You're not the only one, Mac. Ease off on yourself.'

'Sit down, Eddie. I want to help you. It's important to me.'

Eddie sat, and Mac hauled his bulk from the chair. 'I've got some whiskey somewhere. Let me find it, and we'll make a start.'

'Thanks. I guess I'll be meeting Broc Lisle soon, if he's still in a job. Did he come to see you the other day?'

Mac apologized for not phoning Eddie after the meeting. 'There was nothing to tell, in the end. Lisle came to pick my brain in the hope of gathering something on Jordan Ivory. I'm afraid he went home disappointed.'

'Must have been a last gasp, considering today's verdict. Lisle would have known it was coming.'

'Indeed.'

'What's he like?'

Mac returned from the kitchen with a whiskey bottle and two glasses. 'A character. Unusual man, but likable. I feel for him. I hope he holds onto the job after this. They'll try to force him out, of course, but perhaps Buley will take the hit this time.'

'No chance.'

TWENTY-SEVEN

By Saturday morning Eddie and Mave knew everything there was to know about Jonty Saroyan except where he was. Mave had tracked down his parents, two brothers, ex-wife, and most of the people he'd worked with in the past. Mac and Eddie, with some help from Mave, had spoken to all of them.

Sonny called from Turkey to say Nina Raine had heard nothing from Saroyan since they'd split, but she'd had a call from the private detective Jonty was supposed to have paid to help find her son; he claimed Saroyan had paid him nothing of the ten grand they'd got for selling Eddie's pictures.

Nina said Saroyan was an alcoholic. Eddie was told he could be anywhere...on a round-the-world binge or photographing The March of the Cane Toads in Northern Australia. The project title had been Jonty's and, when he was drunk, he had often bored people with his 'project'.

Mac used his contacts to find out if Saroyan had visited Australia since July. "Not using his own passport, he hasn't"

So, twenty-four hours before Scolder's paper was due to go to press, Eddie had some visits to make. He'd have to go and see Kim and Marie and Dil Grant.

As Eddie zipped up his kitbag, Mac rang. 'I thought you might want me to tell Nic Buley in advance about the pictures? He doesn't like surprises.'

'Fuck him. He can find out tomorrow along with the rest.'

'I know you can't stand him, Eddie, but it might make things easier for you if he feels you respect him enough to let him know.'

'Mac-'

'Whoa! You don't actually have to respect him. Just let him believe it.'

'That's worse!'

'Okay. Okay. Let me warn Lisle, then.'

'So he can tell Buley! No! How can you even suggest this shit, Mac?'

'Er, because I care what will happen to you?'

'What will happen to me if I start playing games like that is I will wither inside. That's what'll happen to me.'

Mac went quiet, then said, 'I'm sorry.'

'It's all right. Forget it. Just a return of that old infection, office politics.'

'I think it's my soul that's infected, Eddie.'

'Oh Mac, forget it, will you? Damage limitation's been your default position for the past quarter of a century. It's not going to change overnight. It doesn't turn you into Doctor Evil. Lighten up.'

Dil was in the owners and trainers bar, sitting by the window with two other trainers. Eddie knocked on the window and signalled five with his fingers. Dil smiled and signalled back two and Eddie wandered toward the door to meet him. 'What's up?'

Eddie told him as they walked toward the stables.

'But you weren't giving the tips?'

'A friend of mine was doing the tipping. I was just helping move the cash around.'

'Any of my horses involved?'

'None.'

They walked ten paces in silence. 'You know what pisses me off most, Eddie? I could have done with a few of those tips myself.' He shook back his heavy hair.

Eddie smiled. 'I'm glad you're taking it so well.'

He stopped and touched Eddie's arm to turn him. 'I'm serious,' he said. 'You know how tough things are, running a yard!'

'Dil, listen. I'm sorry for your troubles, but I didn't know the horses. I didn't know what the tips were. I made a point of that, in case something like this Scolder business ever came up. But even if I had known the names of those horses, I wouldn't have told you. The tips didn't belong to me. They weren't mine to give.'

'You could have asked, at least! Who is this friend?'

Eddie reached toward him now and put a hand on his shoulder. 'It doesn't matter who my friend is. If you had something running that you thought was a good thing, would you expect me to be giving that out to all and sundry?'

'I'm not all and sundry, am I, Eddie? I'm the guy that employs you. And you're supposed to be my friend.'

'Dil, I wouldn't care if you were my brother. The tips weren't mine to give and I didn't fucking know them anyway!'

'Keep your voice down, for God's sake.'

'I'll keep my voice down when you get a grip on reality!'

Dil raised his eyes to the skies and his fringe flopped into them and he cursed and pushed it away and leant against the redbrick wall surrounding the stables. He massaged his face with both hands and blew a breath, then looked at Eddie. 'I'm sorry,' he said quietly.

Eddie had three rides for Dil. Grey Heron, the one at longest odds, was in the big race of the day, a handicap hurdle worth £25,000. Grey Heron was a 20/1 shot and Eddie held out little hope until they'd jumped the first flight and Eddie realized everyone was travelling too fast.

No matter how experienced jockeys are, sometimes the wash of adrenaline as the tapes rise in a big race clouds judgement in some, and sows doubt in others. The ground was firmer than the official description of "good". A combination of unexpectedly fast ground, a decent prize and the knowledge that the race was televised across the country, seemed to stir everyone up.

After the first jump, Eddie decided to take a pull and drop out last. By the third hurdle, they were ten lengths behind the pack and Eddie knew that if he'd got this wrong, it would look to some as if he was riding to lose. But Eddie was confident he was right. Often, the best horse does not win the race. Nor does the fastest, nor the one with most stamina or jumping ability. The winner is usually the horse whose energy has been used to best effect throughout the race; the horse who has kept the most even time fractions furlong by furlong.

This racing pack away ahead of him had to run out of steam. Most racehorses can keep up a decent gallop for a while when fresh. But gradually, the effort takes its toll. The less talented and less fit would be dropping away before turning into the straight for the last time. The better ones would hang on longer. But all of them were racing hard. Grey Heron was lobbing along in a lovely steady rhythm, taking little out of himself. Passing the stands first time, the pair were loudly but good-naturedly jeered for being so far behind.

Eddie smiled and cheekily tipped his cap.

On the final bend before the long straight, they began passing the panting stragglers. Straightening up for home, there were still a dozen in front of them, but Eddie kept Grey Heron galloping at the same pace they'd gone throughout. To those watching, it would seem they were accelerating, cutting through the pack. They were not. The optical illusion as the others faded and drifted from a straight line as they ran out of steam, made it look as though Eddie was powering up through the gears.

One to jump. Three in front of them, all wandering across the track, almost exhausted, their jockeys rousting and roaring and swinging whips, but none took the last cleanly…the chestnut almost fell. Eddie could crouch now, and draw his whip and cut them down, but there was no need, and the jeers from the crowd on the previous circuit were fresh in Eddie's mind, so he sat as still as he'd done then, and fifty yards from the line eased past the final rival.

Grey Heron hardly knew he'd been in a race and he galloped on, round the bend. As he began pulling him up, Eddie had a surprising urge to keep going. This might be his last big race win for an awful long time if Scolder had his way, and Eddie became a child again, with visions of jumping the white rails next, and galloping off, heading north through the countryside, north and away, away, away.

TWENTY-EIGHT

After racing, Eddie set off on the long drive to Newmarket to see Kim and Marie. They had arrived home from Cumbria the night before. Eddie had called Marie, and she knew what to expect. She asked him to stay over with them for some family support on Sunday. He'd have preferred being alone, or with Mave, but family had been a word seldom used in Eddie's life and it touched him. Kim would want to comfort him too.

An hour into the trip, with daylight almost gone, Mac called. 'Eddie, Lisle just rang to tell me Scolder's been onto the BHA. He rang Buley for a comment for this story tomorrow.'

'So?'

'So, Buley's in a panic.'

'Good.'

'Eddie, he needs to be able to give some sort of informed response.'

'That'll make a change. Tell him to dip into his buzzword bingo box and haul out six yards of the usual bullshit he talks. He can feed that to Scolder. Why are they ringing you, anyway?'

'To see if I could shed any light on it.'

'To see if you thought I was guilty, you mean?'

'Look, whatever way you take it, Lisle is going to want to talk to you. I'd have thought you'd want to cooperate.'

'I'm happy to cooperate. They should have called me, not you. No offence.'

'I'll tell him that.'

'Please do. By the way, they'll suspend me tomorrow, I expect, so you and I can go fishing or something.'

'I've never fished in my life. Neither have you.'

'True. We can walk the garden paths instead.'

'Eddie, why do you always get flippant at times like these? Your career's on the line.'

'I don't know, Mac. Maybe it's to hear you use words like flippant. Macabre is another one of yours I like. And belligerent. And litany.'

'I give up.'

'See you next week.'

'Call me when you've spoken to Lisle.'

'I will.'

When Eddie hung up, there was a voicemail waiting from Broc Lisle. Eddie pulled into a service station and rang him. They agreed to meet in the morning near Newmarket. Eddie called Mac to update him, then set off again for Marie's place and some peace and quiet and sanity.

Kim's curly hair shone like liquorice under the wide light above the kitchen table. His summer tan remained, making his sparkling smile look like something from a TV ad. Eddie had buoyed myself to come into the house bright and happy, as though the clock hands weren't steadily chipping the edges from his life.

'You should sue this guy Scolder, as well as his paper,' Kim said. 'That would make him think twice before picking on anybody again.'

'I might just do that.'

Marie said, 'You'd think their legal department would have told them to leave well alone, given all these press hacking stories and court cases.'

'Scolder seems a hard man to say no to,' Eddie said.

'Have you met him?' Kim asked.

'Not yet…but I will.' Eddie smiled, and Kim did too.

Eddie told them as much as he could without giving away Mave's secrets.

'So this Jonty guy,' Kim said, 'if you can't find him, they won't be able to find him either, so he can't back up their story.'

'Unless the reason we can't find him is that they have him locked away in a hotel somewhere.'

He nodded, curls bouncing. 'True.'

'But you're right. They've got a signed statement from him saying the pictures are genuine, but I don't know what else that statement says.'

Marie said, 'How can they convince a court or a judge the statement is actually from him, no matter what it says, if he's not there to confirm it?'

'Good point,' Eddie said. 'I'm glad I came here, now!'

Kim looked up at him. 'Will they take away your licence until all this comes to court?'

'I'll probably find out in the morning. I'm meeting their head of integrity, a guy called Lisle.'

'Does he like you?' Kim said.

Eddie smiled. 'We've never met.'

'Meeting on a Sunday? You going to London?' Marie asked.

'Lisle's coming here. Not here to the house, to Newmarket. I'm meeting him at some business place, owned by a friend of his. He assured me it's deserted on Sundays.'

'Newmarket's hardly the best place for you to be, with your picture all over the Sunday papers.'

Eddie smiled. 'Marginally better than Lambourn. I won't be parading around town anyway. I'm seeing him at ten. I should be back here for lunch, then a ride out on the heath with Kim.'

'It's okay. We can give that a miss if you want,' Kim said.

'No way. It's the main reason I came.'

Kim smiled and Marie threw a mock scowl. Eddie reached to touch her arm. 'And to see my lovely sister, of course!'

'Just as well you added that,' she said. 'You'd be getting sent to bed with no dinner.'

When Eddie did get to bed, he considered switching off his phone and leaving it off until this time tomorrow. As soon as those pictures appeared, he'd be blitzed with calls, mostly from reporters but many of the lads Eddie rode with would want to offer a kind word. Eddie stared at the phone...no point in an innocent man going into hiding. Eddie left it on.

TWENTY-NINE

Kim was up at dawn and out for the papers. He bought them all, but only *The Sunday Report*, Scolder's paper had the story. And Scolder had blinked first. Or maybe his lawyers had. The article concentrated on the 'farcical' case against Blackaby, Sampson and Kellagher, under the headline Who are the Villains? Pictures showed Eddie taking cash from Sonny, and Sonny collecting cash from bookies. There was a quote from Jonty Saroyan claiming he'd had them 'under surveillance' for weeks and could conclude nothing else except that Eddie Malloy was getting Sonny to place bets on Eddie's behalf, which was against the rules of racing.

Scolder quoted Eddie correctly: "I was helping a friend and had no knowledge of the cash amounts or the horses". The quote from Nic Buley was non-committal: "In light of possible disciplinary action, it would be unfair of me to comment on Mister Malloy's future." Eddie thought it an unusually bullshit-free statement for Buley.

Scolder's final paragraph: "You can decide for yourself if pictures speak louder than words."

By the time Eddie left to meet Lisle, he'd taken more than thirty calls, giving time to every journalist and telling friends he'd ring back when things cooled down.

Lisle had given Eddie latitude and longitude data to put in his satnav, assuring him he'd need it to find the meeting place. The satnav woman ordered him to head northeast, giving a forecast journey time of twenty minutes.

Lisle had been right about the difficulty of finding the place. It was in a vast forest adjoining RAF Lakenheath. Eddie stopped at the tall wire mesh gates and rang Lisle. 'Come in,' he said, 'park in bay 17, please. I'll meet you there.' The gates swung slowly open.

There must have been thirty parking bays. Only one was taken by what Eddie assumed was Lisle's silver BMW. What the hell did it matter if he parked in any bay? Why 17? But Eddie did as he was told, and as he stepped out of the car, he saw Lisle striding toward him along the length of the single-story dark green building. He seemed to keep dead on track as he walked, five yards out from the wall of the windowless building.

Eddie had seen him a number of times on TV, but mostly just head and shoulders. He looked less imposing in the flesh, Eddie thought, though obviously fit. His brown suit and brogues were impeccable, and Eddie felt like an urchin. This man took serious care of his appearance. The white shirt collar sat stiff and perfectly symmetrical against a shining, clean-shaven throat.

Eddie reckoned Lisle's face had been set in officer mode so long, he'd be unable to smile. But everything went to the At Ease position when he reached Eddie and smiled warmly, holding out his hand. Eddie judged the smile genuine as they shook hands. His instinct gave Lisle a split-second shakedown and pronounced him trustworthy. Mac had been right.

Lisle had a presence that was more than physical and Eddie suspected he was a good deal more savvy than many thought. The ex-soldier had become adept at looking the part, but Eddie sensed it wasn't the real him.

'Sorry for this Secret Service crap,' Lisle said, 'we're not having a great time at the moment, you'll appreciate. We can go inside to a dark room that smells of old boots and sweat, or we can walk a couple of circuits in the sunshine.'

'I get enough of old boots and sweat in the changing room. A walk suits fine.'

The building was laid out in a large T shape, all single story, all green: no windows. Lisle told him it was used for training and evaluation of personnel, and that he'd been an advisor "in a previous life" to the company running it.

He finished the brief history as though it had been a duty, and they walked on, like prisoners in a concentration camp, birdsong the only sound until Lisle spoke again.

'Tough morning for you,' he said.

'I've had better.'

'What's the story?'

'Exactly what's printed. I was helping a friend who was placing bets. I didn't know what the horses were or how much the stakes were, and I had nothing to do with getting the money on.'

'Your friend have a name?'

'Yes.'

They walked a dozen paces without looking at each other, though a smile developed on Lisle's face as Eddie held out. 'Where do we go from here?' Lisle asked.

'That's for you to decide.'

'You'll be up in front of the disciplinary panel. You know that?'

'On what charge?'

'That hasn't been decided yet.'

'Do I keep my licence in the meantime?'

'Depends.'

'On what?'

'On how cooperative you want to be.'

'I just told you all there is to tell.'

'On *your* side.'

'What does that mean?'

'What do you know about Blackaby, Sampson and Kellagher?'

'Other than they're now free to resume riding?'

He looked at Eddie. 'You know they're bent.'

'I wouldn't-'

He stopped and put a hand on Eddie's arm, his head completely still. 'You know they're crooks. I know they're crooks. Everybody in the weighing room knows they're crooks.'

'Didn't a highly respected judge just decide they weren't?'

'They've been fixing races for years. You can't deny that.'

'I concentrate on the races I ride in. Nobody's fixed any of them.'

They walked again.

'Know anything about Jordan Ivory?' Lisle asked.

'He's a bookie, and he must be very smart, and he's probably also very pissed off.'

'Why?'

'Because everyone seems to have decided he's the only man who ever tried arranging fixed races.'

'He's running those three jockeys, anyway, isn't he?'

'I haven't a clue, Mister Lisle. All I know is that he's never done me any harm.'

'I think you'll find the harm is happening through collateral damage. People will lose faith in the sport, no?'

'Punters enjoy the skulduggery stories as much as anyone else. It gives them an excuse for backing the wrong horse.'

'Skulduggery. A euphemism, Mister Malloy. Ivory is a crook. Kellagher, Sampson and Blackaby are crooks. What they've been doing constitutes fraud.'

'Well, the BHA should have done a better job in prosecuting.'

'We'd have had them if somebody hadn't leaked that police payment to the press.'

'Maybe. The real reason the case failed was Buley's ego. He wanted that nice one-year anniversary present.'

Lisle nodded and they walked on in silence, Lisle easing out of his proud stride to put his hands behind his back and stroll head down, like a priest.

'What do you want, Mister Malloy?'

'Fair treatment.'

'I mean what do you want to help us out here?'

'There's no help I can give you.'

'You helped us quickly enough when the chance came up to get your licence back all those years ago.'

'Only because your department was so incompetent they took my licence away. Wrongly, as it happens.'

'But you put everything into it back then, didn't you, when your friend McCarthy asked for help?'

'The situation was different.'

'People were doping horses to make money. They were infecting your sport, same as these guys are doing, but because they're not bothering you, you don't care.'

'It's not my job, Mister Lisle.'

He stopped and looked at Eddie. 'That doesn't absolve you though, does it?'

Eddie couldn't find an answer. Lisle out-stared him then said, 'We're organizing a special sitting of the disciplinary panel for noon tomorrow at High Holborn. Do you intend to have legal representation?'

'Not much point until I find out what I'm being charged with.'

'Who said you'll be charged with anything?'

Eddie raised his eyebrows… 'Best wait and see, then, eh?'

Lisle chaperoned Eddie to his car. Eddie held out his hand. 'See you tomorrow, Mister Lisle.'

THIRTY

On their afternoon ride, Kim and Eddie went steadily among a network of quiet tree-lined roads, never far from falling leaves. The rain that had been threatening all day held off, but the wind was rising. They rode side by side, chatting and listening for traffic.

'Who is this Sonny Beltrami, the man in the pictures with you?' Kim said.

'He's a friend. Well, mostly a friend of a friend really.'

'Won't he speak for you?'

'He's in Turkey. In love. And he's working on something more important.'

Kim watched him.

'Sonny's trying to track down a boy who's supposed to have been kidnapped by his father.'

'Why would a father kidnap his own son?'

'One of these domestic disputes. A marriage gone wrong. A British judge says one thing, a Turkish judge another and you end up with a long distance tug of war.'

'Is it a religious thing?'

'I don't know.'

'Is the boy in any danger?'

'I don't know, Kim. But Sonny's a good man and he's head over heels with Keki's mother, so he'll be doing his best to find him.'

'Keki. I guess that's Turkish?'

'I think so.'

'How big is Turkey?'

'Twice the size of chicken.'

He smiled.

'Hiding my ignorance, mate. I don't know. Was never much good at geography. My final school report card on the subject said "does well to find his way home".'

Kim laughed and his grey horse flicked its ears back.

'Would Sonny come home if you had to go to court over all this?'

'I suppose he would, but I doubt it'd make much difference. He was more involved than I was and he got a fair commission from each bet. They'd class him an unreliable witness.'

'So you need to find this man Jonty, then?'

'I'm not even sure now if that will do any good. He's an alcoholic, and a thief by all accounts. He'd be an even more unreliable witness.'

'Well that works both ways, doesn't it? If he's unreliable for you, then he must be unreliable for this Barney Scolder and whatever he's told him. Especially if Scolder paid him.'

Eddie looked at him. 'I hadn't thought of that. Want to be my lawyer?'

He smiled. 'I'm going to be a jockey.'

'I know you are.'

They trotted on between high green banks thick with trees, listening to the short echo of the hoof beats. 'Does Laura ever call you?' Kim asked.

That caught Eddie unawares. She'd been like a favourite aunt to Kim when they had been together. He'd lived with her and her horses for months up on the northeast coast. 'No, I haven't heard from her in a year. She still calls you, doesn't she?'

'Once a week, usually. Sometimes she says she misses you.'

'Sometimes I miss those days by the sea, when you were safe and happy and I was in love.'

'I'm safe and happy now. Don't worry.'

Eddie turned to him. 'As happy as you were at Laura's?'

His head and shoulders moved to the rhythm of his horse, and the wind stirred the black curls hanging from the side of his helmet. 'Not always.'

'You could go back, you know. Your mother would understand.'

He shook his head. 'I'm too far down the adjustment line. Too many days in the bank to lose them.'

Eddie was about to tell him how proud he was of his mature attitude and his philosophy, when Eddie realized it would be patronizing. Eddie just nodded and said, 'I know the feeling well.'

Kim said, 'And Marie seems to be coming out of her shell. Not so many bad days now. We've had a good summer.'

'How was your trip up north? I meant to call you the other day, then all this crap broke,'

'It was a kind of happy sad trip. I went back to the farm.'

'Your farm?'

Kim nodded. 'Mine. My mum and dad's, but mine now, I suppose. It still hasn't been sold.'

'I'm surprised. That's been a while now, hasn't it?'

'The lawyer sent a letter last month. It's been nearly sold twice, now, then everything fell through at the last minute.'

'It'll sell in time, Kim. And the money's going into trust for you anyway, isn't it?'

'I'm not bothered about the money, Eddie. I'm glad in a way that nobody else is living there. I never knew anywhere else. It was my whole life, and my whole world, and…well, it's hard to explain.'

'I know.'

'Marie showed me the house where Rory used to live, my biological dad. That's an awful cold way of describing somebody who's so important, isn't it? Biological.'

Eddie smiled. 'I suppose it is.'

Kim had lost his adoptive father in an accident on a fierce winter day in the Lakeland hills. Until his death, Kim hadn't known he was adopted. His adoptive mother had died of cancer when Kim was six.

Kim said, 'I mean, they could have come up with something more, well more…something not so much like a science, like it was all an experiment and nothing meant much. I'd like to say real dad but that hurts my memory of dad, and of mum too.

'Marie showed me the places they used to walk, and swim, and sit, and laugh. It was like being with someone my own age, listening to her. It took her right back to her teenage years, and it made me realize that Rory was no different from me. Everything was probably going great in his life then wham, "You can't see your girlfriend ever again. You can't go back to Kyrtlebank. If you're seen on our land again, you'll go to jail."'

'Yep. That sounds like my father, all right. Marie told me she didn't think Rory ever knew about you. She hadn't realized she was pregnant, but mother suspected something. Suddenly she's locked up at Kyrtlebank, removed from school and from life. You're dead right. Everything can change in an instant.'

'But I suppose you can't stay a child all your life.'

'Unfortunate for many, I suppose, that you can't. Though not for me.'

Kim looked across at him. 'I'm sorry, Eddie. I didn't mean anything by that.'

'Hey! I know you didn't. Don't worry. It must have been an emotional couple of days. It'll be on your mind for a while.'

'I suppose.'

They were quiet for a minute, the sounds of hooves filling the silence, then Eddie said, 'Did Marie talk about trying to find Rory?'

'I think Marie was…well, it was always at the front of her mind. But she seems afraid that he might have changed, or that he won't recognize her. Or maybe that he would reject me. My guess would be that she's already been digging around online. She said she'd heard he was a shepherd on one of the big hill farms now. And she seems certain he'll be married and settled, so that's another thing putting her off.'

'It's a tough one. How do you feel?'

'About finding him? I'd like to. My adoptive dad will always be my dad to me, but I'd like to meet Rory.'

'Well, let's see what we can do about it,' Eddie said.

'I'd like to see what he looks like, Rory. Some of the kids at school say I'm like you.'

'You've definitely got the Malloy look about you. Whether that's a curse or a blessing, I don't know.'

Kim smiled. Eddie said, 'At least you're scar free. For now. The jockey's life will soon fix that.'

'I can't wait.'

After dinner with Kim and Marie, Eddie reckoned Mave would be awake by now, and he walked out alone to the end of the barn and called her.

'They haven't locked you up yet, then?'

Eddie told her what Lisle had proposed.

She said, 'Most crimes are solved by snitches. Or by police with snitches, I should say. Throw in Lisle's background, and I guess you wouldn't have been surprised.'

'I was. Bad as the BHA can be at times, they're racing folk and they know better than to ask a jockey to do anything like that.'

'Lisle's not a racing man, though. Nor is Buley.'

'True.'

'What will they do tomorrow?'

'Suspend me, pending a full inquiry, I'd have thought. For PR reasons, if nothing else.'

'Can't be for PR or Lisle wouldn't have offered you that deal.'

'They can't not suspend me, deal or no deal. They'd just have made the suspension shorter and found me not guilty at the end.'

'Well, at least Lisle doesn't think there's much to it if he's happy to trade with you to get those three.'

'A sprat to catch a mackerel?'

'Well, I'd have left of the s at the start.'

'Very funny, Maven.'

'I like to help keep your spirit up. How's Kim?'

'He's fine. He made a good point about Saroyan. I'll tell you tomorrow.'

'Good night.'

THIRTY ONE

Eddie signed in at the BHA office reception and pinned his ID badge to his lapel. 'Please take a seat, Mister Malloy. Someone will be down soon.'

'Thanks. I'll stand.'

Eddie watched this central London street through the big glass doors, amused, as he always was, by the twenty five percent speed increase of life here compared with small towns like Lambourn. Everyone was going somewhere. Even the pigeons walked with purpose.

The one thing missing was a bunch of press men. Any jockey facing a disciplinary hearing in a case like this could expect to be deafened by camera-clicks and shouted questions on the way into the building. Eddie hadn't even bothered checking online for the details of the disciplinary hearing. He took it as read that it would have been announced in a press release in the normal fashion.

Eddie heard the elevator ping and saw Lisle's reflection as he came toward him. Eddie turned. Lisle smiled. Pin-stripe suit, hard-eyed today despite the smile and the reaching hand. He small-talked Eddie up three floors and into a high-windowed office.

'Drink?'

'No thanks.'

Lisle sat. No cosy strolling twosome this time, Eddie thought. A glass-topped table separated them. No notebooks. No recording equipment that Eddie could see. No disciplinary panel. Eddie watched him. Lisle opened his hands and smiled. 'I spoke at length to Nic Buley last night about the threat of acting too quickly here.'

Eddie nodded, resisting the urge to add "like you did in the case you just lost".

'But we need to retain the faith of the betting public.'

Again, Eddie bit his tongue.

'We can't take any formal proceedings until we've interviewed Mister Saroyan.'

'Saroyan's a thief and a liar. He's an alcoholic drifter who could be dead in a ditch somewhere.'

'Why do you say that?'

Eddie told him about Saroyan's Cane Toad Project in Australia. 'He could be lying shrivelled in the outback. Nobody's seen him for months.'

'You seem pretty confident he won't be turning up any time soon, Mister Malloy.'

'He could walk in here tomorrow, for all I know. If you're suggesting I had something to do with his disappearance, at least be straight about it.'

Lisle bit down, flexing his jaw muscles.

'Look, Mister Lisle, I've no doubt you know more about Saroyan now than I do. In any line of unreliable witnesses, he'd be close to the front.'

'Then all we're left with is the balance of probability, and the scales are not in your favour, Mister Malloy.'

Without using their names, Eddie told him about Mave's betting records, and her screen recordings with Nina Raine and about Sonny volunteering to testify that Eddie had not been involved in the tipping or betting. 'My friend has agreed to let you see the programme running live.' Eddie outlined the rest of the conditions.

'Why didn't you mention this yesterday?' Lisle asked.

'Because I want my friends kept out of this, if possible. That betting programme is worth a fortune, and the person who wrote it will be a sitting target. But that person is willing to take a chance for my sake.'

'But you wouldn't be willing to put your friend in danger.'

'There are ways and means.'

He shook his head. 'Eddie, why don't you just do this the easy way and help us get these villains out of racing. Blackaby, Sampson and Kellagher don't care about you or your colleagues or anyone else. They're poisoning your sport. Your sport.'

'You're asking me to do your job, Mister Lisle. You want me to make up for your failure.'

The jaw muscles went again, and his eyes sparked. But he cooled quickly and smiled. 'I don't do failure, Mister Malloy.'

'Well, there's somebody who looks a lot like you doing a damned good impression, Mister Lisle.'

Lisle chuckled, and Eddie believed he was not being sarcastic. He seemed genuinely amused. 'Wait here, please.' He got up.

'Why don't you just bring Buley back in with you?' Eddie said.

No answer. Eddie knew Buley was staying clear because he'd want to push all the blame for this onto Lisle.

Buley was waiting for Lisle who knew that part of Buley's intention with this to-ing and fro-ing was to keep himself out of it. The other part was to make Lisle feel like a message-boy. Buley watched through the glass as Lisle approached, and he signalled him to come straight in.

Lisle told him of Eddie's proposal.

'His friend will demonstrate this betting system?'

'Live. There will also be recordings of previous sessions showing the system making a selection. Miss Raine witnessed those, and indeed took advantage of them.'

'So says Malloy.'

'I've no reason to doubt him.'

'You've no reason to believe him either.'

'Well, we will soon see. He and his friend either demonstrate their case effectively, or they do not. We needn't waive any sanctions.'

'We won't be waiving any sanctions, Mister Lisle, whatever Malloy offers.'

'I think it will prove worthwhile seeing what they have. If there is indeed a fool proof system out there for picking winners, it's best that we not only know about it, but that we know it is in safe hands.'

'And how do you think the press are going to view that? What spin will they put on the BHA effectively signing off punishment against some betting software?'

'The press won't be saying anything, because the system owner won't demonstrate it without the BHA signing a watertight non-disclosure agreement.'

Buley folded his arms on the desk. 'Let me get this right, we pull Malloy in to try and get him onside against those three, and he sets out demands and conditions?'

Lisle's patience was wearing thin, but he composed himself, as always and said, 'I'll tell him no, then, shall I, and we can instigate formal proceedings against him?'

Buley drummed on the table, watching Lisle coldly. 'Tell him to give us sight of this supposed watertight agreement. We can work that way too and get them to sign one, so that if our gullibility ever jumps up to bite us in the arse, we'll have some protection too.'

'So you're willing to do a deal?'

Buley sat back, arms behind his head. 'Tell Malloy the best he gets is that he shows us this system, identifies his friend who owns it and they both sign our NDA. If they do indeed have what they say, then all it buys him is the time it takes for him to round up what sounds like a sorry bunch of witnesses from wherever they are in the world. If I'm not satisfied that all his so-called evidence merits a lesser punishment, tell him he'll be warned off for life.'

Lisle nodded.

The room in which Eddie sat grew warmer, triggering the aircon just before Lisle returned alone. Eddie didn't bother trying to read his face. Buley sat down and put a notepad on the table.

'We need to meet your friend with the betting programme. If we're convinced by the evidence, you keep your licence.'

'No strings attached?'

'None.'

'No conditions that I spy on jockeys or talk about anything that happens in the changing room?'

'You have my word. If everything you've said is true, there is no case for you to answer.'

'I'm happy to take your word, Mister Lisle, but with all due respect, Mister Buley calls the shots.'

'Mister Buley will be guided by me on the best way forward. I don't anticipate any problems on that side.'

Eddie looked at him and smiled slowly. 'You, are a very cool dude, Mister Lisle.'

Lisle smiled.

On the street, Eddie saw a payphone across from Starbucks, but resisted the urge to call Mave. Eddie wanted to think this over on the drive home. She'd be gung-ho for a meeting with the BHA now that she planned to ditch the betting. But that didn't make the programme any less valuable, or her any less vulnerable.

Eddie texted Marie and Kim to let them know his licence was still intact and that he'd call on the landline later. He set off for Lambourn with visions of his peaceful house in the valley away from these crazy city streets.

Eddie stopped off at Mac's place. It was early afternoon, cool, and topped by a long fold of grey cloud hanging low over the valley. As Eddie walked along the path, Mac yelled over the roof: 'I'm round the back.'

He sat in the cast iron chair wearing a thick black fleece and brown corduroy trousers. 'Oh, brown with black, Mister McCarthy. The fashion police will be here shortly.'

'They gave up on me long ago, Eddie.'

'Late in the season for bee-gazing.' Eddie sat on the other chair.

'I'm watching the flowers die.'

'Jeez, you're a bundle of fun.'

'How did it go at High Holborn? I saw online that Buley said they'd be making a statement later today.'

'Well, I've still got my licence.'

'What did Lisle say?'

Eddie told him what had happened.

'Well either Buley has changed his spots, or he has plans to try somehow to confiscate your programme, doubtless for his own use.'

'We'd thought of that. Without my friend's input, for every running of the programme, it won't work.'

'Then…oh, it doesn't matter.'

'No, what were you going to say?'

'I was going to begin a lesson in teaching my grandmother to suck eggs. Forgive me. I was about to tell you how much protection your friend would need. I should have known better than even letting that cross my mind.'

'It's appreciated all the same, Mac. We'll be taking no risks.'

'Well, I hope Mister Lisle's confidence bears fruit. I'd have bet all Lombard Street to a china orange that Buley's sole plan was to shift all the blame for the Old Bailey fiasco to Lisle, and get rid of him. Maybe he's not as smart as I thought.'

'He's not smart, Mac, he's cunning. He's wily. He's devious.'

'The Vicar of Bray.'

'You've got me there.'

'A man who changes his principles as often as necessary to remain in office.'

'They teach you that at Eton?'

'I believe they did, now you mention it.' Mac looked up at the darkening clouds and held out a hand. 'You feel some rain there?'

'No. But then again, you're a much bigger target than me.'

He smiled at that. 'Want some coffee?'

'Please.'

They moved to the kitchen and sat at the table. Eddie nodded toward the row of houseplants on the windowsill. 'You didn't need to go outside to watch the flowers die. You'd better get them watered.'

Mac used the kettle he'd just filled and ran it along the plant line as he spoke. 'If I can offer you some advice on the practical front, your best bet with Buley is to formalize everything in advance of the meeting. Get a good lawyer to draw up that non-disclosure agreement. Make sure Buley signs it rather than Lisle. Tell them the lawyer has to be present at the meeting.'

'Should I build into the agreement that they'll take no action against me after they've seen the programme at work? That's pretty much what Lisle promised me.'

'You can try it, but it would be a pretty public declaration that you don't trust Lisle's word.'

'True.'

'Do you trust him? Do you think it was his TV persona making those promises to you today?'

'If it was, he's bloody convincing. He told me the first time we met that he "doesn't do failure".'

'I liked him too. Perhaps it's time to trust him and see what happens?'

Eddie nodded, then looked up at Mac. 'Lisle's worst has got to be miles better than Buley's best, hasn't it?'

'Let's hope so, Eddie. For everyone's sake.'

THIRTY-TWO

Mave hired the best barrister in the country, Rupert Kingsley. When she told him what it was for, Kingsley said, 'Forgive me, but that is akin to asking a brain surgeon to remove a wart.'

Mave said, 'An apt analogy, Mister Kingsley. We wanted to make sure this particular wart does not regrow.'

Kingsley produced the agreement and attended the meeting to witness proceedings. Buley was unable to hide how impressed he was that Mave had retained the services of such a man.

When all was done, and Lisle was seeing them out, he said to Mave. 'It's been a pleasure to meet you, Miss Judge. Mister Buley seemed much taken with your lawyer. I suspect you have heard the story of John Travolta on set?'

'Can't say I have, Mister Lisle.'

'Ahh, you must have a natural aptitude for such things, then. Remind me sometime to tell you the Travolta story.'

'I'll look forward to it.'

That evening Buley waited until Broc Lisle was the only other person still in the building. He went down one flight of stairs and through the swing doors, then stopped. Lisle was coming toward him, buttoning his overcoat.

'I wanted a word,' Buley said.

'I'm listening.' Lisle stared at him.

'It could take a while.'

Lisle smiled. 'Some other time, then, eh?' He stepped aside to pass Buley, who put his hand on Lisle's arm. 'What's the big rush?'

'I'm visiting my father.' Lisle had told Buley about his father and made it part of his contract that he saw him at the times he specified.

Buley said. 'Well, it's not as though he'll be counting the minutes, is it?'

Lisle tried to keep the anger from his eyes. It was rarely good to show emotion, and your adversary should never be allowed to see it. 'I have a set time to see my father twice a week, Mister Buley. You know that. Now, please excuse me.'

Buley let go his arm. Lisle walked on. Buley called after him, 'Why do you keep going to see him anyway? It's not as if he knows who you are.'

Lisle stopped. He turned and looked at his boss. 'But *I* know who he is.'

Buley blinked. Lisle stared until Buley lowered his eyes.

Buley watched the big glass door swing slowly shut. Oh well, it would have to be Friday, as it had been with McCarthy. At least that would make the weekend less tiresome. He returned to his office and phoned the man. 'Job done?'

'Not yet. It'll be Friday.'

'Why?'

'Things don't always fall into place as we'd like them to.'

'Don't talk to me like that, Buley. Get the bloody job done! If Lisle hasn't gone by close of business Friday, you're finished.'

By Friday, Broc Lisle felt he was making progress. There had been some unpleasantness at Ascot when Kellagher had sneered at Lisle and called him a clown, but given that everything else he'd been working on quietly had come together he felt entitled to a little self-congratulation. Especially so as he sat waiting for Buley's summons.

He pulled from his pocket a soft leather sleeve, inside which was a credit-card sized piece of polished steel. Lisle used it as a mirror. He checked his teeth. He smoothed his moustache and had a sudden crazy wish for a long moustache that he could twirl like a proper pantomime villain. It made him laugh.

Upstairs, Buley heard the faint laughter and he smiled and shook his head. 'Laughing all the way to the scaffold. Clown.' He buzzed Lisle's extension. 'You can come up now.'

Lisle settled in the chair opposite Buley, whose suits and shirts, Lisle thought, were much too tight for good taste. Lisle watched him, knowing that Lisle Senior would have called Buley a corner-boy: a chancer. Someone who didn't even merit the title "opportunist". A corner-boy through and through.

'Thanks for holding on, Broc. I'm sorry to have kept you waiting.'

'No, you're not.'

Buley frowned.

Lisle said, 'The delay was deliberate. Frivolous. Vexatious. A silly tactic aimed at weakening me.' Lisle crossed his legs and leant back and continued, 'You see yourself as a handsome matador, poised to deliver the estocada to a tired and wounded animal. The reality is that you skulk around in your too tight shirt and trousers, hoping your intended victim is so close to death, you need not dirty your hands.'

'I think we are letting you go just in time, by the sound of things, Mister Lisle. Your quirkiness seems finally to have spilled over into lunacy.'

'*We* are letting you go? Who is we, Mister Buley?'

'The BHA.'

'And why would you no longer wish to retain the services of, if I may say so, a diligent, dogged, determined, steadfast employee, especially one with such fine investigation and deduction powers?'

'Because you have failed, Mister Lisle. You failed to gain a single conviction in court. We then have the embarrassment of Eddie Malloy's picture all over the Sunday papers.'

'Ahh, I thought we'd settled the latter? You seemed so taken with Mister Malloy's entourage on Tuesday when signing that agreement.'

'Nonetheless-'

'Nonetheless means nothing to me. It means nothing to anyone, Mister Buley, whatever you follow it up with. Tell me this, who leaked the police payment to the media?'

'Well forgive me for pointing out that your job, until now, was head of integrity. It was for you to find out who leaked it, which you failed to do. Obviously.'

'Ahh, be careful...evidence of absence is not absence of evidence.'

Buley crossed his arms and lowered his chin. Lisle said, 'You met Arni Torland of *The Times* at your flat on the evening of twenty-sixth August, and you told him about the payment to the Met.'

'You have gone mad.'

Lisle pulled an envelope from his inside pocket. 'May I?' he said, picking up the silver letter-opener from Buley's desk. From the slit envelope he took a single sheet of typed A4 and pushed it across to Buley. 'A signed statement from your friend, Torland.'

Buley swallowed and pulled the sheet toward him.

'Dear oh dear,' Lisle said, 'you look on the verge of panic, Mister Buley. Can I get you a glass of water? Some valium? Or perhaps heroin? Does that have a calming effect? I wouldn't know, you see, never having taken it. Your records from that rehab facility in the Tuscan countryside suggest strongly that you could enlighten me on the pleasures of the popular opium derivative.'

Buley sat stiff, staring at the door.

'Thinking of bolting, Mister Buley? I could understand you wishing to be as far away as possible when things get this uncomfortable. What about Australia? Is that far enough? They used to welcome wrongdoers. In fact, I was there last year. At customs they stopped me and said "Criminal record?" I said, "Oh, I didn't realize you still needed one!" Amusing, Mister Buley, don't you think? Of course you managed to escape without facing court there for domestic abuse. What we used to call "wife-beating". Battery, that was another name, wasn't it? Something you specialised in down under, I believe. But once again, bribery came to your aid. You didn't have to spend three hundred grand to get out of that, though, did you?'

Buley had stopped blinking. He stared at Lisle as though the man was steadily receding into the distance and Buley was desperate not to lose sight of him. Lisle said, 'Who is blackmailing you?'

Buley kept staring.

'Mister Buley, who forced you to take that case to court prematurely. You knew it would fail.'

'It was my anniversary,' Buley said quietly, as though alone.

'Nonsense. That was the excuse you gave to Peter McCarthy, who deserved much better and whose loyalty to racing and to the BHA in particular has been unflinching. Who's blackmailing you?'

Buley undid the top button on his shirt and loosened his tie. Lisle said, 'You brought the case to court far too soon. Then, when it looked like all the work I had done was beginning to turn the tide, you dealt the death blow by telling *The Times* about the payment. Are you working for Ivory?'

Buley at last found something to react to. 'I've never met the man in my life!'

'You need not meet anyone face to face these days, Mister Buley. You know that. If it wasn't Ivory, tell me what else, or who else makes sense?'

'I'm not working for Ivory. I'm not working for anybody except the BHA.'

'In the strictest interpretation of the word, perhaps not. But on whose behalf did you act to ensure that case was lost?'

Buley sighed and massaged his face. 'I need some time, Broc.'

'Don't Broc me. I don't respond to your well-practiced "interaction" tactics. Call me Mister Lisle. How much time do you need?'

'The weekend.'

'You've got until this time tomorrow to tell me who found out the same about your past as I did. And why they wanted that case thrown out.'

'Leave it with me.'

'You have twenty-four hours.'

'Then what?'

'That depends.'

'I'll call you,' Buley said.

'Do that. Hopefully I will remember to have my phone line open.' He took his phone from the top pocket of his jacket and held it up so Buley could see that it had been picking up everything.

Lisle said, 'Before leaving my office, I called a voicemail bank I'd previously set up. Everything we've discussed is now lodged there. Should I fail to enter the password to retrieve that recording by a certain date, it will be recovered by my solicitor.'

Buley said nothing but Lisle thought he detected a dimming in Buley's eyes. Lisle picked up Torland's statement and put it back in the envelope. He said, 'You may leave now.'

Buley opened his mouth to object, but stayed silent and got up. Lisle remained seated, smiling. He stopped Buley in mid-stride and said, 'Tell me, Mister Buley, are you familiar with the show, *A Little Night Music*?'

Buley nodded, looking down at Lisle who said, 'Remind me, would you of the title of its key song? Was it Send in the Clowns, or Send out the Clowns?'

Buley left the building. He stood in the blur of a London dusk, barely registering the busy surroundings. The lights of passing vehicles left vague trails on his conscious as though he was immersed in a photograph taken with a slow shutter speed. He turned right, walked half a dozen steps, then turned around and went to the pub on the corner. He ordered brandy and beer, but left both on the bar and went back outside and swiped his card at the main door of the BHA office.

Buley hurried upstairs. Lisle was still in Buley's office, though he'd moved to Buley's chair and was smiling as the man came back in. 'Slightly faster than I thought, Mister Buley. I was prepared to wait one hour. Sit down.'

Buley sat.

Lisle put his elbows on the desk and leaned forward. 'Tell me, am I the rock or the hard place?'

Buley frowned.

'Or don't you differentiate when things get this desperate?'

Buley said, 'It's pointless me talking to the other party now.'

'I know. That's the reason I waited here. The other party's cards are all on the table. The only advantage you have is that they're not yet aware that I know all that they do. But you are going to tell me. You're going to give me the full "heads up", as you would say. You are going to withhold nothing. And when I'm content that you have withheld nothing, I'm going to help you get out of the country so that the other party cannot do you any damage.'

'You have that much clout?'

'I have friends, Mister Buley. True friends. Not contacts…friends. People who trust me. People in whom I trust.'

'What guarantees can you give me?'

Lisle looked at him. 'My word.'

Buley's primal survival instincts had kicked in and they prevented him from showing any doubt about Lisle's honour. 'All right. But no recording, no sworn statements, no signatures.'

'Agreed.'

'And no notes,' Buley said.

'I don't need to take notes, Mister Buley, never have. Those with mental discipline, those who work their minds instead of just their bodies, we do not need to write things down. I'm listening. Please begin.'

THIRTY-THREE

Speculation about Buley's sudden disappearance bubbled away for longer than Lisle had expected. Police had found nothing at Buley's home that suggested he had any plans to leave quickly. His bank balance did not alter. None of his friends or contacts had heard from him. His GP reported that he had no record of any health issues which might have led to a sudden rash decision. His passport was in a desk drawer.

The media interest stretched on over the weeks and Lisle began to think it was simply a matter of time until the stories of Buley's past misdemeanours were sold to a newspaper. But the new winter jumps season arrived without any light being shed on Buley's hidden past. No new CEO had been appointed. The chairman of the BHA, Marcus Shear, announced he was taking temporary charge and that a search for a successor to Nic Buley had not yet been discussed, least of all because of 'our concern for Mister Buley's welfare.'

On one Tuesday evening visit to see his father, Broc Lisle walked the corridors, looking for him. Lisle senior sometimes found his way into another patient's room, but Broc did not want to start a search without asking a member of staff. He spoke to a nurse. She told him she believed his father was being "freshened up" by staff in the toilet in his room.

Broc went to room 15 to find his father being helped from the toilet by two staff members. Broc smiled at them, 'Lily...Martha...Is he behaving himself?'

'Good as gold, Mister Lisle. Not been walking today, nor much yesterday. I think he misses it.'

'I'll get him into his chair and wheel him around a dozen circuits.'

Lily leaned over Lisle senior, 'You'd like that. Mister Lisle, wouldn't you? Shall we help your boy get you into the chair?'

Your boy.

It took Broc by the heart...a long hand reaching through the tunnel of years since his childhood, spinning multiple reels of memories, and settling on his heart. He swallowed.

Pushing the wheelchair at a steady pace along the thickly-carpeted corridors, Broc spoke to his father about the old days, about his mother, about racing. He always told dad about his job in racing now. Someday, a rare shaft of lucidity might open long enough to let him take it in.

Broc pushed the chair, speaking quietly, 'I'm glad you've not been walking, dad. Rest is the thing now. You've walked enough in your life. You've covered a million miles. I can push you the rest. If you still want to be on the move, I'll wheel you around for as long as you want. I just have a few things to mop up in this job, and then, I'll make a deal with you.' Broc stopped and moved to the front of the chair to squat so he was at eye level with his father. 'If you stop wandering these corridors on foot, I'll come every night and wheel you round them. You get to see them in style then. What do you say?'

Lisle senior stared for what seemed a long time, then nodded. Broc offered his hand. 'Good. Let's shake on it!' The old hand reached slowly, rising, shaking, the pearlescent skin marbled with veins...it rested, soft, like a child's, in Broc's gentle grip.

THIRTY-FOUR

Pat Kellagher lived in a small house near the Safari Park just outside the west midlands town of Kidderminster. For more than a year, he had wanted to move to a bigger, better house, but he'd been warned not to. That had frustrated him at first, but when the court case came up, he was thankful that he'd taken the advice…though it wasn't as if he'd had much choice.

Still, he thought, as he pulled up in his driveway, things were getting easier. Once Buley was completely out of the news, he'd been promised that normal service on course would resume.

He unlocked the front door, turned on the hall light, kicked off his shoes, put on his black crocs and went to the kitchen. He switched the light on and gasped and stepped back, his hand still on the switch. Broc Lisle looked up from his seat at the kitchen table. 'Sorry, Mister Kellagher. I didn't intend to scare you. Not this soon, at least'. Lisle stood up. 'I took the liberty of filling your kettle. Would you like a cup of tea?'

Five minutes later they were in Kellagher's living room, drinking tea by the gas fire. 'Heat is so comforting, Mister Kellagher, don't you think? It must be of great benefit to you when the cold gnaws at some of those old injuries you've acquired over the years.'

'How did you get a key for my house?'

'I didn't.'

'How did you get in? The door was still locked when I put the key in.'

'Ahh, remember at Ascot you called me a clown? Clowns know tricks, don't they?'

'What do you want?'

'I want to ask if you'll reconsider the offer of testifying against Jordan Ivory. Turning Queen's Evidence, to use the vernacular.'

'I told you before, I don't even know Mister Ivory.'

'Mister Kellagher. Throughout the case at the Old Bailey, I formed the impression, and I am seldom wrong in these things, that you were the leader of the triumvirate. That you were naturally more intelligent than your two partners in crime. Is that a fair assumption?'

'There was no crime.'

'Let me cut short these tiresome denials.' Lisle took from his pocket a small silver digital recorder. He held it up and clicked the play button. For the next 97 seconds, he and Kellagher listened to Jordan Ivory giving Kellagher orders to fix a race at Warwick. Kellagher sat watching him long after the stop button had been clicked. Lisle smiled and said, 'What say you now, my friend?'

'That's no use to you. We can't be retried. There was no case to answer.'

'Ahh, we used to call them barrack-room lawyers. Changing-room lawyers would, I suppose, be the expression in your business. New evidence, Mister Kellagher. It changes everything.'

'I'm saying nothing, now.'

'Look, I'm not just offering you this opportunity. It's open to Mister Sampson and Mister Blackaby too. They'd be most welcome. The more the merrier.'

Kellagher pursed his lips and crossed his arms. Lisle smiled and said, 'Your lips are sealed but your body language makes an awful racket.' He got up and put the recorder back in his pocket. 'Ahh, well, I thought it would be easier on everyone to have Mister Ivory locked up, so that he can wreak no further havoc. But I guess I will need to change tack and play this to Mister Ivory in the hope he will accept the invitation to turn Queen's, thus keeping himself out of jail. In a way, it's better to have you three back in the dock. At least then, we, the BHA get a rightful conviction. And with Mister Buley gone, the appropriate department will get credit for the conviction.'

Lisle handed him a business card and said, 'I suspect that when you've had time to chat with your colleagues, you might have a change of mind. I'll hold off for twenty-four hours.'

THIRTY-FIVE

On November 2nd, Mave called and asked Eddie to come and see her after racing at Uttoxeter. 'Want me to stay over?'

'That would be nice. Where are you tomorrow?'

'Sedgefield.'

'Good. We can have a pre-dawn walk on the beach.'

'Mave, it's officially winter.'

'That's when the drama starts around here.'

When Eddie settled that night by her fire, with whiskey and a pleasant tiredness, he found out the drama had already started. Mave told him Sonny had flown over to see her on Tuesday, forty-eight hours ago.

'How is he?'

'Pretty desperate, by the look of things. He told me they've now got three different people in Turkey working on finding Keki. They're also burning through cash at a high rate in bribes.'

'Slippery slope.'

Mave nodded.

'So he wants you to start running the programme again so Miss Raine can top up her war chest?'

'Not just that. Sonny knows he won't get on anymore with the bookies since his picture was all over the papers. Nina Raine has suggested her brother could take over.'

Eddie shook his head. 'She's running poor Sonny ragged, isn't she?'

145

'I've never seen him looking so anxious. When he got together with her, he went from that big hangdog expression he had for years, to smiling and laughing like a kid. Now he looks like a junkie.'

Eddie sighed. 'Want me to talk to him?'

'It wouldn't make any difference. If you saw him, you'd know what I mean.'

'So what did you tell him?'

'That I'd think about it and give him an answer by the weekend.'

Eddie said, 'We know what that answer's going to be, don't we?'

She opened her hands. 'How can I say no, after everything he's done for me? It would be like betraying my dad.'

'What about cruel to be kind? The longer he's with that redhead, the harder it's going to be when she dumps him like she did with Saroyan.'

'Saroyan ran out on her.'

'That's her story. Why would he have given her the pictures of me to sell for ten grand? If he was the fly-by-night she painted him as, why didn't he keep the money and take off on his beloved Cane Toad project with it?'

'He was an alcoholic, according to her, and we saw some evidence for that the first time we met him.'

'He functioned well for an alcoholic drifter, though, didn't he? Following Sonny without being spotted. I never knew Jonty was watching us. He got plenty pictures on the racecourse. And though he'd drank himself to sleep that night we got Sonny back, when we all settled down to hear the story, who had the gin glass? Nina…Jonty was drinking water.'

Firelight glinted in Mave's eyes as her logical side took over. Eddie went on: 'Also, when Jonty was cashing in personally on the tips you were giving Nina, why up and run? Why not wait until the tips stopped? He would have made a hell of a lot more by doing that.'

'Good question. Maybe I should have dug a bit deeper.'

Eddie got up to refill the glasses. Mave said, 'So how would she have got rid of Jonty?'

'Well, she seems to find it easy to concoct stories. She could have told him anything…Scared the hell out of him, same as I tried to do with her the first time I met her at Market Rasen.' Eddie handed Mave the whiskey. 'All she's done when Sonny's come along is flitted to the most promising meal ticket. She was probably working on him from the start to give herself options if we didn't pay up.'

Mave put down her glass and massaged her face, groaning softly. 'I'm beginning to wish, I'd never developed this programme.'

'Well, just say no to Sonny. When did Sonny ever care about money?'

'He cares about her.'

'Does he? Or has it just developed into a fear of losing what he thought he had?'

'Whatever, Eddie. It works out the same for me, doesn't it? Do I restart the system and give them the tips or don't I?'

'What would you do if I wasn't here trying to talk you out of it?'

'I'd give Sonny what he wants.'

'Then do it.'

She watched him. 'Just like that?'

'I've screwed up too many relationships in the past by trying to make people do things the way I want them. I get paranoid and controlling. I don't mean to, but I do, and I don't ever want you to be anything but yourself.'

She smiled slowly and sipped whiskey then looked across at him. 'We have a relationship?'

'Spiritual…In a kindred way.'

She nodded slowly, still smiling. Eddie raised a hand. 'Don't let's start analyzing it, please. It's like trying to analyze genius, or art.'

Her smiled widened. 'So we have a genius-based arty relationship?'

'We fit! How many people are in the world?'

She shrugged, 'Seven billion.'

'How many countries?'

'A hundred and ninety six…if you count Taiwan.'

'How many oceans?'

'You don't know how many oceans there are?'

'I do, but it would have broken up this nice rhythm I've got going, as you have just managed to do.'

'Sorry.'

'Rewind?'

She nodded.

'How many oceans?'

'Well, only one, really, but for the sake of your rhythm, four.'

'So throw all those people in all those countries and all those oceans and every living thing into a big barrel, break them all up, and you've got one go at dipping your hand in there and pulling out two things that fit exactly. Dead right. Slot together. Like they were engineered to the finest measurement. What's the odds?'

'Big.'

'Exactly. Well that's us!'

'Oh…Good,' she raised her glass. 'To rhythm.'

Eddie raised his. 'And no blues.'

THIRTY-SIX

Broc Lisle called in at the nursing home. He'd held good to his promise, visiting his father every night and wheeling him for a mile around the corridors. Lisle had used a digital pedometer to work out the distance. His start point was the dining room door. The finishing post the threshold of Lisle senior's room.

The old man had not kept the bargain by choice. The spreading dementia had cut the nerve pathways to his legs. He could no longer walk. Broc knew this. He knew too, that although his father had shaken his hand that night, the old man had been unaware of any deal. He'd reacted automatically to an outstretched hand, as he had done all his life.

Broc knew he had engineered a happy accident that evening, and he was delighted to honour his part of the agreement. The relief he'd found in no longer having to confront his father's pained wandering, his quest for a way back home, would fuel Broc for as long as his father remained alive.

Broc entered his father's room smiling.

It was deserted.

He knocked on the toilet door. 'Dad?' Broc opened the door slowly and the light came on automatically. The toilet was empty. Broc went looking for a member of staff. Two or three were always to be found in the dayroom. Lily smiled when she saw him, 'I didn't realize you had brothers, Mister Lisle!'

Lisle stopped himself from telling her he did not. 'Dad's had new visitors, then, has he?'

'Your brothers are taking him on his usual nightly tour of the corridors. I told them that was what you always did. I thought they'd come to give you a night off.'

Lisle smiled. 'Thank you, Lily, I'll go and find them.'

The building was a long rectangle. Lisle met them on the short, northern leg of it. His father's hands rested on the arms of the wheelchair, his face, as usual, showed no signs of recognizing his son as he approached. Kellagher, flanked by Sampson and Blackaby, stopped pushing the wheelchair and waited for Lisle to reach them. Unblinking, Kellagher slowly turned the chair until the handles were on Lisle's side. Kellagher stared at Lisle for ten seconds, then turned and led the others away.

THIRTY-SEVEN

The first big weekend of the season arrived: Cheltenham. Saturday's feature race was a long established handicap 'chase that used to be known as the Mackeson Gold Cup. It had been won by some great horses. There was no budding champion set for this year's race, but Eddie Malloy was due to ride the second favourite, Playlord, a new purchase by a syndicate of widows.

A good card was scheduled on the Friday too. Eddie had one strongly fancied mount and three others. He left home early as he'd need a couple of hours in Cheltenham's sauna to make the weight for his best ride.

The changing room was already busy. Nobody minded reaching Cheltenham early. It was the home of National Hunt racing, a beautiful racecourse which hosted the big annual festival of National Hunt racing in March. The greatest jumpers in history had run here, and their ghosts still drifted, raising goose pimples on anyone with a racing soul.

Eddie stripped off and joined four of the lads in the sauna, looking forward to the banter, to the optimism, the camaraderie, the collective relish of a new season. Spirits were high, the tales were as tall as ever, old injuries were absentmindedly rubbed and smoothed clean of sweat for a few seconds.

The door opened.

Blackaby, Sampson and Kellagher filed in.

The laughter died. Kellagher looked at Eddie's three sweating companions and nodded toward the door. They rose and left without comment. Sampson pulled the door closed behind them and stood watching the outside through the rectangular glass pane.

Kellagher and Blackaby took the highest bench opposite Eddie. The dark-haired Blackaby turned sideways, swung his legs up and settled back against the wall. Kellagher arranged his towel slowly, like a woman fussing with her skirt hem.

He smiled at Eddie. 'Morning.'

'Morning,' Eddie said.

'Nice out.'

'It is.'

'Is yours running in the big one tomorrow?' Kellagher asked.

'Unless it drops dead between now and then.'

Kellagher smiled. Someone tried to open the door. Sampson held the gap to six inches. 'Later,' he said, and closed it.

'I didn't know you guys had booked an exclusive session,' Eddie said.

'We just wanted a quiet place to give you some worthwhile information.'

'All three of you? You planning to harmonize or something? You should've brought one more for a barbershop quartet.'

'You're a funny man, Eddie,' Kellagher said, smiling still.

'You won't believe the number of people who tell me that, but I never hear them laughing.'

Kellagher laughed, a deliberate mock honking. 'How's that? Feel better?'

'Blissful.'

'Good. I'm pleased to add to your bliss by telling you that Tibidabo will win the big one tomorrow.'

'Well, I'm happy for you. It'll be nice for one of you three to notch a win at a decent track.'

Kellagher nodded. 'And we're happy you're taking it so well. Have a few quid on through your old mate, Sonny.'

'Ahh, well, Sonny's retired, you see, and I don't bet. But I'll be sure to pass your tip on to close friends.'

'Please don't. It's for your ears only.'

'Do the others riding in the race know of your supreme confidence?'

'No need. It's a two-horse race according to the bookies and according to the way a certain good judge sees it. Yours would be the only one that could beat mine. If anything unexpected happens during the race, my colleagues here will deal with it.'

'Good for them. You seem a very efficient team. No wonder you have so many admirers.'

Kellagher's smile gradually faded to leave what he thought was his hard-man look. 'Be good tomorrow and stay out of my way. Tibidabo wins the race. Understand?'

'Thanks for the tip. Now I've got more than an hour to do in this box, and the air seems to be getting toxic since you three came in and started sweating. Why don't you go away and let a few guys in who smell nice?'

Kellagher stood up and looked down at Eddie. 'Have you ever heard the saying "what doesn't kill you makes you stronger"?' he said. Then he ducked low, close to Eddie's face…'They didn't get us. Lisle said he'd finish us. He didn't. He couldn't. He just made us stronger.'

Eddie held his nose and grimaced. 'You certainly smell stronger!'

In what passed for a decent snarl he said, 'You're a fucking idiot, Malloy!'

Eddie smiled. 'A happy idiot, though.'

Kellagher turned toward the door. Sampson opened it. Blackaby swung down from his perch and they walked out, leaving the door open. Eddie got up and called after them, 'Have a nice shower, guys! Use plenty of soap.'

Eddie looked at the other jockeys, who were clad in towels, expecting them to start moving back toward the sauna. They avoided Eddie's eyes. Eddie closed the door and sat down.

What to do?

Tell Mac? Lisle? Those three would see that as weakness. So would Ivory, if he was behind it, as Eddie suspected he was. This had the makings of a long battle. Eddie couldn't risk being seen as weak. And nobody knew what tomorrow might bring.

Eddie would tell no one.

After racing, Eddie left the track in a hurry and broke the speed limit on the way to Lambourn. It would be dark by the time he reached home, and Eddie wanted the house as secure as possible in case he got a visit from Ivory's boys. Turning in off the main road, Eddie went slowly past Rooksnest, the manor house sitting high above his place, then he pulled over and switched off lights and engine.

Vaulting the fence, Eddie slipped into the wood and began working his way downhill. There was little leaf cover left and the bare branches rattled in the wind, but that would help him if anyone was waiting around the house half a mile below. Eddie stood for a minute letting his eyes adjust to the dark. He knew these woods well; his running trails wound through them, and he'd pounded out hundreds of miles.

He set off downhill, smiling involuntarily, as the thrill of potential danger cast its usual spell. It was fear-driven, but addictive.

Eddie circled the house, then settled in the woods for fifteen minutes before deciding all was well. He jogged back up the main track and returned in his car.

Inside the house, nothing had been disturbed. He double-locked doors, and windows and went straight to his bedroom and pulled an ice-axe from under the bed. It's blue and black rubber-covered handle took a full imprint of Eddie's hand in the film of dust.

He had always wanted to try mountaineering, but the thrill of racing kept the mountains in second position. In his wardrobe was a grand's worth of climbing kit, unworn, awaiting his retirement from the saddle. When wondering where to store the axe, Eddie thought he might as well have it to hand in the night.

He swung it slowly, adjusting to the heft, the balance. He took it to the bright kitchen and washed it, testing the spike with a finger through the dish-towel, running his thumb along the blade. For the first time, he understood the attraction of guns. Under attack, he'd much sooner pull a trigger to kill a man remotely than pierce his skull at close range and feel the bone crack and the shock run up his arm and the blood spurt in his face.

At this thought, Eddie put the axe on the table and turned to the comforts of domesticity, filling the kettle and opening the fridge. But he took the axe to bed with him that night and did not hide it. He laid it like a cross alongside him...on the bed now, after two years below it. Ready. Waiting.

THIRTY-EIGHT

With one safe night behind him, Eddie drove to Cheltenham thinking of how best to avoid danger before the big race at 2.45. He felt less threatened than he had when leaving the track yesterday. Kellagher and his crew had either assumed Eddie was bluffing in the sauna, or they'd been too afraid to tell Jordan Ivory that they'd failed to scare him.

Ivory would be betting big on Tibidabo. From what Eddie had heard of him, he'd have wanted to remove any risk to his money. If his jockey trio couldn't frighten Eddie, Ivory would have more persuasive people to hand.

But they'd need to get to him before the race. The easiest way would have been at home last night. If Eddie could make sure he stayed in public view between arriving at the course and leaving the paddock for the big one, he should be fine. What he'd do if Playlord beat Tibidabo…well, he would worry about that later.

Kellagher and his boys drifted around the weighing room and the changing room as though Eddie didn't exist. But when they were called to file out for the big race, Kellagher stepped in front of Eddie, and his partners squeezed in behind.

As they waited for the signal to leave the changing room, Kellagher, in lemon silks, turned and put an arm around Eddie's shoulder, pulling him forward, smiling and putting his head close to Eddie as though wishing him luck. 'Mister Ivory asked me to tell you that he thinks you're a smart and talented jockey who's still ambitious. He says he'd hate to see you having to retire through injury.'

Eddie put his arm around Kellagher's shoulder and returned his smile. 'Tell Mister Ivory I always try to stay a step ahead,' and he put his boot-heel on Kellagher's instep then shifted his full weight onto it. Kellagher's face contorted and his arm came off Eddie's shoulder as he tried to push him away, but Eddie held him there and showed him gritted smiling teeth.

At 2.43 they lined up out in the centre of this vast natural amphitheatre, the packed stands away to their left, the wind swirling across the floor of the gentle valley, ruffling manes and tails as the starter, climbing his rostrum, checked his watch, and missed a step and almost tumbled backwards. Eddie heard a few chuckles, but the starter regained his composure and called them forward. Eddie had a final check to see where Kellagher and his sidekicks were…all on his outside. Playlord's running style until now had been to settle mid-pack and come late; an ideal target for a small gang like Kellagher's to box in and generally mess around.

Eddie had other plans.

When the tape went up he got Playlord away in front.

Eddie and Playlord flew the first fence and heard the others rasp through the black birch. Good pace judgement is vital, especially when making the running. Too fast and your horse has nothing left for the finish. Too slow and you leave the others with enough energy to pass you late on. Dead right and you have a very good chance. Eddie needed the perfect ride: fast enough to draw the finishing spurt out of Tibidabo, but not so fast as to leave Eddie's horse with nothing to give at the end.

The diminishing sound of the pack as Eddie pulled farther clear told him the other jockeys thought he was going too fast, a kind of crowd-sourced opinion from hardened pros. But Eddie couldn't let it affect him. He needed faith in his judgement.

Playlord was in a strong rhythm, and as they ran down the hill with two to jump, Eddie could hear nothing closing. Playlord showed no signs of fatigue. Eddie look behind, ducking slightly to peer through his legs and see an upside-down Kellagher riding frantically on the big grey. They were ten lengths back.

Eddie smiled, but he still had a decision to make…if he drove for home now it might exhaust Playlord halfway up the hill. But it might also increase Eddie's lead just enough to hold on.

If Eddie kept going at the current pace, he was certain they'd conserve enough energy to last home, but he feared Tibidabo's renowned finishing kick and his battling qualities.

It had to be option one.

Crouching lower, Eddie drew his whip and hit Playlord down the flanks, three sharp smacks then he kicked hard for home. Away to his right he heard the crowd respond with a gathering roar that rolled down the hill. Kellagher would hear it too. The favourite leading the second favourite into the final stages guaranteed pandemonium in the stands as punters dumped decorum for base instinct and the scent of the bookies' blood.

Coming into the second last Eddie was on auto-pilot and fired him over the fence, then smacked him three more times as they hurtled toward the last. The PA commentary was drowned in the rising clamour from the stands. The tone of the crowd developed a frantic edge telling Eddie that Kellagher was making significant ground. Normally he'd hear the hoof beats as a challenger approached but the racket now swamped everything, and Playlord took the last cleanly and Eddie was riding for his life.

Head down, whip swinging, kicking and rowing, foam from the horse's gasping mouth flecking Eddie's goggles, Eddie felt him falter. Three hundred yards to go. Eddie push harder, almost weeping in the desperate fear of seeing the grey head of Tibidabo at his flanks.

And slowly, it crept into view.

He was well to the left of Eddie. He had the rail to help him keep straight while Playlord, oxygen-starved, was wandering up the middle of the track. Everything dropped away from Eddie's consciousness. The baying of the crowd faded. The grass below him morphed to a smooth sheet of green, and from the corner of

Eddie's left eye, in what seemed the slowest of slow motion, Kellagher drove the grey in front just before the line.

Finished.

Done with.

Eddie shut his eyes. Gutted. Raging that Kellagher had got another result, as had his paymaster Jordan Ivory. He'd failed by half a length. Failed. Eddie's fault. Eddie's judgement, and the anger would not fade.

His next ride fell and his final mount was unplaced. As much as he loved Cheltenham, Eddie couldn't wait to get away, and he was hurrying through the last of the crowds, when he saw Jordan Ivory alone, head down, counting a wad of notes. Had Eddie been rational, he'd have walked on by…He marched across and blocked Ivory's path.

Ivory, tall, fair-haired, and exquisitely dressed, saw Eddie's shoes in time to look up and avoid bumping into him. Eddie leaned close and said, 'You were a lucky man, today. I gave that everything. Don't *ever* believe that your threats made an ounce of difference to how I rode that race!' Ivory smiled and stepped aside, 'Excuse me. I have guests waiting in my box. They're celebrating, and I'd like to re-join them.'

'You do that. While you can.' Eddie stopped himself from saying anymore. Ivory's facade of cool politeness, his fine clothes, were making Eddie feel stupid and thuggish. And vengeful. Heading for the car, Eddie told himself this was not his fight. Eddie hadn't given in to Ivory, and he never would. That should be consolation enough.

THIRTY-NINE

By the time he'd reached the outskirts of Lambourn, Eddie had decided to call Broc Lisle and offer to testify against Kellagher.

The logical outlook Eddie had acquired in the past couple of years had been almost snuffed out by his anger and frustration, but enough remained to divert him to Mac's place to talk over what he planned to do.

Mac poured him a large whiskey. 'Drink that. Calm down, and stay well away from this.'

They sat by the fire. Mac closed the curtains against the November night. Eddie drank a third of the whiskey in one go and stared at him as he settled in the big chair opposite. Mac said, 'You've got that resentful look about you. The one from the old days. The one that tells me you're going to do something really stupid, and bugger the consequences.'

Eddie nodded.

'Do you want to discuss it, or just tell me exactly what you're planning?'

'I don't know, Mac. I'm disgusted.'

'I saw the race. You rode a peach.'

'A bruised peach. I was half a length out. Half a length that won Ivory, and Kellagher and God knows who else a lot of money. I've never in my life wanted to win a race so much.'

'That's what's clouding your judgement, Eddie. I could see the point of being disgusted and infuriated if you'd given in to them, but you did the opposite. You should be proud.'

'How can I be proud when that crew are doing exactly as they want? When Kellagher and his sidekicks walked into the sauna the other day, everyone else walked out. While those three were in court, the changing room had never been happier. Now they think they're unbeatable. Kellagher was boasting about getting off with the charges. He said "What doesn't kill you makes you stronger". How long am I supposed to put up with that?'

'That's beside the point. What can you do about it? Lisle asked you to help convict them, and you said no. I suppose he'd welcome a change of mind, but why should you take a lone stand? Ivory is a very smart man. He's been pulling bigger and bigger stunts for years and has never been convicted of anything. If he finds out you've done a deal with Lisle, he'll get you...one way or another.'

'Not if I get him first.'

'Then you'd best avoid Lisle and everybody else.'

Eddie smiled for the first time in hours, and looked at Mac. 'What's with you? Your natural response is to tell me to stay within the law and out of trouble.'

'Waste of time and breath telling you that. The only reason I used to counsel you thus, was that I had a position to honour. I never expected you to pay me any heed.'

'Thus. That's another word of yours I like, Mac. I'll add it to flippant, macabre and belligerent.' Eddie toasted him. 'Here's to your vocabulary.'

He raised his glass. 'I'm happy you find me amusing. And even happier that you seem to have calmed down, thus becoming flippant again, not so belligerent and much less likely to do something macabre.'

Eddie laughed. So did Mac, and the world rebalanced itself.

Kellagher's success on Tibidabo went to his head. "What doesn't kill you makes you stronger" became his mantra, and he let it be known in the changing room that there were three more horses running in big races before Christmas which "would definitely win". He seemed to think this would soften everyone up and make his pre-race 'advice' to his main opponent more acceptable than it had been to Eddie Malloy.

The Tingle Creek Chase at Sandown in early December was the next race on Kellagher's list. Eddie spent little time thinking about it as it was most unlikely he'd be riding in it. It was a Grade 1 race, and none of Dil's horses was good enough to run. It would be dominated by the top trainers, most of whom had a retained jockey.

In the weeks leading up to the Tingle Creek, Nina Raine was burning through Mave's tips to the extent that Mave was working the system full time again, and Nina's brother could no longer get bets on. On December 1st, Eddie stayed over at Mave's place. Eddie hadn't seen her for a while. He thought she looked burdened, trapped, and unhappy. The house seemed cold and unwelcoming and she'd reverted to working through the night on a regime of coffee and darkness, living only in the pale light from her PC screen, a ghostly, bodiless head.

'Can I put the lamp on?' Eddie asked.

'If you must.'

Eddie clicked the switch. Now half the room was lit rather than just the halo around Mave.

'I'll get some logs in, eh? Build a fire.'

'If you like.'

Eddie hunkered by her desk and looked up at her. 'You're like a prisoner here. The Rapunzel of North Wales.'

'Minus the tower. And the hair. And the beauty.'

'Minus about half a stone since I last saw you. I wouldn't have thought you'd a pound of flesh to lose.'

Her eyes stayed on the screen, her fingers on the keyboard. 'You're obsessed with my weight.'

'I'm obsessed with your health, Mave.'

'Go and build your fire and let me finish this.'

The flames warmed the room with light as well as heat, and Eddie picked Maven up from the old semi-circular studded leather chair at her desk and carried her to the soft couch by the fireplace. As they crossed the room, she smiled for the first time since he'd arrived, and she mimicked her keyboard action in the air.

Eddie had shopped for bread and butter and ham on the way, as he knew her larder would be empty. 'Eat,' Eddie said, laying down the sandwiches and tea.

'Yes, sir!'

Eddie watched her chew slowly and stare at the flames. 'Mave, I know the last time we talked about this, I said you ought to do what you'd have done if we'd never met.'

'I remember. You didn't want to control me.'

'I don't want to control you. But I don't want to lose you. Believe me, you look ill.'

She nodded. 'I feel like I'm on a hamster wheel.'

'And Nina Raine's spinning it.'

'I'm doing it for Sonny.'

'I know you are, but what's it worth? What's it worth to him? If she had any feelings for him, she wouldn't be sending him on begging missions. Where is this son of hers? How much has she spent trying to find him?'

Mave stared at the flames. 'I've lost count.'

'A million?'

'Maybe…Probably.'

'And not a sniff so far? Nothing in, what, months?'

Mave shrugged.

'Is there a son? Was there ever a marriage?'

Mave looked at him. 'Why wouldn't there be?'

'Because she's spent north of a million employing God knows how many supposed investigators, bribing officials, running Sonny and you ragged for months and not the slightest sign of any son or husband…Maybe it's time to ease off on the programme and do some research into Ms Raine's background.'

'And if she's not who she says she is, what do I tell Sonny?'

'The truth. It's his decision after that.'

'And what if she does have a son?'

'Well, I bet you she hasn't spent a million trying to find him.'

Mave swallowed and massaged her face. Eddie rose from the fireside chair to sit beside her and he put an arm around her shoulder. She moved an inch toward him, her body beginning to relax then she caught herself and straightened again and pushed her joined hands between her skinny thighs. 'Miss Resist,' Eddie said quietly.

'Mister Resistor,' she said, her word-game brain responding automatically.

'Go to sleep,' Eddie said. 'I'll protect you from the Hooded Claw.'

She smiled, and her muscles eased and her tiny bones settled against him, and the old clock she kept in the corner chimed midnight.

FORTY

On the day before the Tingle Creek Chase, Eddie was at Sandown for two rides. Both were at a comfortable weight for him so he'd no need of a sauna. But as he walked into the changing room, Eddie saw five jockeys leaving the sauna box. None spoke. Nobody smiled. Dinky Cobb was one of them. Eddie stopped him. 'Kellagher and his pals just go in there?'

He nodded, firing sweat drops from his nose.

'Who with?'

'Alex.'

Alex Brophy was champion jockey. He was due to ride the favourite in the Tingle Creek. Alex was a tough guy on course; no quarter asked or given. In the changing room he was as close to a loner as you'll get among jockeys. Tim Bellamy, a good friend of Alex's when he'd started riding, had been killed in a hurdle race at Wincanton. Alex pretty much shut down his emotions after that. Everything he did was focused on winning the championship each season.

Kellagher and crew had come along a few years after Alex had withdrawn from the banter and camaraderie of the changing room. They knew little about him except that he was hard to beat in a race, and that would be the only reason those three were in there with him.

Eddie dumped his bag, took off his jacket and went to the sauna. Sampson stood guard. Eddie pushed the handle. Sampson let it open six inches and said, 'Closed for temporary repairs.'

Eddie took two steps back and kicked the door hard, his boot-heel denting the pine just below the handle. The edge of the door slammed against Sampson's ear and he howled and fell. Blackaby tried to catch him as Eddie walked in, but Sampson clattered onto the duckboards, his head hitting the wooden water bucket. All the anger Eddie had felt after losing out to Kellagher at Cheltenham flooded back, and he bent and grabbed Sampson by the hair and turned his bleeding face toward him. '*Nothing's* fucking closed to me! Understand? Nothing!' Sampson's dazed brown eyes searched for his companions. Eddie didn't even bother looking at them. He tightened his grip on Sampson's hair and moved his face close. 'Understand? You fucking moron!'

Kellagher said, 'Leave him alone, Malloy. You don't have a dog in this fight.'

Eddie turned quickly. Kellagher was on the lower bench beside Alex Brophy. Eddie grabbed Kellagher by the throat and hauled him upward, forcing his chin back, feeling massively superior. The rage made everything effortless. Their nakedness rendered them helpless in Eddie's eyes. He could have lifted Kellagher off the floor with that single hand clamped on his windpipe. '*You're* a dog, in this fight, Kellagher. You wouldn't be my dog 'cause you're a fucking cur like your two pals. Now get the fuck out of here…' Eddie threw him with such force that Kellagher couldn't keep his feet and he slithered along the floor of the changing room as everyone watched. Eddie spun and grabbed Sampson and dragged him out and laid him beside Kellagher and as he went back for Blackaby, the jockey hurried out under his own steam and stood over his friends. Eddie held open the sauna door and shouted at them, 'Don't ever fucking tell me where I can and can't go! Don't *ever*! And tell your boss, Ivory, that anytime he wants a fucking sauna with me he can bring it on!'

Nobody laughed. Everyone stared at Eddie as though he were mad. Eddie turned triumphantly to Alex Brophy who was still seated in the sauna. Brophy looked at him and seemed to be wondering if Eddie might attack him next, and some sense of how out of it he was seeped into Eddie.

The changing room door opened and the clerk of the scales looked in. 'Everything all right?' Then he recognized the half-naked bodies on the floor and he smiled and quietly closed the door again. Nobody moved, and as Eddie strode toward the bathroom area, that sense of power, of invulnerability, bloomed once more and for the first time in Eddie's life, he understood how men could become addicted to barbarism.

The sense of utter satisfaction took a long time to fade. Driving home, Eddie still felt as though he could conquer the world. He was convinced he'd finished the criminal careers of Kellagher and co and he laughed out loud at the thought of them squirming, sweating, trying to hold towels around themselves in a final attempt at retaining some dignity. Nobody would fear them now. Nobody.

Except Alex Brophy.

Brophy was due to ride Pearlyman in the Tingle Creek. At nine that night Johnson Carver rang Eddie. Carver trained Pearlyman. When Eddie heard his voice, he thought Carver was about to thank him for dealing with the Kellagher threat. But he didn't. Carver offered him the ride.

'Why? What's wrong with Alex?' Eddie said.

'He's been got at.'

'How? Have they hurt him?'

'Threatened his family.'

'Kellagher did?'

'No. He got stopped a mile from home today, by somebody he thought was a cop on a motorcycle. He had all the gear on and when Alex wound the window down the guy put a gun against his forehead and told him he'd shoot his wife and daughter if Alex won the Tingle Creek.'

'That bastard, Ivory. How the fuck has he stayed out of jail?'

'Eddie, I'm being upfront with you, here. This horse will win tomorrow. I don't want to withdraw him. But I don't want you taking the ride without knowing what the consequences might be.'

'Johnson, tell Alex to go to the police.'

I've tried. He's not soft. You know that. He could have dealt with Kellagher and the other two. But he won't put his family at risk.'

'So what's he planning to tell the press?'

'That he aggravated an old neck injury today and he doesn't feel he can do Pearlyman justice.'

'Bastards.' Eddie wanted the ride, but not at the price of anyone, least of all the Champion Jockey, bowing to these criminals.

I can give you an hour to think about it,' Carver said.

'No need. I'll ride. Thanks.'

'Good. And keep what I've told you quiet, will you?'

'I will.' Eddie realized that Ivory would have to be dealt with outside the law. He'd seen a few like him. Eddie had beaten a few like him. And he was still feeling that power surge from earlier. Eddie decided he'd fix Ivory. No help needed.

FORTY-ONE

Of the three Eddie had thrown out of the sauna, only Kellagher lined up against him in the Tingle Creek on this bright December Saturday. Shorn of his lieutenants and still feeling the humiliation of that sprawling naked slide along the floor, Kellagher did not speak and made no eye contact. Eddie worked himself across and alongside Kellagher as the starter mounted his rostrum, and as Eddie did so, the anger at what they'd done to Alex Brophy bubbled up.

Kellagher wouldn't look at him. Keeping his whip low, Eddie jabbed the butt of it hard into Kellagher's thigh. 'Come anywhere near me and I'll break your legs,' Eddie said. Kellagher stared straight ahead.

Kellagher's mount was a big black gelding called Midnight. He was second favourite at 11/4. Pearlyman was favourite at 13/8 and the others were poorly supported in the betting. Eddie thought back to Playlord and Tibidabo at Cheltenham: favourite and second favourite. This was obviously Ivory's scheme; find a quality race where only two horses have a realistic chance and take the other one out.

Not this time. Eddie promised himself that. Today would be payback for Cheltenham.

Top class two-mile steeplechases are brilliant races to ride in. The horses are all athleticism and muscle and speed. Two miles is the shortest trip in any UK jumps race and these Grade One races were often run at a hell of a pace. Sandown offered the added bonus of seven fences set close together down the far straight. One error there could lose a race.

Eddie's confidence and focus as he pulled down his goggles convinced him he could not lose. The starter raised his flag. Many of the 20,000 people in the stands raised their binoculars.

At the end of the Grandstand, beyond the winning post, stood the four-storey Eclipse Pavilion, housing mostly hospitality boxes. On the roof of the Pavilion, a man lay looking through a single scope. He wore white overalls, which helped camouflage him, though the paint around him was old and grimy. Beside him was a laser rangefinder, an altimeter and a Kestrel wind meter. He looked through a single optic: a Schmidt & Bender scope with 16 x magnification.

In the previous hour, the gunman had taken numerous readings. The wind was gusting up to 15 mph. He believed it was the only thing that might cause him a problem and he had downgraded the target from 'heart' to 'core mass': the triangle between both nipples and the base of the throat.

His equipment estimated a holdover allowance - holdover being the distance between rifle and target - of an eleven-inch drop and a right-to-left drift of five inches. It was almost always the case - aim high.

Kellagher's mount, Midnight, was a front runner with a flawless jumping technique. Eddie's horse, Pearlyman, was a strong traveller who never looked under pressure during a race. He could hold his position at any point regardless of the pace, and on the run-in, he was a head-down grinder, ruthless and relentless, and Eddie was certain they could track Kellagher, join him at the last fence, and outbattle him up the hill.

It developed into a re-run of the Cheltenham race, only this time it was Kellagher and the big black horse trying desperately to hold on. Midnight's coat was sweat-soaked and foam-flecked and his tongue hung from the left side of his mouth. In the final two hundred yards, Eddie edged Pearlyman toward the rail, trying to get right upsides Midnight, to intimidate him.

The gunman on the roof adjusted his aim as Eddie moved across.

Kellagher's black horse snorted air and raised his head trying to take in more. Pearlyman lowered his neck, stuck it out and in the dying strides, they moved ahead. Just before passing the post Eddie turned to his left to smile at the crowd and raise a victorious fist, opening his chest, stretching high…and the cheering stopped as though a switch had been thrown, and a collective gasp from the stands made Eddie look round.

Kellagher was out of the saddle, his right foot caught in the stirrup iron. The horse dragged him. He'd been 'hung up', and jockeys dread it. When it happens, you fight to keep your head away from the galloping hooves. Fear brings the strength to reach as best you can and try and free your trapped foot. But Kellagher did nothing. The bumps and drags and twists made him flop lifelessly and as the tired, frightened Midnight came to a halt, Kellagher ended up face down, arms at his sides, leg held above him in the stirrup as though he was about to kick the planet. Eddie saw on Kellagher's back, above the muddy drag tracks, a small crater of bloody flesh. Around the hole was what looked like a still picture of a raindrop splash, crimson on yellow silks, caught at the moment of impact.

Thousands had left the course by the time the authorities had organized themselves. It took almost an hour to get the weighing room area in lockdown. Uniformed cops moved around trying to look as though they were on guard and in control. Plain-clothes guys whispered in groups. Lisle and Marcus Shear, the BHA chairman, stood with Sandown officials, all nodding and solemn, trying to agree a press statement and a time for a full press conference. Kellagher's corpse remained on the course, surrounded by screens and arc lights, police photographers and detectives.

After the initial jolt of shock in the changing room, a general silence descended. Had Kellagher's sidekicks Sampson and Blackaby not been there, the conversation would have been speculative and animated.

It was eight o'clock before Eddie got back to the car to start listening to voicemails. He rang Marie and Kim first to let them know he was okay. Kim seemed unsure about trying to cheer him up by congratulating Eddie on winning the race.

Millions watched the shooting that night on news channels around the world. Editorial doubts on the wisdom of showing such a brutal act were softened by requests from the police that as many people as possible should see the footage, in the hope that it would help them solve the crime. Each bulletin carried a warning prior to the video.

That evening, Mac called at Eddie's house. They settled in the Snug, but the rain on Eddie's picture window made such a racket they moved to the kitchen and sat at the table, Mac clutching a big blue coffee mug, while Eddie had a glass half full of whiskey and ice. The rain drummed softly on the roof. A few raindrops glistened in Mac's hair.

He nodded toward Eddie's whiskey glass, 'Medicinal?'

Eddie smiled, 'That's my excuse.'

'Remember when I first came to see you in that old caravan full of holes?'

'You make it sound like you were full of holes.' Eddie said.

'You made me sound like I was full of bullshit.'

'I was an angry young man, Mac. Long time ago.'

He looked around the big kitchen. 'Your accommodation tastes are better now, I'll give you that.'

'What about you?' Eddie asked, 'You must miss days like these when the shit hits the racing world fan. Especially when it goes global.'

Mac nodded. 'In a perverse way, I do. Sounds inhumane to say so when a man's lost his life, but I'd like to have been involved in trying to find out who killed him.'

'For his sake, or yours?'

He looked at me. 'Both, I suppose. Mainly mine, if I'm honest.'

'I'd be the same, Mac. So would most men. Especially when you should have been the one running this investigation for the BHA. It's another chance for Lisle to fuck up, so you might get your job back yet.'

'It'll be a tough one for him. What's the talk in the changing room?'

'Not much. We mostly sat and watched the frightened faces of Sampson and Blackaby. Try and imagine what they're thinking. Kellagher was the ringleader. Most of the lads were wary at best and afraid of him at worst, and the other two played on that. At least until yesterday.' Eddie told Mac what had happened in the sauna.

'Do the police know about that confrontation?'

'I told them, to save any of the lads from perjuring themselves.'

'So you're now in their books as having a major grudge against him.'

'Mac, I think I have a pretty good alibi, don't you?'

'Well, the police know where you were when it happened, but they won't discount the possibility of a paid assassin.'

'But hopefully they will discount the fact that I'm not a moron, and that if I wanted someone to kill Kellagher, I'd have made sure it wasn't done in front of twenty-thousand people and a TV audience.'

'That is the real puzzle here,' Mac said. 'Why kill a man so publicly?'

'Also, if the killing was to do with whatever those three have been up to, then Sampson and Blackaby might be next.'

'I'd be interested to know what they said in their statements today.'

'Couldn't you get sight of them, the statements?'

'I suppose I could, if I called in a few favours.'

Eddie had left out his conversation with Johnson Carver the night before. He didn't know if Carver or Alex Brophy had told the cops about the threat to Brophy's family. It wasn't for Eddie to decide who should know about that.

It was also in his mind that Alex Brophy was not soft. He was quiet and deep. He was also absent from the changing room today. But, Eddie asked himself, was he absent from the racecourse? Was Brophy capable, morally and practically, of shooting a man?

Eddie drank and washed the whiskey around his mouth. Mac said, 'There's been some talk that Lisle and Marcus Shear might have offered Kellagher and his pals an amnesty for turning in Ivory.'

'Where'd you hear that?'

'Old friends in the office.'

'Anything to it?'

'Who knows? Could have been said in jest then gathered legs as these things do.'

'So, if there was something to it, your thinking is that Ivory's behind the killing?'

Mac, shrugged, opening his hands. 'You say Ivory had a big bet on Midnight…why have the jockey killed in the closing stages?'

'I had him beat at the time, Mac. He was winning nothing.'

'And what if it had been neck and neck right to the post. You'd have been the man in the sights. The shooter couldn't have got at Kellagher.'

'Well, not if you're assuming the shot came from the grandstands.'

'You said the exit hole was in his back.'

'True.'

'It had to be someone high on the far end of the Grandstand, probably on the roof.'

'If Ivory was behind it, it would have made more sense to shoot me. That way he lands his bet and gets rid of the only one in the changing room who stands up to his boys. And he also gets me back for confronting him at Cheltenham.'

'But you can't put him in jail for twenty years by turning Queen's evidence on him. Kellagher could.'

'So why wouldn't he just have Kellagher quietly killed in a back alley, or in a staged road accident, or something? Think about it…he's got to get a guy with a rifle into one of the biggest racecourses in the country, find him a concealed sniper's point among twenty thousand people. There's a TV blimp overhead, a dozen cameras around the track, and CCTV, I imagine. Then he's got to get him out again. And, *and*, by the way, we're not talking any old gunman here…this is a guy who can shoot stone dead a man on a galloping horse. Granted, Kellagher stood up in his stirrups when he knew he was beat, but if that shot came from the end of the Stand roof, what, a couple of hundred yards away, in a crosswind…'

Mac was nodding as Eddie spoke. 'Perhaps Ivory thought there was no better warning to give Sampson and Blackaby than to kill their friend so brazenly? What do you think those two would say now to an amnesty for turning Queen's?'

'Fair point.'

'And it means Ivory's only had to arrange one killing instead of three. *Pour encourager les autres.*'

'You've got me there, Mac.'

'Sorry. To encourage the others…Irony.'

'I guessed the irony bit.'

Mac smiled.

FORTY-TWO

Eddie had black coffee for breakfast as he scanned the newspapers. Pat Kellagher's picture was on the front of most of them. Only one carried him as a corpse, the others used the shot of him standing in his stirrups a second before he died.

The reports varied little but there was plenty speculation; a betting syndicate hit man; a disgruntled punter, angry at Kellagher being freed by the court in the race-fixing case; an animal rights fanatic. Not one source mentioned the theory Mac had come up with regarding the Queen's evidence rumour.

The Times claimed the shot came from the roof of a building adjoining the Grandstand, one that contained hospitality suites. Eddie wondered if Jordan Ivory owned one of those suites. In the past, Eddie would just have called Mac and asked him to check if Ivory had a box there. It wasn't so simple anymore, but maybe Mave could find out. Eddie sent her a text.

Each of the newspaper reports carried the statement from Jockey Club Racecourses, who owned Sandown, about their shock and sadness etc., and their intention to hold an emergency board meeting and a 'full inquiry'.

Eddie went running in the woods in the Sunday morning rain then showered the mud away and sat at his PC. He'd missed Mave's ping on the private system they used. He clicked and she answered right away. Her webcam pointed at the window. She seldom looked straight at it, but the least Eddie could usually see were her fingers on the keyboard.

'Your webcam's squinty.'

'I'm incognito, today.'

'Let me see you.'

'No.'

'Why?'

'Because I look like shit and you'll nag me for not eating.'

'Still under pressure from Sonny?'

'It's not Sonny, Eddie, it's that woman!'

'Well, if it's that woman, it should be a hell of a lot easier to say no.'

'I don't want to talk about it.'

'Okay…Let me see you.'

She turned the webcam slowly, and stared at it as though she hated it.

'Mave, this is making you ill. I know you don't want to talk about it, but a decision's got to come sometime. Why don't you arrange to meet Sonny here, along with me, and we'll try and get to the bottom of this?'

She put her head in her hands, then pushed back her hair and looked at the camera. 'Will you speak to him, then, and set it up?'

'Of course. I'll call him as soon as we're done here.'

She sighed. 'Okay. Thanks. You texted earlier?'

'I want to know if Jordan Ivory has a special executive box at Sandown, in the Eclipse Pavilion, but there's nobody I can think of to ask. Nobody who's safe, if you know what I mean. Can you take a look at their hospitality database for me?'

'You think Ivory's behind Kellagher's murder?'

Eddie told her about the conversation he'd had with Mac.

'I think it's dangerous to make assumptions here, Eddie. This could be some nut who's just come up with the idea of killing jockeys.'

'Unlikely though.'

'What if it's someone who thinks that bent jockeys should be shot. Literally?'

'That still makes me okay.'

'Not to someone who saw the pictures of you and Sonny in the papers and thinks you've got off Scot-free, just like Kellagher and his friends.'

'That's completely different!'

'Eddie. Cool it. I'm playing devil's advocate. Trust me. Trust logic, not assumptions. Correlation is not causation.'

'I remember you telling me that before, along with the balance of probability theory. What happened to that?'

'Listen, we're not talking about getting some mathematical equation wrong here, we're talking about you getting shot. Dead.'

She wasn't in the mood for debate. Eddie kept quiet.

'Listen, please, Eddie. You've been in plenty of scrapes. You've got out of plenty of scrapes, which tends to make you think things will always be that way. They won't. Someday there will be one you'll go into and won't come back out of. Think about it...seriously.'

'I promise to think about it, if you'll promise to take a break for a while and make yourself something to eat and get some proper rest.'

'I will. I'll check that Sandown database first.'

'Thanks. I'll let you know what Sonny says, but not until tonight. Get some sleep.'

Eddie called Sonny, who told him he needed to see Mave soon anyway and that he'd book a flight to London for the following week.

'Good. Send me the details. I'll pick you up at Heathrow.'

'I'll catch the train, Eddie, thanks. If you can get me at Newbury station, that would be fine.'

'Why don't you stay a couple of days? You must need a break from all that sunshine.'

'I do miss England's rain sometimes, believe it or not.'

'Well I think I can safely promise you a few million litres here in the valley.'

'I'll see how it goes with Nina. I think she'll want me back here as soon as.'

'But you'll stay overnight, at least? Mave will. Plenty of room.'

'Can I drop you an email and let you know?'

'Sure.'

The email came within the hour: Sonny would be happy to spend a couple of days and catch up with Mave. When Eddie told her, she seemed relieved. 'That's promising, Eddie. It's the first time Nina hasn't put him under pressure to get straight back to Turkey. Maybe she's loosening the claws at last.'

'Or Sonny's coming to his senses.'

'I'll tell you one thing, when this is done, it's done. I'm burying this programme for good.'

'Never say never, Mave.'

'Oh, by the way, Jordan Ivory has an annual reservation for the whole top floor of the Eclipse Pavilion at Sandown.'

FORTY-THREE

Throughout the week, the media, in the boring chill of early winter sport, did what they could to ramp up fear for the coming Saturday. The police had made no progress on Kellagher's killing. Racecourses issued strategy statements on security plans. Bookmakers announced they'd contribute to the policing costs.

Eddie rode at four tracks between Monday and Friday and the mood in the changing room had a definite edge. They talked about Kellagher's murder but nobody said much about the prospect of another shooting. Mac found out that Sampson and Blackaby had been 'quietly advised' by the police to accept no more rides until the killer was caught.

But both kept riding.

They looked scared in the changing room. The other jockeys agreed that either Jordan Ivory had ordered them to keep riding, or they'd taken the decision that staying away would imply they had been guilty as charged at the Old Bailey.

Saturday's big race was at Haydock, halfway between Liverpool and Manchester. Dil Grant, Eddie's employer, had two runners in it. Eddie chose the shortest priced one, Solway Sands.

Jockeys had been warned to allow an extra two hours for the security arrangements in place at Haydock. Eddie came upon the motorway warning signs flashing well before the Haydock motorway exit.

Every vehicle was searched. A part of Eddie was reassured, but most of him was pissed off at the delay and what he considered an over-reaction to Kellagher's murder. The racecourses had risen to the media bait. Inside the course there seemed to be more police and security guards than racegoers. As Eddie entered the weighing room, four armed police were on sentry duty. None of this helped ease the tension in the changing room.

Calum Kennedy, the Scot who was third in the jockeys' table watched Eddie dump his kitbag on the bench. 'Have you had your orifices properly searched, Eddie?'

Eddie smiled. 'Way over the top, isn't it?'

'I was fine till I got here. Had talked myself into it being a one off last week. Then I walk in and see all these hard-faced fuckers with flak jackets and machine guns and I'm shitting myself.'

'At least you'll lose a couple of pounds easy. Save an hour in the sweat box.' Eddie said, unpacking his bag.

'Have you seen them? I'd be scareder of them than the guy who shot Kellagher. They all look like they checked their brains in at the gate.'

Eddie smiled. 'Scareder? That a Scottish word?'

'Oh, you're Mister Cool, aren't you?'

'Daddy Cool. That's me.' Eddie said.

'You might be daddy fucking cold on a slab after the big race.'

'Thanks.'

'Well, who knows where this guy is? He could be up on the roof just now, running through the colours to make sure he gets who he's after.'

Eddie finished with the bag and pushed it under the bench. 'Stop worrying, Calum. What's the point? If you were Sampson, you'd have reason to be worried.'

'Say what you like about him, Eddie, he must have balls like a bull to be riding a week after his mate gets shot.'

'Damned if he does, damned if he doesn't.'

'How do they even expect him to give the horse a ride? He'll be plastered along the side of it like a Red Indian bolting from the cavalry.'

Eddie laughed. Kennedy said, 'I'm away to the toilet, before Sampson arrives and locks himself in there.'

One notable difference from the two previous big races, was the lack of any threat in the run-up. No sauna confrontations. No indication that Ivory was betting Sampson's mount. Eddie guessed that this wasn't to be one of their days. The betting was open. Anything could win. Maybe that was why Sampson looked no more nervous than the rest as they made their way to the start.

Eddie's mount drifted badly in the betting, going off at 10/1. Dil had no idea why the market had gone against him. More often than not it's a bad sign and this time was no different.

Solway Sands was never travelling well. Approaching the last fence, Eddie was labouring in sixth when the horse took a tired fall. Eddie rolled over twice in the soft, poached ground and lay still until the final squelchy hoof-beats faded.

As he got up, he heard the same collective gasp from the stands as he'd heard last Saturday, and Eddie looked up the run-in and saw Craig Sampson fall at the winning post. He didn't get hung up like Kellagher, no pummelling drag along the ground. He seemed to slip gently off as though in slow motion to lie still on the grass, his horse galloping away toward the stables.

As at Sandown, the Stewards abandoned the remainder of the meeting. Police sealed the exits, although a couple of hundred people had panicked and run through the gates. Security in the car park mopped most of those up and herded them back in.

Jockeys were confined to the weighing room under armed guard. Once gathered, they all sat in silence for a minute, many with elbows on knees and heads in hands. There was much rubbing of faces and running of fingers through hair as though reality were being checked, some assurance sought that they were still alive.

Clive Banton broke the silence. 'What do we do about this?' he asked.

Kennedy spoke. 'It's not what we do about it, it's what the BHA does. They need to stand Blackaby down so the rest of us are safe.'

Aidan Donnelley said, 'I think you can safely say Blackaby will be standing himself down. Permanently.'

Banton said, 'They got Kellagher and Sampson. If Blackaby is on their list, they'll get him whether he's riding or not.'

Prophetic words.

FORTY-FOUR

On Wednesday 14th November, three days after the Haydock shooting, Roland Blackaby set off for Cheltenham racecourse. There was no racing scheduled, but Jordan Ivory had told him to be there at 10.30 for a meeting in Ivory's private box at the top of the Grandstand. Blackaby had considered not going. He'd spent most of his time since the Haydock shooting looking for places he could run to where the killer couldn't find him.

But he had a wife and three children. And if the rumours were true, and Ivory had set up the hits, it was pointless running anywhere. Ivory would get him. Blackaby knew his big mistake had been going along with Kellagher's idea to scare Broc Lisle. Lisle had threatened to go to Ivory saying all three of them were about to turn Queen's, and Blackaby was convinced that was what had happened. Ivory hadn't hauled them in. He hadn't even asked them about it. He'd just acted the way he always did, thought Blackaby, quickly and effectively.

And shouldn't he be travelling to Cheltenham in hope? He was still alive. Ivory could have had him killed anytime. But he'd asked him along to this meeting in a public place, so there was no threat this morning. Blackaby knew there'd be people around, even though there was no racing. A new grandstand was being built at Cheltenham and the work was well advanced. There'd be hundreds on site.

The man who'd shot Kellagher and Sampson was one of those on site at Cheltenham. He wore blue overalls, a high-vis vest with the contractor's name on the back, and a safety helmet. He was working below the old grandstand. Five floors above him, Ivory paced his box alone, wondering why Major Aubrey Severson had asked for a meeting in such a public place. Severson rarely left his office, content to do most of his ranting on the phone.

In the basement of the stand, the man disabled the sump pump in the pit immediately below the elevator at the south side of the building. He turned next to the thick electric cables, and set about diverting the current into the pit, which was already filling with water. Next, he went back upstairs and took from his leather tool pouch a spool of black and yellow tape. He used it to seal off the stairways in the grandstand and he added pre-written notices apologizing for the inconvenience and asking visitors to use the elevator at the south side. He checked his watch: 10.12, and he moved toward the machine room from where he had a view of the south door entry and the approach from the car park.

At 10.17, he saw Blackaby approaching the building, heading straight for the south entrance.

When Blackaby pushed the button for the top floor, the man took charge of the elevator, sealing the doors and sending the big metal box downward. It registered vaguely with Blackaby that the sensation was of falling, not rising, but he assumed someone in the basement had also pressed the button. He tapped out his impatience with his fingers on the dull metal wall, counting silently. Before he reached eight, the elevator hit the water and the massive voltage consumed the big metal box.

The man left the machine room and drove away from the track in a white van with false number plates.

Jockey Club Racecourses, Cheltenham's owners, confirmed that Mister Ivory had made a special request to use his box for a meeting that morning. A dozen witnesses spoke of seeing Ivory and, later, Blackaby entering the ground floor of the main Stand.

Jockey Club Racecourses announced that work on the site would cease pending an inquiry and a check of all electrical systems. The police were reluctant to classify the death one way or the other. Given the dead man's association with the two murdered jockeys, it had to be considered 'suspicious'. But, had it been anyone else, the only question for the authorities would have been one of negligence on the part of Cheltenham or its contractors.

The good news, as far as jockeys were concerned, was that they could ride races without the fear of a stray bullet or a mistaken identification of colours costing someone his life.

Another good thing, from Eddie's selfish viewpoint, was that the death of Blackaby finally put Ivory under the police spotlight. Ivory had paid retainers to the three dead jockeys. That was above board; it made him nothing more than their employer. But Ivory had no name to offer for the supposed mystery man he was due to meet at Cheltenham, and he denied knowing that Blackaby intended to be at the track.

Between the death of Sampson at Haydock, and the electrocution of Blackaby, Blackaby had taken no rides. Whoever the shooter was, he'd have known that pulling off another public 'spectacular' wouldn't be possible after Blackaby formally announced his retirement.

Once Eddie had read all the papers, he called Mac. 'Your moles in the BHA heard anything on this?'

'If they have, they're not telling me. But oddly, I had a call from Tim Arango half an hour ago, asking for a meeting.'

'He's the big shot at Jockey Club Racecourses, isn't he?'

'Chief Exec.'

'Well, don't be letting him pick your brains free of charge. Remember what I said last time, you're a consultant now.'

'So you tell me. Unfortunately, you're the only one who seems to view me in that light.'

FORTY-FIVE

Come Sunday, Eddie had racked up six winners. His confidence was high, and he was enjoying the atmosphere in the changing room again. Three men were dead, but their threats and their air of menace had died with them. Nobody was afraid anymore.

A heavy police presence still dominated each race meeting, but that was just a precaution on the part of the tracks and the word was that the big off-course bookmakers were now paying all security costs.

Had it not been for the Old Bailey association among the dead men, then racing would have been suspended across the country. The bookies would have been out of pocket, and Britain's sixty racetracks would have been closed.

The media coverage faded, and with it the pressure on the police. Nobody seemed upset or embarrassed that everything was returning to normal.

Eddie hoped that the meeting with Sonny Beltrami would be another item ticked off his list. If Eddie could make Sonny see sense, it would take the pressure off Mave. She seemed determined to ditch the betting programme and that would suit Eddie. Everything that had happened since summer could be tidied up and a new start made without any lasting damage.

Except, of course, to three dead jockeys, and, perhaps, Nic Buley, who came back to Eddie's mind…and lingered. How convenient that Buley disappears, shamed by incompetence and haunted by the dealings of Kellagher, Sampson and Blackaby, and then, one by one, they die. Eddie considered it…Nah. Incompetence was the watchword. There was no way Buley could pull off three killings. Eddie could not visualize him lining up rifle sights, although he wouldn't discount Buley seeking a gun for hire. Maybe worth discussing with Mac.

First, there was Sonny to sort out. Eddie checked his watch. Mave's train was due to arrive at Newbury forty minutes before Sonny's. Eddie set off for the station. It would be good to see Mave in his house again. He wasn't so sure he felt the same about Sonny.

Travelling back in the car, Sonny's mood improved as he talked about Nina. He sat in the passenger seat. Mave was in the back, her feet up, half lying down, seatbelt askew. Sonny told them he and Nina were living in a flat in Istanbul. 'I don't see her much, though. She's forever on the trail looking for Keki. You wouldn't believe the dedication she has to that boy.'

Eddie held his tongue. It wasn't the time to be digging for ulterior motives.

When they reached Eddie's place, Eddie offered to cook for them. Both rejected food in favour of whiskey. Eddie had left the fire burning, and enough embers remained to kindle three more small logs. They settled in the Snug, and Eddie waited for them to unwind and speak their minds. But Maven couldn't overcome her lifelong respect for Sonny, who stayed hidden behind his wall of delusion that Nina Raine was a saint in search of her lost son.

After half an hour, Eddie filled glasses for the fourth time and said, 'The time has come, the walrus said, to talk of other things…'

He shifted back against the arm of the couch and half-turned so he could see them both. 'Sonny, it was me who suggested this meeting. I say Mave's burning herself out. She says she ain't. I say, how long are you both going to carry on here pumping money and energy and time into this?'

Sonny looked at him, and Eddie saw disdain in his eyes. 'For as long as it takes,' Sonny said, 'as far as I'm concerned anyway.' He turned to Mave for support. She said, 'I can't go on forever, Sonny.'

'It won't be forever. We'll get a break soon. Nina's confident.'

'Where's that break going to come from?' Eddie asked.

'It could be from anywhere, Eddie,' he said Eddie's name as a reprimand. 'We've got lawyers, we've got local politicians, we've got a few people on the payroll, hotel staff, taxi drivers, people on the street.'

'You're convinced the boy's in Istanbul?'

'Keki's father told Nina they'd never find them in the big city.'

'And might he have been bluffing…to put her on the wrong scent?'

'She's convinced he wasn't.'

'What do you think?' Eddie asked.

'I believe in Nina. I always will.'

Eddie nodded and drank and said, 'Okay. What about the local press? Have they got his picture? You paying anyone there?'

'Nina doesn't want him paraded in the papers for all to see. She thinks it would increase the chance of kidnap by a stranger, and a ransom demand.'

'So what about the hotel workers, the taxi drivers, have they got a picture?'

'Of course!'

Eddie nodded, watching him, convinced Sonny's anger was with himself. Sonny had been duped and the only way he could find to feel better about it was to keep trying to convince himself he hadn't been. Eddie said, 'Have you got a picture with you?'

'In my jacket.'

Eddie went into the hall and brought back Sonny's jacket. From the inside zipped pocket, Sonny took a wallet.

The picture was of a fair-haired dark-eyed boy; a striking contrast. It wasn't hard to see Nina Raine's bone structure in his face. 'Can I see it?' Mave said.

She held it toward the lamp in the corner. 'Nice looking kid. Happy looking. When was it taken?'

'Three years ago. Not long before the break-up.'

Maven looked again. 'He'll have changed a bit. Maybe a lot.' She leant across and Sonny stretched to grasp the photo, saying, 'That's right. He could have changed a lot. Another reason not to put it in the papers.' He slugged back the rest of his drink by way of punctuation, and put the picture away.

Eddie picked up his glass. 'Same again?'

'No, thanks. It's been a long day.' Sonny said, looking up at Eddie, his eyes softening. 'I'm sorry for snapping at you, Eddie. I'm worn out.'

Eddie smiled. 'Better days ahead. You want to get some sleep?'

'If you don't mind,' he edged forward preparing to get to his feet then looked at Mave. 'You okay if I run out on you again? I promise I'll be in better form in the morning.'

She smiled at him, raising her glass. 'Sleep well.'

He grunted as he rose then took the few steps to where Maven sat, and he bent to kiss her on the cheek. 'Goodnight, Jo.'

'Goodnight, Uncle Sonny.'

He'd used the name he'd called her as she'd grown up. Maven Judge was one she'd chosen in her late teens. She had been christened Jolene in honour of her father's favourite song.

Eddie led Sonny to his room, and for the next half hour Mave and Eddie swapped hushed small-talk by the fire. Close to midnight Eddie asked her to come into the kitchen, well out of Sonny's earshot. They sat at the big table. Mave flinched and cursed when Eddie switched on the main light. Eddie turned it off again. 'Sorry. I forgot you were a creature of the night. I'll put the lamp on.'

'Just leave it. The light from the hallway's plenty.'

They settled in the semi-darkness, facing each other, hands on the table. Eddie said, 'Had you seen that picture before?'

'No.'

'You never asked, did you?'

She shook her head.

'If Sonny came to you, and you'd never met, and he offered you cash to help find Keki, what would you do?'

'Ask for a picture?'

'Then?'

'Run it through Google images.'

Eddie went to the hall and got Sonny's wallet from his jacket and brought the picture back to Mave. Eddie held it out. Slowly, she raised a hand and took it.

'There's a scanner beside my laptop,' Eddie said.

'It's okay,' she said, and laid the picture on the table in the widened slice of yellow light coming from the hall. She took out her phone. Thirty seconds later she held her phone screen toward Eddie. She'd found several matches for Keki's image, all of them photo agencies selling royalty rights. Keki was a professional model known as Julian.

Eddie sat across from her and said, 'Do you want to tell Sonny, or shall I?'

She sighed and cupped her small sad face in her hands. 'Let's rehearse it,' she said.

'Me first?'

'You first.'

'Okay,' Eddie cleared his throat. 'Sonny, there is no Keki. Nina gave you a copy of a stock photo from an agency.'

'No. She'd never do that. It's Keki. His father must have sold his image to the agency.'

'You really believe that?'

'Well, if he kidnaps the boy and goes on the run for two years, it's hardly going to bother him to sell an image to some agency, is it?'

'So you still trust Nina a hundred percent?'

'Why wouldn't I?'

'How much money has she had from you?'

'What's that got to do with it?'

Eddie stopped, and they looked at each other, knowing it was pointless continuing. Mave switched off her phone and pushed it aside.

'Tough love time?' Eddie said.

She stared at the table top. 'I suppose so.'

'Cold turkey?'

She looked up. 'I couldn't do that to him, Eddie. Three more. I'll offer him three more tips and tell him that's it.'

On the verge of seeking a promise, Eddie bit it back, and just nodded.

FORTY-SIX

Over breakfast, Sonny took the news much better than Eddie had thought he would. He watched Sonny as Mave laid out the story. She didn't mention Keki or the picture. She didn't tell him he was a fool. She just said she was exhausted and needed a long break.

By the end of her speech, Eddie realized that Sonny hadn't blown up because Sonny was certain that when the time came, he'd talk her round, as he'd done before. His obsession with Nina Raine had filtered out any emotions he had for Mave. She was a shop girl now, someone who served him when he needed it. Someone who didn't matter anymore. That was how Eddie read it, and Sonny lost him that morning.

Eddie wasn't sure if Mave had sensed the change in Sonny. She was the most logical person Eddie had ever known, but he believed that childhood conditioning creates a world of its own; one where we all want everything to be as it was in the best of times. Mave's desire was to hold that dear. Eddie's was to help Mave preserve its best memories before Sonny damaged them beyond repair.

Sonny flew 'home', as he called it, that afternoon. Mave and Eddie took him to the railway station. She waved as the train pulled out, a child again. Eddie's hands stayed in his pockets. His eyes locked on Sonny's. And Eddie believed Sonny could tell what he was thinking, and Sonny's smile said he held the ace of her heart.

Mave watched the empty track, listening to the ebbing sound of the departing train. She turned slowly to Eddie, then looked at the grey sky. She said, 'I feel that train is dragging this old year away with it, and the year isn't putting up any resistance.'

Eddie put an arm around her shoulder and smiled. 'That's as poetic as I've heard you, Miss Judge.'

'I don't feel poetic. I feel sad.'

'Let's walk,' Eddie said. The automatic exit doors of the station opened and the wind seemed to suck them out and Eddie pulled Maven closer. She ducked her head against his shoulder and put her arm across his back.

At home, in the Snug, Mave watched the rain at work in the shallow valley, its western slopes rising gently from the picture window. 'I'll make tea,' Eddie said.

'Don't. Sit down. Watch.'

Eddie sat across from her. She looked out on the darkening afternoon and Eddie saw the changes of light reflect in her eyes. She pointed up the hill. 'Watch how the rain comes over that ridge, through that little channel between the two humps.'

Eddie moved across to sit beside her and looked where she pointed as the rain gathered and pushed like a power shower through the humps. 'Mother nature,' she said quietly.

Eddie stood. 'Permission to make tea now?'

'Let's go out in the rain first.' She looked up at him.

Eddie nodded. 'Okay. How wet would you like to get?'

'We'll walk to those humps.'

Eddie bowed. 'That'll be from the, eh, sodden menu, then madam?'

'That's fine. I can afford that. Will you join me?'

'How kind! Let me just organize the pneumonia medication for our return, and I'll be right with you.'

Halfway up the hill, her hat blew away. They laughed. She took off her coat and flapped it until the wind caught it like a sail, then she let it go, and they laughed louder. She pointed at Eddie and yelled, 'You now!'

'No chance!' Eddie turned and ran back toward the house with Mave's cries of "wimp" and "coward" sweeping past him in the wind.

Mave took a hot shower, then Eddie had a bath. When he returned to the Snug, Mave's hair was still wet. She nodded toward the window. 'My coat came back.'

It had wrapped itself around the post and rails of the small paddock behind the house, flapping an arm in the dusk. Eddie brought it dripping into the hall. He called to Mave, 'It weighs more with just water in it than it does with you inside.'

An hour later, by the fire, they sat in silence, drinking tea. No television. No music. The big window echoed the rain and reflected the firelight. Eddie thought of Sonny, and of Mac and his late wife, and of three dead jockeys and of how the silent presence of ninety-five pounds of humanity within touching distance made the chaos inconsequential. Of how Maven Judge fitted herself to him without touching, and disarmed the buzzing atoms which had given Eddie's mind no rest through all the years. All she did was be there. All she brought was peace. And that was all Eddie wanted.

'Will you stay for Christmas?' Eddie asked.

'Yes.'

'Will you sleep beside me tonight?'

'Beside you?'

'Lie with me.'

'You were going to say lay then, weren't you?'

He reddened, and smiled.

FORTY-SEVEN

Eddie woke next morning to a text from Mac: "Drop by next time you're passing. News awaits."

Eddie told Mave he'd be back soon, and he drove cautiously on the wet roads knowing that strings of horses would be coming and going at exercise time. Every slow passing of a line of thoroughbreds brought many greetings from riders in that village-sized family that was Lambourn. A family facing another new day, most, despite many disappointments, with hope in their hearts.

There was hope in Mac's too, and in his face, Eddie saw immediately as the big man welcomed him with a smile. 'You look bright on this grey morning, Mister McCarthy. I'm not waiting until the kettle boils for this news. Spill it.'

'Sit down, at least,' Mac said.

They sat at the kitchen table and Mac told Eddie he was back in full employment with Jockey Club Racecourses. Eddie shook his hand. 'So that was what Tim Arango wanted to see you about. Congratulations. Mister Arango has just been added to my very short list of very wise men.'

'Thanks, Eddie. I won't deny it came as a much needed fillip.'

Eddie smiled. 'Fillips are good. I like fillips. What's the brief?'

'They've yet to formalize the title, but essentially it is head of security. A new appointment.'

'Prompted by three deaths at their tracks?'

'Tim was frank about that. Everyone else has looked on the past few weeks as something that's happened in racing, but Jockey Club Racecourses are conscious of the fact that it just might not be a coincidence. They were willing to take a gamble on the shootings, but when Blackaby was killed at Cheltenham, that changed things.'

'So that's the verdict on Blackaby, no accident?'

'Not for publication, but, yes. Somebody tampered with the equipment and the power lines. He was electrocuted deliberately.'

Eddie shook his head slowly. The kettle boiled, and Mac rose to make tea. Eddie got up too and leaned against the sink as Mac poured. 'So Arango thinks that the JCR tracks are meant to be...well, victims, in this, as well as the dead men?'

'Tim and the board simply believe it's better to be proactive than reactive. They're hoping they're wrong and that it's a coincidence.'

'And you're hoping they're right and it's a chance for you to make a name for yourself.'

Mac shrugged as he added sugar to his tea. 'Well, I wouldn't deny that, Eddie. Three men are dead. Whatever the motive was, if I can help find the killer or killers, then I'm thankful for the opportunity.'

They sat and sipped. 'No pastries?' Eddie asked.

Mac slapped his belly. 'Back in the saddle again. Need to look after myself.'

Eddie smiled. 'That horse has long bolted.'

'Never say die, Edward.'

'So what's the next move? I take it JCR will be announcing your appointment formally?'

'Today.'

'One in the eye for the BHA and Mister Nicholas Buley, wherever the bastard is. Get them to add that to your job description, finding out where Buley disappeared too.'

'I'm including it anyway, given that he could be considered a suspect, albeit an unlikely one.'

'Buley could have all the motive in the world, Mac, but he ain't got the guts to go with it. It would be nice if word got out that he's in the frame for this, but I wouldn't be wasting too much time on it.'

Mac stopped mid-sip. 'Just make sure you're not the one who lets slip anything about Buley.'

Eddie held up his hands. 'Mac, it took you a long time to trust me enough to talk so openly, so I'm hardly likely to piss you off for the sake of that little prick. Soul of discretion, as always.'

'Good. Doubtless your ear will be to the ground in your general peregrinations. I'd be grateful for any titbits.'

Eddie smiled, shaking his head slowly. 'Peregrinations, eh? You're in sparkling form this morning, Mac. Once you tell me what it means, I'll do my best.'

'Travels. Wanderings. The latter perhaps more appropriate in your case.'

'Indeed. But I do like peregrinations. As in peregrines, falcons, do you think? The way they fly so easily from place to place?'

'I hadn't considered the etymology, but, yes, you might well be right.'

Eddie got up. 'Etymology…Mac, I'm all worded out for the day and it's not nine o'clock yet. I'd better go before my brain seizes up. Let me know if you latch onto anything. It will be good to be helping each other again.'

'My thoughts, exactly!'

FORTY-EIGHT

On Boxing Day, Mave travelled with Eddie to Kempton, consoling him when he got moody about not having a ride in the King George VI Chase, one of the biggest races of the season.

When they reached the racecourse, the stewards and the clerk of the course were out on the track. Marcus Shear and Broc Lisle were with them and the large group huddled in a small area covered in a man-made racing surface called Polytrack. It was a feature at Kempton, a strip of ground from the all-weather track that crossed the turf course on the bend turning out of the home straight.

Eddie stood with other jockeys watching the unusual gathering. There was talk among the jockeys of a hoax caller, a bomb threat. The group of officials filed away, back toward the stands and before they reached the office, word was out that the race-meeting had been cancelled.

The unofficial word was that a mid-morning anonymous phone caller had insisted that the clerk of the course should walk the track again. The call was ignored, and an hour later the caller rang again offering enough detail to persuade the posse of officials to head out to the area mentioned. Below the sandy surface, a pit had been dug then covered. It easily took the weight of a man, but a field of horses would have smashed through the roof of it and plunged in.

By the end of the afternoon, the press conference staged by Jockey Club Racecourses revealed nothing more than plans for a full inquiry both by the BHA and Jockey Club Racecourses.

As they drove home, Mave took a call from Sonny. One of her selections had been due to run at Kempton. Eddie could hear most of what Sonny said about how much they'd been depending on that, how much it would have meant to Nina, and, most importantly, when would the next tip be? Eddie's anger made him want to grab the phone and rant at Sonny.

Mave fielded questions with a patience that wore thin only when Sonny asked for the third time how soon it might be before the next tip. 'Sonny, I can give you a horse tomorrow. It'll be a seventy-five percent horse rather than ninety-five percent one, but the choice is yours. Quantity or quality?'

Eddie thought there could be only one answer to that, but Sonny told Mave he'd speak to Nina and call back.

Mave ended the call and raised a hand as she turned and saw the fire in Eddie's eyes. 'I know. I know. Just leave them to it, Eddie. Let's get the last three tips to them and wrap everything up.'

Eddie wanted to say many things, but decided to keep quiet.

Shortly after they got home, Sonny rang to say Nina would take the seventy five percent horse. Mave sat at the kitchen table watching steam rise from her coffee, and she glanced at Eddie then said to Sonny, 'Seriously?'

She opened her left hand and raised her eyebrows at Eddie as she listened to Sonny's reply. She said, 'Sonny, you've got three tips left, remember? Don't you think you'd be better waiting for the best I can give you?'

It turned out that whatever Sonny thought, Nina wanted a horse for tomorrow. Mave ended the call and looked up at Eddie. 'Queen Nina rules,' she said.

Eddie shrugged. 'A day closer to freedom for you.'

She folded her arms and stared again at the hot black pool of coffee in the mug. Eddie's phone chirped with a message from McCarthy: "Call when free, please."

Eddie looked at Mave. 'Mac. Wants me to call him.'

She opened her hands and tilted her head in a "who's stopping you?" gesture. Eddie stood up and began pacing as he waited for Mac to answer. 'Eddie, thanks for the quick response. I just wanted some feedback on today. What's the chat in the changing room?'

'Everybody's pissed off that one of the biggest paydays of the year's been lost. No more than you'd expect. A few of the guys, as usual, had sacrificed Christmas dinner to make the weight for today. I needn't tell you their opinion.'

'Are they behind us though, from a safety viewpoint? There was no choice but to cancel. Lives were at risk.'

'I think in the cold light of day, everybody accepts that. But you know a jockey's general approach to risk..."It won't happen to me, or if it does, I'll deal with it".'

'Did Jack Shawcross come and speak to you?' Shawcross was the CEO of the Professional Jockeys' Association.

Eddie said, 'I didn't see him.'

'Would you do me a favour and call him and ask what his plans are regarding a formal statement to the media?'

'Sure.'

'You needn't be too specific.'

'No worries. I'll call him now.'

Eddie rang Jack Shawcross, a former jockey who'd retired just as Eddie was coming into the sport. 'Jack. Eddie Malloy.' How are you doing?'

'I've had better days, Eddie, if I'm honest. What can I do for you?'

'You planning to make a formal statement about safety at Jockey Club tracks?' Eddie asked.

'Your mate McCarthy ask you to call?'

'He's curious.'

'I'm sure. Wherever JCR move the fan, the shit still seems to find it, dead centre. Tell McCarthy we've a board meeting set for tomorrow to discuss it.'

'What do you think?'

'About what we should do?'

'What you should do as boss of the PJA?'

'I think I've learned since my time as a jockey that the number of people who believe their opinions on things like this ought to count more than anyone else's never ceases to amaze me.'

'Jack, you lost me in a blitz of double negatives, or something. Do you think jockeys should be asking if it's no longer safe to ride at the Jockey Club's tracks?'

'Eddie, I used to think that what I thought was all that mattered, since I was chief exec and was in charge. It took me about a week in the job to learn that most of the people who see themselves as being in power, and you can imagine me doing that little quote marks in the air thing there, don't give a flying fuck what I think. And if you believe I should stand by the tatters of whatever principles I have left and resign, I can tell you that the next guy will be no different. So I'm going to suck it up, as our American friends say, and try to go the long way round, which is the only way you have any chance of getting anything done.'

'Er, I think I'll leave you to it.'

'Please do. How old are you now?'

'Thirty four.'

'You're a personable guy. The camera likes you and you speak well. Get yourself in with the TV folks and maybe when you retire you won't have to consider taking a job in racing politics.'

'I'd last maybe three days before shooting myself fatally in both feet.'

'Hmm. Feel free to add "keen self-awareness" to that list of characteristics I mentioned.'

'I will.'

'And tell your pal, he can call me direct in future. I don't bite.'

'Okay.' You don't make much sense, either, thought Eddie as he dialled Mac's number again. He passed on what he'd been told, then turned again to Mave. 'All done. Sorry.'

'Don't worry. My attention's already turning to finding a horse for Sonny for tomorrow.'

'You might want to leave Kempton out of your calculations.'

'You think they won't have the track fixed in time?'

'Even if they do, what else will this guy come up with?'

Mave watched him. 'This scores high on the strangeness scale, Eddie, doesn't it? Somebody having a go at inanimate things like racetracks?'

'I keep saying nothing surprises me anymore, Mave, but this is coming close to it. If you're going to be working, I'll drive up and see Mac.'

'Okay.'

'Lock up behind me.'

'Jeez,' she rubbed her face, 'the reassurance man, right enough.'

'I'm sorry. Want me to stay?'

'No. Go. I'll be too busy anyway to get scared. Wrapped up in the search for a seventy-five percent horse.'

'For a one hundred percent ungrateful redhead.'

'So it goes, Eddie. So it goes.'

FORTY-NINE

Mac seemed surprised to see Eddie at the door. Eddie said, 'You sounded on the phone like you needed some moral support.'

They sat in the gloom of Mac's living room. A tall, ancient standard lamp with a ribboned lemon shade lit the corner and little else. The place was cold. Mac had his long coat on, though he'd loosened his tie and poured a drink. He splashed some whiskey in a crystal glass and handed it to Eddie.

'Want me to build a fire?' Eddie asked.

'I'll do it. Let me finish this drink.'

'You'll get your suit dirty.' Eddie balled up some old newspapers and drew wood from the stack which rested against the stove. As the fire struggled into life, Mac rubbed his chin, the crackle of his beard shadow clear above the sparking logs. Eddie sat back. 'There. You've got something to stare at now.'

He managed a tired smile.

'You look…befuddled. Is that the right word?' Eddie said.

He nodded. 'Along with four or five others.'

'Back in the saddle again, Mac. Now the blisters remind you of the downside.'

Mac raised his eyebrows then drank. Eddie said, 'Whoever took you on was dead right, wasn't he? Somebody's targeting Jockey Club Racecourses.'

Mac laid his head back on the chair and stared at the ceiling where the flame shadows flickered. Slowly he lowered his chin until he was looking straight at Eddie. 'Listen to this,' he said, and he pulled from his inside pocket a slim grey machine with a thin wrist-cord. He held it toward Eddie who saw the small regular holes of a circular speaker. Mac clicked a switch on the side: "Mister Bletchley?"…"Yes?"…"You need to walk the course again."…"Who is this?"…"Listen, you need to walk the course again, particularly the track intersection."…"Why?"…"Just do your job." Mac clicked the off switch.

Eddie recognized the voice of Ken Bletchley, clerk of the course at Kempton. The other speaker had sounded like a female robot. 'Bletchley got that call this morning?' Eddie asked.

'Five past ten,' Mac said.

Mac was still holding the machine at eye level. 'Is there more?'

He lowered it. 'No.'

'Did Bletchley walk the track again?'

Mac shook his head.

'So our man called somebody else to warn them?'

'He called the Press Association.'

'In that robot voice?'

'In a normal voice.'

'Recorded?'

Mac shook his head.

'So why at Kempton? Why did Bletchley record the call?'

'Standard practice on all Jockey Club tracks ever since the bomb scare at the ninety-seven National. If anyone calls the switchboard and asks for an official without identifying himself or herself satisfactorily, the operator records the call.'

'A good idea, on the face of it. But this one could rebound big style.'

He nodded.

'How long do you think you can keep it from the press?'

'We'll probably announce it tomorrow.'

'You'll see a massive shitstorm for not giving it out at the press conference today.'

'That was a decision made in alliance with the police.'

'The leader of this alliance being JCR?'

'We needed time to think. To try and unscramble the digital disguising of the voice.'

'I'm guessing it stayed scrambled?'

Mac nodded, and drank some more. Then finished it off. 'Want me to pour you another?' Eddie asked.

He grunted as he rose. 'I'll get it. You?'

'No. Thanks.'

Mac reached to rub his back above his belt, then turned it toward the strengthening flames. Then he leant forward, hands on knees, and groaned softly. The second of his chins drooped, firelight glinting in the sweaty crease. Eddie said, 'Maybe retirement wasn't such a bad idea after all, Mister McCarthy.'

He looked at Eddie sideways and smiled.

Eddie followed him to the kitchen where he took off his coat and hung it on the open door. 'Mac, who's heard that tape?'

'Me, Bletchley, Tim Arango, and the police.'

'Anybody reached a conclusion other than this guy knew the pit had been dug?'

'The only thing that made sense to us was that the informant was somebody close to whoever's targeting JCR. The police believe that a broadcast of the tape tomorrow, alongside an appeal for that person to come forward might pay dividends.'

'That's a bad idea, Mac.'

He pushed the top back into the whiskey bottle. 'Why?'

'Because if it is an informant, then your man is going to know who it is. Not only that, he's going to know how determined this guy was to prevent carnage on the track. You might suddenly lose your informant.'

'True.'

'Then you not only don't have a foot in your man's camp, you've got another murder to deal with.'

'True, also,' Mac said, and drank.

'So?'

'I'll call Tim.'

Eddie prompted him with raised eyebrows and by leaning toward him, as though that would make him reach for his phone. Mac said, 'I'll call when you've gone.' His smile said that he knew if he called now and didn't get the response Eddie thought he should, then Eddie would spend another hour giving him grief.

'We've got to know each other too well, Mac.'

'Thankfully…For me, at least. Will we return to the fire?'

Back in their chairs, Eddie said, 'Play that tape again.'

He reached for the recorder and clicked it. Eddie listened, twice, then said. 'Play that end comment a couple more times.'

"Just do your job". "Just do your job".

Even though it had been digitally altered to sound robotic, the nuances remained. 'Mac, that's a pretty definite command. Even disguised, you can hear the firmness, the tone.'

'So?'

'Well it doesn't sound like some scared informant sneaking on his boss. Maybe it was the man himself.'

'Why would he set up a disaster then try to prevent it?'

'Maybe all he wanted was the abandonment of the meeting. That would have been pretty damaging to JCR in its own right, wouldn't it, especially on top of everything else that's happened?'

'Not as damaging as dead horses and badly injured jockeys. And why would he suddenly develop a conscience after killing three jockeys?'

'Maybe he justified those killings because Kellagher, Sampson and Blackaby were crooks.'

Mac shifted in his chair, the fire getting too warm for him. 'It's a strange conscience that can live with a triple murder over a few bent races.'

Eddie paused and watched him. 'Mac, let's go back to Blackaby's death at Cheltenham. We are certain the killer was there that morning. He had to be. So isn't it strange that it was at exactly the time Ivory was there. And it turns out pretty helpful to Ivory that the last man who could have turned Queen's evidence against him died that morning. And didn't Ivory also claim that he didn't know this mystery caller who was supposed to be meeting him in his box? He has got to be favourite now.'

Mac half-stood and used his legs to push the big chair farther away from the fireside. He settled again and said, 'But why wouldn't he just have had Blackaby shot the same as Kellagher and Sampson?'

'Because Ivory's a bookie. With three deaths, he'd have been risking either the BHA or the Professional Jockeys Association pulling the plug completely on racing until the killer was caught. No racing, no income.'

Mac nodded, looking into his whiskey glass. 'True. But how would he have known racing would carry on after the second shooting? How could he be sure the plug wouldn't have been pulled when Sampson was shot?'

'Because Ivory knew that everyone in racing was working with the same sum. He could be certain that those who added two and two would come up with the right answer. Especially the jockeys. And that was confirmed when Blackaby said he had no plans to ride in the near future.' Eddie became aware of his tone of certainty strengthening.

Mac said, 'But if the sums added up so nicely, every jockey would have taken comfort from the news that Blackaby had also been shot, if, of course, he had been.'

'And maybe that was Ivory's initial intention, but remember what I just said. Blackaby wasn't getting back on a horse again, was he?'

Mac set aside his drink and clasped his hands in his lap. 'Okay…let's go with Ivory as chief suspect. He has removed all three threats to his liberty. He can safely resume business, both bookmaking and whatever else on the nefarious side. Why would he want Kempton abandoned on one of the biggest betting days of the year?'

'He wouldn't. Ivory has no conscience. The man who dug that pit tried to warn the clerk of the danger before anyone was injured.'

'So whoever dug the pit didn't kill Kellagher, Sampson and Blackaby?'

As that sank home, Eddie nodded slowly. Mac said, 'So that means that despite the killings all taking place on Jockey Club tracks, today's disaster wasn't linked to them? Which then dictates that we have two people doing their best to discredit JCR. Does that seem logical?'

Eddie sighed and stared at the fire. 'No, it doesn't seem logical. I can't even see the logic in one person attacking the Jockey Club, never mind two.'

'Nor can we. But today took everything that's happened recently beyond coincidence, don't you think?'

'I suppose it did. In a way, it strengthened the pattern but kind of broke the mould, if you know what I mean?'

'Eddie, I don't know what anyone means anymore. And nobody at JCR does either. We haven't the faintest idea which front to try and defend, because we don't know what or where the next target will be.'

Eddie watched him. 'Any regrets?' Eddie asked.

'About taking the job?'

Eddie nodded. He shrugged. 'Not really. I just thought I might get a few weeks to adjust, to get back up with the pace. You know what I mean. I'm ring-rusty. I feel old.'

'And I guess it's a much different Jockey Club from the one you worked for all those years ago?'

'Much less restrictive. The stuffed shirts have pretty much all gone. When we lost the responsibility of running racing I was quite despondent. But everything changes, doesn't it? Lord knows we've learned that during this year. But things move much more quickly now at JCR. It's all commercial, even though they're non-profit. Everyone seems focused.'

'Well, you can bet they'll be focused on steadily pushing the blame for what's happening in your direction.'

'We'll see. I'll be no worse off than I was, whatever happens.'

Eddie got up. 'Well, you know I'll help you if I can, Mac.'

'I do,' he sighed, 'I do,' and he got to his feet and followed Eddie to the door.

They shook hands. 'Do you think Kempton will go ahead tomorrow?' Eddie asked.

He shrugged. 'They're working under arc lights just now to see if everything can be made safe. It would be ghastly to lose two days.'

'It would. I'd wish you a good night's sleep, but somehow I think I'd be wasting my breath.'

He smiled wearily. 'Sound sleep's a distant memory. The demons who don't get you in daylight, tend to be waiting their turn after dark.'

FIFTY

Mave and Eddie were at the breakfast table when they heard on the radio that racing at Kempton would go ahead. BBC 5 Live summed up the Boxing Day events there, then introduced Marcus Shear, who picked his way carefully through an interview on behalf of the BHA. No reference was made to Jockey Club Racecourses and Eddie realized that JCR had been the only ones so far to conclude that their tracks alone were being targeted, rather than racing as a sport.

'Coming to Kempton with me?' Eddie asked Mave.

'I don't want to jinx the horse I've given Sonny. I've never been to the track when one of my tips was running.'

'Well maybe you'll bring some luck with you. Not much point staying here on your own.'

She played with the slice of toast she'd been pushing around her plate for the last five minutes. 'I suppose so. I just wish I could get this over with, you know. I wish I could have given Sonny three horses today and shut up shop.'

'Well, if Nina Raine's willing to take the seventy-five-percenters, you might get it all done and finished before the New Year. Fresh start.'

'It won't stop me worrying about Sonny.'

'Mave...Sonny's almost twice your age. Whatever decisions he makes, for whatever reasons, he can live with. You're not his mother.'

'I know. I know. It's stupid, and it's even more stupid that I've got this feeling, this wish that everything will still work out all right with him and Nina.'

Eddie smiled. 'You were logic personified when I met you. You were a female Mister Spock. Now look at you…from cynic to hopeless romantic.'

'I know how it will end, Eddie. And I didn't think it would matter much to me. But it does. It will.'

'No matter how many times he comes back for more tips?'

'I'm going to destroy the programme.'

Eddie looked at her. 'Completely?'

'Irreversibly.'

'How many years of your life are in it?'

'The journey proved much more enjoyable than the destination. I've hated having the responsibility of money. Hated it. It's not me. I've felt as though I've been living with a disease.' She pushed her plate aside and opened her palms on the table and twirled her late mother's wedding ring on the third finger of her right hand, watching it turn on her skinny finger. She looked up at Eddie. Her eyes did. Her chin stayed low. She said, 'You know how we are, you and me? We fit together?'

Eddie nodded.

'Money gives me the opposite feeling. Since I started accumulating more than I need, I've never felt right. I thought I'd adjust, but I knew I wouldn't. I knew I was kidding myself.'

'Fine. Ditch it.'

'I intend to.'

'If it's making you that unhappy, finish now. Tell Sonny no more after today.'

'No. I'll see this out.'

'Then what?'

'Sell the house.'

'And move in with me!' Eddie said with mock excitement.

She smiled sadly. 'We need each other too much for that.'

Eddie opened his hands and slid them across. She put hers in his and their fingers closed with the same gentle pressure until they were linked physically as well as emotionally and spiritually. Eddie stopped himself asking her never to go too far away. Her independence meant as much to him as it did to her.

At Kempton, Eddie introduced Mave to Dil Grant and the Black Widows syndicate of three. They owned the horse Eddie was riding in the first race, Domacorn. Mave, as ever, wore a thin short jacket and trousers which tried to be tight but were defeated by her boniness. The widows encircled Mave in the windblown paddock, their fake fur coats nestling her as though she were a chick. 'You must be freezing, you poor soul!'

Eddie smiled as he caught Mave's eye above their shoulders. She could do with some mothering. She also needed something to take her mind off the tip she'd given Sonny. It was a grey horse called Stalbridge Colonist and, along with nine others, it was an opponent of Eddie's in this race.

Mave had asked if it was all right to give Sonny the selection. She and Eddie had agreed she'd never tip a horse in a race he was riding in. But everything was ending soon, and the tip was the best she could come up with that day. It had hit seventy-two percent on her chart, and she'd warned Sonny of this. But he'd told her not to worry.

She'd passed on Eddie's warning too that all was obviously not right at the Jockey Club courses. None of this affected Sonny. He had his "fix", for Nina. That was all that mattered.

Eddie's mount, Domacorn, was having his first run on a right-handed course. Some horses have a preference for racing clockwise; some hate it. It turned out Domacorn didn't care much for it at all, and never seemed comfortable. He made several early jumping blunders and Eddie considered pulling up for his safety and the horse's. But he decided to try and nurse him round, to accept they wouldn't be winning, but to try to give Domacorn a bit more confidence in himself on right-handed tracks.

With three to jump, they were second last, a long way off the grey, Stalbridge Colonist, who'd led throughout. Eddie took some comfort in the fact that he wouldn't have to fight head-for-head with Mave's tip.

In the straight, from a long way back, Eddie watched the grey increase his lead galloping toward the second-last fence. A winner for Sonny and Nina…he had mixed feelings.

Alex Brophy was on the leader and as he charged toward the second-last he saw a group of men in high-vis jackets ducking under the rail. Three carried checkered wooden boards with big directional arrows to guide riders round a fence. The men tried to lodge these in the turf, while the other three stood blocking the approach waving checkered flags and shouting 'Pull up! Pull up!'

Brophy looked round to see how the other jockeys were reacting, but his closest opponent was fifteen lengths behind. If he pulled up and this turned out to be some kind of stunt, he'd look a fool, and he'd be throwing away a winner and plenty prize money.

But if he carried on and it turned out that this was all official, he could face a lengthy ban from the saddle. He was also aware that there might be some danger beyond the fence, especially given yesterday's problems.

He leaned back, bracing against Stalbridge Colonist, and managed to pull him up to a trot as he reached the race Marshalls. He recognised three of them and immediately felt better. Looking round, he saw the others pulling up too.

A Marshall told them there had been an emergency radio message through their headsets warning of severe danger if horses went near the final fence. The jockeys walked the runners back to the paddock past baffled crowds and curses, Stalbridge Colonist had been well fancied. But better safe than sorry.

It took twenty minutes of talking and arguing and questioning among officials before it was discovered that someone had hijacked the radio network and issued a false instruction. The race was declared void.

After a delay of more than an hour, it was announced that racing would continue. Eddie didn't have a ride in the second race. He stood with Mave on the steps of the weighing room. 'Sonny been on the phone yet?' Eddie asked.

'Oddly. No. But I'm back to square one. I'm going to have to give him another horse to make up for that one. What do you think?

'It's your call, Mave. I don't suppose one more will matter.'

She pinched her chin, looking at the ground. 'I'm going to tell Sonny I've set a self-destruct code line into the programme, one that will execute at midnight on December thirty first.'

'And have you?'

'Not yet.'

'I think that's a good idea. It gives him a chance to plan for the New Year once Nina dumps him.'

She nodded, still pondering. 'Maybe he could live in the Shack?'

'Maybe he could. It would suit him well.'

'Save me having to sell it, too.'

'I'd be sorry to see it go. I'd probably buy it off you if you decide to sell.'

She smiled and looked up at him. 'What would you do with it?'

'Use it for holidays.'

She laughed. 'You wouldn't know how to holiday. You'd need to go to holiday college for about ten years to learn. Even then, you'd fail your exams.'

'True.'

The jockeys for the second race filed past them and cut through the gaps among circling horses. Mave watched them fan out, moving toward the groups of connections. She said, 'What's the betting on what will happen in this race?'

'For the first time in my life, I'm kind of glad not to be riding.'

The bell sounded and the jockeys moved to mount. Some would make a circuit of the paddock, adjusting stirrups, getting the horse settled. Others would want to exit onto the walkway toward the course as soon as possible and get their horses cantering to the start.

As the last horse left the paddock, a big iron-grey gelding halfway up the line reared and squealed. Charlie Crilly was riding him and the right arm of his purple silks reached forward to pat the horse's neck to help calm him. Then the same arm came up to shield Charlie's eyes and he lurched to his right and the horse reared again and unseated Charlie.

The groom kept hold of the grey and Charlie rolled under the rail and quickly got to his feet. He ducked back under and onto the walkway and raised his hand to stop the jockey behind, John Davidson.

Charlie was gesticulating, pointing to his eyes. The groom, still trying to calm Charlie's horse, spoke to Charlie then turned the horse around toward the paddock. The five horses who'd been behind the grey were also turned by their jockeys and walked back toward the paddock. Charlie jogged past them to meet Ken Bletchley, the clerk of the course, who was hurrying across the lawn.

The other runners were recalled to the paddock. Eddie told Mave he'd be back soon.

Charlie was in the changing room, already telling everyone that someone had shone a laser in his eyes and probably in the horse's eyes first. After a fifteen minute Inquiry, the Kempton Stewards abandoned the remainder of the meeting.

FIFTY-ONE

As Eddie drove down the track toward his house, he turned to Mave, 'Looks like I'd better get used to arriving home while there's still some daylight.'

'Or just avoid taking rides at JCR tracks. There were no incidents at the other three meetings today. That's two days in a row where only Jockey Club Racecourses have been targeted.'

Eddie pulled up in the drive and they took the conversation inside. 'What's your take on this, Mave? This JCR stuff?'

'I don't have a "take". It looks like the rest of the world is only just beginning to realize that racing per se isn't the target here. The one thing that doesn't sit right with me is why JCR themselves decided so early that the campaign was against them and hired McCarthy to help.'

'You think somebody at the Jockey Club had been warned in advance?'

'Maybe. Or they could just have picked up on something internal. Who's bearing grudges within the organization? What's the politics at board level? How much does Mac know about all that?'

'I'll ask. Want some coffee?'

'Yes please.' She took off her jacket and wandered toward her room.

Eddie called after her as he filled the kettle, 'What did you make of the Black Widows?'

'They made me sad,' she closed the bedroom door behind her.

Over dinner, they agreed that Eddie would go and see Mac, while Mave sat through a Skype session with Sonny and Nina. 'Was that Sonny's suggestion?' Eddie asked.

'After half a dozen pretty desperate phone calls.'

'You told him about the self-destruct?'

'I did.'

'Well, at least they're taking you seriously now. I don't mind hanging around for moral support. She's going to throw everything at you. Is it a video call?'

'It is.'

'Be prepared for lashings of wet mascara and her holding up pictures of her so-called son like some poor refugee on an Iraqi mountainside.'

'I have the considerable advantage of knowing she's a lying bitch.'

'That was a good decision last week not to tell Sonny about the picture.'

'One of the few things I've got right.'

Eddie put his elbows on the table and rested his chin in his hands. She watched him. He said, 'I'm sorry to see you so unhappy.'

'And I'm sorry for being a miserable cow.'

'Things will get better, Mave. Everything passes in time.'

'You've been raiding the cliché cupboard again, haven't you?'

Eddie smiled.

Mac was still wearing his coat when Eddie arrived. He sipped tea. Eddie got the makings of a fire together and squatted at the wood burner. Eddie said, 'I could have been a fire maker in one of those big country houses in the nineteenth century.'

'I'm not sure they employed boys just for fire making. You'd probably have to have climbed up the chimney too and hauled the coal and logs. Doubtless you were one of those firebugs as a child?'

'I was. Managed not to burn anything down other than an old dead Beech tree, which I've regretted ever since.'

'Why?'

'Because when I walked that field the next day, the one the tree had been in, it was the first time in my life I didn't see it against the skyline and it set me thinking that maybe thousands of people had seen that tree over hundreds of years, and I'd been the one to put an end to it.'

'How old were you then?

'About ten.'

'So you've always thought too much?'

Eddie smiled as he struck a match. 'I suppose so.'

The fire got stronger. Mac loosened his tie. Eddie switched on the ancient lamp with the ribboned shade, then settled with a mug of coffee across from McCarthy. 'Well, how high is the panic meter now at Jockey Club Towers?'

Mac managed a tired smile. 'Even though most of the stiff upper lips have gone, they still don't do panic. Not yet, at least. But frustration is rising.'

'Was it Tim Arango who first got suspicious about JCR tracks being targeted?'

'I think there'd been a general discussion at board level after Blackaby's death. I don't know who suggested that the campaign might be against JCR alone.'

'Can you find out?'

'I can ask. Why?'

'Because nobody else seems to have picked it up. Well, they have now, but usually a reporter or somebody on social media would have latched on at least as quickly as JCR did. Could there have been some sort of warning you've not been told about?'

Mac sat back, resting his head, and looked at the fire. 'I don't know. I can't see why that sort of thing would have been kept from me.'

'So, what now?' Eddie asked. 'The next JCR meeting is Monday, isn't it? Haydock?'

He nodded. 'Due to be.'

'Meaning?'

He looked at Eddie. 'We spoke earlier of relinquishing our fixtures until we've caught who's behind this. Another death on one of our tracks would be…well, unthinkable.'

'When you say relinquishing fixtures, transferring them?'

'It would take a bit of planning, but Tim's due to meet Marcus Shear in the morning to discuss how quickly we could structure it.'

'Meaning no more racing at JCR tracks until this guy is caught?'

Mac opened his hands. 'What else can we do?'

'But if you're not racing, whoever's behind this is not on your racecourses. That's going to make it a hell of a lot tougher to find him.'

'If a dozen cohorts of policemen, multiple ranks of security officers, TV video tapes etcetera couldn't nail him at Sandown or Haydock, what chance have we when he's one of twenty thousand people on a couple of hundred acres, with a laser pen?'

'But think about it, Mac. What did we say last night? A man who kills two jockeys in cold blood and arranges the electrocution of a third is hardly going to be phoning warnings in or lasering jockeys on the way out of the paddock. If he wants real carnage, he aims the laser at the horse's eyes approaching a fence at full gallop.'

'That was mentioned in our meeting.'

'So that's twice he's tried to prevent loss of life. It's two different people, Mac. It has to be.'

He clasped his hands. 'That makes it worse then, doesn't it?'

We looked at each other. 'Yes. I suppose it does,' Eddie said, 'have you spoken to the families of Kellagher, Sampson and Blackaby?'

'No. Why?'

'Maybe we're just making too many assumptions. Let me make another one…there's only one guy behind this. He had something personal going on with the three jockeys and he's got something not quite so personal with JCR. Maybe the first issue led to the second one. You'll get nothing from Ivory, we already know that. But maybe you'd have more luck with the people who were close to the dead men.'

'Perhaps. But, going back a step, how could somebody not have something pretty personal against JCR to be trying to get them to stop racing?'

'Okay, maybe I should have said less personal. He ain't killing people anymore.'

'But what could he have against JCR? It's not some monstrous commercial conglomerate trampling all over people. We're a non-profit. Every penny goes back into racing. We're eco-friendly. Our PR profile, especially measured against the BHA is saintly. Who'd want to damage us?'

'So, what's the motive? If JCR is damaged, who suffers? Who'd be hit hardest?' Eddie asked.

'Who is there to hit? We've no shareholders, we haven't-'

'But you do have shareholders, in a way, don't you, through that bond issue a couple of years ago?'

'Bondholders, yes. But that's a one-off transaction. The bonds don't rise or fall in value. They can't be traded.'

'So how do the people who bought the bonds benefit?'

'They get an annual guaranteed return on their investment.'

'How much?'

'I'm not sure…around five percent, I think.'

'How much did JCR raise through the bonds?'

'Twenty five million.'

'So they need to find over a million every year just to pay the interest?'

'One point two five.'

Eddie watched him as Mac seemed to take in the implications. 'So if you stop racing, and stop earning money, how long will it take you to go bust?'

'I wouldn't even want to think about that, Eddie. Why would anyone want to ruin JCR?'

'Maybe it's the bondholders they want to ruin. If these can't be traded and things go tits up, the bonds are worthless, are they not?'

'Well, the short answer is yes.'

'So who are the big players? Who invested most?'

'I don't know, but I'll find out.'

'Mac, hasn't this angle been raised at your meetings in the past few days?'

'Not in my presence.'

'Does the scenario make sense?'

'On the face of it, yes. But I've a feeling that there was a limit on the amount you could invest, to give as many people as possible a chance. So nobody would take a huge hit. If that's the case, it kind of weakens your theory.'

'Find out who the big guys are and how much is at stake for them.'

'I'll do my best.'

'And if they haven't already prepared a statement, you'd best get your PR guys ready for questions from the press about these bonds. If you announce that you're transferring all your fixtures, that'll be one of the first you'll be hit with.'

'I'll call Tim.'

Eddie got up. 'I'll let you get on with it. Give me a ring if you get some info on those bondholders.'

FIFTY-TWO

Mave looked dazed. She sat on the four-wheeled office chair at the PC. Her legs were folded beneath her in a yoga pose, though she wasn't meditating. Eddie touched the edge of the chair back, setting it off in a gentle spin on the wooden floor. She smiled wearily. Eddie spun her again, then squatted to her eye level and watched as she turned. 'You're in orbit,' Eddie said.

'I'd rather be in an obit, I think.'

'Your Skype session didn't go so well?'

'No worse than I'd expected.'

'Come sit by the fire and tell me about it. But do not exit the ride until it comes to a complete halt, or whatever they say at fairgrounds these days.'

They drank tea and shared a banana. Mave broke small pieces from her half of the fruit and stared at the burning logs.' You and your fires,' she said.' What would you do without them?'

'Life would be duller. Mine would, anyway. When dad made me live in that old barn, I used to lie at night thinking of being by a fireside where everybody was happy. I promised myself that when I grew up, I'd get married and have kids and we'd always have a log fire and we'd sit around it every night, all feeling safe and secure.'

'You've over-achieved on the fire part. You're leaving it late for the kids.'

'And the wife,' he said.

'And the wife.'

Eddie smiled. 'Tell me about Sonny and his beloved.'

'You kind of had to be there so I'll save you the histrionics and tell you the deal. They want the last three horses all on the same day. They're going to stake whatever they have left on a win treble.'

Eddie shook his head slowly. 'Say it ain't so, Jo.'

She smiled at hearing him use her real name. 'That can't be said, Ed.'

'Well the outlook seems grave, Mave.'

'You have me beat, by virtue of selfishly having just one name.'

'I was counting on that.'

Maven had gone through the percentages with Sonny and Nina, shown how their chances of success diminished greatly by staking all on a treble. 'Sonny, got it,' she said. 'I think he even agreed with me. But he wouldn't speak against her.'

'But they agreed to quit the pressure after you've given them the last tips?'

'She did. Sonny doesn't matter, and he doesn't want to matter. He just wants Nina to have what she asks for.'

'You told them the software dies with this old year?'

'Not that poetically, but they know.'

'So you have four days to find them three horses?'

She nodded and tipped the final piece of banana over her thin lips. 'Four days. Eleven race meetings.'

'You can take out one of those, and probably three.' Eddie told her about the JCR cancellations.

'Brilliant. They own the best tracks. Eighty percent of my selections have been at the best tracks. The odds for this treble are dropping by the minute.'

'That's their problem, Mave. Their choice. Their problem.'

She got up. 'I'd better get to work.'

Halfway across the room, she stopped and turned. 'Sonny's going to realize there's something wrong when I don't give him anything for Haydock or Wincanton. Can I tell them what you've told me about what's going on at JCR?'

'You might as well. It's going to be in the press tomorrow, unless the Jockey Club has a change of mind.'

She didn't move. She just stared past him through the big window.

'You okay?' Eddie said.

'She nodded slowly. 'I'll be so glad when this is done.'

FIFTY-THREE

JCR went ahead with the announcement next morning. Their CEO, Tim Arango, battled his way through questions from reporters in admirable fashion. When the bonds issue came up, he was asked who'd be most affected if the police could not catch whoever had mounted this vendetta, and JCR were unable to honour their liabilities. He got political then and did everything but answer the question. But the squirming was obvious, and Eddie thought that reading between the lines would never be easier.

Jack Shawcross was quoted on behalf of the Professional Jockeys' Association: "We consider this a courageous and pragmatic step by Jockey Club Racecourses. It's refreshing to find an organization which cares about the welfare of all its stakeholders. Our members will miss riding at JCR tracks, but we applaud this directive as its primary aims encompass the protection of jockeys."

Eddie knew that was another political statement. The truth was that most in the changing room were pissed off at the potential loss of opportunities and maybe prize money too. The JCR fixtures were to be auctioned among other tracks, but none needed to provide the JCR level of prize money for each race.

Marcus Shear's statement on behalf of the BHA was sympathetic and conciliatory. Eddie had expected some gloating given the public hammering the BHA had taken over the balls-up in the Old Bailey trial. But Shear was a different character altogether from Nic Buley. That thought set Eddie wondering again about Buley's disappearance, and the motives of whoever was behind all this.

Eddie had a winnerless day at Uttoxeter, and by the time he got home, Mave had chosen her last three horses and sent them to Sonny. 'Two at Doncaster, one at Kelso,' she told Eddie. 'Last day of the year.' Eddie crossed his fingers and held them up. She smiled. 'Soon be over,' Eddie said.

Mave flopped down on the couch. 'I'll see the New Year in with you, then head back to the Shack and start planning for the future…If that's all right with you?'

Eddie sat beside her. 'Of course it's all right. Stay on. Do your planning here. There's no need to go back right away.'

She turned to him. 'Symbolic, though, innit?' she smiled wearily. 'I thought you'd appreciate that.'

'I do. I just don't appreciate losing you.'

She closed her eyes, and massaged her face then said, 'I'm too tired to talk about it, Eddie. I think my brain is finally burning out.'

'Nah. Couldn't do. They say the sun is halfway burnt out, but it still has five billion years left.'

'I think I've got about five weeks left.'

Eddie put his hand on hers. 'I'll come north with you, if you want. Help you start your planning.'

'Thanks, but it's a solo job, this one. A solo job for the soul.'

Dil Grant had just one runner at Doncaster on the last day of the year. Normally, Eddie would have packed his bag as usual and driven up there. But Mave's anxiety over Sonny's final bet prompted him to ask Dil if he could stay home. Dil agreed. The horse had little chance anyway. Eddie came off the phone and turned to her, 'I'm yours for the day.'

'Oh, glory be! You'll regret it. If these don't win, you will not want to be within a mile of me.'

'Mave, you've done your bit. Leave them to it. Your betting career is over now. Your tipping time is done. You want to travel, don't you? Let's not go anywhere near a betting shop. There's a big motorhome dealer near Cheltenham. I've passed it a few times. Why don't we drive up there and pick one for you for your round the world trip?'

And that's what they did. While Mave moved wide-eyed from vehicle to vehicle, while they had lunch and turned the pages of glossy brochures showing glorious beaches, and sunsets, and Roman ruins, the first two of Mave's selections had won at 5/1 and 9/2. From what Sonny had told her, they'd managed to place bets totalling £10,000; all straight win trebles where one loser would bust the bet. But the victories of those first two meant that Sonny and Nina had £330,000 running onto a mare called Glad Rags in the final race at Kelso.

Glad Rags was 4/1. Had the mare won rather than losing by a neck, they'd have gone into the New Year with a pay-out of £1.65 million pounds. But the length of the winner's neck meant Sonny and Nina lost every penny of their ten grand stake.

Eddie and Mave were back at his place by the time they found all this out. Mave was sad, but relieved. She took out her phone. 'I'll just text Sonny to say sorry I didn't come through for him.'

Eddie's hand began rising to stop her, but, remembering his control freakery, he stopped himself, although he couldn't hold his tongue. 'Mave, you have nothing to apologize for.'

She looked at him. 'He'll be desolate, Eddie.'

'He'll learn his true worth to Nina Raine. He'll need all the affection you've built for him over the years. He'll need you when she dumps him. But if he's desolate, it's because of the decisions he made. You don't have to say you're sorry.'

She had watched him silently, her sad frown fixed, and when Eddie finished talking, she said quietly, 'But I want to say I'm sorry.'

Eddie shrugged and turned away.

'Build a fire,' she said softly.

Later, as the final minutes of the year leaked away, they followed what had become Eddie's ritual since moving into this place. They sat in the sun house in the cold, wet garden and raised toasts to the fact that they'd survived another year and that Mave had settled on the motorhome she wanted, and that soon she'd be driving away, trying, as this year was, to leave the sadness behind.

They huddled together as the sweeping second hand of Eddie's watch moved toward midnight. 'Boom!' said Mave, as it struck 12. 'There goes my programme, in a digital blast. The sound you hear is from a millstone finally cut from the neck.'

FIFTY-FOUR

The big meeting on New Year's Day had always been Cheltenham. Not this year. It was one of the JCR tracks and the fixture had been hastily transferred to Newbury. Dil had two runners there. Mave had wanted to catch a train home. Eddie said, 'Mave, it's New Year's Day. How long do you think you'll spend waiting for trains to get you to your godforsaken part of the world?'

'It's not as if I'm doing anything else, is it?'

'Come with me to Newbury. My final ride's in the third race. We'll get away straight after that. I'll drive you home. I'm at Catterick tomorrow, so I'll stay over with you. If that's okay?'

'Of course it's okay. I just don't want to be on a racecourse. Not today. Not anytime.'

'Then stay here. I'll be back by four.'

When Eddie returned from Newbury, Mave was in the Snug, curled up on the couch.

'You built a fire,' Eddie said.

'All by myself. Amazing, eh?'

'Blazing amazing. I don't suppose you stretched to making yourself a meal too?'

'I did actually. I had some pasta and tuna for lunch.'

'Building your strength for this globe-busting trip, ain't you?'

'I am.'

'I'll grab a sandwich and we'll head for your place. If you're ready, that is?'

'I'm ready, Eddie.'

The drive was a five-hour gauntlet through torrential rain. Rain so heavy, Eddie told Mave he didn't believe that a cloud could hold so much before bursting. The farther north they travelled, the less respite, and as they made the final turn on the road to Mave's place, Eddie was confident he wouldn't be riding next day. Catterick would be flooded. The only other meeting scheduled had been Exeter, another JCR track. They'd been unable to rearrange that fixture.

Eddie parked close enough to the door to give them a chance of staying relatively dry. 'You got your keys?' Eddie had to shout as raindrops battered the car roof. Mave held them up, swinging them. Eddie smiled, and they jumped out.

But the key wouldn't turn in the lock. The wind drove the rain at their backs and Eddie tried to cover her as she fumbled. 'It won't turn!'

Eddie reached for the key and tried. She was right. Without thinking, Eddie tried it the other way…It turned. It locked the door. Eddie unlocked it and urged Mave through, then pushed it closed on the wild weather. Mave was reaching for the light switch. Eddie stopped her. 'Mave, the door was unlocked. Unless you forgot to lock it when you left, I think you'd better prepare yourself before you turn the light on.'

She flipped the switch.

Her eyes went past the general mess the burglars had left straight to her desk. 'PC's gone,' she said.

She ran her main programmes on a big desktop PC. The monitor, keyboard and mouse were on the desk. The PC unit was missing.

Nina.

Sonny.

Had to be, Eddie thought, but he knew better than to say anything. Around the old stone-flagged floor, lay scattered rugs and many of Mave's personal things. Drawers from her desk had been turned over. The kitchen was a mess. Her bed mattress lay on its edge between the bed-frame and wardrobe. Eddie followed her silently from room to room.

In the bathroom, the side panel had been ripped off, exposing the underside of the bathtub.

She turned to Eddie. 'You want to start the biggest fire of your life?'

Eddie waited for the satirical smile. It didn't come. 'What do you say?' Mave asked.

'Are you seriously suggesting we burn the house down?'

'Seriously.'

'Mave, what we need to do is call the police. Once whoever did this finds out they can't run the programme without your input, they'll come after you next.'

'Nobody can run the programme, remember? It ceased to be at midnight.'

'Wouldn't your PC have to have been set up and running for that to happen?'

'No. Everything was in the cloud. That's why I could run it from your place.'

Eddie looked around again. 'All this for absolutely nothing, then. So what will happen when they turn the PC on and try to start the programme?'

'The usual. They'll be asked for a password.'

'And if they get some super geek, could he break the password?'

She stared coldly at him.

'No offence intended, Mave. I'll take that as a no.'

Mave went outside. Eddie followed her and put an arm around her shoulder. 'I'm sorry, Mave. We need to find a safe place for you. Whoever did this is not going to believe you destroyed the programme. They'll be looking for you.'

'But I'm not going to be here, am I? I'll be on a campsite in Morocco or somewhere.'

'There's no way you're travelling anywhere on your own after this. Not until these people are caught.'

She looked serious as she stared at him. She said, 'I'm only going to tell you this once, okay?'

Eddie nodded.

'Sonny wasn't involved in this.'

Eddie watched her. She raised a finger, 'You believe what you want, Eddie.'

Eddie turned and went downstairs and stood in the middle of the messed-up living room. A couple of minutes later, Mave came through the doorway, jaws clenched, breathing through her nose, trying to control her anger but each fast breath flared her nostrils and pumped her thin chest. Eddie said, 'Want to find a hotel somewhere?'

She nodded.

They got a room in a hotel on the outskirts of Abersoch, high above the beach, and the sounds of the wild night roared up at them. Eddie hung their wet coats from the showerhead and they sat on the bed listening to the steadily decreasing drips hit the bath. Mave's hands were clasped, resting on her thighs.

They sat together, bodies touching, but didn't look at each other. Eddie said, 'Mave, I'm in a bad position here, and I don't know what to do.' He saw her short nod of acknowledgement from the corner of his eye, but she said nothing, and they both kept staring at the floor.

Eddie said, 'I told you a couple of days ago that I never wanted to control you. Ever since we got close, I made myself always ask one question when it came to any disagreement...I'd ask myself, what would she do if I wasn't here? If we'd never met? But I don't know what you want to do. Were you serious about just taking off?'

'I'm serious,' she said quietly, 'but I don't trust myself anymore. I've made some shit decisions in the past seven years. Every single one seems twice as bad as the one before it. It's like one of those pyramids of acrobats that starts with the top one tumbling, misjudging just one step, then as everything beneath him goes, it just spreads in layers. That's what my life has come to, and I just need to get away from it now. Leave everything. Wipe it all out. Try to start again. Go away.'

She hadn't looked at Eddie, but the quiet despair in her voice tore him up. Eddie saw a blotch of wetness on the blue denim of her right thigh, a teardrop. He turned to her, put an arm around her shoulders and drew her close. Her weeping was quiet at first, then came a gulping for air in that lump-swallowing grief that engulfs before the dam bursts. Then the low helpless wails, and she tried to work herself closer to him, and it developed into a silent choreography as they understood what was needed, and she turned and Eddie eased her across until she lay in his lap, and he rocked her gently, like a child.

Her distress eased slowly as they moved, and Eddie realized that the steady rhythm was comforting him as much as it was Mave. And the sea below thundered on, and the coats in the dark bathroom dripped, and they rocked in the pool of light from the bedside lamp until all sense of time was lost, and even when she fell asleep the rocking would not stop.

FIFTY-FIVE

They woke to TV news pictures of flooded roads, fields, and houses across northern England. Computerized graphics showed the whole of the UK. It was wet everywhere, but it looked like some giant had grabbed John O'Groats with one fist and Land's End with the other and squeezed until the water pooled in the middle. No race meetings had survived. This was their first piece of luck. Mave had agreed to let Eddie take care of things, to take care of her until her confidence returned.

She was in danger. She accepted that. Whoever had the PC would soon discover that Mave's password couldn't be broken. The fact that the programme no longer existed made no difference.

Eddie couldn't look after her twenty-four-seven, unless he stopped being a jockey and went full time trying to find who was behind this. But if he could get Mave to a safe place, he could put all his spare time into tracking down whoever was behind the burglary. For all Mave's protests, Eddie had no doubt it was Nina and Sonny. Nobody else knew about the programme. Nobody else had been benefitting from it. And nobody else knew it was about to be destroyed. Case closed.

Eddie was sure Sonny hadn't done it willingly. He believed that even with Nina driving him, Sonny wouldn't go so far as to harm Mave. But Nina would know this too, and she'd have other men to do these things for her. That made Eddie think again…perhaps

Mave was right after all. If Nina had a few people doing her dirty work, all she'd have needed from Sonny was Mave's address. This was running through Eddie's mind as Mave showered. She came out wearing a long red bathrobe. 'You could fit about six Maven Judges in there,' Eddie said.

She flapped the wide sleeves. 'I feel like little Red Riding Hood's little sister's little sister.'

She dried her hair with a towel. 'Mave, I need to make some plans. I don't want to upset you, and I don't doubt what you said about Sonny, but Nina has to be behind all this. She probably didn't even tell Sonny she was going to have your place raided. Nina and Sonny were the only ones who knew about the programme. I'm happy to take Sonny out of the suspect side if you're happy for me to go after Nina.'

She stopped with the towel and turned to him. 'Sonny wasn't there when they broke in. I'll tell you why...whatever Nina Raine asked him to do, Sonny would rather die than scatter my personal things all over the floor. If only the PC had gone, you might have persuaded me Sonny was involved.'

'Fine, I'm sorry I-'

'*And...* they were not the only ones who knew about it. Remember the demo we had to give to the BHA people, the ones who signed the NDA?'

Nic Buley and Broc Lisle. Eddie had forgotten about them. 'You're right. Sorry.'

'That's okay,' she turned up the collar on the dressing gown and the edge went close to the top of her head. 'You're the boss, now. I feel better having shoved all my responsibilities on to you. I'll just drop in the odd fact or opinion if I think it's going to be helpful.'

Eddie smiled. She sounded more like her old self. He said, 'And I'll still ask your opinion on my theories, especially the crazier ones, if that's okay?'

'That's fine, but I'm guessing you're already ruling out your two BHA guys?'

'I'd trust Broc Lisle way ahead of Buley. But we don't know where Buley is, so he's got to be in the picture.'

'What about Lisle?' Mave said. 'You sure about him?'

'I've no reason to be sure other than instinctively. I don't know, Mave. I can arrange a meeting and tell him what's happened and see how he reacts.'

She crossed her arms and shook the still damp hair away from her face. 'Your call. I'm going to get dressed.'

'I promise not to watch.'

'I don't know whether to take that as a compliment or an insult, Mister Malloy.'

'It's respect, Ms Judge. R-E-S-P-E-C-T.'

She smiled wide and Eddie realized how long it had been since she'd done that, since he'd seen that crooked-toothed happiness. She said, 'Congratulations, that's the first song quote of the New Year.'

'Let's aim for one a day.'

'Deal,' she said, and returned to the bathroom.

Eddie's phone rang, offering Eddie's first seemingly psychic experience of the New Year. It was Broc Lisle.

'Mister Malloy, Happy New Year to you.'

'And to you.'

'It's been a while since we spoke. I'd planned to travel to Catterick and see you, but the rain put paid to that.'

'What can I do for you?'

'Well, I'm hoping we can do something for each other, but it's best talked about face to face. Mobile networks can be very public places. Are you in the north at the moment?'

'I'm in the north west.'

'Could we meet for lunch?'

'That would be difficult. I'm setting off soon to travel south. I could meet you tonight near Lambourn.'

'That would be helpful. Where and when?'

'You're welcome at my house. About eight-thirty?'

'That's fine. What's your postcode?'

FIFTY-SIX

Mave settled in the passenger seat. They'd bought a soft woollen blanket in racing green. Mave liked to travel wrapped up. She was still trying to shake off the nocturnal habits she'd built up over years working on her programme. As soon as they left the winding coastal roads, she'd nod off.

Eddie had expected an argument from her when he'd told her his plans. But she accepted everything. Reluctantly, Eddie knew. But she'd promised to let him take charge, and she wouldn't go back on her word.

They were on the way to Newmarket. Eddie's sister Marie had said she'd welcome female company for as long as Mave needed somewhere to hide out. It would be an experience for Kim too. Eddie knew Mave would get on well with him.

After ten miles on the M6, Mave dozed off. Eddie glanced across, happy to see that sleep had wiped the worry lines from her face, and reminding him how easy it was for humans to adapt. Eddie had grown used to seeing Mave frowning, and had forgotten how calm and confident she'd looked when they'd first met and her 'project' was the focus of her life.

Whoever wanted the programme would now want Mave. Nina was still favourite in Eddie's book, and she'd dump Sonny and send someone with no emotional attachment. Somebody who she believed would be able to handle Eddie. She'd have learned a sharp lesson from her partnership with Jonty Saroyan…maybe he was a promising co-conspirator and no doubt he was a talented photographer. But he was not a hard man, and Nina would know a hard man was what she needed. Eddie found himself smiling at the thought. He leaned to look full-face in the rear-view mirror just to see himself smiling.

Ever since that first lawless pursuit of Gerard Kruger all those years ago, Eddie's appetite for danger had never faded. It was different from the risks that came with riding steeplechasers every day. In doing that, Eddie was invariably trying to catch someone, another jockey, another horse, before the ever-closing, relentless deadline of the winning post.

With this, someone was trying to catch him at exactly the same time as Eddie was trying to catch them. For the most part, neither knew where the other was. In this case, Eddie didn't even know who the other was. But that would reveal itself. Or Eddie would reveal it. The latter would be the safest option. But Eddie didn't mind either way.

As he passed the road sign that told him he was entering The Valley of the Racehorse, Eddie checked the odometer. He'd set it to zero on leaving Mave's place that morning, heading on the long road southeast. Then he'd come west toward home, Lambourn…385 miles. Driving down into the valley, it was cold and wet and dark. Eddie hadn't spoken to McCarthy in a couple of days, and he had an hour in hand before his meeting with Broc Lisle. Eddie took the narrow road toward Mac's house. Maybe Mac could offer a clue about what Broc Lisle wanted.

But his place was in darkness. High on the downs, in the car on Mac's drive, the wind sucked and blew. Eddie dialled Mac's number: voicemail. 'Happy New Year, Mac. I'm parked outside your house. The noise you can hear is the wind trying to spit me back out onto the road. I'm heading home. It's half-seven. Give me a call.'

It was much calmer in the dip of the soft cone of woodland where Eddie's house sat, the trees filtered the power of the night wind, raising noise, but leaving an unusual stillness in the air as Eddie got out of the car.

Slight as she was, Mave's absence seemed to leave a big hole in the house. Eddie noticed it each time she'd come and gone. The longer her stay, the bigger the void when she went. So Eddie did what he always did to try to fill the gap in his heart, he built a fire. By the time he heard the engine of Lisle's car, the fire flames were putting on a show and the water in the kettle was hot.

Lisle chose coffee, and complimented Eddie on finding such a quiet place to live. 'Do you feel safe here?' he asked as Eddie steered him toward the Snug and the welcoming fire.

'Why do you ask?'

Lisle smiled. 'Just my old training kicking in, I suppose. We were taught to evaluate everything, constantly. Your life becomes a never ending risk assessment.'

'No bad thing, I suppose,' Eddie said. 'Take a seat. You might be best at the far end of the couch until the fire dies down a bit.'

Lisle put his coffee mug on the low table and took off his coat. 'Just sling it over the back of the couch,' Eddie said.

Lisle settled, leaning forward, elbows on knees, cradling the coffee. 'I'm impressed by your lack of curiosity,' he said.

'Everything comes to he who waits.'

'If only.'

Eddie watched him. That square-jawed, serious face took shape, the one Eddie was so used to seeing on TV, and he waited for Broc Lisle to put down his coffee. Lisle did, and Eddie allowed himself a small self-congratulation. TV directors had taught Lisle to use his hands a lot when explaining things and when he crossed into that mode, Eddie had guessed habit would prime his limbs for full theatrical effect.

He said, 'Remember Jonty Saroyan, the guy who couldn't be found when we needed to question him about your involvement in that betting caper?'

'I do.'

'Can you recall when you last saw him?'

'I can recall it exactly, and it's not changed since I recalled it the last time you asked me.'

'I forget what you told me. Forgive me.'

'You're forgiven. I last saw him with a hangover...his, not mine...at a house he shared with a woman called Nina Raine. A place near Chaddesley Corbett, south of Birmingham.'

'When was that?'

'July. Late July.'

'Can you recall when you last saw him on a racecourse?'

'I never saw him on a racecourse. Or, at least, I never noticed him. He saw me though. Try Barney Scolder, the reporter. He did the deal for the pictures with Saroyan. I think. Nina Raine might have been driving things, rather than Saroyan. I believe he was more a puppet. Or a muppet, depending how kind you want to be.'

'Well. He's a dead puppet. And he's been dead for a long time.'

'How do you know?'

'Because I saw him yesterday. Saw his corpse. There wasn't much left of him.'

'Murdered?'

'We don't know yet. No obvious signs of assault.'

'Who found him?'

'The maintenance man who does the servicing at Haydock Park. Mister Saroyan was in the boiler room. On the floor, below the boiler.'

Eddie's first thought was for Mac. Haydock was a JCR course. 'I think you've got yourself a proper man on a mission here, Mister Lisle. He's done all he can to get JCR to shut down their tracks, and even when they give in and do that, he still won't let up on them. Who told the maintenance man to check the boiler so soon after JCR announced a suspension of racing?'

'Nobody. It was the scheduled six-monthly check by an independent contractor.'

'And nobody goes into that boiler room in between checks?'

'Not formally, no.' Lisle opened his hands for the tenth time since he'd put down the coffee. Eddie realized Lisle was watching him with some kind of expectation. Eddie said, 'Apart from the fact that Saroyan was one of a pair who were trying to blackmail me, why are you telling me this?'

'I'm investigating the case. That's my job. I know you won't take it personally when I say you had a strong motive for Saroyan to stay missing.'

Eddie laughed. 'Sorry…I'm not mocking you, but how does a man not take a statement like that personally?'

Lisle smiled and opened his hands again, this time in concession. 'Fair point.'

'Look, I'm sure Jonty Saroyan had a family or loved ones somewhere, and I'm sorry for them. But if anything, this exonerates me, don't you think? I mean, someone is on what looks like a mission to rip JCR apart. He's killed three jockeys and it now looks as though he might have killed Saroyan. If Saroyan was into blackmail, what else was he into? How did he get mixed up with the guy who's blitzing JCR? Any sign of an association between Saroyan and Jordan Ivory or with any of the dead jockeys?'

'It's early days.'

'That's one of those straw-clutching comments, Mister Lisle. A Buley special. And what about him? Wouldn't Nic Buley have a motive for damaging JCR? I know they use their influence pretty quietly, but they're the biggest racecourse group in the sport. They must have had some say in firing and hiring at the BHA.'

'Motive perhaps. Guts, no.'

'Ah, a personal opinion? At last! Join the club. Anti-Buleying we should call it.'

Lisle smiled. 'Very good, Mister Malloy.'

'You guys ought to look out too, on the off chance Buley found some guts and decided to take revenge. He wouldn't have killed Kellagher or the others, I grant you that. But he could have hired someone to do it. That would not have troubled his conscience in the slightest. And once he's done with JCR, maybe the BHA will be next.'

Lisle remained impassive. He said, 'Do you mind if we return to Mister Saroyan?'

'Return away, Mister Lisle. There's nothing more I can tell you. Have you spoken to Peter McCarthy?'

'I have a meeting with him tomorrow.'

'He's one of the good guys. I know you got his job, but he stepped out of that voluntarily because he knew what was going to happen if that case went to court too soon.'

'So I hear.'

Eddie looked at him. 'You were the patsy, Mister Lisle. Buley's patsy.'

Lisle nodded. He didn't look upset. 'I don't do politics. Another part of my training. My job description was clear enough, and that's all I care about.'

'You don't do politics and you don't do failure.'

He smiled. 'You remembered.'

'I did. And I admire your capacity for not being seriously pissed off at your employers for playing you as a mug.'

He shrugged. 'People say and do things on the spur of the moment. If I commit to something, I like to see it through. If it does get to a stage where I'm no longer wanted, then at least I can say I never quit.'

'Once a soldier...' Eddie said.

Lisle nodded. Eddie said, 'I'm sorry there's nothing I can help you with, but if I can offer you one piece of advice...trust Mac. He's a good man. I'm afraid he does do politics and he does do failure, but he doesn't enjoy either. He doesn't do resentment, and he'll help you all he can. And you'll be helping him, which makes me wonder why the BHA are back into this? With JCR being bombarded, all the pressure's off you guys. How come you're back in it?'

'As I said, I don't do politics. Let's just say that Marcus Shear accepts that the BHA and JCR should stand shoulder to shoulder here.'

'Well, if Shear accepts that, rest assured his true motive will jump up and kick you in the balls sometime soon. And it'll be laughing hysterically and yelling "You don't do politics. Eh!"'

He smiled and stood and reached for his coat. 'Thanks for your time, Mister Malloy. I needn't tell you that the police will want to speak to you too given the blackmail stuff with Saroyan.'

'Well, they know where I am.' Eddie walked him to the door.

Lisle buttoned his coat, and reached to shake Eddie's hand. Eddie said, 'I hope you get more out of your meeting with Mac tomorrow than you got from me.'

'I got what I expected. Confirmation that you're a decent man with no sides to you. Often that's worth quite a lot.'

'Thanks. And you seem pretty decent yourself. I'd go so far as to say honourable.'

'That's kind of you. That increases my confidence that you're a very good judge.' He smiled warmly.

'Tell me this…would you say that honourable men should sometimes be dishonourable if the circumstances demand it?'

'Highly hypothetical. Any specifics?'

'Would you say that a man who'd signed a non-disclosure agreement covering a betting software programme should always honour that commitment?'

He watched Eddie in the gloom of the porch. 'I would say so, yes.'

'And would you describe Nic Buley as an honourable man?'

'I think I made it clear what my personal feelings are about Mister Buley. Can I ask what prompted your initial question?'

'Curiosity.'

'Isn't that what prompts every question?'

Eddie smiled.

'Well,' he said, 'if there's ever anything you feel I can help with, give me a call.'

'Formally or informally?'

He straightened his coat collar. 'I'll leave that up to you.'

FIFTY-SEVEN

Eddie tried contacting Mac again. Since JCR had taken Mac on, it was almost as though whoever was behind all this had really turned up the heat, as though Mac was the target rather than JCR. Eddie left him a much shorter message this time, then he called Mave and told her about Jonty Saroyan.

'Oh, God! Poor man! So much for him having disappeared to Australia.'

'Can you remember who suggested that, the Australia trip?'

'We spoke to a few people when we were trying to track him down…I don't recall. Maybe Sonny will. Have you spoken to him?'

'Not yet.'

'Jeez…I wonder how Nina will take this. She's got to feel some level of guilt, hasn't she?'

'Why would she? She's hardly the type, for a start. And it was Jonty who ran out on her and left her penniless, so she says.'

'Still, he was her partner.' Mave said.

'Her slave, more like, before Sonny. Question is now, did Jonty come to his senses and leave, as she claimed he did, or did one of these deals they were doing backfire?'

'What deals?'

'Well if they were blackmailing me, what else were they up to? Maybe they thought the racing game was easy meat. Whoever's after JCR knows racing inside out. He, assuming it isn't Nina Raine herself running riot here, is a serious criminal, which keeps bringing Jordan Ivory back into the frame, and maybe Jonty and Nina tried to hit him for something.'

'So why kill Jonty and leave Nina alone?'

'Because after she made the mistake of getting directly involved in my blackmail, she decided to stick Jonty's head above the parapet and keep hers down.'

'How did he die?'

'They don't know yet. Or they're not saying. JCR's problem is that whoever's behind this is not letting up. They've suspended their operations. He hasn't suspended his.'

'This is getting crazy, Eddie.'

'You said it. Have you heard from Sonny?'

'Not a word. Nothing since that last horse lost. It's the first time in my life he hasn't rang to wish me Happy New Year. I know you think she's changed him, Eddie, but that worries me.'

'That he hasn't called?'

'Yes.'

'Why don't you call him?'

She hesitated. 'It wouldn't feel right.'

'Mave, you did everything you could to give Sonny what he wanted. Why do you think he's going to be angry with you?'

'I don't think he will…I suppose I'm just afraid that he will.'

'Because that would mean he'd changed.' It was a statement.

'Yes. I suppose it would mean that.'

'And if he'd changed, you might have reached the wrong conclusion about who burgled your house?'

'That would be the least of my sadness, Eddie,' she said quietly.

'I'm sorry, Mave. But you need to call him. Jonty was mixed up with Nina. He's dead. Sonny's mixed up with Nina. You haven't heard from him at New Year, for the first time in your life.'

'Oh, don't even think that, Eddie! I'll call him now!'

'Mave! If you speak to him…don't tell him where you are.'

'I won't.'

'He might ask.'

'Eddie!'

'Okay. Okay. Ring me when you've spoken to him.'

Eddie tried to remember if he'd ever told Sonny about Marie and Kim. He wondered if Mave had ever mentioned them to Sonny, and his impulse was to call her straight back. He stopped himself…There were a million combinations of possibilities in this now, now that Jonty had closed the circle and established a link between Eddie and Mave and whatever was going on with the JCR vendetta.

FIFTY-EIGHT

Sonny sat in darkness on the bleached roof terrace of the grubby apartment in the back streets of Istanbul. He had acclimatized and had gone from marvelling at the locals wearing sweaters to buying one himself. He wore it now, its tie-dye multi colours which had promised so much at purchase, helping his mind drift easily to the late 1960s, to youth and vigour, mocked him on this winter evening.

His phone rang, and he watched Mave's name, bright in the gloom, and he set the phone on the cheap plastic table to let it ring out to voicemail. Then he picked it up again. 'Jolene.'

'Uncle Sonny. Are you all right?'

'As all right as I'm ever going to be, Jo.'

'Happy New Year.'

He closed his eyes and his face creased and frowned in shame. 'God! I'm so sorry! How could I forget to call you? This New Year of all New Years, after everything you've done. I'm sorry, Jo. Happy New Year.'

'It's okay. It doesn't matter. So long as you're alive and kicking.'

'It does matter. It matters a lot. I'm so sorry.'

'Sonny, please! It's not as though you missed my wedding or something. Forget it!'

'I'll make it up to you.'

'There's no need. I just wanted to be sure you were all right. How is Nina?'

He sighed. 'Absent. That's how Nina is.'

'I'm sorry. I'm sorry about that. I did my best.'

'Don't be sorry. She left before I even put the bet on, said she couldn't take the pressure. And she hasn't come back. A blessing in disguise, maybe.'

'Have you and Nina split up?'

'You'd have to ask Nina that.'

'Oh, Sonny, I'm sorry. I know what she meant to you, what she means to you.'

'We're a sorry pair, Jo, you and me. All we've been tonight is sorry, sorry, sorry.'

She laughed. 'I know. Better days ahead, eh?'

'We can but hope.'

'Do you know if Nina's heard the news about Jonty Saroyan?'

'What news?'

Mave told him. He said, 'That's grim. That is grim. I didn't really know the guy, and for all that silly kidnapping stuff in the summer, I think he was harmless. Poor sod. How did he die?'

'They don't know yet. Or at least they haven't told Eddie.'

'How is Eddie?'

'The same one-off he's always been…always will be.'

'He's a good man.'

'He is.'

'Send him my salutations for the New Year.'

'I'll do that.'

Sonny stared at the faraway harbour lights, at the scythe blade shape the dark ocean gave to them. Mave said softly, 'Why don't you come home?'

'Jo, if I knew where home was, I'd be there, believe me.'

'Come and stay at the Shack. Rent-free. And we never close.'

He smiled sadly. 'Thanks. You never know, the sea might carry me back there someday.'

'Seriously…if things aren't going to work out for you over there, well, you're better around people who love you.'

Sonny cleared his throat. 'There's not much to you physically, Jo, but you're a rock, and I love you.'

'I love you too, and I'll always be here for you. It's important to me that you know that. Nothing's changed.'

Sonny looked at the stars. 'No, I suppose you're right. Nothing's changed. I thought it had. I thought it would. I believed we would be different. And you only have one life, don't you? Better to have loved and lost and all that jazz.'

'All that jazz…I miss your music.'

'It's been a long time since I played. A long time since I sang. I should have known from that alone, eh? They say actions speak louder than words. It kind of works out even more convincingly the other way round, doesn't it?'

'Come home.'

Sonny stood, and turned slowly on his heel, feeling like he was surveying the whole earth and all the sky. 'I might just do that, Jolene. I might just do that.'

Mave called Eddie and told him about Sonny.

'Poor sod. But at least he's seen the light. Do you think he'll come home?'

'I do. I think if she stays away from him, he will. If she comes hip-wiggling back with some other scheme, well, I wouldn't bet on anything.'

He said nothing.

'Eddie?'

'Sorry, Mave. I was trying to recall if I'd told Sonny about Marie and Kim. Did you ever say anything to him about them? Can you remember?'

'I wouldn't have discussed your past with anyone. It belongs to you.'

'I'd never looked at it that way. Thanks. Did he ask where you were?'

'No.'

'If Sonny hasn't seen Nina since New Year's Eve, could she be here, in England?'

'You thinking aloud or asking me a question?'

'Sorry, Mave. I think I'm thinking aloud.'

'Do you still believe she's behind the break-in?'

'Well it's either her or Nic Buley.'

'But not Broc Lisle?'

'No. Not for my money. But you keep mentioning him.'

'He's the only one we know is here, in England, alive and well and functioning, and not in the best of jobs if he ever wants to be a millionaire. Why are you so certain he's not in the frame here?'

'Well, first, he's not the type. I don't think he is a money man. He's a respect man. He's a look-up-to-me man. He's somebody who, in his own eyes at least, thinks he's special and that he's here on earth for a purpose.'

'And second?'

'He wouldn't have left your place in a mess. In fact, but for the PC going missing, you wouldn't have known he'd been there.'

'You seem sure about that.'

'I've made plenty mistakes, Mave, but I usually get people right. I've never found it hard to tell the good from the bad. Lisle's one of the good guys.'

'Would you be upset if I did some digging around anyway?'

'Not at all. He's in fighting with us now, after lying low for a while. I'd believed the BHA were just making the best of having the spotlight off them and on JCR. But they've thrown Lisle into it, hopefully to help Mac.'

'So they've got their problems, and we've got ours…Or to be precise, I've got mine.'

'We, Mave. You were right the first time. We.'

'We. Me. You. Whoever…we're in limbo. We can't do anything, make any decisions, because we don't know who we're up against or what they're going to do next.'

'So we do the only thing we can, we wait. You're safe. That's the main thing. They can't do anything without you, and they don't know where you are.'

'But they know where you are. And they know you'll know where I am.'

Eddie smiled. 'So they can bring it on, Mave. I'm ready.'

'How can you be ready when you don't know what you've got to be ready for?'

'That's the readiest you can get. Nothing ruled out. As long as you and Marie and Kim are safe, I'm happy.'

'I hate waiting. I hate having nothing to do.'

'Do that digging you mentioned. You've got your laptop, haven't you?'

'Yes.'

'See what you can find in the guts of the JCR communications system.'

'I will.'

'And give Marie and Kim my love.'

'I will. He's a fine boy, Eddie.'

'He is. And I heard somewhere the child is the father of the man, so he should be okay.'

'I love it when you talk philosophy to me!'

He laughed. 'Go and do your digging. Spadeless digging. The best kind.'

'Okay! I'm going, I'm going before you peel off into your Irish ploughman ancestors nostalgia wallow.'

'Ha! Call me tomorrow.'

'Okay.'

'Just thinking about that, should we go back to the cheap throwaway phones for communications? Just to be on the safe side.'

'Probably. I'll get one today.'

'Me too.'

FIFTY-NINE

Sonny was shouting at Nina and she was screaming at him, and, as in past rows, he felt his energy draining. Nina was capable of sustaining these verbal attacks at such high pitch that he had never managed to outlast her. He'd always given in. This time…this time, he had to make her see.

'There is no more, Nina! It's done! Gone! You've leached the life out of me and out of Jo, and you still don't stop!'

'I'm fighting for my child! My son! What would you do? I'll never stop. You knew that at the start. I told you I'd do anything. Anything!'

'And that anything includes selling your pendant, obviously.'

'I told you, I didn't sell it! I lost it. I lost it and I'll find it.'

'You sold it. That was for eternity. My gift to you that was supposed to remind you of everything we had, long after I'm dead. And you sold it.' His voice was weakening. He moved away from her to sit on the bed.'

She was relentless, standing, hands on hips, feet apart, knees slightly bent as though waiting on the baseline of life to smash back the next aggressive service. And she saw him fade. A tactical change was needed.

She softened and moved toward him and hunkered to try and take his hand, but he balled it into a fist, and wouldn't look at her.

'Sonny. Sonny, Sonny, Sonny…how have we come to this? A new year…we should be closer to happiness, to finding Keki. I'm

253

sorry for leaving on Tuesday. I couldn't stand to be here, to wait and see Keki's future resting on the back of that horse. And I'm so grateful for you taking it all over. So grateful. I just needed a few days on my own.'

Slowly he raised his head and looked at her. 'On your own? Were you on your own, Nina? Maybe the pendant was ripped off you by whoever you were with. Maybe you sold yourself instead of the pendant.'

She stared at him and said quietly, 'The same worm turns every time, eh? This is nothing to do with me selling anything, or asking you to ask Jo for more help…it's that old devil called jealousy. Again. Again. Again. The insecurity that's been with us since the start. That dread of yours that you couldn't hold out against my generation. My generation of men.'

Sonny got up and turned his back on her and walked to the window.

'That's it. Turn. Walk. Stare out at the past and see if maybe the young Sonny Beltrami is out there. What would he have done?'

Sonny didn't face her. He said. 'Young Sonny would have walked away from this a long time ago. A long, long time ago.'

She straightened gracefully and went to stand beside him, the morning light showing the dull redness in the whites of his eyes. She said, 'That's the saddest thing I ever heard.'

She walked away, and opened the door to leave.

'Jonty's dead.'

She stopped, still holding the handle, the door half open. She turned, 'What?'

'Jonty's dead. They found his body at Haydock racecourse.'

'Choked on his own vomit? I always said that's how it would end for him.'

'I don't know. I don't know how he died, but so comforting for his spirit to see how upset you are.'

'How I feel about anybody in death depends on how they treated me in life.'

'Ha! That's encouraging. All Jonty did for you that I could ever see, was exactly what you told him to.'

'And what about the time we spent together before you came on the scene? What would your all seeing eye know about that?'

He looked at her. 'My all seeing eye would notice that the spots on the leopard had not changed.'

'Fuck you, Sonny.'

Sonny began packing his gear in an old canvas holdall. If he could get away to the airport while the hurt still drove him, if he didn't look back, he could make it all the way home.

He stopped just once, on the way out, to look in the mirror as he pulled on a beat-up sun hat. He didn't need the protection it offered, not on this January day, but he thought he suited it. He smiled as he settled it at the right angle over his white hair. His tan had deepened enough for him to pass as a native. He tipped the hat at his reflection and wished himself luck.

SIXTY

While Kim and Marie slept, Mave had returned to habits of old. She was in the bedroom where Mrs Malloy had died the year before. Even in the daytime, the dark surroundings and heavy curtains enclosed Mave in a way she found comforting.

This was the first time since helping Eddie with the Jimmy Sherrick case that she'd lost herself in the art of probing the security of an IT system. The tougher it was, the better she liked it. The defences of the BHA and JRC had been easy to crack, but she felt compensated by the richness of the content as she roved through it, an expert tracker in a digital world where the landscape was new but the signposts familiar.

Long before dawn, she had sent Eddie a secure message: "Much news on JCR. Ping me."

Eddie saw the message at 6.30, as the first coffee of the day brewed and he wrapped the heavy black dressing gown around himself. He smiled, and poured the coffee then hit the secure connection link. Mave answered right away. 'Morning.'

'And to you, Miss Judge. A fruitful night?'

She looked at the webcam. 'You been reading PG Wodehouse in bed, or something?'

He laughed. 'You look well, Mave, back to your old self. Though it's bloody dark there. Turn a light on, will you.'

'No. I won't. And you can't make me because you're on the other side of the country. So there!'

Eddie laughed again. 'You're miles better, Mave. I'm glad. What have you got?'

'I have got a charming fellow called Major Aubrey Severson in bed, figuratively speaking, with your man Jordan Ivory.'

'Do tell me more.'

'The major is chairman of The Jockey Club, as you no doubt know, and from what I can find was the man behind this Jockey Club Bond that launched a couple of years ago.'

'Behind it, meaning what, it was his idea?'

'It was his idea, or so he claims, but he stayed behind it all the way through. Actively, I mean. There's plenty documentation where he's pushing and shoving and nagging and negotiating. Not typical behaviour for the chairman of any established company. Usually they'll approve a project and let the management get on with it. Old Aubrey looks like he was on it full time.'

'Go on.'

'You're familiar with this bond, right?'

'I spoke to Mac about it. It was the reason I asked you to take a look.'

'Why?'

'Because I was trying to come up with a motive for these attacks. Whoever's behind them wouldn't be out to damage the company itself. A company doesn't care one way or the other being, well, not alive, I suppose. You know what I mean…it has to be an attack on someone who'd lose out in some way if the company went bust. It has to be something to do with people, not companies.'

'Well, you might well be right. The bond was set up to raise twenty-five million for investment, mostly to help build the new stand at Cheltenham.'

'Correct.'

'Anyone could apply. The annual interest rate to bondholders was five percent with some other goodies thrown in like free entry to tracks etcetera. Companies were invited to buy blocks, but were limited to a maximum of a hundred thousand pounds investment.

Fifty-seven companies invested the maximum. Fifty of them are owned jointly by Major Aubrey Severson and Mister Jordan Ivory.'

Eddie drew a long breath. 'You…are a genius.'

'I…was astounded at how easy it was to get into their system. Breaking through the facade of the shell companies was marginally harder, but they were sloppy enough to use the same incorporation agent for all fifty companies.'

'One of these Cayman Island dodges, or something?'

'No. Canada. It's actually a hell of a lot easier to find an agent who'll ask no questions in the bigger, supposedly well regulated countries. Anyway, bottom line is that, between them the chairman of the Jockey Club and a large bookmaker of questionable morals have put five million sterling into a vehicle guaranteeing them five percent return with no perceived risk. At the time, at least.'

'How many companies applied?'

'There were a hundred and twenty eight submissions requesting the full hundred K. Ninety two were companies.'

'So why did those two stop at fifty companies?'

'Maybe that was all they had to invest, or all they wanted to invest.'

'Okay. So who else found this out before you did? And why didn't he just give it to the press if it's some sort of vengeance mission?'

'Well, I'm not certain, but it could be that the legal side of it has enough gaps in it for them to wriggle through. It wasn't a stock market transaction. The bonds have no tradable value. Inside information wouldn't have mattered. The regulatory side probably consists of little more than caveat emptor. Besides, if your man wants to make these two sweat long and hard, he has the satisfaction of knowing they're suffering financially, perhaps terminally from a financial viewpoint, and, he's planted the seed with them that he knows what they've done.'

'That answers one of the other questions in my mind, why did JCR react to this before everyone else? Why take on McCarthy at a comparatively early stage? Old Aubrey must have been shitting himself and Ivory would be squeezing him too.'

'The big question for me is, how does a man, assuming our perp is male, come to terms with killing three people by way of doling out financial damage? Which leads on to why he then turns all the way around and begins warning tracks about potential accidents.' Mave adopted a robotic voice, 'Does not compute.'

'Agreed. Two different people. It has to be.'

'So where's the killer gone, and has he finished killing?'

'Well that depends a lot on how Jonty Saroyan died.'

'Jeez! I'd forgotten about him. So it could be four murders?'

'At least.'

'What next, Edward?'

'I think a meeting with Mac's the best bet.'

'You going to tell him everything?'

'I'll think about it.'

'Want me to do anything else?'

'See what you can find out about the galloping major, especially where his association with Ivory might have started.'

'I'm on it!'

SIXTY-ONE

Sonny's taxi dropped him in Abersoch as the afternoon light faded. The coastal winds cut at him as though they knew he was a deserter and that his time away had weakened him. He hunched against it and ducked into a charity shop where he bought an old Barbour waxed jacket. It was short in the sleeves but it tamed the wind.

His three-mile walk up onto the headland warmed him, and he wondered how long it would take to rebuild immunity to the British winter. Mave's Shack was visible a long way off, but Sonny saw no lights. He assumed Mave had curtained the place off against the night.

But as he drew closer, seeing only the hulk of the Shack against the sky, no trail of smoke from the chimney, he knew it was empty. He remembered that the last time he'd seen Mave was at Eddie's and he cursed himself for not checking she'd come back. Then again, that would have killed the happy homecoming surprise.

No point in knocking...Sonny turned the handle. The door opened. He stopped, and considered phoning Mave. But what if something was wrong? He hurried in and switched on the lights.

A mess. A stomach-churning mess.

Only his head moved as he tried to take this in. Then he dropped his bag and ran upstairs calling Mave's name.

Two minutes later he sat on the bottom step taking in the aftermath of the burglary. How the hell was he going to break this news to Mave? Maybe a call to Eddie would be best. He'd know how to handle it. Eddie could tell her face to face.

'Sonny,' Eddie said, 'Happy New Year.'

'And to you, Eddie. Listen, is Mave with you?'

Eddie judged the question to be too quick and too straightforward to carry an ulterior motive, but care was needed. 'Not at the moment. Is everything all right?'

Sonny told him about the break-in.

'Jeez, Sonny, that's grim news. What are your plans? Can you stay there until we try and sort something out?'

'Sure. Sure, I'd hoped this would be a surprise visit, anyway. I'll stay as long as I'm needed.'

'Good. Let me speak to Mave and call you back.'

'Should I ring the police?'

'Not right away, I don't think. Let's see what Mave says.'

'I'm sorry for pushing this onto you, Eddie. I'd tell her, but-'

'Don't worry. She's in pretty good shape at the moment. I think she'll handle it.'

'Call me back, will you?'

'Of course.'

Eddie ended the call and ended his doubt about Sonny being involved in the break-in. Mave had been right. He called her on the throwaway phone and told her.

'Did you ask him if the PC was still there?'

'It crossed my mind, but I didn't want to put him on the defensive. Defending Nina, I mean.'

'I know what you mean…'

'Do you think he's back for good?'

'Judging by how low he was yesterday on the phone, he could well be.'

Eddie hesitated, then said. 'We should either tell him we suspect Nina, or ask him about the PC and leave him to draw his own conclusions on it.'

'The latter.'

'Okay. He also asked about calling the police.'

'Well, we don't want that, and he can't live in that mess, so the answer's no, we want to see what we can find out ourselves.'

'Okay. He's going to ask when you're due back.'

'Oh…buggeration!'

Eddie smiled. 'That's a new one on me, Mave. Effective, all the same.'

'Listen, we're going to have to tell him, aren't we? I can't stay hidden without him knowing why.'

'It'll put him on the spot with Nina.'

'I know. I know…'

'Look, that could work in our favour. I'll arrange to meet him and we can take it from there. If he's really finished with her, and we might have to take it on trust, then maybe he can help us nail her.'

'That is, of course, assuming that it was Nina who broke in and not Buley or his cronies.'

'True. Let's see what he says. If he can't be truthful about her now, he probably never will be.'

'Okay. Let me know what he says.'

Sonny hadn't moved from his seat on the stairs, surveying the torn cushions, the broken books, the smashed drawers as though they were so many hypnotic objects.

His phone rang.

'Eddie.'

'Sonny, I spoke to Mave. Listen, we need to meet, you and me.'

'Did she go crazy?'

'No. No, she's fine, she's okay under the circumstances. But all sorts of shit's been going on while you were away. Mave won't be back at the Shack anytime soon. I'll explain everything when I see you. I'm at Ludlow tomorrow. You still got that caravan in Stourport?'

'If I can find the keys, yes.'

'Can you get there for late afternoon tomorrow?'

'Should be able to.'

'Okay. I'll come straight there after racing.'

'Mave's not been hurt, has she?'

'No. She's fine. We're just taking precautions.'

'Good…that's good, Eddie. Give her my love. Tell her I'm sorry.'

'I will.'

'You think it'll be okay for me to spend the night here?'

'If you can clear a space, by the sound of things.'

'I'll tidy up as best I can. Assuming you don't want me to get the police in?'

'No. No point. And if you could get the house back into some sort of order, that'll make things easier when Mave comes home.'

'Sure. Sure, I will. See you tomorrow.'

'Okay. Oh, Sonny…is Mave's PC unit still under her desk?'

'Hold on…No. No, Eddie, it's not,' Sonny's tone was dropping, fading. 'The PC's gone,' he said.

'Shit.'

Sonny stayed silent. Eddie said, 'Well, look, there's nothing we can do about it now. I'll see you tomorrow.'

'Yes,' Sonny was whispering. Slowly, he put the phone away. He buried his big tanned face in his hands and massaged it and groaned and pushed his fingers back through his hair until he gripped the jacket collar, and he tried to haul it forward, wishing he could draw it all the way over his head and down his body like some magical soft eraser, capable of deleting the past.

He did not move for a long time, then another groaning sigh seemed to galvanize him and he rose muttering 'Where to start? Where to start?'

He began picking his way through the jumble, setting chairs upright, refitting cushions, collecting books. Three lamps were smashed. Sonny got bin bags and a brush and dustpan from the kitchen.

When the solid objects had been cleared from the living room floor, Sonny set to shaking out the tumble of rugs and laying them in the order and shape he thought they had been in. From the blue fireside rug something fell and tinkled on the stone flags. Sonny looked at it. He took his right hand from the corner of the rug and bent to pick up the pendant he had given Nina.

Sonny held it delicately by the clasp and raised it carefully to eye level. As the kinks in the gold chain freed themselves, the diamond slowly turned, sparkling in the light.

SIXTY-TWO

Eddie had resisted calling Mac, but come morning, he realized there was little choice. Care was needed. The major was Mac's boss. The phone he was using was JCR issue. Eddie was due to ride out for Ben Tylutki before leaving for Ludlow, so time was tight. He drove to Mac's place before dawn and was relieved to see a light on as he pulled into the driveway.

Mac heard the engine and opened a curtain. He waved Eddie in.

'You smelt the coffee pot, didn't you?' Mac said.

'From a mile off.'

'What's new?'

Eddie told him about Major Aubrey Severson. Mac didn't say a word all the way through. Eddie looked at him. 'You seem to be kind of absorbing this in slow motion, Mac, if you don't mind me saying.'

'I don't know if I'm ring-rusty or my brain hasn't woke up yet. Let me just make sure I've got this right...' He summed up what Eddie had told him.

'That's a fair potted version, Mac. I don't know where it leaves you, and I was in two minds when to tell you, but, we are where we are.'

Mac stared into his coffee mug, then swirled the liquid slowly. He said, 'How are you for time? Can you help me try and break this down?'

'I've got half an hour.'

'Right. The chairman of the Jockey Club is a crook, leaving aside the merits of legal arguments on shareholdings and insider dealing etcetera. He's a crook, in spirit, if you like.'

'Agreed.'

'He's involved with another crook, by all accounts, in Ivory.'

'Correct.'

'It seems highly likely that he prompted Tim Arango to recruit me, way ahead of the time when anyone could have reasonably concluded this was a JCR only issue.'

Eddie made one fist of both hands, rested his chin there, and nodded. Mac said, 'Tim Arango is not someone you'd file under "dimwit", so how much does Tim know, if anything? And if he is not in on it, what questions did he ask of the major when my name came up?'

Eddie said, 'There's no indication that Tim's involved, or that he's hiding anything.'

'Right. So who took the decision to cease operations? Was it Tim, and did the major object, or was the suspension of racing instigated by the major?'

'The major, according to meeting minutes.'

'So, he believes it better to, in his lingo, retreat and regroup than to carry on against an unknown enemy.'

'Fair comment.'

Mac nodded slowly, then drank, staring at the table. He looked up at Eddie. 'I don't mind telling you that I haven't a bloody clue what to do now. Your friend has found out pretty much all there is to know on the inside. It's gobsmacking, and it's immensely helpful to me personally in watching my back, but, with due respect to your friend's hard work, it does not put me one step closer to finding out who's behind this.'

'True. But at least it gives you a motive, or what looks like a motive. If we accept that the motive's correct, then we're looking for somebody with a major grudge, no pun intended, against Ivory or the major or maybe both. Not only that, but it's someone who knows what they're up to. Now, I think it's a reasonable assumption that the major and Ivory have told no one about this, and it's hardly the kind of thing you stumble across. Whoever's behind it, not only holds a grudge, but he has access to the same skills my friend has used, and I can guarantee you that those skills are as rare as a Motown song without a tambourine in it.'

Mac looked puzzled. 'I'm afraid I'm not up with popular culture, Eddie.'

'True. That was a comparison I should have saved for my music-minded friend. But believe me…' Eddie hesitated, furrowing his brow. 'Having said that, my friend did say that accessing the IT systems at JCR and the BHA was ridiculously easy.'

'He looked at the BHA side, too?'

Eddie was on the verge of telling Mac that his 'friend' was a woman, but given the potential danger Mave was in, he resisted. 'That's right. The BHA were handling the case before you were brought in, remember?'

'Of course. Anything worthwhile there?'

'Not so far. But I don't know how deeply that was dug into. The big discovery was a showstopper, I suppose.'

'Would you ask your friend to have a good root around on the BHA side?'

'Sure.'

'Good. Thanks.'

'What are you going to do?'

Mac picked up his coffee mug and looked at Eddie. 'I haven't the faintest bloody idea.'

'One thing worth thinking about. This is personal, isn't it? The guy could have asked for a King's ransom to leave off JCR, and there hasn't been a single word from him. It's personal. Big time.'

SIXTY-THREE

Even though none of his four mounts was placed, Eddie enjoyed riding Ludlow. To him it seemed the quintessential small English racetrack, and only the clothing of those attending gave you some idea what decade you were in. The main thing jockeys riding there noticed was that police levels were almost back to normal.

Eddie sensed some element of guilt among his fellow riders that since the killings of Kellagher, Sampson and Blackaby, the atmosphere in the changing room had been much more relaxed and friendly. Nobody mentioned the dead men.

As dusk fell, Eddie drove from one small town to another, twenty miles east, Stourport-on-Severn, where Sonny waited in his caravan by the riverbank.

The site barrier was closed. Eddie called Sonny who said he'd walk up with the swipe card. Ten minutes later, they stood in the warm kitchen of the long caravan, all curtains drawn, the radio playing quietly and the kettle bubbling.

'A change from the delights of Turkey,' Eddie said.

'A welcome one for me, Eddie. Once the tint on the rose-coloured glasses started to fade, everything seemed grubby and hollow and kind of hopeless. There's no fool like an old fool, right enough.'

'Not your fault, my friend. Love doesn't discriminate in age or anything else.'

Sonny smiled sadly as he made coffee. 'And that's a fine thing…so long as it's on both sides.'

Eddie offered a sympathetic shrug. Sonny said, 'Let's sit down. I've got something to tell you, though it might not be the biggest of shocks.'

They settled in the U-shaped lounge. Sonny said, 'It was Nina who broke into Mave's house.'

'She confessed?'

Sonny drew the broken pendant from his shirt pocket and held it up. 'She left this there.'

Eddie nodded. Sonny said, 'You knew?'

'Had a fair idea.'

'And you knew it had happened before I told you last night?'

'Yes.'

'Mave, too.'

Eddie nodded. 'We went there three days ago.'

'And you thought it was me?'

Eddie watched him a while. 'I did. Mave bet her life you weren't involved.'

Sonny's look confused Eddie. He seemed partially relieved and a little amused, and he said, 'What is it with women, Eddie? No matter what I did to Jo, no matter how much I changed, she never lost an ounce of faith in me. And no matter what I did for Nina, no matter what I gave up, she never gave a fuck about me.'

'One of them knew you. The other didn't.'

'You knew me.'

'I'm not a woman.'

Sonny smiled sadly, 'Which brings it round full circle.'

'It does. But where do we go from here?'

'God knows.'

Eddie drank and watched him. 'You in or out?'

'Of what?'

'Of this. Of trying to stop Nina. Mave would understand if you want to just lie low and stay neutral.'

'How the fuck can I be neutral, when she's trying to harm a kid I've loved and protected all my life!'

Eddie, expressionless, watched and waited. The fire went from Sonny's eyes. 'I'm sorry. That was uncalled for.'

'It's okay. Any idea who was with Nina at Mave's?'

'None.'

'What about her brother, the one who was placing bets?'

'There was no brother. That was another piece of deception I should have said no to.'

'So you weren't stopped by the bookies from placing bets?'

'I was, but it was a friend of Jonty's who took over. We just thought it would seem more confidential if she conjured up a brother.'

'What's the friend's name?'

'Stefan. Stefan Gerraro.'

'Could he have helped Nina in the break-in?'

'I suppose so.'

'Where does he live?'

'I don't know.'

'What did she say when you told her about Jonty?'

'She said she'd always believed he'd choke to death on his own vomit.'

'Charming woman. Was that it?'

'Pretty much.'

'Did you tell her he was found at Haydock?'

'Yes.'

'That must have surprised her.'

'She didn't question it.'

'Didn't you find that strange?'

'I wasn't particularly thinking straight at the time, but, yes, I suppose it is.'

'Did you get the impression when she said about the choking thing, that she knew that was how he'd died?'

'Not really. It was just one of her assumptions. She's good at assumptions, Nina. Did Jonty die of choking?'

'I don't know. They haven't announced anything, but what Nina says makes me very curious.'

Sonny's head went down. Eddie said, 'Listen, I think we need to have a three-way conversation about what to do next, you, me, and Mave.'

Sonny nodded.

'What are the chances of Nina contacting you?'

'Slim, I'd have thought. I'm a meal-ticket past its expiry date. And the last time we saw each other I cut her enough to sever all ties. Not literally, I mean, verbally.'

'But if she thinks she can still get something out of you, she'd forgive you, if I can put it that way?'

'Probably…Definitely. Why, what's in your mind?'

'I need to speak to Mave first. We both do.'

'I can't wait to see her again.'

'I think we'd be better doing it by secure link, online, for now. You still got a laptop?'

'In my bag.'

'I'll get Mave to set you up.'

'There's Wi-Fi here on the site.'

'I doubt she'll risk that. Let's see what she says.' Eddie stood. Sonny got up. 'Can I call her,' he asked.

'Best not until we've figured out what to do. There's other crap going on.'

'What other crap?'

'Nothing to do with Nina, but maybe twice as dangerous. Look, can we agree for now that you'll stay here? Don't call Mave. Ring me on this throwaway phone if you need to and buy yourself one of these tomorrow. And if Nina happens to call you, can you kind of leave the door open with her, for now, at least?'

Sonny nodded, then rubbed his face and sighed. 'Okay.'

'Jet lag,' Eddie said.

'I wish. Life lag, it is,' he sighed again, long and loud, and it seemed to relax him. 'Life lag, Eddie.'

SIXTY-FOUR

When Eddie got home that night, Mac was waiting for him. The big man got out of his car as Eddie pulled in behind him. Eddie still had his lights on full beam and Mac frowned and raised his arm, looking to Eddie like a monochrome flashbulb picture of some mob boss.

Eddie got out, smiling. 'Dazzling, ain't I?'

'Well, your car certainly is.'

'Been waiting long?'

'Half an hour.'

'Come inside. You should have rang me on that number I gave you this morning.'

'I was going to. But I'm bloody paranoid now.'

Eddie made tea, and sat Mac down in the Snug. 'Talk away, while I get a fire going. Hard frost on its way, I hear.'

'We got the results on Mister Saroyan's autopsy.'

'And?'

'He died of sulphur dioxide poisoning.'

Eddie stopped his fire building. 'How does that happen, do you know?'

'Quite a few avenues, apparently. Heavy industry, agriculture, sewage treatments, bleaching paper or wood pulp, food processing. It can build up through physical contact, but not to deadly levels. It's the gas element, inhalation, that kills.'

'Any estimates on how long he'd been dead?'

'Months.'

'Jeez, he must have been a grim site in that boiler room.'

'He was. According to Broc Lisle.'

'Was it him who told you?'

'Yes. We met the other day, just to exchange thoughts. He rang me late this afternoon.'

'On your JCR number?'

'Yes. Why?'

'You might just want to be careful in case the old major's listening in.'

'Oh…'

'So the cops have added Saroyan to their list?'

'Reluctantly. They've made no progress whatever on Kellagher, Sampson or Blackaby.'

Eddie returned to the logs and firelighters. 'No surprise, there. No contact from the killer. No witnesses. No informants, unless it's the same guy who was pulling the laser pen stunts etcetera.'

'Which brings me to my next point. How long can we hold off from telling the police about the major and Ivory?'

'Well, how long do you want to spend dissecting the legality of what they've done, and who's going to do that for you and how will you keep it all away from the major and his pal?'

'Question is, is that really our job, or is down to the police?'

'Whatever, Mac. Open it up and the one thing you throw away is the advantage of knowing something when those two think you don't. Let's just keep it quiet a while longer, eh?'

'I'm getting edgy.'

Eddie struck a match. A firelighter flared. He turned to the big man. 'Keep your nerve, Mac. The police can occupy themselves with Saroyan. How long had he been in that boiler room? Not for months, surely? A guy who announces some vigilante campaign by shooting a jockey in front of twenty-thousand people is hardly going to have quietly planted a corpse months before it, is he?'

'Unlikely.'

'So why did he kill Saroyan, if indeed he was killed? Why go to the trouble of poisoning him when a bullet in the brain would have been easier, and why store him for months then dump him at Haydock, in a very private, very secluded place?'

Mac had been nodding slowly all the time Eddie had been talking. Eddie said, 'Does that sound like our man's M.O.?'

'Nope.'

'Then maybe the cops should be looking a lot more closely into Mister Saroyan's past affairs.'

'Fair point. I'll see what Broc thinks.'

'He riding shotgun with you, now, then?'

'He's a pleasant man, and a bit of a character. I can think of worse partners.' Mac's eyes narrowed. Eddie was well acquainted with the big man's mischievous smiles. 'Mac, you wait and see how Broc Lisle is when your backs are to the wall before you desert your old pal!'

They laughed.

SIXTY-FIVE

Mave, so long unused to company, began feeling more settled with Kim and Marie. She'd taken to helping with the four stallions they had in, and Kim had been protective of her around the horses.

She enjoyed Kim's company more than Marie's. The bitchiness from her schooldays had left marks she had thought she was over. But she found herself uncertain and guarded when Kim wasn't around and Marie was, even though Marie was always polite and welcoming.

That evening, in the dim light of a corner stable, she watched Kim groom Garamond, a big bay, still covering mares at the age of nineteen. Kim worked rhythmically with the brush, showing Mave the areas where Garamond was sensitive, smoothing those parts over softly.

'Why don't we go on a ride at the weekend?' Kim asked.

'Because I'd fall off and break something.'

Kim stopped working and looked at her. 'Haven't you ridden before?'

'Your uncle warned me to steer clear of them. He says they bite at one end and kick at the other.'

Kim smiled, 'He was just kidding!'

Mave squatted in the straw and pointed to Garamond's hind feet. 'Er, excuse me, aren't those hooves? With the equine equivalent of Doc Marten boots on?'

He laughed. She shuffled sideways toward Garamond's head. 'And isn't that a row of one-inch teeth under those big lips?'

'You'd be fine, Mave. I'll teach you. We can start lessons on Saturday.'

'That's good. You have a Shetland pony hidden away then?'

'We'll find you something docile. Marie has plenty friends with horses.'

'I'll think about it. I'll check and see if I can find my docile meter before Saturday.'

'Ha! You'll love it. I promise. It's the greatest feeling to be part of something where you're both sensing things from each other and kind of reading each other's mind and trusting each other. The horse is always learning and you're always learning. It's never boring.'

'Okay. Okay. You've convinced me. And if you decide the jockeying game isn't for you after all, you'd make a hell of a salesman, and a fine husband, to boot.'

'Don't be daft. This has got nothing to do with girls.'

'That's what you think.'

Kim worked his way to the other side of Garamond, where he could see Mave if he ducked or stood on tip-toes. 'What about you and Eddie, if you want to talk about girls! He seems mad about you. It's him that'll be making a good husband.'

'Your uncle will never marry.'

'No way! Of course he will! He's still young and once he's done riding, he'll settle down, with you. I'm sure of that.'

'Well that'll be most gracious of him. I can't wait.'

Kim stopped brushing, unsure, straight-faced. 'Sorry, I didn't mean to be patronizing.'

She laughed. 'You weren't, Kim. I'm just kidding you.'

'I just sort of took it for granted you were a couple.'

'We are. In our own way. An odd couple.'

'Do you love him?' Kim kept up the steady sweeps, not looking at her. Mave found herself holding her breath. 'I…hadn't analyzed it quite that deeply.'

'That means yes,' he said brightly.

'It does?'

'Yep.'

Mave put her hands on her hips. 'Well blow me down!'

Kim ducked low and blew hard toward her and she took a mock tumble in the dry straw, laughing in a way she had never laughed before, overcome for a few moments by a sense of utter freedom.

Mave smiled at the webcam. 'Your nephew is some kid.'

'The boy's a diamond. I don't know about him wanting to meet his father, I certainly would. And, God, how I wish I'd known his step-parents. There can't be many who've made a better job of raising a child. I envy him what he had, Mave. I wouldn't tell anyone else that, but I do. And it guts me, when I think about how he must have felt losing them both.'

'I know. But he'll be all right, Eddie, He'll be fine. They say kids are resilient. Kim just seems to handle everything and care for everyone. He's a real gem.'

'I'm glad you're getting on so well there. I was worried.'

'You were worried! Well, it shows that it's an ill wind that blows nobody good right enough. Out of all this bloody chaos, I've learned that locking myself away from the bitches and the bad guys means I miss out on all the good folk too.'

Eddie took time to look at her. And she looked at him. He said, 'Maybe there's a lesson there for me too, Mave.' She shrugged and raised one eyebrow.

Eddie said, 'Seems strange moving back to the depressing side, but Mac was waiting for me when I got home…'

He told her about Jonty Saroyan.

'Sulphur dioxide?' Mave asked.

'Plenty sources, apparently.'

'One of them is a darkroom.'

He looked at her. 'As in photography darkrooms?'

'As in the place they locked Sonny up in. The place where you backed straight out of when the door opened. What caught your throat was sulphur dioxide.'

'So why isn't Sonny dead?'

'Because most of the time, the room was properly ventilated.'

'So, if Jonty took such care with ventilation, why is Jonty dead?'

'Good question.'

Half an hour later, Mave had connected Sonny securely to the conversation, but only in audio.

Trying to work back through the timeline on Jonty was getting complicated. Sonny said, 'Mave, I never went back to the house after you guys got me out of there. Yes, I was seeing Nina after Jonty disappeared, but she'd come to Stourport or we'd meet in Worcester.'

'But she was still living in that house they took you to?'

'So far as I know.'

Eddie said, 'Sonny, can you recall when it was that Jonty went missing?'

'Late August, I think, or early September. That's when Nina and I were talking about going to Turkey.'

'What about the house? Did she sell it?' Eddie asked.

'It was a rental.'

Mave said, 'Must have been a long bloody rental if he'd built a darkroom in it.'

'I don't know,' Sonny said.

Eddie looked at Mave through the webcam, raising his eyebrows. Mave nodded to him and he said, 'Sonny, Mave and I put a possible plan together earlier. You're the one who'd have to make it work, and it could be dangerous.'

'I'm listening.'

'And it could put Nina Raine in jail for a long time.'

After a moment's hesitation Sonny said, 'I'm still listening.'

SIXTY-SIX

Nina Raine woke up in her flat in London, a home that was now one hundred percent hers. The mortgage had been paid off with the winnings from the bets and the fine flat and the free flowing cash had given Nina a taste for property speculation.

She'd stolen Mave's PC more in hope than confidence. She knew nothing of the software world but she'd grown accustomed to what she believed was a charmed life. The men she had needed, for whatever task was in hand, had always seemed to turn up. She was now on the hunt for a software engineer or a hacker. A Russian made plenty appeal.

She checked her messages and saw one from Sonny. She sighed and said aloud, 'This is getting fucking tiresome.'

She played it: "Nina, I found the pendant. It was at Mave's place. You left it there when you broke in. If you can think of any reason why I shouldn't tell Mave, and then the police, call me."

Her fingers went to her neck, touching her collarbone, where the diamond had rested. She stared at London's cityscape. Her future lay out there among the high fliers and the big deals. Now this.

She undressed, and went to the shower to try and work things out.

Ten minutes later, hair still wet, she sat on the edge of the bed again, looking through the picture window. She brought up

Sonny's number. She needed no mental or emotional preparation. She'd done this a hundred times.

He answered, 'Oh, Sonny, what are we going to do! I got your message. I'm so sorry. So, so sorry. I know how much that pendant meant to you and you couldn't live long enough to figure out how much it meant to me. I was heartbroken. I know we fought about it. I know I was a bitch, but believe me, I've never stopped thinking about it, or about you.'

'Listen, Nina-'

'Please, Sonny. I know you mentioned the police and, well, if it comes to that, I deserve it. But at least the pendant's safe.'

'Nina, it's not about the pendant anymore, for God's sake! You broke into Mave's house. You stole her PC!'

'Sonny, darling Sonny, you know how desperate I am to find Keki. You know I'd risk anything. I'd rather it wasn't breaking the law and it wounded me to have to betray you and Mave, but I had to try. You know that. More than anyone in the world, you know that! Mave must have been devastated. I'll crawl on my hands to knees to her, honest to God, I will!'

'She doesn't know. Thank God. She doesn't know yet.'

'How can she not know?'

'She's away. Remember she said she was giving up and travelling?'

'Well, that's a blessing. At least you'll be able to prepare the poor woman, and maybe tidy the place so it's not so much of a shock.'

'You're kidding me! You want me to tidy up my dearest friend's house, that you broke into, that you messed up!'

'Sonny! Sonny, don't shout at me, please! Don't let's start another fight, please. I'm so very near the end. So very close to just…just finishing everything.' She frowned and raised a bare foot to rub at some old nail polish on her toes.

'What do you expect, Nina? What about me? What am I supposed to do?'

'Darling, why don't we meet?'

Mave set up the evening conference call. Again, Sonny was on audio only. Mave and Eddie could see each other.

'So she bought it?' Eddie said.

'She did, but left me thinking, as she usually does, that it was me who'd fallen for something.'

Mave said, 'Sonny, if this is, well, too soon for you, we can leave it a while.'

Eddie glanced at her, wondering if she was serious. She didn't look at him. Sonny said, 'No. I'm on a reparation job now, Jo. Anything I can do to help put things back the way they were…that's what I want to do.'

'Okay. But you don't have to. I want you to know that.'

'I know it. And I appreciate it. But this is the right thing to do.'

'Well, let's hear it.' Mave said.

'She wants to meet me in Liverpool. She asked if I was still at the Shack. I told her I was back in Stourport and that Worcester would have been easier. But she said she had a special weekend in mind. There's a holiday property bang in the middle of Aintree racecourse. It's called Steeplechase Cottage. They rent it out on non-racing days. She's booked it for this weekend.'

When the conference call ended. Mave immediately reconnected with Eddie. He was waiting, looking right at her via the webcam. Both were silent for a few seconds, and serious-faced. Mave said, 'Looks like your hunch was right.'

'It does. The trouble is, how do we protect Sonny?'

'We're going to have to tell him, aren't we?'

Eddie thought about it. 'Probably. But we'll still need back-up…something formal.'

'Mac?'

'Mmm…might be a bit risky for him.'

'We can't get the police in, can we?'

'I don't know, Mave. I'd rather not, but there's no way of knowing what she's got planned.'

'Could we watch the place? You and me?'

'Let me think about it. Maybe I will talk to Mac. If it goes the way I expect, he'd be the next man in anyway.'

Mave looked at the clock in the corner of her PC screen. 'I'll be around for a while. I'm going out to help Kim with evening stables.'

'Good. I thought you'd suit each other, you two. Kim's still quite formal with me, and kind of adult, and manly, but it sounds like he's himself with you.'

'He seems to be. And, oddly, I'm myself with him. I only realized that last night. His appetite for life, after all he's been through, his ambition, in the best sense of the word, is just, well, inspiring. It's definitely infectious. I felt like a girl again, last night. All my own old hopes and dreams seemed fresh again, and real, and achievable.'

'Youth. I suppose we forget how simple everything seemed then. How straight the road ahead looked.'

'Kim won't let anybody forget that. I'm for my first riding lesson on Saturday, apparently.'

'I hope you can steer a horse better than you can steer a car.'

'You're not the only one.'

Eddie decided to drive to Mac's place.

Mac was stepping away from the burning stove as Eddie settled in the chair. Mac said, 'Thought I'd get your favourite fire going to thaw you out a bit.'

'Frost's all in the air, just now. Be in the ground overnight. Plumpton are inspecting in the morning, and I don't think Hexham are confident.'

'Well, it's January. We haven't lost many meetings so far, so we can stand a few, I suppose.'

Eddie looked at him. 'You mean you haven't lost many to the weather. How many have JCR cancelled now?'

'Twenty-seven. But bear in mind that twenty-one of those were transferred and all future ones, until we get going again, should also be run elsewhere.'

'Happy days, then?'

'Worse things have happened.'

'I know, Mac. Maybe we can start to make some kind of headway now.'

Mac grunted as he flopped back in the chair. 'That's good to hear. Please elaborate.'

Eddie told him the story of Sonny and Nina, then said, 'Now that's by way of background. She's arranged to meet him on a JCR property at the weekend, a holiday cottage on Aintree racecourse. That backed-up a hunch I had, no pun intended.'

Mac smiled.

Eddie said, 'Saroyan's body at Haydock seemed so far out of line with everything else that's happened to JCR that it set me thinking. The first time I came across the guy was when he got into this blackmail stunt with Nina Raine. Saroyan then disappeared. She said he'd stolen money and run out on her, but that made no sense because my friend was feeding them tips at the time. Why wouldn't Jonty Saroyan have waited until the tips dried up? Anyway, the last one to see him was Nina Raine.'

'To see him alive, you mean?'

'To see him at all. But that's her story. Now, maybe Jonty died by accident in his darkroom, and whoever is behind all these attacks was also associated with him in some way and decided to use him. But if that were the case, he'd have done it much sooner. Jonty died months ago. So, was Nina there when he died? Did Nina have something to do with his death, and she saw the whole JCR thing hitting the headlines and thought that Haydock's boiler room would make a nice place for a red herring.'

Mac's hand was on his chin now. He was nodding, prompting Eddie to go on.

'So we gave her the chance, as she'll see it, to get herself out of trouble by finding some way to shut Sonny up. Now, my guess is that she'll try the let's get back together pitch first. But if it doesn't work, Nina's plan B might be leaving JCR with another corpse in Steeplechase Cottage.'

SIXTY-SEVEN

On the evening before Nina was due to arrive in Liverpool, Eddie drove to Sonny's caravan. Sitting in the U-shaped lounge, they finalized preparations. Eddie said, 'CCTV's been installed all around the cottage, inside and out.'

'Well disguised, I hope?'

'Mac assures me it is. Obviously, the big question is, will she bring someone with her? Or will that someone be arriving at a certain time? And will it be the guy who helped her move Jonty's body? And, will he be armed?'

'Or will she be armed?' Sonny said.

'What do you think?'

'I'm beyond surprise with her, Eddie. I don't know.'

Eddie opened his kitbag and brought out the blue and black ice axe he owned. 'I couldn't get you a gun. This is the best I can offer.'

Sonny's hands were clasped, his elbows resting on his knees. 'You seriously think I'd be capable of hitting her with that?'

'It might be a him, Sonny.'

Sonny raised his eyebrows and slowly reached for the axe. He surprised himself by laughing. 'Where am I going to keep this, Eddie?' He tried mimicking Nina, "Is that an ice-axe in your pocket, or are you just pleased to see me?"'

Eddie smiled. 'I know. It's hardly portable. I'd a half hour argument with Mac before I could get him to agree to it. I'm dropping it off to him on the way home tonight. He'll be at the track in the morning, and he'll place it on top of the wardrobe in the main bedroom.'

'And I'll just have to hope that's where we are when the shit hits the fan.'

Eddie got serious. 'Look, Sonny. You don't need to go through with this. I shouldn't tell you, but Mave's already regretting agreeing to it. She'd be much happier if we call it off.'

'No, Eddie. Tell her I've got no doubts on it. I'm not quite as sure as you are that she's got anything drastic planned. I think the gig she has in mind is trying to persuade me to get the software access off Mave.'

'That might well be it, but you're going to say no, aren't you? The key here is to make her believe she's in deep shit and you're not going to pull her out.'

'But she's so damn sure of herself, she won't have a plan B. Up until that fallout over the pendant, I'd never given her anything except…obedience. That's the only word for it. Canine grade obedience. She'll think this is a no-brainer, believe me.'

'I hope you're right.' Eddie noticed Sonny's two phones on the coffee table. 'Which is the secure one?'

Sonny picked up the smaller of them. Eddie said, 'Stash it where she won't find it. We won't call you on it unless it's life or death.'

Sonny nodded, looking beyond Eddie now, all the way back to what might have been.

Sonny waited at Lime Street Station, too nervous to sit. He walked the windy platform, coat collar up, the warm Istanbul air a distant memory.

He had to keep moving.

She'd be wearing that tight red dress he loved. She was the only redhead he could recall who wore clothes the colour of her brilliant hair, and she carried it off like a catwalk model. Seduction would be the plan, he was certain. He smiled at the imagined graph of his sex drive over the years…the last five had seen it drop like a ski-ramp. Then came Nina, and Sonny soared once more.

But even with her, it lost its power much more quickly than in his younger days. He could not physically recall that feeling now, that hour-by-hour subconscious sexual foraging…at work, in the street, on holiday, watching TV…The mental memory was there, as though he'd maybe read about these feelings. The physical recall had returned briefly with Nina, then faded once more.

But it wasn't the sex he grieved for, and it wasn't his youth. It was the loss of another love. The first had happened in his late teens, then, despite the years of searching, nothing more till Nina. And that was his life… topped and tailed by heartbreak.

There was no red dress. She was in black. Without makeup, her face was bare and white and stark. Her hair could not be dimmed, but Sonny was shocked when he saw her.

She raised her head for a kiss, offering her cheek, and gripping his arm with her black-gloved hand. 'Are you all right?' Sonny asked.

She nodded, looking down. He gently touched her chin, lifting her head to look in her eyes. She'd been crying. 'Has something happened?' Sonny asked.

'Just…everything came home to me. I've thought of nothing except how I've hurt you. And I was so full of dreams after we talked. I booked the cottage and planned my outfits and thought about a whole weekend together with no pressure, no searching and waiting and worrying. Just you and me. But my mind kept bringing back that horrible fight we had, and the hateful things I said, and…and I just knew it was hopeless.'

'I'm sorry, Nina. I'm sorry for my part in it, and-'

She put her fingers to his lips. 'It was my fault. Nobody else's. Mine. I tried to find a way of shaking off the responsibility for it, then I realized that's all I've done all my life. Seek excuses. Shift blame,' she looked up at him. 'No more. No more.'

She asked if they could go straight to the cottage. 'I couldn't' face being in a restaurant full of happy people.'

Downlighting on the white outside walls gave Steeplechase Cottage a mystical look in the hard air frost. It was softly lit inside too. Warm and luxuriously decorated.

In an ice bucket on the glass coffee table stood two bottles of champagne. Soft classical music played through invisible speakers. Nina had volunteered to sleep in the smaller room, but Sonny said he'd feel better if she took the four-poster.

She came out of her room as she'd gone in. Sonny had expected, at least, some makeup, some sign of a plan. She'd caught him out at the station, but this all had to be one of her games, surely?

She sat, then reached slowly to touch the cork of the champagne bottle.

'Want me to open it for you?'

She smiled sadly. 'I suppose they drink at wakes, don't they?'

He smiled. 'They do.'

'What about you? Will you have a glass for old time's sake?'

Was this the first step in the seduction? She knew how rarely Sonny drank. His diabetes had ensured he'd never developed a taste for alcohol.

'I'll risk one.'

She leaned forward, touching his arm, looking concerned. 'You sure? You've brought your meds haven't you?'

'I've been managing this all my life. I'll be fine.'

'But have you brought enough medication?'

'Nina, I'll be fine, I promise.'

'No. Leave it. I won't bother.'

'Don't be daft. I'll get the glasses.'

'Get your meds first. I want to make sure you've got enough.'

He was walking away. She called after him, 'Sonny! Get the meds!'

Sonny brought the glasses and his diabetes medication, which he shook out onto the table. 'Happy now?'

'Just a glass then, okay?'

But Nina took over the pouring and one glass led to one more, then a third and by the time she emptied the second bottle, her shoes were off and she was stretched on the couch, and they'd talked and laughed and cried.

Nina noticed Sonny checking his watch. 'What's up? Your coach going to turn back into a pumpkin at midnight?'

'Nearly there,' Sonny said quietly, and on the stroke of midnight, he drew a jewellery box from his pocket and gave it to her. The pendant was inside.

She stared at it. 'I got it repaired. The clasp had broken,' Sonny said, quietly.

Slowly she raised her head, 'Could you get us repaired?'

Sonny looked down, joining his hands, elbows on knees.

'We broke, too, didn't we? Didn't we, Sonny?'

'I suppose we did, Nina. I suppose we did.'

'Call me darling…'

He looked at her.

'One last time…'

He sighed and laid his head back as though talking to the sky, 'How did we get to here? How did it come to this?'

Clutching the box, she swung her feet onto the floor and leant toward him. 'Maybe we can get it back, Sonny! It doesn't have to be lost! If I can only find Keki, I can give the rest of my life to you.'

'Keki. Keki. Keki. God help the poor boy, Nina, but if he's not been found by now…I mean, at some point you're going to need to face the prospect that he'll never be found.'

'I'm his mother. His mother. How can I accept he's lost forever? How can I? If we can pay enough people to-'

'Nina! How many people? How many searchers, so far? How much money burned through?'

'Money's nothing, Sonny. It's nothing to me. It's a tool to help find my boy. That's all. And how can I stop? The next person I can pay might find him the day after. If Mave had only held on a while longer. If that last bet had only come up.'

'Nina-'

She jerked forward, eyes wide. 'See! You see now why I was reduced to bloody burglary out of desperation? Common sense told me the programme would be protected, that I wouldn't be able to use it, but desperation always overrules common sense. Can you understand that?'

'I can understand it, but it doesn't overrule other people's common sense. You can't expect them to keep on and on and on.'

She got to her knees on the floor in front of him. 'Sonny. Look at me. I'm begging you. I'm begging you to ask Mave to give us the password or the key or whatever it is we need. She doesn't have to do anything more after that. She can go on travelling. We can do it all. I can. I can!'

Sonny covered his face with his hands.

'Sonny…I am begging you.'

He sighed and drew his fingers back through his white hair. 'It's over, Nina. All I'm going to tell Mave when I see her is the truth. I owe her that. It's the least I owe her. She's not mean. She won't want revenge. She won't report you to the police. I'll ask her not to do that…but she needs to know the truth.'

Nina slumped forward, till her elbows rested on the rug and her head went down, splashing her hair across its whiteness.

Sonny rose. 'I'm going to bed. I'll take you to the station in the morning.'

Two hundred yards to the rear of the cottage, on the old grand-prix track that runs inside The Grand National course, a white minibus was parked. It was the Aintree courtesy vehicle for transporting those who arrived on the helipad.

Inside the bus were Eddie and Mac.

Mac said, 'I do wish I'd brought that second hot water bottle.'

'I wish I'd brought a first hot water bottle.'

'How much longer, do you think?'

'Who knows, Mac?'

'We could be here all bloody night. In January! Can't these people commit their crimes in summer, for God's sake?'

Eddie smiled. 'Like the Flat season? You get Flat season criminals. Nina's a jumps fan, by the look of things.'

'Well, if she was stuck out here with the bloody icicles, she'd soon change her allegiance.'

'At least you still have a good head of hair, Mac. It could be worse. Most body heat escapes through the head, you know.'

'That's a bloody fallacy, too! Well, it's not a fallacy, but it's silly. Of course heat escapes through the head, but not because it's at the top of your body, it's because it's the only part that isn't bloody clothed! Doesn't that tell-'

'Mac!' Eddie raised a hand.

They stared through the frost-rimmed porthole in the window that Eddie had spent so much time wiping.

Nina was leaving.

Sonny sat up in bed, in the dark, listening to the key turning in the back door. A minute before, he'd lain still while Nina had taken his phone from his jacket and all his medication from the dresser.

SIXTY-EIGHT

McCarthy and Tim Arango were the only ones in the offices of
The Jockey Club in Newmarket that Sunday afternoon.

'A woman?' Arango said.

'Nina Raine. Early thirties. Been involved in attempted
blackmail, burglary, and, possibly, the killing of Jonty Saroyan.'

'Have you evidence of that?'

'Only circumstantial. Saroyan became a liability, as did Sonny
Beltrami, the man involved at Aintree yesterday.'

'And?'

'She effectively left Sonny for dead. She took away the
medication he needed for his diabetes and locked him in a building
when nobody knew he was there. If he'd taken a hypoglycaemic
attack, after drinking alcohol, it could have resulted in ketoacidosis,
which is often fatal.'

'But our staff at Aintree knew that she had booked the cottage,
is that not correct? She's hardly going to kill someone in the place
she's reserved in her own name.'

'She could have told any story…that she booked it on behalf of
someone else. That she'd thought better of it and told Sonny she
wasn't coming.'

'I thought you said everything was on CCTV?'

'It is. But she wasn't to know that.'

Arango frowned. 'You think we have enough to give her name
to the police?'

'I think we should at least discuss it formally.'

'I'm not sure it's a decision I'd be comfortable making. Are you happy for me at this point to get the major's view?'

'Of course.'

That evening, after the call from Arango, McCarthy rang Eddie. 'Guess what, the major prefers to keep it in-house for now.'

'There's a surprise. What does in-house mean exactly?'

'Apparently, the major knows some reliable private agencies who are extremely discreet, and might be able to find Miss Raine in the hope she can help.'

'Discreet private agencies? I'll bet. The Ivory Agency, no doubt, will be first on the list.'

'Well, that's the way you saw it panning out, isn't it?'

'It is, Mac, but now we're winging it. Nina Raine's winging it too. So far, she's been dealing with amateurs. If Ivory finds her…'

'Well, I wouldn't be too concerned for her welfare. Mister Ivory seems a pragmatist. If all she's been involved in on the JCR side is with Saroyan's body, then he'll let her go, I should think.'

'And if not?'

'Mmm. We shall just have to wait and see.'

'Waiting's the hard part.'

SIXTY-NINE

Nina Raine was waiting too. She'd flown from Liverpool to London in the early hours of Sunday morning then onwards to Turkey. Four days later, she sat by the pool at her villa in Yalikavak, on the Aegean coast, wondering what had happened to Sonny.

She'd been scanning the news channels and the online versions of the Liverpool newspapers. Was it possible he hadn't been found yet? Had he got out? She doubted he had or he would have come raging in pursuit.

Maybe the JCR people were keeping it quiet? Nobody from the booking office at Aintree had tried contacting her.

She'd much rather know one way or the other. If the authorities, were onto her, so be it. At least she could make plans. Morocco was a short flight away. She hadn't yet used the tiny apartment she'd bought there, in Agadir. Maybe it was time she moved in for a while. It had been a 'distress purchase'. Nina had hoped she'd never need to take refuge in it, in Morocco, a country with no extradition treaty with the United Kingdom.

Nina went inside to pack. When she came back out, Jordan Ivory was sitting by the pool.

She stopped, and pushed her sunglasses onto her head and frowned. There was no point in folding right away. There was just a chance that this might have nothing to do with Sonny.

'Who are you?' Nina asked.

Ivory removed his sunglasses and slotted them into the top pocket of his linen suit. He smiled, 'I am the ghost of Christmas past, Miss Raine.'

'Pardon me?'

'Come and sit down. I am not a policeman. I'm not here because you tried to kill Sonny Beltrami. I'm here because it seemed much more civilized than having you dragged kicking and screaming back to London. Sometimes the mountain must come to Mohammed.'

Nina set the wheeled luggage on its end and put her hands on her hips. 'What on earth are you talking about?'

Ivory got up from the low chair in one long easy movement. She was surprised how tall he was. He strolled toward her, smiling, and she sensed the threat rather than saw anything in his face, for his smile didn't change as he grabbed her hair at the nape of her neck and wound it around his fist and dragged her toward the pool and threw her in.

She surfaced blinking and drew a deep breath as Ivory bent at the waist from the poolside. His smile had faded. 'Nina. Don't be tiresome. Don't be time-wasting. Don't cause trouble. The three Ts. Remember them. Commit to them. You will reap the benefits, as will I. The most important thing to bear in mind in the coming days is that time, to me, is extremely precious. Once spent, it cannot be got back. Our lives are limited, constrained by time. Understand?'

Treading water, oddly fascinated by this man and his speech rhythms, she nodded. 'Help me get out,' she said.

'No.' He went back to his chair.

She climbed the steps and stood dripping, a hank of hair gleaming on her shoulder like seaweed.

'Get changed. You have five minutes. Be thoughtful.'

She went inside. Was there any point trying to leave by the French doors? No, he'd have men at the foot of the stairs. Could she call anyone? Her phone was outside, in her bag. Time was better spent trying to figure out how to handle this guy. She stripped and dried her body, and changed into sawn-off jeans and a short white blouse.

Still towelling her hair, she walked back out into the sun. Ivory was looking at his watch. 'Good. Three minutes thirty-seven. Come and sit down.'

She moved across and sat facing him, still towelling her hair.

'Enough. Put the towel down.'

She stopped, looked at him, then obeyed.

'In forty-five minutes my driver will take me to the airport. Four of my people are downstairs, two men, and two women. They will stay here when I go. The terms of your imprisonment will depend greatly on how truthful you are with me. Understand?'

She nodded.

'Then I'll begin.'

In the airport lounge, Jordan Ivory phoned a man he called his project manager. 'Dalton. I want you to find a woman called Maven Judge, also known as Jolene Cassidy. She might be travelling, possibly in a motorhome, probably in the UK, maybe in Europe. She's close to a jockey called Eddie Malloy and a man called Sonny Beltrami. I have details on Beltrami which I'll send on. I have little on Malloy and will leave that to you. Do not pick her up. Do not lose her once you've found her. Give me daily updates on this number only.'

SEVENTY

On his third daily phone update since briefing Dalton, Jordan Ivory, told him to hold. Ivory left his desk and went to close his office door. 'Go ahead, Dalton.'

'Been working on Maven Judge's phone records. Stretching back, they're mostly from her home in North Wales. A few over Christmas and New Year were made from Malloy's place. One last week was from a mast in Newmarket. She was either passing through, or she stopped using the phone after that call. No calls have been made on that number since. Bit of a shot in the dark, but I'll probably send someone to Newmarket to dig around. We have Malloy's place wired, along with the three caravans belonging to Beltrami. Should have some better news for you tomorrow.'

'Thank you, Dalton. Malloy has form as a bit of a daredevil, all amateur stuff, but worth bearing in mind.'

'Thanks, Mister Ivory.'

That afternoon, Mac drove to Taunton racecourse. He'd considered sending someone into the changing room to find Eddie, but he was too nervous about the implications, mostly because he didn't know the scale of those implications. Events seemed to be overrunning him. He felt he'd never got up to the required pace since joining JCR, and his confidence was suffering.

Although he could have walked into the changing room himself, Mac didn't think that would be smart. But he had to speak to Eddie.

He scribbled on a page of his diary, and ripped it out. Standing near the paddock entrance as the jockeys filed past for the next, Mac handed the note to Eddie. 'Keep moving,' Mac said.

After the race, Eddie did what Mac had requested and hurried to the stables, away from the crowd. He wore a jacket over the pink colours he was due to wear in the next. Mac had been pacing while waiting for Eddie, and as he saw him approach, he found he couldn't stop walking, couldn't stay still.

Eddie dropped in alongside him. 'What's up?'

'Broc Lisle came to see me. Somebody's going to a lot of trouble trying to find a woman called Maven Judge. Broc assured me that you would very much like to know about it, urgently.'

'Who's looking for her?'

'Jordan Ivory's people.'

'How did Lisle find out?'

'My guess is that he has contacts in GCHQ. He worked there for three years.'

'The government place? The spy place?'

'Well, intelligence and security, in their lingo.'

'Why didn't he come straight to me?'

'He assumed I knew about Miss Judge.'

'Mave is the friend I've mentioned, the IT genius.'

'You said it was a man.'

'You assumed it was a man, Mac. Anyway, it doesn't matter. Did Lisle say they'd caught Nina Raine?'

'He didn't. I got the impression he had to be very selective. Or chose to be. Do you want me to ask him?'

'No. There's no point. You got your phone?'

Mac took it from his pocket. Eddie asked him to dial Marie's landline number, then to cover him. It was ringing. Mac passed him the phone and stood in front of him, blocking Eddie from the view of anyone in the stand.

'Marie, it's Eddie. All well there?'

'Fine, Eddie. What's wrong?'

'Is Mave around?'

'She's upstairs. You sound like you've got bad news for somebody.'

'Not really. Kind of good news, in a way, depending on how you look at it, I suppose. Listen, before I speak to Mave, if you and Kim had to leave there temporarily, but very quickly, could you do it? Could you place the horses somewhere?'

'How quickly?'

'Today. Soon.'

'What's wrong?'

Eddie told her. She said, 'My God! I'll call Mave.'

'What about you, Marie? And Kim?'

'Well, I know you're worried, Eddie, but isn't it Mave they're trying to find.'

'It is. But even if Mave's not there, if and when they come there, I want you two safe as well.'

'Why? What do you mean safe? We're not involved. From what you say, you're not even involved, not really.'

'If they know Mave has been there, they'll think you know where she's gone.' She didn't reply. 'I'm sorry, Marie.'

'This isn't our fight, Eddie, mine and Kim's. We're only just getting our bloody life together!'

'I'm sorry.'

'I'll get Mave.'

Eddie stepped sideways and peered past Mac, nervy. He checked his watch. 'Fuck!' he said.

'Pardon?'

'Sorry, Mave. Listen…' Eddie told her.

'All right,' she said, 'I'll fix something.'

'You got access to the money, as much as you'll need?'

'Yes.'

'Don't tell me where you plan to go. Don't ever tell me where you are until we get Ivory. Okay?'

'Okay.'

'Don't tell anyone. Don't talk on the phone. Call me once a day at nine p.m. from the throwaway, just to say you're all right. Get half a dozen more phones. Cycle them for the calls to me. Speak to nobody else.'

'What if you need to get in touch with me?'

'I don't know. I need to think about that. You've got to get out of there as soon as possible. Try and talk Marie and Kim into coming with you.'

'They'll be safer well away from me, Eddie.'

'I don't think they will, Mave. If they won't go with you then I'm going to leave my place and move in with them until this is done.'

She was about to speak, then reeled it all back and just said, 'Okay.'

'Call me tonight. Nine o'clock.'

'I will.'

'Good. I have to go.'

'Eddie. I need to tell you something…'

'I'm listening.'

'I love you.'

He stood still, staring straight ahead, unblinking. Mave said, 'Goodbye, Eddie.'

Marie had been standing at the open door of the kitchen, biting her lip, watching Mave talk, until that last part. Marie had lowered her head, and backed away, sorry to have witnessed what seemed a sad intimacy, a last goodbye.

When Kim got home from school, Mave was waiting. She'd packed one case. After an argument with Mave, Marie had agreed that he had the right to know what was happening. He was old enough. He'd been a victim himself of Eddie's enemies. Mostly, Mave wanted him to know that she would never have considered leaving, but for this.

He listened, blinking steadily, as though storing each part of what she said away in his brain for safekeeping. When she was finished, Kim turned to look at Marie, then back at Mave. 'You can't go on your own! Marie, tell her, tell Mave! She can't go on her own!'

Mave reached to touch his arm. 'I'll be fine, Kim, honestly.'

'You won't be fine. Even if you are fine, it's not right! We're not throwing you out like this!' He turned again to Marie, and the anger in him shocked her. Marie said, 'Kim! Kim! Mave's leaving of her own accord. We're not throwing her out!'

'It's the same, Marie! It's the same thing. We're her friends! We're almost her family! She's not going alone. End of!'

Mave reached for him again, 'Kim-'

'You are not going out to God knows where from this house. No! I'm going with you.' He stood straight and tall and looked at Marie. 'So are you. Come on. Get ready. Let's get moving.'

Marie folded her arms. 'Kim! Listen-'

'No, Marie. No more listening. No more excuses. No more desertions. No more abandonments of people we love. This family changes, and it changes now! Now!'

One of Dalton's men checked in with him. 'The names you gave me, Malloy and Beltrami, along with the phone records...there's a Malloy in Newmarket on the voter's roll, it looks like she's Eddie Malloy's sister.'

'Says who? Are you in Newmarket?'

'Not yet. Online search brings up a news story from a while back with both of them mentioned, and a picture of the family. Parents both dead. Small stud in Newmarket left jointly to Eddie and Marie Malloy. Stud feeds off that phone mast where the single call was logged.'

'Get down there.'

SEVENTY-ONE

Eddie had talked Mac into coming back to his place straight from Taunton. He had been struck by Mac's bewilderment. While talking to Mave he'd been watching Mac who had seemed to Eddie almost like a lost child. In all the years he'd known the big man, he'd never seen him look so nakedly vulnerable. Eddie wondered if some sort of delayed grief over Jean's death had suddenly caught up with his friend.

'So strange to see your house dark and fireless', Mac said, as he followed Eddie inside.

'Ahh, well they don't do takeaway fires at the drive-through, Mac. Believe it or not. I actually build those fires with my bare hands. Anathema to you, I know...' He stopped and watched the big man.

'Anathema, I said, Mister McCarthy. AN-ATH-EMA.'

Mac nodded, half smiling, 'Indeed. You're correct. Manual work has never appealed.'

'What about my mental work? Learning that word? Just for you?'

'What word?'

'Anbloodyathema! I downloaded a dictionary app and I'm learning a word a day. Starting at A. Just for you.'

'Commendable. Admirable. Good idea.'

'I give up! Whiskey? While you watch me build this fire?'

'Splendid!'

'And spagbol?'

'Perhaps later.'

At nine, Mave rang. 'All well?' Eddie asked.

'Perfect.'

'You sound pleased.'

'Kim and Marie are with me.'

'Thank God for that! She changed her mind, then?'

Mave told him what had happened. 'Your teenage nephew is now officially in charge and ruling with a rod of iron.'

'He is a hell of a kid.'

'You'd best not call him kid, Eddie.'

'I'll be calling him boss by the sound of things. He's a walking wonder, that boy. You've done brilliantly to tie everything up and get away. Who took the horses?'

'We did.'

'You're kidding?'

'Nope. Kim wouldn't leave them behind.'

'You're travelling in a horse-box?'

'We are. And you'll be glad to hear I am not driving.'

'I am…I am.'

'What's up?' Mave asked.

Eddie sighed, 'There are questions I want to ask that I can't. For your sake. For all your sakes.'

'I know. It's okay.'

'Mave, if we get away with this one, I promise. Never again. Never.'

'Pointless promising, Eddie. Trouble finds you. Or us. If I'd never written the programme we wouldn't be here.'

'If I'd noticed Jonty Saroyan when I should have, we wouldn't be here either.'

'Spilt milk, as Sonny once told us. How is he?'

'Lying low. Licking his emotional wounds. Don't tell him where you are, Mave.'

'I won't. I won't, but give him my love.'

'You can do that yourself when this is all done. Mac's here. We're going to figure out a way to get these people, to get the police involved.'

'I thought Mac's hands were tied because of this Major Aubrey whatever?'

'Well, the major's in partnership with Ivory in the bond scam. He'll have to be outed sooner or later. It's just a matter of deciding when. Mac and I will work it out.'

'Okay. At least we're doing something. You're looking after everything there and your nephew's looking after everything here.'

'Give him my love.'

'I will.'

'And Marie.'

'Of course....'

'And you.'

'Oh, I'm sorry about this afternoon, Eddie. It all felt so, well, terminal at the time.'

'Don't apologize. I'd always want you to say what's on your mind.'

'Always?'

'Er, I think.'

They laughed.

Sonny lay in the dark in the small bedroom of his caravan. He'd spent the day in bed, rising only to use the toilet, before taking refuge once more beneath the covers.

He thought of racetracks. He pictured a seven furlong race and thought of the verse from *Macbeth*:

> Threescore and ten I can remember well
> Within the volume of which time I have seen
> Hours dreadful and things strange; but this sore night
> Hath trifled former knowings.

This sore night…This sore life…This short race which found him now at the furlong pole, six tenths of it gone. Nina had failed to kill his body but had murdered all they'd had. Slaughtered his hope. He had betrayed Jolene, his best friend's daughter who had become just as dear a friend as her father had been.

He thought of Jack Cassidy. 'You were lucky, in a way, Jack,' he whispered, 'we were not made for growing old, you and I.'

Sonny had amassed one hundred paracetamol tablets. He had left them in a cupboard, because the memory had come to him of a woman he had known in the music business, a woman who had overdosed on paracetamol, but not enough to kill her.

Sonny had gone to see her in hospital and watched her lie in what looked like a huge incubator. Her skin, at 30, was grey, her pillow wet with drool, and her system so toxic she would never regain consciousness. And he had watched her family disintegrate in arguments over when the life support was to be switched off.

That could not be risked. And ends remained to be tied. Jo's place must be left as it had been before the misery. The Shack must be cleaned. A note must be left.

He rose, and got dressed. He held his motorcycle leathers in front of him…he thought of them as friends, as protectors, comforters and, gently, he eased them on for the last time.

SEVENTY-TWO

Broc Lisle made his second call of the week to Cynthia. 'That information proved most helpful to my friend. Thanks.'

'My pleasure.'

'I'm going to ask you another favour, if you don't mind?'

'I could never live long enough to repay you for all you did for me.'

'Not at all. You were born to do good things. It was my duty to help, and I took, and still take great personal satisfaction from it.'

'I know you do. I know. What can I help with?'

'Well, this is a bit unusual. Are you free in about an hour?'

'I can easily arrange to be.'

'My father is dying. I need to go and discuss the arrangements for his end-of-life care. I'd very much like the comfort of a companion at the meeting, and you were the only one who came to mind.'

'I'm so sorry to hear that. Of course. I'll be honoured to be with you.'

The senior nurse welcomed them into her large office. Broc Lisle shook her hand warmly and introduced Cynthia as a family friend. The nurse led them away from her desk to a comfortable corner unit built around an oak coffee table. They politely refused drinks. The nurse sat and opened a folder, taking out some papers.

'Mister Lisle, I'm sorry to have had to call you so late. The doctor was delayed and he did not see your father until after six o'clock.'

'That's perfectly all right.'

'I gave you the briefest of details on the phone, and again, I apologize for that. But I didn't want it to be a total shock when you got here.'

Broc nodded. The nurse scanned a page from the folder. 'You know your father's had trouble with this stringy mucus, these awful choking fits, for some time now?'

'I accompanied him to hospital myself that first day,' Lisle said.

'Of course. I'm afraid the doctor is convinced that dementia is the cause. The brain has ceased communicating with the swallowing muscles. Your father is unable safely to take in food or water, other than intravenously, and the doctor believes his chances of surviving surgical intervention to set up the intravenous feed are outside the risk-reward boundaries. It's unlikely your father would survive such surgery.'

Lisle nodded. Cynthia reached for his hand.

The nurse said, 'The doctor would like to commence a nil-by-mouth regime to bring a relatively quick and peaceful end to your father's suffering.'

Lisle drew on reserves of old, on memories of strong times, on blocking recollections from childhood, and the nurse explained in detail how the coming days would be.

After the meeting, Lisle and Cynthia walked along the corridor toward his father's room. 'I've covered many miles on this carpet,' he said, and Cynthia smiled.

Cynthia took the chair at the far side, but Lisle said 'Let me bring that round for you. We can sit together.'

And they sat, side by side. Lisle reached for his father's hand. The old man's eyes were closed, his breathing ragged. 'They've got everything organized, father. All will be well.'

The old man did not stir.

Lisle turned to Cynthia. 'Are you okay to sit a while?'

'As long as you are here, I will be too.'

'I'll see you safely home afterwards.'

'Thank you.'

In Cynthia's flat, she spooned loose tea leaves from a caddy into the pot, while Lisle took off his jacket. 'Too warm?' she asked.

'A little.'

'I can open a window.'

'No, thank you. I'll be fine. The tea will cool me.'

She smiled. 'By the way, your friend Mister Buley's name came up today.'

'What's he been doing?'

'Trying his hand at brokering arms deals with some of the smaller Syrian groups.'

'A bit spicy for him, I'd have thought.'

'I suspect he won't be in the business for long. He's been trying to build contacts at the Embassy, though it seems a panic measure.'

'They say every man reaches his level of incompetence and stops there. I suspect Mister B has gone a step beyond.'

Cynthia carried the tray across. 'I bought you an Empire biscuit.'

He turned to smile at her. 'Lord, it's years since I've tasted one of those!'

'Well, by the look of you, the calories will do no harm.'

Lisle broke the iced biscuit into small pieces and feasted, smiling, on each morsel.

Cynthia said, 'Isn't it odd the tiniest of things that can make one happy?'

'It is. The years without make the minutes with all the more precious.'

'I meant me, actually. I have rarely been happier than when watching you enjoy so much the smallest of gifts.'

'A gift in itself, being able to take joy from such things.'

She watched him collect, with a dampened fingertip, the remaining crumbs. 'I'd very much like to sit with you during the vigils with your father.'

'I'd like that too,' he said.

'I can rearrange my hours. Normally, I'd be working through the night. I'll be returning to the office once you've gone home. I'll make the necessary alterations to my schedule.'

'You were always one for the night hours.'

'As night follows day…I sometimes picture it doing just that, slowly tracking the daylight as the world turns, always shrouding half the earth.'

'Shrouds. They await us all.'

SEVENTY-THREE

Ivory's secure mobile phone rang. It was Dalton. 'Sorry to call you so late, Mister Ivory. We just polled the audio at Malloy's place. I think you should hear one section. In private. I can mail the file.'

Ivory took from his briefcase a small laptop, which ran only on the 'dark net', so that no file was traceable and every deletion from the PC was total and immediate.

He clicked to open the MP3 file Dalton had sent. Only the relevant section had been pasted into the file. Dalton was well acquainted with Jordan Ivory's hatred of timewasting.

"Well, the major's in partnership with Ivory in the bond scam. He'll have to be outed sooner or later. It's just a matter of deciding when. Mac and I will work something out."

Ivory rang Dalton. 'Who's Mac?'

'I'm sorry. I thought you knew. It's Peter McCarthy, ex BHA, currently working for the Jockey Club.'

'Is he still with Malloy?'

'I don't have a man there just now, but I can poll the audio at one minute intervals.'

'Do that. And get someone down there. Send a team.'

'I will.'

Sonny knew that choosing the best jumping point from the cliff would be vital to success, though success seemed to him a strange word to use. He had walked out there in the dark, in the icy wind, and found that a determination to die did not make his body immune to the weather.

His eyes watered. His face stung. He ducked trying to avoid the worst of it, and was careful not to go too close to the edge. Death would be fine. Living out his final years as a paraplegic would not.

The rocks two-hundred-feet below in Hell's Mouth bay, would stop his falling body from a hundred miles an hour to stationary in a blink. Their granite ridges would crack his skull and pulp his organs…if he got it right.

Getting it wrong, landing on sand, leaving a wrecked burden for Jolene to worry about, to nurse…that couldn't be risked. He pulled his collar up and returned to the Shack. He would do it at first light, when the rocks could be seen and the take-off point decided.

He had made the Shack as tidy as he remembered it…one important wrong righted.

He'd ripped up three suicide notes, and thrown them in the cold grate. Maybe he should speak to Jo. He'd like to hear her voice again. How comforting it would be to know, to *know* that she had forgiven him. And yet he could not risk her realizing what he had planned. He wanted no cavalry to come charging along this headland at dawn. Just him, and the birds, and the sound of the sea.

Sonny watched the grandfather clock in the corner. He took his pen and began another note. But he did not finish. He balled it up and set it on the table, and he rose and walked the room. On the wall above the fire was a black and white picture of Sonny with Jack Cassidy, Mave's father. They were young and slim, dark-haired and full of life and hope, and plans.

Sonny walked on, around the room, around the house. There were no more pictures. Not a single one of the owner of this house. No trace of her past.

He returned to the picture above the fireplace. Looking at it, he took out his phone and dialled Mave's number.

It woke her. She sat up in the makeshift bed. Sonny's name flashed on her screen. She thought of Eddie and his stern warnings. The safety of Kim and Marie edged into her mind too. And she did not answer.

It could wait for morning.

She lay down. The wind sounds that had lulled her to sleep had not lessened. Their pattern had changed, the gusts stronger and longer, and she stared at the ceiling of this new home.

What could Sonny have wanted at this time? Had Eddie told him she was on the run? Maybe something had happened.

She got up and took from her bag one of the six throwaway phones. She dialled Sonny's number.

He thought it could only be her, but the number was unknown. 'Hello?'

'Sonny?'

'Jo!'

'Are you all right?'

'Yes. Yes, it's great to hear your voice.'

'Where are you?'

'I'm at the Shack, the famous Shack on the cliff, recalling summer walks and better days.'

'Sonny, what's up? Why are you there? Is there somebody with you?'

'No. No. I'm alone. I just wanted to make a final clean-up.'

'Final?'

'Well, you know what I mean. I wasn't sure if I'd got everything last time. Remember, when I came to surprise you, but you weren't here?'

'Were you hoping to surprise me tonight, too? Haven't you spoken to Eddie?'

'Well, yes, I suppose I was hoping to see you, to surprise you. And no, I haven't spoken to Eddie.'

Mave knew from his tone that something was wrong. Could Ivory's men have him? Were they trying to find out where she was? Eddie would go crazy at her for calling Sonny. Maybe they were analyzing what was coming in on the mobile network, trying to track this call.

'Sonny, the battery's almost dead on this. Let me charge it up and call you back, okay?'

'Sure. But if for some reason you don't get me, don't feel…I mean don't worry about it. Okay?'

'Okay.'

'I love you, Jo.'

'I love you too, Sonny.'

She ended the call and dialled Eddie's throwaway.

No answer.

Eddie returned from the toilet. Mac was putting on his coat. He told Eddie about the missed call. Eddie checked the number and suspected it was one of Mave's phones. He looked at his watch: a minute after midnight. He pressed to return the call.

Mave answered. 'Eddie, I think Sonny might be in trouble with Ivory's people.' She told him what had happened.

'But why would they take him to the Shack, Mave?'

'Because the PC was there? Because they thought I'd be there?'

'If they believed that, they'd be searching for you. No point wasting time with Sonny.'

'But if they had a gun to Sonny's head, they're going to get all they want from me.'

'Mmm.'

'Eddie, there's something wrong there. I'm certain. I can hear it in his voice. And I think he was going to say that if I didn't get him when I called back I shouldn't feel guilty.'

'Want me to drive up?'

'No! You don't know what you'd be driving into! Phone the police.'

'Mave! What would I tell them?'

'Everything that's happened.'

'They'll think I'm a crank!'

'Mac could speak to them, couldn't he? He's got contacts.'

'He's still here. I'll ask him, and call you back.'

'Okay.'

Eddie looked at Mac. 'I don't know if you got the gist of that?'

'I think so.'

Eddie went through it again. 'Mave wants us to call the cops.'

Mac raised his eyes, then bent at the waist and put his hands on the back of the big fireside chair. 'Eddie, I know how much you respect Mave. That's clear from listening to you tonight. But, this is no more than a hunch, after a one-minute phone conversation, and on the back of hours of fleeing these people. Anyone, even someone superhuman would have their judgement clouded by that.'

'I'd like to agree with you, Mac, but I'm not used to her being wrong with anything.'

'Then maybe Sonny's just somewhat tired and emotional? It's hardly been an easy time for him either. Perhaps her concern for him is making her sense something that isn't there.'

Eddie shook his head slowly and looked at his watch. 'Mac, I can't just do nothing. It's not an option.'

'And I can't get the police involved in this without speaking to Tim Arango, and, forgive me, but it's an extremely shaky premise on which to get Tim out of bed.'

Eddie pushed the phone into his pocket. 'I'll drive up.'

'To North Wales! At this time of the night?'

'There'll be no traffic. I'll do it in a couple of hours.'

Mac buttoned his coat. 'I'll come with you.'

'No need, Mac. I'll be fine. You'll just moan about me driving too fast.'

'If I'm preventing you from sending the police, the least I can do is come with you.'

'Okay. Give me a minute.' Eddie went upstairs, then stopped before going into his room and cursed as he remembered that his ice-axe was probably still on top of the wardrobe in Steeplechase Cottage.

He hurried back down and unhooked an old metal baseball bat from the coat-stand. Mac watched him. 'That's a bit out of left field, if you don't mind me saying.'

Eddie turned and smiled and pointed at Mac. 'That was pretty good, for you.'

'A compliment indeed.'

Eddie put the silver bat under his arm. 'Been carrying this around for a long time now, Mac. It has hung from many pegs.'

'Well, I can only say that I hope it returns to that peg tomorrow free of dents and bloodstains.'

'Let's go. I'll ring Mave on hands-free.'

The man in the woods watched Eddie's car climb the track as he waited for Dalton to answer. 'Malloy and McCarthy have just left Malloy's place.'

'Good. I'll poll the audio.'

'Want me to take a look inside?'

'Not yet.'

SEVENTY-FOUR

Two hundred miles north of the man in the woods, Sonny had finally completed a suicide note he thought was okay. He knew he could write a million words and never find the right ones. This was a compromise, but it was the best he could do.

Between now and first light, there'd be no sleep. He recalled the time he'd considered joining a monastery. The simplicity, the isolation, the frugal living, the silent melancholy had all appealed. But that strand of hope stretching back to Kathleen, that long umbilical cord from the birth of love had never been cut. It had nourished him with just enough hope to keep going, to keep searching.

Until Nina.

His obsession with her had included a search for the meaning of her name. For the Quechua people of South America, Nina meant Fire. That had made Sonny smile. Fire and Raine.

And that set him thinking on another suicide note, one for her. His purpose with Jo's was to try to ensure she felt no guilt.

With Nina, he'd have wanted guilt spilling over her like pus from a wound. But guilt was an emotion she was incapable of. He knew that. He got up. He would see out the final hours on his feet, walking this room, pacing the stone flags like a monk, but one unburdened by prayer.

He walked.

The deserted Lambourn roads were icy, and Mac flinched as Eddie overtook a gritting truck, its orange light flashing slowly. 'Eddie, go easy will you? The gritted parts are now behind us. The slippery sections are ahead.'

'I just hope the motorways are clear.'

'Well, go steady. We'll be of no use to your friend if we're wrapped around a tree.'

Eddie braked at a junction, and felt the back end waltz to the right, pulling them over the give-way line. 'See!' Mac said.

Eddie eased off.

On the motorway, Eddie gave in to Mac's frequent warnings and settled at a speed that kept the big man calm.

'Mac, we're looking at a three or four hour drive. We might as well try untangling this mess from the start. I'm missing something. It's been nagging at me for the last couple of days, but I can't nail it.'

'Untangle away, my friend, I'm listening. Beginning at the start's a fine idea, the trouble lies in identifying the start.'

'Well, the start, for me, was when Sonny went missing that summer night, after we'd met in the churchyard at Slad. The start was Jonty Saroyan taking secret pictures.'

'But where was the start for Mister Saroyan?'

'Good question. Almost certainly when he met Nina Raine.'

'And where was the start for Miss Raine?'

'Torturing kittens in kindergarten, I suspect.'

Mac laughed. Eddie said, 'You know her trouble? She's got the nerve for it, and she's got the sociopathic skills...she just doesn't have the brains for it. She's a female Jordan Ivory without the cunning. No, I take that back. She's naturally cunning, but not smart cunning, if you know what I mean?'

'Her morals meet the low-water mark of cunning but her wit does not reach the high mark.'

'That's it. Ivory seems the complete package. He's been in court a few times, but has no convictions.'

'And he has contacts. The major speaks for that.'

'They make me laugh these guys who hang on to their military titles long after leaving the forces. What's the point?'

'There used to be lots of them in racing in my younger days. Many ran the racecourses. A race-meeting was seen then as primarily an exercise in logistics. Organized military men seemed ideal for it, and once the infiltration started, the old boys' network sprung up quicker than you can say "Present arms!"'.

Eddie smiled. 'What do you know about the major? He obviously rates you if he told Tim Arango to recruit you.'

'I've bumped into him many times, over the years, but I recall nothing more than an exchange of pleasantries. One thing that sticks out was his attitude to the Jockey Club handing over most of its powers to the BHB, back in the '90s. He'd been a Jockey Club member since he was a young man and he was convinced they were the best people to run racing.'

'Well, history shows he might not have been far wrong.'

'I think the major would agree with that. They'd been in sole charge of racing for nearly two-hundred and fifty years. It was lack of good PR more than anything else that saw them unseated.'

'Now commercialism runs rife and a hundred fingers are in the pie.'

'Well, there's no going back now, Eddie.'

'Nope. So the major decides if you can't beat 'em, join 'em, and he throws in with Ivory.'

'Yes. It will be interesting to see how the major reacts to all this, once it's out. He might fall on his sword, literally, I mean, for the honour of the Club.'

'Kill himself?'

'It wouldn't surprise me. He's led what seems an unimpeachable life. He might not be able to deal with the shame.'

'He must have known the risks, Mac. Or maybe he was convinced by Ivory's lifetime record of avoiding jail.'

'Broc Lisle knew the major well. They served together in Northern Ireland. Broc says he was an absolute stickler for minimizing risk, for intricate planning.'

Eddie looked at Mac. 'Lisle served under him?'

'Alongside, I think.'

'Could the major have recommended Lisle as a replacement for you?'

'Every chance. The BHA are always careful to listen to the Jockey Club's point of view on 'new signings', as your friend Buley used to call them. Come to think of it, there was talk that the major played a part in recruiting Buley last year.'

'You're kidding! I thought you said the major was keen on minimizing risk!'

'Ha! You detested Buley since the day you met him, didn't you?'

'Wouldn't you have? Do you remember that meeting in that house in Stratford where he seemed to mistake me for the butler?'

Mac laughed. 'I remember it well! Buley could have featured that in one of his favoured staff training videos…How not to get off on the right foot.'

'Mac, honestly! Leave aside the fact that he's an absolute prick…he's never a chief exec in a million years. Never. Not of anything. He's a chancer. Always has been, always will be, wherever he's scuttled off to.'

'Well, he did have some unusual ideas.'

'Not the least being sacking you so he could bring a hopeless case to court. That shows you how far up his own arse he was. You wouldn't even need to have been a cop to realize how poor the odds of a conviction were. One of these bloody what do you call them, community officers, could have told him!'

'Well, you know my position. You'll get no argument from me.'

They passed the road sign for the M54. Mac glanced across. Eddie said, 'I'm going to carry on up and take the fifty-six, stay on the motorway as long as possible. Those back roads up into Wales will be grim.'

They travelled on in silence for a while, then Eddie said. 'If the BHA checked recruitment decisions with the Jockey Club, wouldn't Buley have spoken to them before firing you?'

'Possibly.'

'Especially if the major had recommended Buley's recruitment in the first place. If that's true, there's no way Buley lets you go on the eve of a huge case without speaking to the major.'

'He might well have spoken to him, Eddie. But it doesn't change anything. The major could have taken the view that I was no big loss.'

'But he then gets Tim Arango to recruit you to try and clear up the JCR mess? It makes no sense, Mac. None at all.'

'Unless they wanted the case to fail.'

'Why would the Jockey Club…' Eddie stopped.

Mac said, 'Those three jockeys were Ivory's boys, weren't they?'

'Yeehaa!' Eddie slapped the steering wheel, and reached to grab Mac's shoulder and shake him. 'That's it, Mac! You got it! The missing link. That's what's been hovering around the edge of my mind for days. We'd been so taken up by the bond scam, and Nina Raine, and Sonny, we'd forgotten all about Kellagher and Sampson and Blackaby, and the bent races they were organizing for Ivory.'

'So Ivory got the major to tell Buley to bring the case to court while there was insufficient evidence.'

'Correct! I knew it! I knew even Buley could not be that fucking stupid! And getting rid of you was part of the plan. The major obviously rated you, and so did Buley. So they couldn't have you anywhere near the case. Then when things go tits up for JCR, the major wants you on his side.'

'I'm somewhat torn between logic and flattery, Eddie.'

'It's totally logical, Mac. And I'll bet the major did not rate Broc Lisle.'

'Well, Lisle did say that they seldom saw eye to eye when serving together.'

'And Lisle had developed this over-the-top TV persona as a military and security advisor who everyone thought was a clown.'

'Broc Lisle, is no clown, I can tell you that. I spoke to one or two old friends after Broc came to see me that first day at home. More because I'd found him an entertaining and unusual character than anything else. But he was very highly thought of in his younger days at GCHQ. I think that's where his skills would have been best used. But he had an appetite for action, apparently, so into the army he went.'

'But the major told Buley to get Lisle in your place. One, because he didn't rate him, and, two because Lisle knew nothing about racing.'

'The trouble with that is, Buley would have known that he himself was unlikely to survive the failed court case. That the pressure on the BHA, the accusations of incompetence and bribery would mean he'd have to go.'

'Mac. Maybe that was part of the grand plan. A catastrophic failure by the BHA would have let the major argue for the Jockey Club to take back the reins of racing.'

'A bit drastic.'

'Maybe, but not impossible.'

'No. Not at all.'

'Then somebody scuppered those plans by killing Ivory's jockeys, and laying waste to JCR's business.'

'Buley?'

'No way.'

'Eddie, the trouble all started after Buley disappeared. And if the major was running the bond scam, maybe Buley knew about it. Not even Buley would blindly follow the major's instructions to ensure the acquittal of those three.'

'But if Buley knew about the major, he probably knew about Ivory too. It was common gossip that those three were Ivory's boys. Even a sight of Ivory would have Buley shitting himself, so I'm not buying that. Not Buley. Honestly, can you seem him shooting jockeys? From a skill viewpoint, never mind the guts?'

'I could see him organizing it.'

'No way, Mac. He hasn't the balls for it.'

'So where is he?'

'I suspect Jordan Ivory knows the answer to that.'

Jordan Ivory was sitting beside Dalton, who was flying the helicopter. They had just crossed the Welsh border at 15,000ft.

SEVENTY-FIVE

As they turned at the end of the headland, Eddie was reassured by seeing light from the windows in the Shack, just over half a mile away. He steered down a narrow shale track to a small car park used by tourists and dog-walkers.

'Best on-foot from here, Mac, until we know what we're up against.'

Mac groaned as he pushed himself off the seat out into the frosty air. 'Glad I brought my coat.'

Eddie took the metal bat from the back seat. 'And I'm glad I brought this.'

'And I'll be glad if you find no need to use it.'

'Me too.'

They headed for the lights in the Shack. Eddie couldn't remember being out in such darkness up here. He recalled that right on the cusp of a summer night, the hulk of Mave's place was easily seen against the sky. But they had only the lights to guide them now.

Mac spoke quietly, 'Perhaps we should have spent some time discussing what exactly we might do if Jordan Ivory is here.'

'Well, we'll skirt the headland. We've seen no vehicles on the road up. They're not easy to hide out here. If it's only Sonny's bike at the Shack, there's every chance he's alone. But we'll check all the way round the perimeter before getting closer.'

'Ivory or his boys could have been dropped off.'

'True. But if they're waiting for somebody to come running in panic, they'll be expecting arrival by car. We'll be able to get close enough to listen, to check through the windows. The curtains aren't closed. There's too much light coming out for that.'

Ten minutes later, they were scouting the Shack, walking quietly, close to its walls. Sonny's frost-covered bike was in the yard. Eddie edged closer to the living room window. The lawn rose away from the window in a gentle slope. Eddie turned to Mac and pointed to the fence twenty yards back. It was set eighteen inches higher than the grass at window level.

Eddie crept toward the fence. Reaching it, he stood straight and looked through the window. Sonny was inside, asleep, a book resting on his chest. Eddie smiled. He raised a thumb to Mac and hurried quietly toward him. 'Sonny's okay,' he whispered. 'Let's just have a look through these other windows.'

They checked the two other rooms where lights showed on the ground floor. Eddie whispered, 'Not a sound, not even a snore from Sonny. I think we're okay.'

'With respect, if someone is lying in wait, you wouldn't expect to hear a sound, would you? Why don't I wait here until you've gone in?'

'Fine. I don't mind.'

'Just a precaution.'

'Of course. It's a sensible idea. Here, take the car keys.'

Mac took them. Eddie went to the front door, slowly turned the handle, tightened his grip on the metal bat, and opened the door.

The sound of Sonny's breathing.

Something stopped Eddie from stepping inside. He called out, 'Sonny!'

Sonny opened his eyes and sat up and Eddie knew immediately that he had not been asleep and Dalton stepped out from behind the door and pointed a Kalashnikov rifle at Eddie's face. 'Put down the bat.'

Eddie threw it backwards in a low loop onto the lawn. Dalton took three steps more until he could see Mac. 'Inside. Both of you.'

Sonny stood as they came in. He was in tears. He opened his arms and Eddie hugged him. 'I'm sorry, Eddie. So sorry.'

Eddie patted his shoulder. 'It's okay.'

Ivory came down the stairs. 'Very touching, gentlemen.' He walked, in that graceful way he had, to where Mac stood, and he offered his hand. 'Mister McCarthy. Nice to meet you.' Mac reached slowly and shook his hand.

Ivory walked to the window, resting his elbow on the deep ledge. 'Sit down, please. Sit beside your friend.'

Mac and Eddie sat on the long couch with Sonny. Ivory smiled. 'The three unwise men.'

Sonny stared at the floor, tears dripping onto the rug. 'Why are you crying, Mister Beltrami? You'll be no worse off than before Dalton and I arrived, isn't that correct? Come, get your note and show your friends.'

Sonny, red-eyed, looked across at Ivory. 'Get the note!'

Sonny pushed himself to his feet and went to the fireplace. He lifted the note from the mantelpiece.

'Let them read it.'

Sonny walked in baby steps back toward the couch and held the note out to Eddie. He took it, and read it. Mac read it. Ivory crossed his arms and said, 'It's the only thing that mitigates this inconvenience. Considerable inconvenience. Mister Beltrami's dawn suicide plan is the only silver lining on this very dark cloud, gentlemen. That, and his call that brought you running. That brought us running too, or should I say flying? And that was no coincidence. It was the result of the usual excellent planning by Dalton here. I wouldn't like you to think we simply got lucky.'

Eddie read the note again, and shook his head then looked at Sonny.

Ivory said, 'Indeed, Mister Malloy. Indeed. But the note, along with your call to Mister Beltrami earlier, does simplify matters. Mister Beltrami will, of course, go ahead with the planned suicide, and, unfortunately, you two knights of mercy, will plunge to your death trying to save him. The note will make a fine postscript for the police.'

Eddie tore it twice and threw the pieces on the floor.

Ivory didn't move. He smiled, and shook his head. 'Defiant to the end, Malloy. Childish, but defiant.' He walked over and picked up the four pieces. 'They add pathetically to the others Mister Beltrami wrote and then dispensed with. Your silly act has simply increased the credibility of the scenario.'

'You're a fuckwit, Ivory,' Eddie said.

Ivory smiled again, shaking his head slowly, 'Dear oh dear, Malloy, more juvenile by the minute. I-'

Ivory stopped mid-stride and came alert. He turned to Dalton. 'Did you hear that?'

Dalton shook his head, narrowing his eyes and watching Ivory, who said, 'You sure? Did you check it was just these two?'

Dalton looked doubtful. 'Go and check, now,' Ivory said.

Dalton hurried outside, Eddie rose quickly and went for Ivory, then stopped as the tall man pulled a pistol from an under-arm holster. 'Despite all you've seen tonight, despite all that's happened, you still think I'm a fool, Malloy? You believed I'd panic and send Dalton out with the only weapon?'

Eddie retraced his steps and sat down. Ivory said, 'You know what really upsets me? Anyone who knows me would confirm this...the waste of time. I detest wasted time. I understand your perfectly sensible wish to do the job properly, Mister Beltrami, but to wait three hours for daylight would make me very angry.'

Dalton came in, 'All clear,' he said. Ivory nodded. 'Go and check those coordinates.'

Dalton left.

Ivory settled again at the window, pistol hanging from his right hand. He slipped it off and placed it carefully on the ledge, then he put his hands behind him and leaned against the wall. He said, 'Dalton is utilizing some of the equipment he always carries. Night glasses and a GPS. If he can get safe access to the beach, he will take the GPS coordinates of the largest rocks, and he will return to the cliff and match those coordinates with an exit point. Two hundred feet below that exit point, will be where you gentlemen might be found. *Might*. Much depends on the vagaries of the tide.'

He checked his watch. 'You know, I detest giving up even the twenty minutes or so it will take Dalton to measure things out. But it's much better than three hours. Wouldn't you agree?'

Eddie glared at him. Mac looked afraid and exhausted. Sonny began weeping again.

SEVENTY-SIX

At 4.47, all five men left the shack and walked westward toward the cliff edge, Dalton checking their heading every ten paces. Eddie had been battling with the decision whether to make a go of it and risk being shot.

But if he made that choice, to rush them, Mac might die too. And there was still the slim chance that the fall might not kill them. Ivory had mentioned tides. Did the water sweep over those rocks? How high did it come? Was the tide on ebb or flow? Might the sea save them? Maybe Dalton's coordinates would be out and they would land on the beach?

Eddie flinched. Two hundred feet onto the softest of surfaces could still kill them, or leave them paralysed.

A deep flowing tide was the best chance. High waves. A hundred metres from the edge, he knew he should at least be hearing the crash of them by now. Nothing…

They reached the cliff edge…the sound of the sea was distant. The tide was out. Eddie raised his eyes to the clear sky, the sliver of moon away out over the water, the stars, sharp and glinting here on the tip of Britain, far from the city lights. This big stage, he thought. This final curtain call…

The five stood. Dalton said, 'There's a fair margin of error, Mister Ivory.'

'Good. Mister Beltrami? Only fair for me to say, after you?'

Eddie reached to turn Sonny away from the sea. 'It was good knowing you, Sonny.'

Sonny could not speak for weeping. Eddie looked at Mac, 'You've been a fine friend to me. I'm proud to have known you. Very proud. Maybe I should have dropped you off at home, eh?' Eddie smiled.

Mac did too, as he shook Eddie's hand. 'At least I'll be with Jean again.'

Three hundred metres behind them, on the flat roof to the rear of the Shack, the gunman was not as confident as he'd been at Sandown, or at Haydock. The wind was down. That was good. But the nightscope's efficiency was blunted at this distance. A kill shot would be best, but he might have to compromise.

The likely trajectory was measured by the ancillary equipment he carried, but the final judgement would be his. That equipment suggested nine inches up and three and a half to the right for Ivory. The swing to take Dalton would have to come from experience. A touch of artistry was required, but the gunman's well-worn motto had seldom failed him, and it was always in his mind at the squeeze point: aim high.

Ivory said, 'Mister Beltrami, please!' and as he reached toward Sonny, a bullet entered Ivory's rib cage halfway down his left side, the impact carrying him off the cliff. The gunman anticipated that Dalton would turn toward the sound of the shot. He did, and his bullet took him in the throat, the peak of the gunman's core-mass area…but every one counted.

Mac's knees gave way, and he folded to the ground as Eddie grabbed Sonny and hauled him away from the edge. 'Down, Sonny! On the ground. Stay low!' Eddie crawled to Mac, felt for a pulse. Had a shot ricocheted and hit him?

His pulse was strong. Eddie edged upwards to listen to Mac's breathing. It was level and easy. Poor Mac, must have fainted with shock, he thought. Sonny tried getting to his knees, crying loud now, sobbing, out of control. Eddie gripped his collar from behind. 'Down! Stay off the skyline! Don't even move, and you need to shut up, Sonny! He'll pinpoint the sound! Shut up!'

But Sonny could not, and he lay crying until shivering took over. Eddie did not know how much time had passed. Mac had come to, only to be pushed flat again by Eddie. 'Down, Mac. You're okay. It didn't happen. They're dead. They went over the cliff.'

When the cold grew unbearable, Eddie got to his feet and stood shivering for a minute before he'd let the others rise.

SEVENTY-SEVEN

It took the police an hour to get there. Firearms officers had to be flown from Liverpool. They landed on the beach beside Ivory's helicopter. Eddie counted nine vehicles with flashing lights. While waiting for them, Eddie had told Sonny they'd need to be honest with police from start to finish. The attempted suicide could not be covered up.

'My fault, Eddie. I'm glad to still be here to take responsibility.'

Mac had argued weakly for a chance to warn Tim Arango, to at least try to manage the PR side. Eddie had stopped him. 'This is way too serious, now, Mac, to be doing anything even close to breaking the rules. And who's to say Arango isn't in on it? He could warn the major.'

On the Shack roof, the police found only a body length mark in the white frost, already turning pale once more.

The major was not warned. He was arrested before he finished breakfast. From the combined hours of repeated statements from Sonny, Eddie and Mac, the police asked Interpol to try to find Nina Raine. They never did.

The major spent less than forty-eight hours in custody, before his lawyer won him bail. There was, his lawyer argued, no case whatsoever for holding his client in connection with the murders on the Welsh coast. As for the major's business involvements with shell companies, what crime, asked his lawyer had been committed? And, indeed, if a crime had taken place, what evidence was there other than hearsay that his client had knowingly been involved?

And Eddie's family, which now, Kim had decided, included Maven Judge, would never go back to live in the south. When Eddie, Mac and Sonny were released by the police after seven hours' of questioning, Mave, Marie and Kim took an almost manic delight in giving Eddie directions, from place to place on his way to find where they had ended up.

They forced him to stop off at what they called checkpoints and phone for the next set of instructions. Sonny was with him. Mac had gone to meet Tim Arango. Normally, Eddie would have ranted and raved at this crazy chase east then north, but he hadn't yet rebalanced his senses.

He had not anticipated life beyond the cliff edge. Every single moment passed in what seemed to Eddie a different dimension from what he was already thinking of as his previous life. Sonny had said little throughout the journey, and after an hour, Eddie stopped asking if he was okay.

As Eddie stooped to ring for his final set of instructions, he reckoned there was less than an hour's light remaining. He had also figured out where they were, or at least he would bet on it: Kyrtlebank, his childhood home. He accepted that it would have been a sensible choice. It was remote enough, and anyone who knew anything about him, or, more importantly, who searched online for old news stories, would realize it was the last place he or his family would have run to for refuge.

He was deep into Cumbria, had just come off the motorway, and as he waited for Mave to answer, he knew he would play along, they all seemed so excited.

Mave put him on loudspeaker and, as they'd done with previous calls, each of them shouted a line of directions. When he ended the call, he did so with great relief. They were not at Kyrtlebank.

The final turn he made using the instructions he'd noted, was down a single track, high in the Cumbrian Fells above Lake Ullswater. It had once been a proper road. But was overgrown and pot-holed. He noticed freshly broken branches on the hawthorn hedges and assumed the horsebox had done the damage.

A mile along, around a gentle bend, he saw the horsebox parked. A flaking sign on a low brown wall read Felltop Farm. Eddie pulled up at the end of the driveway and turned to Sonny. 'This is it, my friend.'

They got out and closed the door and stood at the bottom of the drive looking at the long-fronted sandstone farmhouse. A *For Sale* sign had been uprooted and lay in the grass behind the brown wall. There was no sign of life until smoke suddenly began rising from the chimney. A side door opened in the farmhouse and Mave, Marie and Kim came running out shouting and screaming and laughing down the driveway toward the two men.

Kim grabbed Eddie round the waist. Marie hugged his neck, Mave reached up to Sonny who seemed ready to fall forward and crush her. But he steadied himself and opened his arms and the tears came again.

Inside, Eddie discovered they had spent twenty minutes wrestling the smaller of the two tables from the big kitchen into the living room so they could all sit facing the fire and look out of the huge side window to the fells as dusk descended.

'Guess where you are!' Kim said, when they'd all settled with hot drinks.

'Your farm.'

Kim looked disappointed. 'How did you know?'

'From the way you used to talk about it. The road you described when you told me how you learned to ride a bike. And the same road you described when you told me about your first pony. And the same road you described when you were walking home from school each day. It kind of etches itself in the mind.' Eddie drank tea and added, 'Oh and the for sale sign dumped on the lawn helped.'

'Oh no! I forgot about that!' Kim covered his face.

Eddie looked at them, one by one. 'The Cumbrian air's worked wonders. Or maybe Kim's become infectious, if you know what I mean…you look like children again.'

Kim said. 'We're staying, Eddie. We're not going back to Newmarket. We've got the horses. Mave's going to buy the farm. We're all staying here, and we want you to as well!'

'And Sonny,' Mave said quietly, reaching to touch his arm.

Eddie looked quizzically at his sister. Marie smiled and nodded. He turned to Mave. She did the same. 'No travelling?' he asked.

'It can wait.'

'We're going to be a family,' Kim said. 'A proper family. We're all going to start over. You're our family. You can't be head of the family because there's not going to be a head of the family. We're all going to be equal.'

Eddie said, 'You've thought a lot about this, haven't you?'

'We've talked about nothing else,' Kim said, 'Have we?'

'We haven't,' the women said.

Kim looked at Eddie. 'Will you come and live with us here?'

Eddie watched the boy as his past life fast-forwarded in his head: the wounds, the dreams, the hopes, the determination, the solitude, the hurt, the daily defence of…he didn't know what…of permitting himself to be alive. Then the confrontation with death in the early hours of that morning. Still his face stayed calm, perhaps even peaceful as he answered, 'Yes. I will.'

Kim got up and jumped. He jumped and raised his fists and he shouted, then he began bouncing round the perimeter of the table and everybody laughed. Sonny too.

Mave rose and stood behind Sonny, her hands on his shoulders. 'Will you join us, Uncle Sonny? Uncles are needed in every family.'

He reached up and took her hand, and he nodded. Kim was at Eddie's side, watching. 'No nodding allowed, Uncle Sonny! You need to say "I will!" It's like vows, like "I do".'

'I will,' Sonny said. 'I do.', and everyone cheered again, and Eddie thought of Mac.

SEVENTY-EIGHT

Mac had not wanted to leave voicemails for Broc Lisle, but he tried so many times, he thought it best in the end to leave a message. Lisle returned his call just after eight o'clock. 'I do apologize, Peter, it's been rather fraught lately. My father is very ill. I'm spending as much time as I can by his bedside.'

'Oh, I am sorry, Broc. This can wait. I was unaware of your father's illness. It must seem an awful intrusion. Please, I'll let you get back to his side.'

'Not at all. Cynthia, a good friend of mine, is with him. What can I do for you?'

'I was hoping to see you to thank you for that tip-off on Ivory. It seems rather rude to do this by telephone, I'm sorry.'

'Not at all. It was a pleasure to help. I heard a little about your ordeal. I cannot even imagine what it must have been like.'

'Well...' Mac dried up.

Lisle said, 'Look, are you still in the office? Are you in London?'

'I am. Just heading home now.'

'Why don't you stop off here at the nursing home and sit a while? Cynthia needs to get back to work. I'd be grateful for the company.'

'Of course. I'd be pleased to.'

The lamp in the corner of Lisle senior's room was low. Lisle turned to Mac, 'He looks at it, the lamp, even though it can cause him discomfort at times. The eyes of the dying seek the light, Peter. I'd heard the saying. I've seen it proved during these vigils.'

'Are you his only family?'

'After mother died, yes. My solitary son, that's what he used to call me.'

Mac nodded. Lisle bent forward to wet the drying lips, then sat back, showing the moist tissue to Mac. 'They're really well prepared. The wooden case there, below his bed, contains any medication he needs. Just in case, they call it. All the staff are trained to administer it. There's a muscle relaxant, diamorphine and these very effective patches. See that one on father's neck? They dry up this bloody mucus before it can build.'

'He's been ill for some time, then?'

'Three years now. I almost didn't take the BHA job, but they agreed on the conditions I needed for father. He'd have been quite proud of me getting that job, you know,' Lisle reached to touch Mac's arm, 'apologies for the circumstances, of course.'

'Not at all.'

'You see he was a racing man himself. Won the Grand Military Gold Cup many years ago, when I was ten. The memories are vivid. He'd have been proud to see me working in racing. One of the reasons I found it worth persevering through such a trying year.' He smiled warmly, 'You'll be glad now, you did lose that bloody job, eh?'

And Mac kept vigil with him, and talked about his own childhood, something he'd never done with anyone but Jean. And beside them Lisle senior faded steadily. His breathing would stop and start. He would rally, and try to raise his head, and his son comforted him and talked to him and moistened his lips and held his hand until the old man drew his final breath. Lisle checked his watch. 'Three fifty-six a.m. on the twenty-seventh of January.'

Mac put a hand on Lisle's shoulder. 'I'm so very sorry.'

'Eighty-eight years, eleven days. I wish I knew what time of day he had been born. I get comfort from precision, Peter. I don't know why.'

'I'm certain you'll be able to find out, Broc. Certain.'

'It makes the value of a life so much more, what's the word I'm looking for...tangible? No, more solid. Something you can wedge accurately and precisely into its time slot in the turning of the universe. Do you know what I mean?'

'I do.'

The friendship between Mac and Broc Lisle strengthened over the following weeks. Mac attended the funeral, as did Eddie and Sonny, Mave, Marie and Kim: the family. Eddie's house in the valley was up for sale. He had moved north. Part of his plan had been to persuade Mac to join them, to be one of that family.

And Mac admitted that he might have done it, had it not been for his growing attachment to Broc Lisle. Mac had never had a male friend with whom he'd felt he could be himself, not even Eddie. They were too different.

And Lisle too found comfort in Mac's company. It was a different comfort from that offered by Cynthia. He'd been seeing her often since his father's death, and the friendships had calmed his fear of the future. Of aging. Of following too literally in the footsteps of his father.

The search for the killer of the three jockeys and Ivory and Dalton lost what little impetus it had. To help Mac as much as he could, Broc discovered through Cynthia that Nina Raine was in Agadir, living with a man who had worked for Jordan Ivory.

The major resigned as chairman of the Jockey Club, but remained free pending fraud investigations. Racing began again on all Jockey Club Courses, without incident.

SEVENTY-NINE

Come April, and the end of the winter jumps season, Eddie was well settled in Felltop Farm. The sale had been completed, the money put in trust for Kim, and two extensions built, so everyone had their own living space. The stallions were back in operation and Kim was trying to persuade Eddie to consider retirement and swap his riding licence for a training licence.

'Maybe next year, Kim.'

The women proposed a housewarming celebration that was to last a weekend. The first night was close friends and family only. Mac had travelled up and Eddie had taken no persuading to agree that Broc and Cynthia should attend, and the three arrived in the warmth of what seemed an early summer.

The day was spent eating and drinking and walking in the fields and laughing and making plans and Eddie had never imagined that life could hold so much promise. Promise that was nothing to do with riding winners.

Marie and Mave had insisted that they would not be cooking dinner. That job would be left to caterers. And they made a hard and fast rule that everyone was to dress properly for dinner. Eddie argued tamely. He couldn't remember the last time he'd worn a suit and tie. But he was overruled. Sonny did not admit it, but he was looking forward to being in a suit once again. To stand tall and tanned and handsome and remember past days.

So the dining room was lit. Fine china and silver was on the table, and champagne, which Sonny stared at transfixed for a few seconds when it was offered. He declined quietly.

Kim sat directly opposite Broc Lisle who was the most enthusiastic man Kim had ever met. The boy was fascinated by the fine clothes, perfect manners and the impression Lisle gave of being a sort of ideal father from a time long past.

After dinner, Kim invited Broc Lisle for a full tour of the farm. He showed off the stallions, and asked Lisle if he wanted to see the hayloft where he'd hidden when the police had been searching for him after the death of his dad.

'Of course,' Lisle said, 'Lead the way.'

Kim looked up at him, 'You might get your suit a bit dirty.'

'Not at all. Let's get climbing.'

In the loft, Kim opened the doors and they settled on hay bales while Kim pointed out the different fields and what had happened in them over the years. 'And see the road back there, the smooth one you drove along, before you turned onto our track?'

'I see it.'

'That's where I first learned to ride a bike, when I was five. And I did my first proper rising trot on exactly the same bit on my first pony.'

'Something you'll always remember, I'm sure. Things that happen in childhood will stay with you all your life.'

'Well, I've already decided that when we get our first horse in training, I'm going to ride him along that exact same stretch.'

'I hope that brings you some luck, and he wins for you too.'

Lisle looked toward the horizon. Kim said, 'It must be great to work in racing. Have you always done that?'

'No. On the contrary, I'm a rookie, I'm afraid. The army was to me what racing is to you. Since I was a boy, I always wanted to follow my father into the army, though he loved his racing too.'

'Were you in any wars?'

Lisle hesitated, smiling sadly. 'Well, not wars in the formal sense of the word. I carried out what they call special duties in different conflicts around the world.'

'Spying?'

'No, not spying, though I worked with some spies early in my career.'

Kim paused, then said, 'Did you ever have to shoot anyone?'

Lisle, still staring into the distance, nodded, 'I did,' he said quietly.

'Was it…hard? Was it a difficult thing to do?'

Lisle turned to him. 'In a way. But you must do your duty. You must protect your ideals, and what is dear to you.'

'Like your country?'

'Your country. Your beliefs. Your loved ones.'

Kim stared at him. Lisle stood up and said, 'Anyway, enough of me, what about you, I guess jockeying will be your game, like your uncle?'

Kim got up, smiling again. 'Uncle Eddie was Champion Jockey at twenty-one. I'm planning to be Champion by my twentieth birthday!'

'Well that is the best way to achieve anything, Kim. Never settle for second best. I've tried to live my own life that way, in the footsteps of my father. My motto has always been the one he taught me when I was your age. And I have lived by it.'

Kim watched him as Lisle's gaze turned once more to the view across the land. 'What is it? The motto?'

Broc smiled and reached to put a hand on Kim's shoulder. 'Aim high.'

22618562R00202

Printed in Great Britain
by Amazon